SILVE S

FALLING DOWN

BASED ON A TRUE WWII STORY

OF A B-24 PILOT AND CREW

BY YVONNE KAYS

Silver Wings Falling Down

Published by St. Helens Press
Toledo, Washington
www.sthelenspress.com

ISBN 978-1-963467-08-6 print
ISBN 978-1-963467-10-9 ebook

Cover design by Kathy Campbell

Publisher's note: All the names, missions, dates, and many of the stories in this book are true. As a storyteller, not a novelist, the author created the settings and conversations after extensive research. While the book contains elements of fiction, it is based on a true story.

Subjects: Novel / Historical Fiction / World War II / Twentieth Century / Christian Fiction

Preface

"We shall not settle for less than total victory.
That is the determination of every American
on the fighting fronts. That must be, and will be,
the determination of every American here at home."

President Franklin Roosevelt, July 28, 1943

This story has been on my heart for a very long time.

Just a child, I lay on my parents' bed by my twin brother, Dan. My mother, Ruth, stood at the end of the bed ironing my dad's shirts. She began to tell us a story.

"Your Uncle Dub is a hero. He was the pilot of a huge plane, a bomber in the war. One day the enemy shot down his plane. He and his men parachuted out of a burning plane, and he landed in a country far away called Yugoslavia. We didn't know if he was dead or alive for months. He walked the soles off his boots hiding from the Germans."

I didn't know what a hero was, but I knew my mother was very proud of her brother.

This is my attempt to tell that true story as best I can.

Lt. W.T. Eaves with his B-24 bomber crew

This book is dedicated to my heroes:

My uncle, 1st Lt. William T. Eaves, and his crew,
Silver Star recipients

And
All who served in WWII who did not come home to their families,
paying the ultimate price for our freedoms.

And
Those who have followed in their footsteps,
stepping up to fight for our country.

My twin brother, SP4 Dan A. Hale,
Vietnam War Army veteran, Bronze Star recipient,
whose own story remains a closed book.

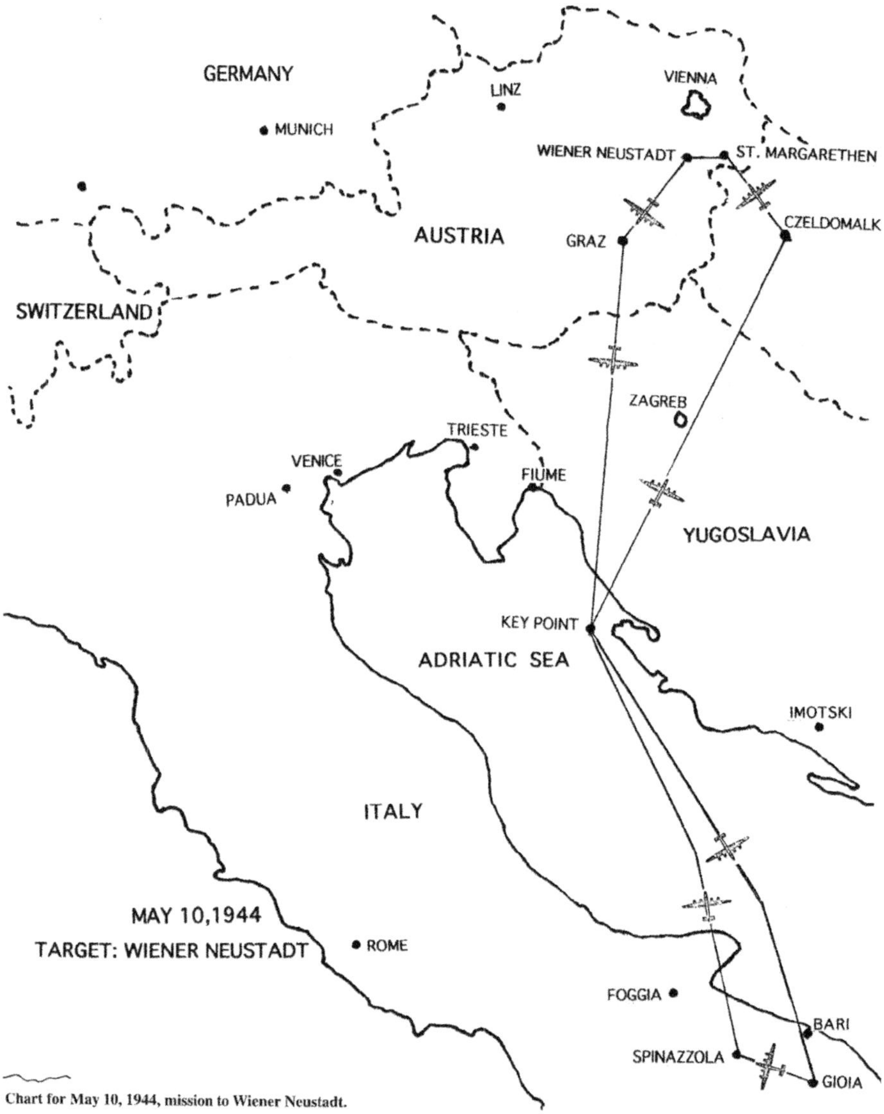

Chart for May 10, 1944, mission to Wiener Neustadt.

Courtesy of *The 464th Bomb Group in World War II: In Action Over the Third Reich with the B-24 Liberator*

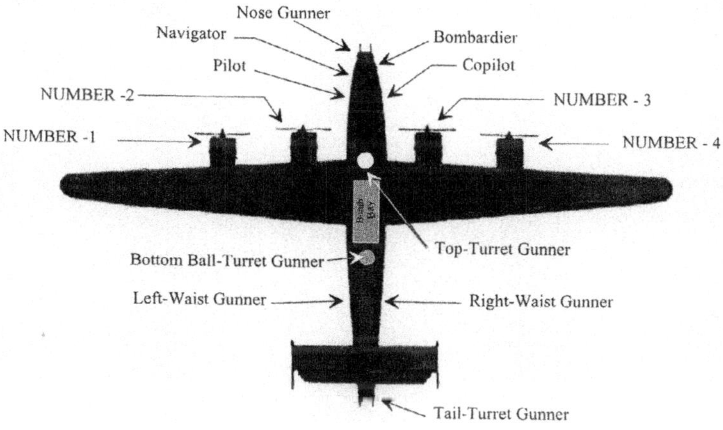

https://449th.com/b-24-aircraft/

List of Characters

The crew of 1st Lt. William. T. Eaves:

Position	**Name/rank**	**Home state**
1—Pilot	W.T. "Red" Eaves, 1st Lt.	Texas
2—Copilot	Dan Sherman Jr., 2nd Lt.	New York
3—Navigator	Bob Haverkos, 1st Lt.	Ohio
4—Bombardier	Lawrence Lambert, 1st Lt.	Michigan
5—Flight Engineer	James Elder, S/Sgt.	Wisconsin
6—Radio Operator/Gunner	Bill Christel, S/Sgt.	Wisconsin
7—Left Waist Gunner	Joe Linneman, Sgt.	Missouri
8—Ball Turret Gunner	James Petrone, Sgt.	Connecticut
9—Right Waist Gunner	Sylvester Fangman, Sgt.	Texas
10—Tail Gunner	George Masterson, S/Sgt.	Illinois

Jean Webb Eaves—Eaves' sweetheart and wife, in Galveston, Texas
Ollie and Bill Webb—Jean's parents, in Galveston, Texas
Gert and Bud Brandt—Eaves' friends in Galveston and Pocatello
1st Lt. James Tudor—Eaves' best friend in 464th Bomb Group, former copilot
Colonel Bonner—Commanding officer of the 464th Bomb Group
Sgt. Ryskeciski—Crew chief for *Target for Tonite*
Colonel Goodrich—Senior American officer of *Stalag Luft III*
Actual names—All mentioned 464th airmen and lost aircraft

Mrs. Brown—Widow in Pocatello, fictional character
Sam Smith—POW in Stalag Luft III, fictional character
Eddie Jones—Fellow American airman in Yugoslavia, fictional character
Hawk, Scout, George, Bara—Partisans, fictional characters

Chapter 1

3 MARCH 1944—NATAL, BRAZIL

SWEAT TRICKLED DOWN HIS FOREHEAD. He strained to pull back on the yoke. The bomber dropped lower, dangerously close to the waves. The B-24 wasn't responding.

Dark menacing waves crested below, looming closer like tentacles of a demonic sea monster reaching toward the plane. Seething ocean waters stretched to the horizon.

We're going down!

Lt. W.T. Eaves' eyes popped open, his heart racing, his gut in a knot. Body sticky with perspiration, he struggled in the bedding wrapped around him on the cot. The odor of damp canvas and stale cigarette smoke filled his nostrils.

A dream—thank God, it was only a dream.

Closing his eyes, Eaves leaned his head back on the thin pillow as he blew out a long breath and willed his racing pulse to slow. The distant roar of the surf and the unfamiliar bird calls of the Brazilian jungle washed over him. Closer to his ear, he heard the buzz of a pesky mosquito cruising through the tent. Muffled voices and a truck motor told him the base was stirring.

The nightmare had probably come because of Cumming's plane. Only two days ago, Lt. Cumming and four of his crew members were killed when their B-24 had gone down on the way to Belem, Brazil. A man he'd trained with, a good pilot. If it happened to him, it could happen to anyone.

Only four months since the 464th Bomb Group had been formed. They'd already lost three planes and more than twenty men in training. Some of the guys muttered about a bad luck unit. He didn't believe that, but nothing was safe about this business.

Opening his eyes in the warm dark, he looked across the tent. Gentle snoring told him he hadn't awakened his fellow officers.

On the closest cot, deep breathing came from his navigator, Bob Haverkos. A Cincinnati native, the strapping six-foot athlete reportedly pitched a wicked fastball and had boxed as a Golden Glove Heavyweight champion—a great addition to the crew.

The snoring emanated from the bombardier on the far side of the tent. Lawrence Lambert hailed from Dearborn, Michigan, a quiet, serious guy who kept to himself and did his job well.

The newest crew member, Dan Sherman, sighed and rolled over on his cot. The dark-haired New Yorker had joined the crew as copilot a few weeks ago in Florida.

Eaves took another deep breath and exhaled slowly, trying to shake off the alien feeling of dread, residue from the dream.

As the twenty-two-year-old pilot of a B-24 bomber, he wore his silver wings proudly, ready to do his part to battle the evil powers striving for world dominance and the destruction of everything he held dear. Pearl Harbor had ignited an intense anger and passion to defend his country. Inspired as a lad by Charles Lindbergh's daring flight across the Atlantic, he'd chosen to enlist in the Army Air Corps. Receiving his wings fulfilled his boyhood dream.

Freedom, and keeping his family safe—that's worth fighting for. He sighed. All this waiting grated on him. Time to give Hitler a taste of American muscle.

He focused his thoughts on the day ahead. His biggest challenge yet—piloting his crew of nine men over the two thousand miles across the Atlantic to the African shore.

Coming from Florida, they'd hopscotched across the Gulf of Mexico to Brazil in three days. An overnight in Puerto Rico, then on to British Guinea, with another fueling stop in Belem before arriving here in Natal on the eastern tip of Brazil.

Crossing the Atlantic was another story. No landing spots between them and the African coast. Plus, severe weather conditions frequently encountered over the Atlantic increased the danger. The flight would be ten to twelve hours of airtime, the longest he'd ever attempted.

The Liberator was a "man's plane," a huge four-engine bomber managed by a pilot's strength and endurance. Although he'd been flying B-24s for over a year now, was he strong enough, wise enough, to pilot this "flying boxcar" over the Atlantic?

Please help me do my job and get us there safely, Lord. Thank You for the crew I've got, not a slacker in the bunch. And watch over Jean and keep her safe. My wife—still can't believe I have a wife.

Jean's lovely face floated into his mind. His hands clenched as the ache to hold her filled his chest. Didn't know he could miss someone so much.

He exhaled deeply, forcing his body to relax.

Yesterday the crew had christened their B-24H *Target for Tonite* and painted a shapely, gorgeous girl as nose art while they waited in Natal for their orders to fly overseas.

The name fits. Get this job done and the target is home—back to Texas and his gal.

Eaves ran his hand through his short-cropped hair and over the stubble on his chin. He'd have to shave close today. Would need the oxygen masks if the plane hit turbulent weather.

They'd be packing a heavy load—all the gear and supplies needed to set up a temporary base in North Africa. His orders specified a wait at the Oudna Airfield in Tunisia until air strips were ready in southern Italy.

For the past three days the chronic bad weather over the Atlantic had forced his bomb group to stay put on the eastern-most tip of Brazil, waiting for a clear day to launch toward Africa. But what a place to be delayed—Natal, a favorite resort city of Brazil.

Miles of dazzling white sand beaches stretched around them. Crystal clear azure waters beckoned, and he dove into the surf whenever the blazing sun popped out.

Some of the guys worked on getting a tan and flirted with the local beauties. Eaves endured a lot of good-natured ribbing about being the only crew member with a ball and chain, but he didn't mind. He felt completed. Jean was a blessing from the Lord.

On trips to the local open-air markets, he'd discovered delicious Brazilian cuisine. Empanadas, little pastries filled with shrimp, meats, and cheeses, were delicious snacks whether fried or baked. Another favorite—*feijoda*, a pork 'n black bean stew, served with rice.

Vendors hawked jewelry and souvenirs, colorful squawking parrots and shrieking squirrel monkeys, all creating the aura of a tropical vacation that he longed to share with Jean. War seemed far away.

But . . . now the day had come to step closer. He sat up and slipped into the uniform he'd laid out the night before.

"Okay men, time to rise and shine. Can't be wasting daylight," he said in a loud voice. Eaves smiled inside. His daddy had gruffly roused him with that same verbiage so many mornings back home in West Texas.

One muffled groan as the other officers stirred awake.

Eaves poured water from his canteen into his steel helmet to shave, lathering up his face with bar soap. After scraping off the stubble, he patted his cheeks dry.

"Briefing at 0600." He laid his already-packed barracks bag on his cot. "See you guys at the mess hall." Lifting the tent flap, he stepped out into moist tropical air.

The base at Natal hummed with activity in the predawn light. Trucks filled with equipment and young airmen rumbled past spewing gasoline fumes. Outside the olive-drab tents, men piled footlockers and barracks bags as crews prepared to leave the jungle airbase.

Eaves savored the alone time as he strode toward the mess tent, contemplating the recent news from Italy and the daunting tasks ahead.

His bomb group was part of the new wave of bombers joining the Fifteenth Air Force in Italy, tasked with pounding Germany into submission. With Mussolini deposed in July, the U.S. infantry had reportedly dug in, fighting hard to push the Germans out of northern Italy. The Army Air Corps engineers and ground crews had gone ahead by ship to prepare airfields in southern Italy.

The 464th Bombardment Group was a formidable fleet of forty-eight B-24s, comprised of four bomb squadrons. Eaves' 777th Squadron, along with the 776th, 778th, and 779th, were all scheduled to cross the Atlantic in the next few days to join the war effort. Each plane would travel individually to reach Dakar, Senegal, the closest base on the West African coast.

Crossing the "pond" would require several hours of dreaded nighttime flying. He couldn't rely on his natural senses but would have to rely solely on the instruments. A shiver tingled through him.

Eaves looked up. A clear sky arched overhead, a great day to fly.

Remember your training, Eaves.

His mind flashed back to the many required hours of "hooded" flights, when all he could see were the gauges and dials inside the cockpit. He straightened his shoulders as he entered the mess hall.

With Your help, God, I can do it.

His tent mates soon straggled into the mess hall. The other three officers each grabbed a tray and filed through the line. They joined Eaves at the end of the long table.

He slid the salt and pepper toward them. "You'll need this," he said with a grin.

Haverkos laughed as he sat down and grabbed for the ketchup. "That's for sure, Red. At least the hash browns and toast don't look too bad."

Steaming mugs of coffee helped wash down the dreadful powdered eggs and fried Spam. The men seemed subdued, the usual banter gone.

Sherman spread marmalade on his last piece of toast. "Long trip ahead."

Eaves nodded. "Yep. Hope we get an early leave time. That would help cut down the hours of night flight." He needed to reassure them and himself that all was ready. "Glad to have those extra fuel tanks in the bomb bay that the ground crew installed back in Nebraska. We're gonna need 'em."

"They know what it takes. It's a long hop across the pond." Haverkos wiped his lips and threw the napkin on his plate.

Eaves took his last swig of coffee and picked up his tray. "Let's head to the briefing and get our orders."

The six enlisted men on his crew joined the officers inside the briefing room. Lanky James Elder, the flight engineer, strode in with little Bill Christel, the radio operator, both from Wisconsin. The waist gunners Sylvester Fangman from Texas and Joe Linneman from Missouri playfully pushed ahead of the ball turret gunner, Joe Petrone, the smallest man on the crew. George Masterson from Chicago fittingly brought up the rear, the crew's tail gunner and "old man" of the team at age twenty-four.

"Sir, I got some fresh fruit and goodies from the locals yesterday," Joe Linneman, the left waist gunner said with a lopsided grin. "Otherwise, all we'll have to eat are those lov-er-ly K-rations." Always an entrepreneur, Joe kept fun and food and women clearly in mind at all times when he wasn't on the gunnery range. He and Fangman had been the force behind stowing several cases of cheap rum in the plane before they'd left Puerto Rico.

"Good idea, Joe. Is everyone's stuff packed and ready to go?" Eaves asked.

"Affirmative, sir."

✈✈✈

Hurry up and wait—the mantra of the Army Air Corps. After the briefing, most of the crew sprawled on the ground around their gear waiting for the ride to the plane. Linneman and Fangman pulled out their mitts and played catch until the cargo truck finally arrived to take them to the tarmac. The pilots and the navigator headed to their specialized briefings to lock in final instructions for the long haul over the Atlantic.

After loading all the equipment into *Target for Tonite* and checking every serial number off on the inventory sheets, the crew learned from Eaves that they still had another two hours to wait before their designated time to start engines.

Eaves walked the length of the plane with his checklist, charged with visually inspecting every area from the tail gunner's station to the nose turret. Final accountability rested with him, and he knew each crewmember's duties well enough to perform them himself. But he had confidence in his crew and trusted each man to fulfill his responsibilities.

In the nose turret, he found Haverkos seated at his chart table with his sharpened pencils, checking calculations with his maps spread out around him. If the navigator erred by as much as one degree, they would end up in the Atlantic instead of Dakar.

Eaves smiled. He knew Haverkos was good, very good at his job—one of the best navigators in the squadron. "Ready, Bob?" he asked.

"You bet." Haverkos turned to squint up at him. "But don't let anything get us off the 64-degree heading or—we could be in for a dunk in that big bathtub out there."

They locked eyes briefly. They both knew that the Liberator was known to break apart upon attempted water landings.

"Do my best," Eaves said.

Leaving the nose turret, Eaves crouched down and crawled through the front wheel casing. He straightened up to enter the flight deck and stepped into his seat on the left side of the plane. Dan Sherman was already in the copilot's seat to the right.

Taking a deep breath, Eaves thought of the first time he'd sat in the pilot's seat and had stared in bewildered amazement at the twenty-seven gauges, the twelve levers controlling the throttle, turbocharger, and fuel mixtures, and the four buttons above the windshield that feathered each of the props on the four huge engines. Now it felt like home.

Eaves checked his watch again. Finally—time to start their engines. He signaled Elder, the flight engineer, to fire up the "putt-putt," the single-cylinder gasoline-powered unit in the B-24 that boosted the batteries.

Then Elder opened the top hatch and stood to observe the engines carefully for any fuel leaks. He signaled all clear.

At Eaves' order, Sherman flipped the switch to start the first 1,200 horsepower Pratt & Whitney engine and an incredible roar filled the cockpit. As each engine sprang into life, Elder continued standing to watch for any sign of fire.

The crescendo of noise increased, making conversation impossible except on the intercom.

There it was—the flare to begin takeoff. Eaves gave the order. "Release brakes."

As the bomber began to move, Elder remained head and shoulder outside the plane. Neither the pilot nor the copilot could see the wheels of the plane or the taxi strip, and it was the flight engineer's job to guide them.

No rear-view mirror on a bomber, either. The tail gunner and ball-turret gunner were his rear eyes. Flying a B-24 took a team—and a whole lot of trust.

"More to the right," Elder called into the intercom.

Eaves steered with the propellers, reducing power on the right-side engines and speeding up the ones on the left wing.

Once on the runway, *Target for Tonite* rumbled to a halt as Eaves and Sherman tromped down on the brakes and revved the engines for take-off. When the engines reached maximum power, the roar was deafening as the plane vibrated and shook, feeling like every nut and bolt could fly off in a thousand directions.

Eaves called out the final checklist to Sherman. *Target for Tonite* was next in line for take-off. He waited, heart thumping, adrenaline pumping.

Every takeoff in a B-24 bomber was an adventure. It always felt like the "flying boxcar" would never gain enough speed to lift off the ground, but its prowess was undeniable. Once in the air, a B-24 flew faster, longer and carried more weight than its more famous cousin, the B-17. He'd learned to trust his ship.

The B-24 in front of them lifted off the runway. Eaves and Sherman waited the required twenty seconds before releasing the brakes.

Target for Tonite thundered down the runway, picking up speed ever so reluctantly. Sherman called out airspeed. "130 miles per hour."

They'd reached the end of the runway and Eaves pulled up on the yoke.

With the plane barely skimming the ground, he ordered, "Wheels up." Sherman hit the switch to hydraulically raise the landing gear. "Flaps up." The copilot brought up the wing flaps, and with less drag, *Target for Tonite* nosed upward.

The tail gunner came on the air. "Masterson here. Those waves almost kissed our tail."

Eaves circled, and the heavily loaded B-24 bomber slowly climbed into the sky, like a huge pelican that appeared too heavy to fly.

The exhilaration of flight, the glorious sense of freedom coursed through him.

Here we go—into the wild blue.

And the unknown.

Chapter 2

4 MARCH 1944—MID-ATLANTIC OCEAN

"CAPTAIN, ARE WE STILL ON COURSE?" Linneman's voice crackled over the intercom.

Only five hours out and the crew had repeated the question over and over. Eaves sighed, and pushed his throat mic, "Roger to that. How 'bout breaking out the snacks, Joe? Bring some up to the nose turret and flight deck."

"Yes, sir. Be there in a jiff."

Even with the waist gunners' windows closed for flight, the B-24 was cold and drafty. The waist gunners were assigned to the radio compartment right behind the flight deck for take-off. Since they only had room to stand back-to-back in their area behind the bomb bay and the ball turret, Fangman and Linneman had stayed there today with Christel, the radio operator, for the long flight.

Time for check-ins. Eaves pressed his throat mic again. "Christel, status?"

"A-OK, sir. Linneman, Fangman, and I have just been playing a little poker to pass the time. Masterson and Petrone are napping in the tail."

"Navigator, check-in."

"Just rechecked our heading. All seems well. Lambert has his nose in a book—as usual."

Elder, the flight engineer, stood behind the pilots, helping monitor fuel mixtures and instruments. He turned to reach for the meat *empanadas* and a small sack of oranges offered by Linneman and helped himself before passing them on to the pilots.

Eaves put the plane on autopilot as the mouth-watering smell of the flavorful treats reached his nostrils. He quickly devoured two meat-filled pastries, then peeled the orange and bit in. Sweetness flooded his taste buds and he wiped the juice from his chin.

"Thanks Joe," he said into the throat mic. "You're right—sure beats K-rations."

Squinting, his jaw tightened as he noticed dark clouds looming low across the horizon. The characteristically bad weather of the Mid-Atlantic lay dead ahead.

"Navigator, storm ahead. We'll have to go around it. What is your recommended heading?" He checked the altimeter. *Target for Tonite* was cruising at 8,000 feet.

May have to go up to avoid of the worst of it. That'll cost us fuel.

Billowing black clouds soon towered into the sky, sharp nails of lightning crashing down. Eaves clenched his hands on the yoke.

The Liberator began to buck and sway in the strong winds. Eaves took *Target for Tonite* off autopilot and pulled up on the yoke as the plane flailed downward in the turbulence.

"Navigator here. Adjust heading 4 degrees north."

Suddenly the tenor of his voice changed. "What's that thing doing here? Oh no, get off my charts! Get him Lambert!" Haverkos hollered into the intercom.

Eaves' stomach lurched. He pressed his throat mic. "What's going on?"

"It's a monkey. Someone smuggled a monkey onboard and he's sick—throwing up and pooping all over my maps."

Eaves sucked in his breath—his heart thudded against his rib cage. Those maps were critical to successfully navigating the Atlantic. Steely cold, his voice burst over the intercom, "Who brought that monkey onboard?"

Dead silence.

"There he goes!" It was the bombardier. "Just missed him."

Minutes later an olive-gray creature with orange arms and legs popped up on the flight deck close to Elder's feet. Eaves glanced down to see dark eyes peering up at him, ringed by a white face topped with a gray cap. The mischief-maker's whip-like tail dangled down longer than its body. Shrieks and yowls emanated from its mouth, and a putrid smell of urine and feces filled the air.

Elder reached for the little critter, but the squirrel monkey ducked and scrambled up into the cockpit, bumping levers as it tried to escape out a window. Sherman attempted to catch it, but the monkey nimbly leaped over his arm, landing closer to Eaves.

Without warning, the plane lurched in the storm, then dropped like an elevator cut loose. Momentarily suspended in the air, the monkey suddenly crashed down, landing on the fuel-mixture control levers of the instrument panel. Elder pitched forward, fell to his knees. Sherman gripped onto the yoke, knuckles white, struggling to stay in his seat.

"Dan, take over controls," Eaves ordered.

"Got it," Sherman replied.

Making a quick grab with his right hand, Eaves reached out and collared the monkey firmly. It writhed in his grasp, twisting and squirming. With his left hand, he slid the cockpit window open.

"Sorry monkey, hope you can swim," he said, and with a pang of remorse, he thrust the struggling monkey out the window and released him.

Eaves exhaled. Can't feel guilty. That monkey was endangering the lives of everyone on the plane. He'd deal with the culprit who brought it onboard later. For now, he had to focus on the damage done.

"Elder, stabilize those fuel-mixtures. Keep them lean," he ordered as he scanned the instrument panels. "Dan, I'll take the controls now. Wipe down all the levers and dials."

"Yes, sir." Sherman's face looked pasty as the Liberator bucked again in the strong winds. His hands shook as he cleaned the instrument panel fouled by the monkey, then he leaned over and retched into the empty paper bag the oranges had come in.

Eaves pulled back hard on the yoke and the nose of the plane edged up. He watched the altimeter as the aircraft gradually gained altitude, soaring up and plunging like a rollercoaster.

"Crew, this is the pilot. Put on your oxygen masks. We'll have to climb to hopefully get out of some of the turbulence. Navigator, how're things in the greenhouse? Reconfirm our heading."

"Lambert and I are okay, just bruised a little. Will get my maps picked up and cleaned off. Get back to you as soon as I can."

"Christel, status?"

"Rolling around a bit back here, sir. Sure woke up Petrone and Masterson. None of us much worse for the wear. Fangman's got a little cut on his head, so we broke out a first aid kit."

Light was fading and the clouds enfolded them. *Target for Tonite* hurtled into the blackness and the storm, a seething ocean stretching endlessly below.

✈✈✈

Haverkos wiped cold sweat from his brow as he pulled out the Fairchild A-10 sextant used in celestial navigation—the sole method of overwater navigation he could use to start a new point of departure.

The constant refrain from his navigation classes resounded clearly above his anxiety. "Never change a heading unless you know your current location."

They'd have to clear the storm before he could set a new heading. To find their current location, he'd need to look through the sextant for six minutes and track the positions of three different stars or planets.

He studied the maps as he wiped off the monkey's feces and putrid-smelling vomit, his seat sliding almost out from under him as the plane lurched again. Going north was their best bet. The closest emergency base was on the Canary Islands.

His gut tightened. He alone was responsible for directing the ship through the night and the storm. All their lives were in his hands now.

Remember—all the practice and drills, the extensive training in dead reckoning. He knew his job. His instructor's voice echoed in his mind, "If you've trained adequately, you'll respond automatically, even in the stress of battle."

And this was a battle—not yet against the Germans, but a battle against the elements. His confidence surged and a prayer winged upward.

With Your help, we can do this.

✈✈✈

Eaves' shoulders ached from fighting the yoke for so long and his body screamed from being cramped. He glanced at his watch. Twelve hours in the air now. The tropical storm was behind them. Moonlight gleamed on the dark Atlantic and hundreds of twinkling stars filled the sky.

His eyes scanned the gauges. Altimeter read 9,000 feet. Thankfully the oxygen masks had come off. He sucked in a deep breath and let it out slowly. But where were they? Eaves had to trust his navigator and believe that somewhere, out there in the inky darkness, lay the Canary Islands and a landing strip.

He peered into the night. Nothing. No glimmer of light.

Twelve hours of flight time—they were pushing the plane's limits. "Elder, how much fuel is left?"

The engineer stood behind the pilots, constantly monitoring the flow of fuel to each engine. "We're hovering toward empty in our final reserves now."

Eaves swallowed hard. "Navigator, what's our location? How many miles to destination?"

"According to my calculations, we're twenty miles from the Canary Islands."

Eaves' gut twisted as he scanned the endless darkness. Minutes ticked by.

"We're losing engine two," Sherman said as he tapped the gauge monitoring the engine revolutions per minute.

"Feather it," Eaves called out.

The copilot hastily pulled back the lever and pushed the overhead button that turned the massive propeller blades knife-edge to the wind, cutting the drag.

"Elder, adjust fuel levels to the other engines. We'll have to make it on three."

Another engine coughed and sputtered, this time outboard on the right wing.

"Feather engine four," he ordered.

Sherman complied. Elder immediately cut the fuel to that engine.

Target for Tonite lumbered on, toiling to stay in flight with just two engines. Sweat drops formed on Eaves' forehead and upper lip, tension ratcheted up his shoulders and neck.

Suddenly Eaves saw Jean's beautiful face and thought of his family back home. He clenched his jaw, feeling cold sweat run down his back.

Can't disappoint them, disappearing into the Atlantic without dropping even one bomb on the enemy.

Each of his men flashed through his mind.

They're depending on me.

"Fuel levels on zero. We're flying on fumes," Elder said, his voice cracking.

Eaves scanned the horizon frantically. Only darkness.

God, help us. Keep us in the air long enough to get to a landing strip.

Eaves watched the altimeter fall as *Target for Tonite* dropped lower and lower in the sky. Only two engines at full power, not enough to maintain altitude.

The dream flashed back into his mind. The dark waves reaching for them. He gritted his teeth, straining to pull up on the yoke. Is this the way it would end?

Wait, what was that?

He leaned forward.

A faint glow, straight ahead.

"Sherman, do you see it?"

"Lights—yes, I see them!"

Relief flooded over him. Thank God, land in sight! Haverkos had come through.

"Canary Islands straight ahead, boys. Christel, make radio contact. Tell 'em we're coming in on two engines and to prepare for an emergency landing. Elder, move back to the waist area with the rest of the crew."

He scanned the instruments. "Attention, all crew members. Brace for emergency landing."

More lights flared before them. Now the pilots could clearly see a runway, lined with flare pots. Eaves cut back on the throttle and they dropped toward the center of the steel mats that made up the runway.

"Lower landing gear. Flaps," Eaves ordered. "Hit the brakes as hard as you can when we touch down, Dan."

Sherman flipped the switch. "Roger. Gear down."

As the wheels gently touched down, another engine slowed to a sputter. Both pilots leaned back, stomping on the brakes as hard as they could.

Reaching the end of the runway, *Target for Tonite* trembled, lurching to a halt as the last engine slowed and the propellers stopped rotating. Emergency vehicles surrounded them, lights flashing.

Eaves leaned his head on the yoke, his arms like jelly, a prayer of thanks in his heart.

Couldn't have been closer. Not even enough fuel to taxi off the runway.

Chapter 3

EIGHT MONTHS EARLIER, JULY 1943—GALVESTON, TEXAS

"JEAN, HONEY, I COULD USE YOUR HELP PLEASE." Her mother's voice rang out from the kitchen.

"Be there in just a moment." Jean finished powdering her nose and patted her dark hair where a stray curl poked out of place. Humming Dinah Shore's popular song "He Wears a Pair of Silver Wings," she glanced in the mirror one last time. She lifted her arms to an imaginary partner and twirled in a circle, the navy cotton skirt swirling around her legs.

Closing her eyes, she pictured the appreciative look in his brilliant blue eyes the first night he saw her across the dance floor. She flushed remembering how handsome he was in his uniform. And that red hair. A prayer of gratitude flowed from her heart.

Please keep him safe, Lord. This flying business can be so dangerous. And thank You for the promise I read this morning in Psalm 34, that You will give us the desires of our hearts if we delight in You. I think he's the one. But only if it's Your will, Lord. You know the future. I don't. Please make it clear to me. Thank You for bringing us together, even in this terrible time of war.

Oh, those butterflies in her tummy were back again. He should be here soon.

She closed the door to her room and quickly joined her mother in the kitchen, pulling on a flowered apron to cover her dress. "What do you need me to do?"

"Please set the table before you finish your cake. It's cooled long enough to frost now."

Jean picked up the plates and silverware. After carefully setting the table, she slipped back into the kitchen and gathered the things she needed for the icing.

"Thanks for giving up our entire sugar ration for the cake, Mama. Red said coconut cake is his favorite, one of the things he missed most from home." She lifted the eggbeater up to check the egg whites. Yes, thick enough for peaks to form. "Must be hard to be away from his family for more than a year."

She whipped the vanilla into the egg whites and sugar, trying to ward off the thought that followed—him leaving soon for overseas. Sadness pricked at her heart, but she took a deep breath.

Think about the present, not the unknown.

Across the room, her mother smiled at her. "Well, tonight we'll give him a taste of good home-cooked food."

✈✈✈

Eaves nervously fingered the tiny box in his pocket as he hopped off the trolley and strode down the boardwalk. Pink crepe myrtle blossoms swayed overhead. The constant wind brought a hint of jasmine drifting by on the humid salt air.

Grey-brown waves crashed onto the shore, stirring the piles of seaweed strewn about the beach. He eyed the seventeen-foot sea wall, erected after the Big Storm of 1900. Over six thousand lives had been lost, the city of Galveston decimated.

The island community had rebuilt and constructed the sea wall. But Galveston lost out to Houston as the premier port of the Gulf when oil companies outflanked the demand for cotton. So—Galveston carved its own niche as the Gulf's exclusive resort town where the rich and famous flocked to drink, dance and gamble. Even Frank Sinatra and Benny Goodman performed here.

Last night he had taken ten bucks into the backroom casino of the famous Balinese Room. He'd made enough to take Jean out on the town for a show and a night of dancing.

He smiled at the thought of her softness in his arms. His heart did that funny pitter-patter he'd felt the first night her saw her. He couldn't get her out of his mind.

His grip tightened on the ring box in his pocket.

Was it fair to ask her to marry him before he left for the war? She deserved someone who would be there for her, take care of her. Would this love last—or would it be taken away from him too?

He sucked in a deep breath and straightened his back.

One step at a time. First, dinner at her house.

Clutching the bouquet of red roses in his left hand, he turned away from the shore and strode down Avenue S½. He spied the single-story bungalow on his left, a large magnolia tree covered with white blooms by the stoop, its sweet fragrance flavoring the air.

He rapped on the door. Bill Webb, Jean's father, opened it, his tanned face cracking into a slow smile with warmth that filtered up to his blue eyes. "Welcome, son. Come on in."

"Good evening, sir." Eaves held out the roses as he stepped into the living room. "These probably need some water."

"Jean, Eaves is here. Come get these flowers."

Jean swished into the room, carrying two glasses of iced tea, a shy smile on her face.

Eaves' heart beat a little faster.

"Oh, thank you so much! They are lovely—you really shouldn't have," she said in a breathless rush. She handed him the tea and took the roses into her arms.

Eaves gratefully accepted the drink. His palms were so sweaty, he feared the glass would slip out of his hands.

Jean closed her eyes as she inhaled the lovely fragrance. "I'll put them in a vase." She gave Eaves an even bigger smile before turning back toward the kitchen. "Dinner will be ready in a few minutes."

Eaves sank down onto the sofa beside the blue easy-chair where her father sat. "How's the ship building going, sir?"

Bill grunted. "Keeps me busy. Different world now, working with all those women. Rosie the Riveters." He shook his head. "Actually, they do a pretty darn good job. And I'm doing my part, supporting the war and all. But if I were young again, I'd be with you on the front lines."

Eaves heard the mix of admiration and regret in his voice. "I'm sure you would, sir."

Bill cocked his head to look at Eaves. "About finished with that anti-submarine training?"

"Yes, sir." Eaves took a deep drink. "Yesterday one of the other crews thought they spotted a German U-boat and dropped depth charges on a poor whale." His lips curled into a smile. "Don't know if they were just bored or really mistook a whale for a U-boat, but I'm sure glad we don't have a mistake like that on our record."

Now's the time, while the girls are in the kitchen.

He swallowed hard, took a deep breath, and calmed his mind.

"Sir, I have something important to ask you." He cleared his throat and looked the older man in the eye. "I want your permission to ask your daughter to marry me. I want her to be my wife." His voice broke a little. "I love her—with all my heart, and I promise to do everything in my power to make her happy."

Bill did not look surprised. He looked down at his drink. Seconds passed before he spoke thoughtfully.

"I appreciate your respect in asking me for her hand in marriage. It's no secret that all she's ever wanted is to be a wife and mother. And I see the way she looks at you, her eyes all lit up." He raised his glance to look Eaves in the eye. "Life is short. I worry about the war, but sometimes you have to grab happiness by the tail. You're a good man, Eaves. If she'll have you, I'll be proud to have you as my son-in-law."

Eaves' eyes misted. Something about the older man's confidence and acceptance astounded him.

"I'll ask her, and if she says yes, I'll try to make you proud."

"You already make me proud to know you, son. Just wish this confounded war was over." He cleared his throat. "What do you think about the operation in Sicily? At least we got a toehold in Europe now."

"Mussolini better get ready. We're headed his way, and he'll be the first to fall. Then—on to Berlin."

"So many losses . . ." Bill took a drink of his tea and changed the subject. "How's your day off been going?"

"Tried to play a round of golf with my buddy this morning but couldn't believe the wind." Eaves grinned. "When I teed off on the second hole, the wind was blowing so hard the ball lifted straight up and swooped right back at me, rolling to a stop at my feet. Never saw anything like it!" He shook his head. "I thought our West Texas wind was bad, but you got us beat. Doesn't it ever let up?"

Bill laughed out loud and slapped his thigh. "Wish I could have seen that!"

"Dinner's served. You boys need to wash up." Jean's mother, Ollie, stood in the doorway, smiling. Mouth-watering smells drifted into the living room.

"Yes, ma'am. You don't have to call us more than once," Bill said with a wink.

✈✈✈

Soon they were all gathered around the dining room table, the red roses beautifully arranged in a crystal vase in the center of a gold-colored tablecloth.

Platters of Southern fried chicken and fried okra were piled high beside bowls of pinto beans and potato salad. Delightful odors filled the air.

"True Southern comfort food, just like my Aunt Minnie used to fix," Eaves said.

"Let's thank the Lord for this bounty." Bill stretched out his arms, as the family all joined hands and bowed their heads.

"Thank you, Lord, for this good food and the hands that prepared it. We are grateful for Your provision. We pray for all the young men in harm's way today. May You protect and guide them as they fight for freedom and country. Grant them success. In Jesus' Name. Amen."

"Now, tell us about your Aunt Minnie," Bill said as they passed the food around the table. "Do they live out in Iraan, close to your folks?"

"Oh, no. Aunt Minnie and Uncle Otto don't live in Texas. They live on a farm up by Marlow, Oklahoma." Eaves hesitated, flashing back to that faraway place and time as he carefully ladled some beans onto his plate. "I was born in Oklahoma and was only eighteen months old when Mama died. My older sister Ruth and I first went to live in town with our Grandmother Gray, but she had a tiny house and my two uncles lived there too. So, Aunt Minnie and Uncle Otto took us in. We loved the farm, and Aunt Minnie was the world's best cook."

He set down the bowl of beans. "They became our second parents. Lived with them till I was six I reckon. Then Daddy remarried and came to get us." He paused. "Salt of the earth, they are. Never will forget their kindness and love. 'Bout broke their hearts when Ruth and I left. They never had any children of their own."

They all ate in silence for a few minutes. Tears glinted in Jean's eyes.

Embarrassed that he'd made it pretty obvious it had broken his heart too, Eaves ducked his head and finished his last bite of fried chicken.

Bill cleared his throat. "More fried okra or potato salad, Eaves?"

"Yes, sir." He smiled, glad to focus back on the food. "Haven't tasted anything this good for quite a spell." He dished up another helping of fried okra.

"Well, you better save room for dessert." Jean rose from the table. "Made it special." She soon returned with two plates of cake and served him and her father first, returning moments later with two more servings.

After Eaves devoured his first bite, he looked at her with admiration. "My favorite—coconut with lemon filling. Best I've ever had."

She blushed and looked down. "Glad you like it."

The cake quickly disappeared. "Thank you so much." Eaves turned his gaze to Ollie. "You don't know how much it means to eat a good home-cooked meal." He glanced back at Jean. "I hate to eat and run, but we're supposed to meet the Brandts at the Balinese Room in half an hour for the show tonight."

Jean's mother smiled as she stood up and shooed them away from the table. "You're as welcome as the flowers in spring. Don't worry about the dishes, Jean." She started clearing the table. "Y'all just go on now and have a grand time."

✈✈✈

As they left the house, Eaves reached for her hand.

Jean loved how her fingers curled inside his, like they belonged there. They walked hand in hand toward the seawall. His hand felt strong, but so gentle.

The warm moist wind tossed her hair and carried the scents of the sea and the oleanders.

"I appreciate your folks so much, opening their home to me," Eaves said. "You are lucky to have such loving parents."

Jean nodded. "They're the best. I'm so thankful to be blessed with folks who love the Lord and walk with Him every day. I know it means a lot to them that you join us at church on Sundays." She looked at him. "Tell me more about your parents."

He hesitated for a moment. "Daddy is a hard worker. I appreciate him teaching me to always do my best, to never quit or be a slacker. He and my stepmother took us to church every Sunday and were strict about us doing what's right. I learned to do what I was told and not talk back." He laughed. "That's been a help in the Army Air Corps."

"Did they talk about Jesus?" she asked.

"Well, we always said grace. And they wanted us to get baptized as soon as we were old enough to understand what that meant."

"I know we've only been dating about a month, but I remember you once said you didn't feel close to the Lord. Can you tell me more about that?"

"I believe He died for my sins. Sometimes, I wonder though . . . "His voice trailed off as they reached the Balinese Room pier.

Jean's heart sank. What did he wonder about? Didn't he believe like she did? It's really important to not be unequally yoked.

"I'm not perfect. Maybe I don't deserve His love."

"You don't have to earn His love." Jean squeezed his hand as they arrived at their destination. She looked deep into his blue eyes. "He died for you and loves you just the way you are."

Eaves smiled at her words and tightened his grip on her hand as they stepped onto the rough planks of the pier.

The Balinese Room sat at the end of the six-hundred-foot partially-covered pier jutting out from the seawall into the Gulf. Meant to be impressive, it was the most glamorous spot in Galveston. As they strolled down the long wooden pier, waves crashed below and the cry of a seagull pierced the air.

Eaves held the heavy door open for her and Jean stepped into another world. From hot and humid, the air surrounding her suddenly became dry and cool. She reveled in the new sensation of air conditioning, with intriguing odors hard to describe—mysterious, musky scents of sea-soaked wood and bamboo.

In the first room, the wild carpet swirling with tropical leaves drew her eye. Colorful fish flashed in large water displays, and tropical bird calls filled the air, transporting her to a South Seas paradise.

The next heavy door opened to the dining room. Known for their exquisite food, the Maceos family served the rich and famous elegantly. Bone china plates, with crystal glasses and silver flatware glittered on white linen tablecloths. Jean's eyes feasted on the dazzling splendor.

Moving on, Eaves had more doors to open. They passed through exclusive gift shops and several lounges before finally reaching their destination, the Grand Ballroom.

Stepping inside the immense room, Jean gasped at the sight of the beautifully painted murals covering every wall. Beautiful Polynesian women graced ocean beaches, surrounded by palms and flora, all framed with delicately carved wood molding.

In front of the bandstand, two intricately sculpted palm trees held up fish nets and floats intertwined with twinkling blue lights above the highly polished wooden dance floor. Tables filled the room, with flickering candles and bowls of fresh flowers centered on elegant white linen tablecloths.

Their friends, Gert and Bud Brandt, waved from a table close to the bandstand. Eaves took Jean's elbow and guided her to the table, pulling back a chair and sliding it under her.

"How are you two doing?" Looking smart in his dress uniform, Bud reached out to shake Eaves' hand,

"Just had one of the best home-cooked meals ever," Eaves said as he pumped Bud's hand and turned to smile at Jean.

"I'm still trying to learn to cook," Gert said ruefully, shaking her brunette curls. "Afraid I burned the roast tonight and put too much salt in the greens, but Bud is patient with me." She gazed at him with love and adoration in her brown eyes.

Jean knew they had just been married a month or so. A lot of couples were tying the knot before the guys shipped out.

Bud laughed. "Not the worst thing in the world." He sat down and glanced around the room, which was quickly filling with many other men in uniform and civilians in glamorous attire. "Glad we got here early. Slipped the maître d' a couple of bucks to get these seats. But it's worth it. Phil Harris and Alice Faye are the headliners tonight."

"Oh, she is so beautiful," Jean said with a sigh, picturing the glamorous blonde star. This night was definitely a dream come true.

She looked at Eaves.

Yes, more than she dared hope for.

✈✈✈

They leaned on the pier rail, gazing up into an inky black sky with pinpoint sparkles twinkling down on the end of a perfect evening.

"What a magnificent show," Jean said. "Thank you so much for bringing me."

The constant warm wind tore at the menu fluttering like a moth in Jean's hand. Eaves reached out to secure it for her. "Careful," he said.

"Thanks. I wouldn't want to lose the menu Alice Faye signed for me. That was so gracious of her." She looked up at him, clutching it close to her heart. "And it means even more as remembrance of this special night we had together." She paused, looking out over the dark water. "It's like a fairy tale come true. If I pinch myself, will I wake up and find it was just a dream?"

"It's no dream, sweetheart."

Eaves tipped her chin up and slowly lowered his lips to hers. He gently kissed her, wrapping her in his arms. He could feel her heart beating against his chest and fought to control his rising passions. He lifted his head and gazed into her dark eyes.

Now—it's the perfect time.

Stepping back, he reached into his pocket and located the tiny box. Going down on one knee, he took her hand and looked up. In a husky voice, he said, "Jean, I love you with all my heart. I know we haven't known each other long, but I want you to be my wife. Will you marry me and wait for me to come home after I do my duty for our country?"

Jean appeared to be stunned. She opened her mouth and her heart spoke for her. "Yes, darling. Oh, yes!"

He opened his hand and offered a tiny box to her.

She fumbled to open it and stared at the gold ring with the glint of a diamond. "Oh . . . it's so beautiful."

"A wedding as soon as we can," he said, rising to his feet. "A promise sealed with a kiss." He pulled her into his arms as their lips met again.

Chapter 4

23 July 1943—West Texas

"I'M SO GLAD THEY APPROVED YOUR LEAVE." Jean watched the graceful mesquite trees and prickly pear cactus of the Texas landscape blur together as the car whizzed along. "But I'm a little nervous meeting your folks and your family. What if they don't like me?"

She chewed on her lip, remembering her nervousness when they told her parents that they wanted to get married now, before he had to head overseas. They'd been supportive, glad to accept Eaves into the family. But what about Eaves' parents? They'll probably think this is happening too fast.

"Don't you worry about that." Eaves stretched out his right arm to pull her closer to his side. "They can't help but love you."

She smiled at him, and cuddled close. "You're a little prejudiced, I think. But I love it."

She stared out the window, thoughts still swirling.

I'm so lucky to have this time with him before he leaves for the war.

She shivered slightly. Who knows what the future holds?

The flat plains with fields of cotton and maize gave way to the bluffs of West Texas, dotted with dark cedars here and there. Some deer lunched on green grass in the bottom of the ditch.

Scattered about the hills, pump jacks with giant hammer-like heads rose and fell, drawing the black gold from the earth. The odor of fresh oil floated through the car as they drew nearer to Iraan, the tiny West Texas town where Eaves grew up.

A post office, drugstore, barber shop and grocery store lined the streets surrounding the town square. "There's the theater," Eaves pointed. "It's only open on Saturday nights."

"And Iraan High School, my old alma mater," he said as they drove by the two-story red brick building, the football field prominent beside it. "Left a lot of sweat and tears on that field in the four years I played football there." He laughed. "The whole town showed up on Friday nights. Football and church, that's what brings the folks together in a small town like this."

Jean could almost imagine the seats filled with cheering students and parents, little ones playing tag behind the bleachers. She felt a little envious. "You know I went to that all-girl Catholic school in Galveston, mostly because my friends did. It was an excellent school, but we didn't have any sports. You'll have to teach me about football."

"No problem, if you want to learn." He kept driving, leaving the small community behind. "Camp One is three miles south of here. The Ohio Oil Company owns the houses—the folks just rent. Daddy's a maintenance man and a gauger. I was working for them as a roustabout when the Japs bombed Pearl Harbor. I'd come home from college because of a knee injury during football."

"Roustabout?" Jean cocked her head. So much she didn't know about this man she was about to marry. "What's a roustabout?"

"Oh, that's just an oil driller's helper." He grinned. "You get to do all the really dirty work."

"I see. And you played football in college?"

"Yes, at Hardin Simmons in Abilene for two years on an athletic scholarship. Played center for them till I got hurt and came home to heal up. Then Pearl Harbor happened." He paused, looked out the window before continuing. "My best friend John and I decided to enlist in January. He was declared 4F, but I passed the physical and was thrilled when I made it into the Army Air Corps. Always had a dream of flying."

He smiled. "The whole family came to Jones Field at Bonham when I graduated as an air cadet on the 4th of July that summer. My sister Ruth and her husband, Marcus, were there too. You'll get to meet them today. They're coming down from Lubbock. Marcus enlisted in the Army and is stationed there. Ruth is head cashier for the PX. I spent a lot of time with them when I did my advanced flight training in Lubbock."

As Eaves talked about his family, Jean remained silent, a raw place in her heart aching as her thoughts flew to her brother. She still missed him so much. "Must've been nice to have family there," she murmured.

She swallowed the lump in her throat. She should tell him. "Did I ever tell you about my brother John?"

Eaves' eyes widened. "No . . . I didn't know you had any brothers."

Tears pooled in her eyes. "It's still hard to talk about." She took a ragged breath. "He was my only sibling. Both of us were born in March, just a year apart, and we were always close. John was just twelve when he came down with a horrible stomachache. My folks finally rushed him to the hospital, but he died anyway." Tears flowed down her cheeks. "They said it was appendicitis, that it ruptured."

Eaves drew her closer and squeezed her shoulder. "I'm so sorry, sweetheart. That must have been terrible for you and your folks to lose him like that."

"That's why I think it is so special that you have two brothers and three sisters to share life with." Jean sniffed, and pulled a handkerchief out of her purse. "When we get married, I'll have brothers and sisters too." She attempted a smile, wiped the dampness from her cheeks, and looked out the window. They rode in silence for a few minutes.

"Losing your only brother." Eaves shook his head. "I can't even imagine losing my sister Ruth. And you were so resilient—your faith shines through all that pain." He blinked his eyes. "Yes, you'll have brothers and sisters to love soon."

Enough sniffling. She didn't want to ruin the happiness of this day. "So," she said, taking another deep breath, "how long were you in Lubbock doing that advanced training?"

"Oh, about three months. I received my commission as a 2nd Lieutenant on November 10th. That was a red-letter day, the day I got my silver wings." He paused, then grinned. "Daddy and my two younger brothers attended the ceremony, and afterwards Marcus went with us guys to see Texas Tech play Texas A&M. First time my brothers ever got to see a college football game."

Eaves slowed down as they entered Camp One, and turned on the first street lined with little houses that all looked alike. He stopped in front of a small white cottage with a green roof. "Here we are."

The front door flew open, and a freckled-faced kid ran toward the car.

Jean smiled. *Another redhead!*

Eaves swung open the car door and stepped out in time to give the youngster a hug that lifted him off his feet. "My youngest brother, Lyall." He ruffled Lyall's red hair. "This is Jean."

Lyall shyly ducked his head.

"Red, can we go golfing?" he blurted out. Then, as if remembering his manners, he turned and ducked down to look at her through the car door, "Nice to meet you, Miss Jean."

"Golfing? We'll see," Eaves said with a laugh as he walked around the vehicle and opened the car door for Jean. Taking her elbow, he guided her toward the house as more family members streamed out the door.

She took a deep breath, hoping to keep the names of his siblings straight.

"This is Levon," Eaves said.

Jean saw a lean young man with a quiet smile and brown hair coming toward them, and she knew he was the next oldest son. Two young teenage girls followed him.

"My sisters, Lou Ann and Laverne," Eaves said.

Lou Ann also had red hair and freckles, and an engaging smile. Laverne, her older sister, was a dark-haired girl with angular features.

Behind them appeared his stepmother, Gladys, wiping her hands on a dish towel, with a flowered apron over her cotton housedress.

"Hi Mom," Eaves said.

"Welcome home W.T.," she said softly.

Slight of build with her reddish-brown hair pulled back in a bun, she seemed reserved as she gave each of them a brief hug.

Eaves' dad appeared in the doorway. Tom Eaves was an imposing figure, coal-black hair and dark eyes with a square jaw and high cheek bones, his leather-like skin darkly tanned. He strode to his son, and looked at him proudly as he gave him a hug. "Good to see you, son."

Then he turned toward Jean, looking her up and down as he said, "So this is Jean."

Jean smiled but felt her legs wobble a little. She reached out and put an arm around Eaves' waist, leaning against him for support.

Immediately she noticed Gladys' eyes narrow and her lips purse.

Uh-oh . . . a moment of panic slipped through Jean. Had she done something wrong?

Just then a blue Chevy pulled up behind their car. A dark-haired beauty leaped from the passenger side and ran to Eaves. "Red, it's so good to see you!" She wrapped her arms around him and Jean, giving them both a big hug. "And you must be Jean, the one I've heard so much about. I'm Ruth."

Jean felt a strength and a warmth surrounding Ruth that she liked. And so physically un-like Eaves, with dark brown-black hair and dark eyes—why, she and Ruth could be sisters.

A slender man with thinning brown hair and a big smile stepped out of the driver's side door in his Army uniform. Jean knew three stripes on his shoulder meant he was a sergeant.

"Hey Red—great to see you." He looked at Jean. "I'm Marcus, Ruth's husband. Glad to meet you."

Marcus smiled at Eaves and winked. "Looks like you lucked out, brother."

Jean blushed. Ruth looked at Marcus and shook her head. "Men! Come on now, let's get out of the sun." She linked arms with Jean and walked toward the swing on the porch.

Grateful for the suggestion, Jean suddenly realized how hot she was, moisture beading up on her forehead as the West Texas sun beat down on them. She and Ruth settled down on the porch swing as the family gathered around, the kids sitting on the steps and the men sprawled in the other chairs.

"I'll get y'all something to drink," Gladys said. She soon returned carrying a tray with glasses and a pitcher of fresh lemonade.

"Thank you. This is delicious," Jean said, after slaking her thirst with a long drink.

Jean learned that two years ago Ruth had been the home economics teacher at Iraan High School and Marcus the history teacher. The school board actually changed the rule forbidding married couples to teach at the same school when they fell in love and planned to marry.

"Yeah, they didn't want to lose two of their best teachers," Eaves said with a twinkle in his eyes. "Would you believe the Friday they chose to get married was Halloween? Only had the weekend for a honeymoon. Monday when they returned to school, the seniors shivareed them—carried them both out of their classrooms and dunked 'em in a stock tank. A Texas way to start a marriage."

Everyone laughed, but Jean's heart lurched. She hoped that wouldn't happen to her.

"Then, a month later—Pearl Harbor," Marcus murmured. "The whole world turned upside down." A sobering quiet descended over the family as each remembered the shocking news and the uncertainty of the future that loomed over them all.

"By the way, Marcus, are your brothers overseas yet?" Eaves set down his glass.

"Well, Don is somewhere in the Atlantic serving as a pharmacy mate on the USS Pastores. Spike joined the Army Air Corps, and is in Sioux Falls about to complete radio operator/mechanic training. Being prepared to serve on a bomber, but we don't know where yet. Keep an eye out for him—maybe he'll be headed your way, who knows?"

Eaves nodded. "Could be . . . it's a small world."

Ruth cleared her throat. "Did Red ever tell you about the road trip he and I took the summer of '41?"

Jean shook her head. "No, where did you go?"

"I'd just bought my first car, a black '39 Chevy. Two of my best friends and one of their younger brothers joined us for a trip to California. We all pooled our money and camped along the way. Swam in the Pacific Ocean and ate clam chowder at Fisherman's Wharf. Crossed the Golden Gate Bridge as we left San Francisco and drove up Highway 101 through the Redwoods. Went all the way to Seattle, Washington."

"Don't forget we cut over to see Crater Lake," Eaves said. "The bluest lake I ever saw. Won't ever forget it."

Ruth smiled, nodding in agreement. "From Seattle we drove to Yellowstone, then down to Pikes Peak in Colorado."

Jean noticed Eaves stiffen and looked down to see his hand clench when Ruth mentioned Pikes Peak.

"What an adventure," Jean said. She'd never been outside of Texas and couldn't help feeling a bit envious.

"Yes . . . and then do you know what my sister did?" Eaves had a sharp edge in his voice. "She didn't think I was able to drive her precious car up Pikes Peak. She spent good money to hire a driver." He glared at Ruth, angrier than Jean had ever seen him except when he talked about the Germans and the Japanese.

"Whoa," Ruth said. "It was my first car. And we saw so many cars stalled with their hoods up and radiators steaming from trying to drive up that mountain." She looked pleadingly at him. "Don't be angry, Red. I know you are a very capable driver, but they recommended a professional."

He just shook his head. Jean could see how stubbornly he stuck to his guns when he felt insulted. And his sister Ruth was equally strong in defending her decision.

Eaves looked at his brothers and Marcus. "Let's get the golf clubs from the shed and go play a round." He glanced back at Jean. "Are you okay staying here with the gals?"

She nodded, even though her gut tightened. She forced a smile. Tension lingered in the air with whatever had ruffled his stepmother earlier. But she felt comfortable with Ruth.

He popped the trunk and took out his clubs. His younger brothers ran ahead to open the shed door as Marcus strode over to get another set of clubs.

"Bet I beat you this time," Marcus said laughing, as he tugged the bag of clubs firmly up onto his shoulder.

Tom Eaves walked over to open the front door and stepped back into the house. Gladys leaned over to Jean and spoke quietly but firmly. "Please, we don't have any unnecessary hugging or kissing in front of the children." Then she turned and looked at Lou Ann and Laverne. "Please come help me fix dinner." The girls followed their mother into the house.

Seeing Jean's stricken expression, Ruth patted her hand. "It's okay, Jean. They're just old school. I'm sure you didn't do anything wrong."

Coming from a family where affection was often expressed physically, Jean realized Eaves' parents had a formality and a coldness she had not expected. "I hope I haven't offended them."

"Don't worry about it," Ruth said. "Now, tell me about the wedding plans. Red wrote that you're getting married the first week of August."

"We're planning a small wedding in Galveston at the church with my parents and a few of our friends." She looked into Ruth's brown eyes. "I'm so sorry you and Marcus can't be there."

"I'm sorry, too. Red and I are extra close because of losing our mother when we were so young." She took a deep breath. "But Marcus couldn't get any more leave. And we're
shorthanded at the PX."

Ruth took a long drink of lemonade. "By the way, did Red tell you that I got to represent our PX when Brigadier General Walter Kraus came? We sold more war bonds in Lubbock than anywhere else in a three-state area, and he presented us with an award." Her eyes sparkled. "I was thrilled to see all that support for our troops."

Jean looked at her with admiration. "No, but Red told me you were the head cashier. That's a lot of responsibility. I wish I could contribute like that."

"Just glad to have the job, and to be close to Marcus." She smiled warmly at Jean. "I'm so glad Red has found someone he loves to share life with." Ruth squeezed Jean's hand. "Welcome to the family."

Chapter 5

8 NOVEMBER 1943—POCATELLO ARMY AIRFIELD, IDAHO

"YOU BUNK HERE, SIR." The orderly pointed to the nearest barracks. Eaves nodded and hopped off the jeep, shouldering his duffel bag.

He dropped the bag on the cot nearest the door. Weary from the flight, he hoped to be here in Pocatello for a while, long enough for Jean to come. The last month in Utah had been so lonely without her. Just thinking of her triggered a deep longing inside and he felt his pulse quicken. He perched on the side of the cot and pulled out her picture. Her dark eyes looked into his, her softness awakened desire to hold her close.

He shook his head, remembering. Seemed like a dream. Just three months ago yesterday, they had stood before her folks and a small group of friends as the pastor declared them husband and wife. They only had weekends together, so every moment counted, and special memories flooded over him. Maybe they could be together again here in Pocatello, while his crew was being formed and the final trainings completed . . . before the day came to fly overseas.

"It will work out," she had said. She always had faith, talking about Jesus being right there with them, and believing He would help them be together regardless. Sometimes her sweet love felt like a dream, as fragile as a bubble that could pop and disappear.

Lost in thought, he was startled to hear the barracks door open. A decidedly unfeminine voice interrupted his reverie.

"Lieutenant Eaves?"

He turned to see a short second lieutenant entering the barracks door, duffel bag on his shoulder. "Yes."

"Tudor, Jim Tudor, sir." He strode forward and held out his hand. Eaves noticed the silver wings on his left chest, the firm handshake and friendly smile.

"You must be my copilot. I go by W.T., but my friends call me Red."

Jim laughed. "I can't imagine why," he said as he eyed the color of Eaves' hair. "But thanks for deciding to call me 'friend.'"

Eaves chuckled.

Noticing the frame in Eaves' hand, he asked, "Who's the beauty queen?"

Eaves' face warmed. "My wife, Jean."

Jim gave a low whistle. "She's a looker." Then, locking eyes with Eaves, he said, "Bet you miss her."

Eaves nodded. "Hope to go out tomorrow on our day off to see if I can rent her a room in town. She's found a ride with some other Air Corps wives driving up from Galveston."

"Wish you luck. Heard it's hard to find a place sometimes." He put his duffel bag down on the bed near Eaves and started unpacking.

✈✈✈

Early the next morning Eaves caught a ride into town and picked up *The Idaho State Journal* from a young boy hawking newspapers on a street corner. He noticed a lot of other men in uniform out on the town.

Quickly he scanned the "Rooms for Rent" section and started knocking on doors. Everywhere he went, the message was the same. "Sorry, I just rented it."

At the last house on the list, as he shared the need to find a room for his wife, the kind older gentleman seemed to sense his discouragement at another "no."

"Say, why don't you come to our church tomorrow morning? I'm sure someone might open a room for her."

"Thank you, sir. I'll be there." Eaves quickly scribbled down the time and directions on the margins of the newspaper.

The next morning, Eaves arrived early at the church. The older gentleman and his wife greeted him at the door.

"Glad to see you made it," he said, shaking Eaves' hand. He nodded toward a gray-haired woman in a blue dress standing in the vestibule. "I was just telling Mrs. Brown about the room you needed. She's a widow, got a big house and could use some company. Let me introduce you."

Eaves noticed her twinkling blue eyes and infectious laugh. Seemed to be a down-to-earth kind of person. Soon he'd made arrangements for Jean to stay with her. As the service started, Eaves found a seat in a back pew, bowed his head and gave thanks.

Jean was right. The Lord had provided—again.

✈✈✈

15 November 1943—Pocatello Army Airfield, Idaho

Eaves and Tudor walked toward the B-24 waiting at the hard-stand for their training mission.

"Feels like we've been flying together more than just a week. By the way, how long were you with the 10th Anti-submarine Squad before you were transferred here to the 464th?" Tudor asked.

Eaves thought for a minute. "Well, got assigned to Shoal Field in Galveston in December of '42. I completed the anti-submarine certification and got my promotion to first lieutenant right after Jean and I married, so late August, '43. Then mid-October all the anti-sub units were transferred to Boise. So . . . about eleven months, I reckon." Eaves grinned. "Speaking of Boise, did I ever tell you about time the brass wanted to go pheasant hunting?"

Tudor shook his head.

"They asked me if I wanted to fly on my days off, so I said sure. We dropped down into Pierre, South Dakota, where a friend of theirs took us out to some corn fields. Boy, shooting those ringnecks was great fun. And they were pretty tasty too!"

"Better than the chow here, I bet." Tudor turned to look him in the eye. "I want you to know, Red, that I sure appreciate flying with you. All that great experience under your belt with the airtime you built up chasing those subs. And the crew you brought with you . . . all top-notch gunners."

The compliment warmed Eaves' heart. Tudor was a skilled pilot and becoming a good friend.

"Well, have to say I'm glad to have you in the seat next to me too." He smiled back at Tudor. "And I was grateful they kept the team together. You're right—all of them take care of business and are pretty good Joes."

He looked off in the distance. "Did you ever hear about the first time Linneman met Christel?"

"No, but I know Linneman can talk nonstop and pulls some pranks. What happened?"

"Well, when he and Fangman joined the crew as waist gunners, Linneman nods toward Christel and barks, 'Who's the little shrimp?' pretty loudly to the other guys and then laughs. Christel heard him. Didn't appreciate the derogatory remark about his height."

Tudor grinned. "I reckon."

"What he didn't know was that Christel had just been made staff sergeant and outranked him. He put Linneman in his place in a hurry!"

Tudor laughed out loud. "Would love to have seen that! Christel is even shorter than I am, but underneath that quiet exterior, he's a tough cookie."

"And a great gunner." Eaves rubbed his chin. "Have to tell you about my initial impression. I was on the gunnery range in Galveston, training with two other officers. Thought I'd made a respectable showing, twelve hits, with my buddies scoring eleven and thirteen. A group of enlisted men stepped up next. Most hit the target only six or eight times, with ten hits the highest until a short sergeant stepped up to the line and scored sixteen hits." Eaves shook his head. "Sure impressed me. Was glad to find him assigned as our radio operator and nose gunner when the anti-sub crews got formed."

Tudor whistled. "Whew! That's some shooting. Nice to know we have a gunner who can hit what he aims at."

As they arrived at the plane and started to climb up into the bomb bay, they overheard Linneman talking above them.

"I think we're going to be great friends, Christel," he said.

"Why do you say that?"

Eaves looked up to see Christel giving Linneman a skeptical glance.

"Because you're the only guy here on the crew that hasn't told me to shut up," he replied.

Christel just smiled a crooked smile.

✈✈✈

18 NOVEMBER 1943—POCATELLO, IDAHO

Jean sat watching out the front window of Mrs. Brown's large two-story white house for Gert's car. Time dragged between weekends, the only time she and Red had together. This mid-week opportunity to visit the lounge on the base would be a highlight in an otherwise very long week.

She liked Mrs. Brown and enjoyed her company. She'd taken to joining her in the sitting room as they each pulled out needlework to help pass the time. And she accompanied Mrs. Brown to the ladies' meetings at the church, where they worked on projects that supported the war effort. This week they'd cut and rolled strips of cotton for bandages.

"There's my ride," she called out to Mrs. Brown. "See you at supper time."

"Have a good time, Jean."

She pulled on her heavy coat, wrapping the warm woolen scarf that Mrs. Brown had given her over her ears and around her neck. Pocatello was much colder than she'd imagined, quite a contrast from sunny, warm Galveston weather. And winter was just beginning.

She hurried down the sidewalk to the car, hopping in the passenger side.

"Hi Gert. Thanks for the ride." She smiled at her friend. "How's the gas holding up?"

"Hey, glad we can go together." Gert returned her smile and glanced at the gauges. "Got enough gas for today. Hope my ration card gets here soon though." She sighed. "Everything's rationed now. But . . . we've got to be thankful for what we have."

"I know. I'm down to my last pair of nylons." Jean laughed. "More important than looking good, they help my legs stay warm. These icy winds cut right through me!"

Gert nodded in agreement. "A lot colder here than winters on the Gulf."

Jean looked at Gert. "You've been such a good friend." Her eyes misted. "You don't know how much it meant to have you and Bud stand up with us the day we tied the knot."

Gert reached out and squeezed her hand. "We felt honored to be asked. We think the world of you and Red."

Soon they passed through the gate at the base and were directed to the officers' club. Parking quickly, they hurried inside, anxious to see their husbands.

Jean spotted Eaves by the front door, a big smile on his face and books in his arms.

"Hi, sweetheart." His eyes tenderly searched her face and he gave her a quick kiss. "How's your week been going?"

"Thanks for finding me such a good place to stay. Mrs. Brown is a dear. I went with her to the women's meeting at her church on Tuesday. We rolled bandages this time."

He nodded. "They'll be appreciated, I'm sure. Do you have everything you need?

"Yes. Gert's hoping her gas card arrives soon. Do you think we could help some with the cost of the gasoline? I sure appreciate her willingness to drive."

"I've got a little cash I can slip to her before you leave." He pointed to two chairs by the window. "Let's sit over there and maybe you can help me study for the test I have tomorrow."

Jean noticed that many wives had books in their lap and were quizzing their husbands. She was glad to do anything helpful.

The time flew by as she asked questions about navigation and terms totally unfamiliar to her but not to Eaves. She was amazed at his memory. Reluctantly she realized it was almost time to leave.

"Mom has decided she is going to call you Sug," she suddenly announced.

Eaves looked at her quizzically. "Shoog? What's that about?"

"Well, she said it's because you are sweet as sugar," she said, smiling.

He laughed but seemed pleased. "Well, I guess she can call me whatever she likes. Your mom is one special lady. Think about her as my own mom now."

Jean's heart warmed, blessed by his response. He and her mom did seem to have made a very unique connection.

She looked up to see Gert and Bud heading toward them.

"Hi, Bud," she said. "Sure am glad we're all here together."

He smiled at her and pulled Gert closer, his arm around her waist. "Yep. Nice to have our best friends with us." He eyed both the girls. "You two stay out of trouble now, and we'll see you this weekend."

Eaves spoke up. "Thanksgiving is coming up next Thursday. Heard we'll have turkey and all the trimmings." He paused. "We do have a lot to be grateful for."

Jean's thoughts flew to home. This would be the first Thanksgiving she would not share with her folks. Her first as a wife, beside her husband. Still hard to realize she was married to the love of her life.

Yes—together for the present. A blessing, for sure.

Chapter 6

14 December 1943—Pocatello Army Airfield

"MISERABLE WEATHER," TUDOR MUTTERED.

Eaves nodded in agreement. "At least we got one training flight in today."

Snow and ice had grounded most flights that week. His crew only needed a couple more missions to complete Phase Two training and the delay was aggravating.

They hustled toward the mess hall. After being up in the air for more than four hours practicing long distance navigation and then a required hour and a half of instrument training, Eaves had worked up quite an appetite.

"Glad to finally get assigned to a squadron," Eaves commented as he hunched his shoulders against the cold.

Ten days ago, thirty-six more crews arrived from Mountain Home Army Airfield. Headquarters proceeded to assign all crews to one of four squadrons in the 464th Bomb Group. Eaves and his crew had been assigned to the 777th Bomb Squadron.

"Just wish we had a designated plane," he added. The older olive-drab B-24s used for training were not very safe and often in the shop for repairs. He was forced to fly a different Liberator for practically every training flight.

They squeezed into a crowded mess hall and got in line.

"Yeah, and a permanently assigned navigator would help too. Seems like we always get a rookie," Tudor said. "By the way, a reliable source from headquarters told me that crews who complete Phase Two training will be given leave for Christmas."

Eaves grabbed a tray. "That long-distance bombing flight is our last main requirement. I hope the weather stays clear long enough for us to complete it. Would love to have that leave."

Tudor scanned the mess hall for an empty table. "Yep. Pokey isn't first on the list of places I'd choose to hang out during Christmas holidays, but I can celebrate anywhere if we get leave."

Eaves nodded. "Too hard to get a ticket home on a bus or train. We'd just use up all our leave getting there. Plus, all this ice and snow is making travel almost impossible." He set down his tray and pulled back the chair. "Jean and I never had a honeymoon, so this could be the next best thing."

Tudor grinned. "She is a trooper, Red. If you're gonna have a ball and chain, she's a good one!"

Eaves smiled back, savoring Tudor's comment, glad his copilot, and now good friend, saw Jean that way. The familiar longing to see her welled up inside. He wished there was married housing here on the base. Their time together on weekends flew by.

After dinner they headed back toward the barracks in the dusk as light snowflakes drifted down. A rowdy chorus of "Pistol Packin' Mama" echoed from the officer's club. Eaves hummed along. Wartime America couldn't seem to get enough of the catchy tune, which had been the unofficial theme song of the former anti-sub crews and now morphed into a favorite of the 464th.

As he trudged through the snow, thinking about the tough, rootin'-tootin' Texas gal out for revenge glamorized in the song, he reflected on the striking contrast between her and the sweet little Texas gal God had given him. He silently vowed to never give Jean reason to doubt his love.

The snowstorm grounded all planes the next day, but after supper Eaves saw the flight list posted. As he scanned it, he found his name. They were scheduled for that final training flight the following morning. His attitude brightened, and a brief prayer winged upward.

Lord, please keep the skies clear one more day and help us successfully complete the assigned mission.

✈✈✈

Morning broke clear and bright. Runways had been plowed and all training missions a "go."

Eaves studied the flight plan calling for a simulated bomb run on a target in the Pacific Ocean about a hundred miles due west of San Francisco. It would be a long flight, a minimum of six hours, and they would drop fake bombs from 12,000 feet.

Once again, they had a rookie navigator, only his second training flight.

Eaves and Tudor went through the checklist. Elder, the flight engineer, popped the hatch to guide the B-24 as it taxied from the hardstand to the main runway.

Soon the B-24 rolled down the runway, reluctantly gained speed and lifted off.

Three hours later, Eaves licked his lips in concentration as they reached the Initial Point, the designated turning point onto the bomb run. Precision here was essential.

Eaves pressed his throat mic. "Bombardier, your plane."

The bombardier had control of the plane now. In a real attack, once the plane reached the IP and turned onto the bomb run, there could be no evasive maneuvers. Once on the bomb run, the plane had to remain straight and level until the bombs were dropped.

Moments passed. The plane lurched upward as the bombardier confirmed, "Bombs away! Your plane, sir."

Tudor gave Eaves a thumbs-up as the dummy bombs splashed down right on target. All requirements of the mission completed.

Now, all they had to do was fly back to Pocatello and land.

As they left the Sacramento area and headed northeast, dark clouds filled the horizon. Winds buffeted the plane. A storm front had moved in. Soon they were flying in solid clouds.

The plane suddenly leapt upward several hundred feet. An updraft! Then, they dropped in a free fall. In the extreme turbulence, the ship bobbed like a kite on a string.

Eaves managed to stabilize the plane and decided to try to fly above the storm, even though it meant using more fuel.

"Going up. We'll try to get out of the turbulence." He pulled back on the yoke.

Clouds grew only thicker.

"Ice forming on the wings," Tudor noted.

Minutes later, Eaves could no longer see the lights on the ends of the wings. Ice was building up fast. He struggled to keep the plane level as the accumulation of ice began to affect controls and altitude.

The B-24 had deicers on the edge of the wings but he was reluctant to use them except as a last resort. The deicers were rubber bladders that would expand when activated to break the ice off the leading edge of the wings , but he'd learned in training that the ice chipped off unevenly, leaving a jagged surface that affected air flow and lift.

He had to make a decision. "Going down—we'll try to drop below it."

At five thousand feet the clouds thinned and the icing appeared to stop. Eaves leveled out the plane, eyeing the needle and ball gauge that told him when they were flying straight. His shoulders ached from tension and fighting the wind.

"Navigator, what's our location and estimated time of arrival?"

"Mm . . . let me check the maps and get back to you, sir."

Eaves swallowed hard. He scanned the horizon, hoping they were past any high peaks in the Rockies.

"Elder, how are the fuel levels?"

The flight engineer quickly responded. "Below a quarter tank, sir."

The storm had slowed them down. Eaves looked at his watch. They'd been in the air for more than six hours now. Should be close to Pokey.

His gut clenched. Landing a B-24 on an icy runway in gusty winds would be a challenge.

✈✈✈

Jean put down her novel and looked out Mrs. Brown's big picture window. The wind whipped the bare tree limbs and moved the snow into sheets of ice crystals, creating new drifts across the sidewalk. Her wonder in the beauty of snow had faded as days stretched into weeks of frigid cold. Nothing like this in warm Galveston.

She sighed. Tomorrow morning she'd have to bundle up and shovel that front walk. Jean so appreciated Mrs. Brown's kindness and hospitality. She looked for anything she could do to be helpful.

An uneasy feeling slipped over her. Again, she wondered what Red was doing today. Only two more days before she could see him again.

Christmas was soon approaching, and thinking of her folks filled her with a deep longing for home. She closed her eyes and pictured herself seated by her parents in their little church on Christmas Eve. She could hear the Christmas carols as the children dressed in their parents' robes marched down the aisle. Shepherds coming to worship the King of Kings. Little angels with tinsel halos singing "Silent Night." She shook her head. Thanksgiving had been difficult. How would she get through Christmas without them?

Pray.

Startled, the word broke through her reverie.

What should I pray about, Lord?

Silence.

The uneasy feeling increased, her chest tightened, and she realized she was holding her breath.

Is Red in danger?

She dropped to her knees and turned to face the couch, her head bowed and her hands clasped before her.

Whatever the danger is, Lord, keep Red and his men safe. Thank You for providing all they need for You hold all things in Your hand, and You are faithful and true. Be with them Lord, give them wisdom and skill to overcome whatever is affecting their safety. If they are in the air, please put Your hands under the plane and guide it back to the airfield here at Pocatello. Help them to land safely. Send Your angels to be with them. In Jesus name, Amen.

She hastily got to her feet and climbed the stairs to her room, pulling her well-worn Bible off the nightstand and opening to Psalm 91. Sitting on the edge of her bed, she began to read aloud the words she had underlined, so familiar, so comforting:

"He that dwelleth in the secret place of the Most High shall abide under the shadow of the Almighty. I will say of the Lord, 'He is my refuge and my fortress, my God, in him will I trust.' Surely he shall deliver you from the snare of the fowler, and from noisome pestilence. He shall cover you with his feathers, and under his wings shalt thou trust; his truth shall be thy shield and buckler."

Yes, Lord. Cover them with Your feathers, lift them with Your wings.

She resumed reading.

"Thou shalt not be afraid for the terror by night; nor the arrow that flies by day; nor for the pestilence that walketh in the darkness; nor the destruction that wasteth at noon-day."

Even now, oh Lord, protect them against whatever threatens them.

"There shall no evil befall thee, neither shall any plague come near thy dwelling. For he shall give his angels charge over thee, to keep thee in all thy ways; they shall bear thee up in their hands, lest thou dash thy foot against a stone."

Yes, Lord, may no evil befall them. And please, please send your angels.

"He shall call upon me, and I will answer him. I will be with him in trouble; I will deliver him, and honor him."

She closed her eyes again and bowed her heart.

Thank you, Lord, for Your Word, for promises we can stand on regardless of the dangers around us.

Peace slipped over her heart and she clutched her Bible to her chest.

✈✈✈

18 DECEMBER 1943—POCATELLO, IDAHO

She saw him striding up the walk. Jean ran to the door and threw it open before Eaves could knock.

"Hi, sweetheart," Eaves murmured as he stepped forward and pulled her into his arms for a quick kiss.

She lingered in his arms, so grateful to feel his tender strength cradling her against his broad chest. "Oh Red, I'm so glad you are safe," she whispered.

Eaves cocked his head to look down at her. "Why wouldn't I be?"

She shivered and pulled him toward the living room. "Let's get out of the cold air."

He stomped his boots and bent to untie them. "Whoa—let me get these boots off so I don't track up Mrs. Brown's floors. By the way, where is she?" He slipped off the clunky boots.

Jean's smile grew even wider. "She's gone to her son's house for Christmas. She said she wanted us to have some privacy." She blushed and looked down.

"Well, bless her heart! She is a dear." He took Jean's hand in his and tugged her toward the couch. Pulling her down into his arms, he gave her another kiss, deeper and more passionate than the first, and she eagerly responded, losing herself in her love for this man.

After a moment, he lifted his head and gazed at her tenderly. "Now—what is this about me being safe?"

"Well, on Thursday the strangest thing happened. I had this terrible feeling you were in some sort of danger that afternoon. I got down on my knees and prayed for you and your men. Then I got out my Bible and read Psalm 91 out loud, claiming God's promises for safety for you. When I finished, a deep sense of peace washed over me, and I felt that whatever threatened you was over."

Eaves' eyes widened. "Well, you were right about the danger. We had been on a training mission when we ran into a bad storm on the way back. Gusty winds, dense clouds. Ice started coating the wings. Had to fly low to keep the ice from building up, and I was worried about landing on an icy runway. But a strange thing happened—the winds suddenly died down as we flew out of the clouds just south of Pokey. Amazingly, the runway was clear, no ice."

He leaned back and gazed deep into her dark eyes, a questioning look on his face. "How did you know we were in trouble?"

She shook her head. "I didn't—the Lord knew. And He prompted me to pray for you. His Holy Spirit is always right there with us, if we will just listen."

Eaves looked away, as his arms tightened around her. "You're a gift, you know. The Lord sure knew I needed someone with faith like yours."

"Hasn't He spoken to you like that sometimes?"

Eaves just shook his head.

"I'm not special, sweetheart. It says in His word that He is always speaking to His own—we just have to listen." Tenderly she touched his cheek and turned his face toward hers so she could look into his blue eyes. "He wants to talk to you too. Just tell Him whatever is on your heart, read His Word, and—listen."

He squeezed her tighter. "Listen. I'll try." He cocked his head. "I know He listened to you and answered your prayers, that's for sure."

He paused. "And I have one more thing to tell you, darling."

Was something wrong? Jean searched his face.

He grinned. "We completed all our trainings, and I have leave for the next two weeks. We get a honeymoon!"

Chapter 7

24 December 1943—Pocatello, Idaho

WARM AND FESTIVE, CANDLES GLOWED in centerpieces placed on every table in the small restaurant. The smell of fresh-cut pine boughs and Christmas carols filling the air helped Jean almost forget how much she missed not being home for Christmas.

Jean glanced at the laughing faces surrounding her. Eaves had invited all the crew for a Christmas Eve dinner on the town. These men seemed like family now, a band of brothers who had learned to respect and care for each other. She missed Gert and Bud, who left town to spend Christmas with family.

Tudor leaned across the table. "Say, Red, did you hear about the plane that went down? Lt. Gitt's crew, eight men lost. Said the cause of the accident was probably carburetor icing." He shook his head. "This weather has been something else. Guess we've been fortunate in not losing more men and planes in this deep freeze—ourselves included."

Eaves nodded solemnly as he glanced at Jean sitting beside him and reached out to cradle her hand in his. "Read about the crash in the Journal. Don't know how the maintenance guys manage to work on the planes in this kind of weather, especially out on the hardstands without any cover. It's amazing there haven't been more accidents."

Jean's hand tightened in his. The ice storm on the last training flight. It could have been so different. She silently breathed a quick prayer.

Thank You, Lord, for Your mercy. And please, please comfort the families that just lost loved ones. Such a devastating loss, right at Christmas.

Tudor nodded. "By the way, I joined the guys in the officers' club this afternoon to hear Roosevelt's radio address. He announced that General Dwight D. Eisenhower has been appointed to oversee the invasion of Europe. Not afraid to let the Krauts know we're coming for them." He took a drink of water. "Our bombers in England are already softening them up. Taking the battle into Germany itself, right to Berlin."

"Yep, and I think Ike's a good choice," Eaves said thoughtfully.

Jean noticed they sidestepped the recent news reports of the heavy losses of Allied bombers, the highest rate so far for the war. Not something she wanted to dwell on tonight, not on Christmas Eve.

Just then a trim brunette waitress wearing a red dress set a plate in front of her. It overflowed with traditional Christmas foods—moist turkey breast with dressing, mashed potatoes, green beans and cranberry sauce.

Jean smiled as she noticed the effect the pretty young girl had on the guys, who all began vying for her attention. But Eaves' eyes stayed locked on her own and her heart fluttered with the love she saw in them.

Lifting the napkin that covered a basket of warm rolls, the delicious scent of fresh yeast made her mouth water as she plucked one out. "Could you please pass the butter?" Jean looked at Lt. Tudor, who sat across the table from her.

"Yes, ma'am." He smiled at her as he passed it over. "I want to thank you for inviting all of us to share a Christmas meal with you and Red."

"We're so glad you could join us." She appreciated his respectful, direct ways and knew how much Red valued his copilot.

Fangman and Linneman sat next to him. She knew they were both waist gunners who had been with Red since Galveston, and that Fangman was also from West Texas. Linneman talked nonstop in his Missouri-drawl, telling jokes that kept them all laughing. Christel, the radioman, sat next to Linneman, and he laughed the hardest.

She whispered to Red. "Who did you say the other two gunners are that are sitting by Elder at the end of the table?"

"Sgt. Masterson, the guy with brown hair, is our tail gunner, and the little guy is Sgt. Petrone, our ball turret gunner. He has to be small to squeeze into that little bubble!" His eyes twinkled. "A great crew—couldn't ask for better men to fly with."

She smiled. "I'm so grateful you have confidence in them." Knowing they were all young and single, she appreciated the polite and considerate conduct extended to her and although about their same age, felt rather motherly toward them.

"Great party at the USO Club last night." Tudor winked at Eaves. "Swell time with a cute little blonde. She could really cut a rug!" Then, more seriously, he added, "The town folks are so darned supportive—always someone ready to listen and to dish out those delicious homemade treats."

"Yes, down-to-earth, always make you feel welcome. Jean and I stopped by to dance to the live music they brought in last weekend. And we took in a couple of movies too." He stopped to swallow a bite of turkey. "Saw *Song of Bernadette* and *A Guy Named Joe*."

"Oh, you had time for that?" Tudor laughed, giving Eaves a knowing look.

Eaves flushed but just smiled. "Well, Pokey has a little more action than my hometown in West Texas but not much more. And with all this snow and ice, sometimes you just have to stay in."

Jean smiled demurely and changed the subject back to movies. "My favorite was *Casablanca*. Such a good film, even though it was sad."

Soon the meal ended and choruses of "Merry Christmas" rang out as everyone bundled up and left the restaurant. Linneman hung back, apparently to share a few more words with the pretty little waitress.

Eaves wrapped his arm around Jean as they walked toward Mrs. Brown's house. Jean snuggled close, grateful for the lovely evening and the wonder of Christmas. She would choose to treasure this special time together . . . and consciously pushed away darker thoughts of an uncertain future.

✈✈✈

21 JANUARY 1944—POCATELLO ARMY AIRFIELD, IDAHO

Bad weather continued to plague the 464th in January with training runs all scrapped the first week. Time dragged. The only good thing—it meant more time with Jean. Eaves treasured every Saturday night and Sunday with his sweetheart.

Finally, the weather broke a little the second week. A series of full-scale practice sorties sent the whole group flying bombing missions to specific target cities. Eaves flew one mission to Las Vegas and another to Salt Lake City.

Gunnery missions focused on helping the gunners sharpen their aim on the move. On bombing missions Lambert dropped real practice bombs on isolated targets, mostly in remote areas of South Dakota. Tension to be ready pulsed through Eaves, and the crew jelled into a competent team as time drew near to complete Phase Three.

"Did you hear that the pilots flying with Colonel Bonner this week had some real concerns about his odd behavior?" Tuder glanced over at Eaves as they hiked back toward the barracks. "He seemed fine as long as everything went according to the book, but when they ran into some gusty winds, he panicked."

"Yeah, heard some talk about that." Eaves paused and gazed into the distance. "Another officer mentioned to me that he didn't want to fly with the colonel anymore after he tried to land under the recommended airspeed and flared out about ten feet higher than he should have." He shook his head. "I'm sure he's done a lot of things right to be in charge, but I'm glad we haven't had to fly with him."

"Dangerous enough as it is. Can't believe we've lost three planes and sixteen men just since the first of the year." Tudor cleared his throat. "Yesterday really hit home. One from our own squadron."

Eaves swallowed hard and set his jaw. Seven young men they knew, just gone. They'd crashed only eleven miles south of the base. Training in these older B-24s could be as fatal as combat.

Jean's face flashed before him. He'd noticed the dark circles under her eyes as news of each plane crash escalated her worry about his safety. He tried to reassure her, but she admitted that sirens made her cringe. She knew too that their time together was quickly drawing to a close, every weekend precious.

Eaves' arms ached. He felt like a pin cushion after all the vaccinations he'd received earlier that morning—typhoid, tetanus, smallpox, typhus, yellow fever, and cholera. Before the upcoming overseas travel, all airmen and ground crew were required to go through a mandatory series of physical exams carried out by the medical department. He'd waited in long lines to be poked and prodded till they checked off every item on his medical record.

"Heard that Elder ended up in the infirmary after all those shots. Him and a lot of other guys." Tudor winced as he rubbed his upper arm. "I'm sore, but glad I didn't get that sick."

Eaves nodded. "All the pressure to complete the training schedule, and now the overseas physicals—can't be long now. Rumors flying that we head out soon. And I'm ready to go. Wherever they send us, I believe we can help win this war."

Only days later the rumors proved true. The Ground Echelon received orders to start packing for the trip overseas.

Action around the Pocatello Army Airfield was nonstop. Everything from tools to typewriters were stenciled with the group number and transported to an area designated for packing onto railroad cars. Still, no one knew if they were going to the Pacific or to Europe.

Finally, on 3 February, the order came. Ground Echelon would leave by train for Camp Patrick Henry, Virginia. One mystery revealed—the 464th Bomb Group would be heading for the war in Europe.

✈✈✈

As he walked up the steps to Mrs. Brown's big old house, Eaves took a deep breath. The time for goodbyes had come. This would be the last weekend he and Jean would spend together for months . . . maybe forever.

Focus, Eaves. Enjoy the time left and carry those special memories close to heart.

Hours flew by and all too soon it was the time to part.

"I'm glad you'll be with your folks. I won't worry 'cause I know they'll take good care of you." Eaves looked deep into her dark eyes as he prepared to leave. He kissed her gently and held her close. "Be brave for me, darling. I'll be back as soon as I can."

"I appreciate Gert letting me ride back to Galveston with her and a couple of other wives tomorrow. So, I won't be alone." Jean looked down and drew a deep breath. "But I hate to leave you. I'm so thankful for every single moment we've had together, Sug."

Eaves saw the glint of tears under her pretty lashes.

"Now, don't cry sweetheart." He patted her shoulder.

"It's just . . . I, I had hoped . . ."

"What? What had you hoped?"

"That I might be . . . you know . . . in the family way."

Eaves laughed aloud. "Don't worry darling. Plenty of time for that. I want us to have a big family, three or four kids for sure." He squeezed her tight and then tilted her chin up for another long kiss.

Please, Lord, let it be.

A deep ache settled into his gut as he turned and steeled himself to walk away. Turning to look back one more time, he waved from the sidewalk and etched the sight of her standing in the doorway on his heart. Didn't know he could feel so lonesome.

Back at the base, Eaves found his orders waiting. Transfer to Lincoln, Nebraska, on 5 February—the staging area for all bomber crews preparing to leave for overseas.

✈✈✈

14 FEBRUARY 1944–LINCOLN ARMY AIRFIELD, NEBRASKA

Nothing like it. Eaves breathed in deeply, settling down into the pilot's seat. A brand-spanking-new B-24H, all their own. Better than a new-car smell. So different from the older planes they'd used in training, always reeking from odors of aviation fuel, hydraulic fluid, and human sweat.

Every crew member was onboard, checking out their area and their equipment thoroughly.

"Wow, feels great to have a plane of our own, right off the assembly line!" Tudor patted the console. "No more worn-out, hope-we-can-make-it-back-to-base piece of junk for us."

Eaves nodded. "Yep, sure feels good to have reliable wings under us as we head out." He turned to look at his copilot. "And I'm sure glad to have Haverkos assigned as our navigator."

The tall, athletic Midwesterner from Cincinnati took his job seriously and had been a welcome addition to the team, completing the crew. In the three instrument training flights they'd had in the new plane, Eaves was impressed by his professionalism and accuracy.

Extra tanks had to be installed in the bomb bay to carry the fuel they'd need to cross the Atlantic. And a brand-new plane required a thorough check from nose compartment to tail turret.

Right off the bat, Eaves liked Sgt. Ryskeciski, their crew chief. Knew his business. Eaves felt confident he and the ground crew would go over the plane with a fine-tooth comb before it left for combat. And while they prepared the plane for overseas travel, Eaves and the crew were pleased to receive a few days of leave to check out the sights in Lincoln, the capital city of Nebraska.

Eaves climbed to the top of the capitol building for a panoramic view of the plains. Wandering down "O" Street, he and Tudor found a nice little café that served a fine home-cooked meatloaf meal with piping-hot coffee for practically nothing.

Some of the guys chose to stay in the Cornhusker Hotel downtown—pretty luxurious compared to the accommodations on the base—but Eaves declined.

If only Jean were here.

He pictured her in the snug little Galveston cottage, safe and sound, with her folks there to keep her company.

Then . . . on 18 February the order came—APO 520. Fly to Morrison Field, Florida, final staging.

This is it. The last leg in the States on the way to war.

Chapter 8

14 March 1944—Oudna Airfield, Tunisia

After the crossing of the Atlantic and the close call at the Canary Islands, Eaves was glad to be back on land, but Oudna was nothing like he'd anticipated.

Chilled to the bone, Eaves looked disgustedly at the three inches of muck sticking to his boots as he slipped and slid his way toward their olive-green tent, sagging dejectedly beneath the weight of the pelting rain.

The 464th had arrived at the airfield during the rainy season. About ten miles south of Tunis, the capital of Tunisia, Oudna Field sat on a flat plain, a vast sea of mud. Nothing resembled his vision of windswept sand dunes and arid desert in broiling sunshine.

Engineers had laid steel matting to create the runway and taxiways, but they were dangerously slippery when covered with this adobe-type clay and pools of water. No electricity here. Torches lit the runway at night.

All forty-eight Liberators had survived the crossing, but inclement weather had kept the 464th grounded for a week.

Eaves threw back the tent flap and ducked into the semi-darkness. The smell of wet canvas, stale cigarettes, and aviation fuel permeated the air and assaulted his nostrils, but warmth greeted him, emanating from the stove they'd patched together. Created from a fifty-five-gallon drum, it sported a four-inch-pipe smokestack protruding through the tent roof. A matrix of copper tubing funneled in fuel from an airplane wing tank sitting on stilts outside. Not pretty, but it did the job. Warding off the damp cold, the stove kept the tent more comfortable, the coffee hot, and heated water for shaving.

Eaves reluctantly made the announcement. "Dig out your pinks, boys. Colonel Bonner has ordered a formal inspection in Class A uniform."

Haverkos looked up from his cot, total disbelief written across his face. "In this weather? You're kidding."

"Nope. Them's the orders. Parade ground, 1500."

Lambert chimed in. "What's the matter with the head honcho? He seems to major in the minors. Just yesterday in the officers' club, the guys were mumbling about his nitpicking style."

Eaves shrugged. He might not like it, but not his place to criticize the brass. He grabbed his flight bag and dug out the dress uniform. Finding it on the bottom of the bag, it was a wrinkled mess.

No ironing board here—they'll just have to do.

Soon the 464th stood at attention, a rumpled and disheveled lot, mud splatters on every pant leg and several men without shoes, sucked away by the voracious mud.

Colonel Bonner appeared late, arriving in a jeep that fishtailed as the wheels spun out-of-control in the gooey gumbo. He frowned, struggling to maintain his composure at the spectacle before him. Obviously dismayed, he said little and quickly dismissed the men.

"Bet this is the last formal inspection Bonner orders here," Sherman said as the officers trudged back to their tent. They quickly shed the muddy pinks in disgust, bagging them up to be sent to the laundry tent manned by Italian POWs.

Eaves had learned the POWs freely roamed the base, happy to be no longer engaged in the war. They also served the food in the mess tent. A small tent, it was only big enough to be used for cooking and the buffet table. A tarp out front covered the single serving line for all ranks, first-come first-served. Everyone was expected to take his food back to his own tent.

Home always on his mind, Eaves pulled out a V-mail. Victory Mail, a small letter and envelope combined, would be filmed on microfilm and reduced to one fourth its size when printed. Saving the government space and money in shipping, V-mail sometimes didn't feel like a "real" letter, but free was a good price for the airmen. He scribbled a note to Jean, remembering to write big.

Dear sweetheart,

Trusting you made it safely back to Galveston, dear. Mail hasn't caught up with us yet. Missing you more than you can know. Rain coming down in sheets here, and weather grounded us for a week. Mud so sticky it cakes on our boots three inches or more, and some guys lost their boots in it! Playing a lot of cards and dreaming of my darling. Thinking of you in my arms every night and praying you are doing okay. Love you so much. I'm glad you are with your folks—give them my love.

All my hugs and kisses for you
Sug

He folded his V-mail with the address outside and set it aside to take to mail call. Nothing here for the censors to worry about.

Braving the rain and wind, the four officers headed for the chow line. After waiting his turn, Eaves balanced his tray carefully and hunkered down to protect it from the pelting raindrops as he hiked back to their tent.

Lost in his thoughts of Jean and home, he perched on the end of his cot, quickly slurping down the bowl of now-cold soup and chewing on the hard tack. The only good thing was the real coffee. What a place.

18 MARCH 1944—OUDNA AIRFIELD, TUNISIA

Mail call was better than he expected. Eaves had two V-mails from Jean, one from his sister Ruth, and one from his folks. He deposited his V-mail to Jean in the mail drop and hustled back to the tent to savor his letters.

He squinted at the tiny writing in the letter from home first, news about school events and the warm West Texas weather, "already in the 90s." Ruth wrote of the constant wind in Lubbock, her job at the PX, and Marcus wishing Eaves was there for a golf game. He smiled ruefully. No golf here, that's for sure.

Saving Jean's letters for last, he opened her first one . . .

Dear Sug,

So grateful to catch a ride back to Galveston with Gert, but what a long ride it was. Had a tire blow out. Only with God's help and the kindness of a rationing board in Oklahoma were we finally able to get another tire. I'm missing you terribly and pray constantly that the Good Lord keeps you and your crew safe, right in the palm of His hand. Mother and Dad are glad to have me home, but my heart is with you, darling. Mother started a book drive at church for the USO clubs and we were pleased with the number of books given. V-mail says no lipstick

or fragrances but know this is sealed with a kiss, just for you. Praying this finds you strong and well.
Hugs and all my love,
Jean

Eaves folded the V-mail, closed his eyes and pictured her lovely face. He whispered, "Love you too, sweetheart." Her second letter had been written two days later and included a promise of a care package on the way. Just getting letters from family boosted his morale and intensified the longing for home. He read each one of them again, savoring the connection with his loved ones.

He pulled out some blank V-mails. He'd better get to work if he wanted more mail.

✈✈✈

The next day the weather broke. Every clear day the crews began training missions to sharpen navigational skills and practice the combat tactics of the Fifteenth Air Force. Hour after hour, they flew in tight formation, wing tip to wing tip, the best defensive protection against German fighter planes. With the war over in North Africa, only dummy bombs splashed down into the Mediterranean, but morale improved as they prepared for battle.

Then, once again, tragedy struck the 464th. On 27 March, Eaves and his crew watched in horror as *Monin Lisa* crashed on takeoff during a routine training flight and burst into flames. Three men were killed, six seriously injured.

Another accident. Eaves sighed. If only Sgt. Ryskeciski and their ground crew from Lincoln, Nebraska were here instead of traveling by ship to Italy. The maintenance crews here did their best but were stretched thin. He couldn't help but wonder if that contributed to the tragedy.

The bad luck wasn't over. Only days later, one of the GI-rigged stoves exploded in a tent, burning four men severely.

Discouragement loomed like the dark clouds hovering over the base.

✈✈✈

9 April 1944—Oudna Airfield, Tunisia

Easter morning dawned another dismal, gloomy day. Sheets of rain fell. The scheduled formation training flight was canceled.

After breakfast, Eaves heated water in a small tin can, shaved and put on a clean uniform before heading to the mess tent for the Easter service. He pictured Jean in the little church in Galveston, worshipping with her folks on Easter Sunday. He fingered her last two letters in his pocket, already tattered from him reading them over and over.

One by one or two by two, men slogged through the ankle-deep mud from all over the base to the service and the small tent soon overflowed. Rolling up the sides so all could hear, the men crowded together, many standing in the rain. Eaves saw Christel squeeze into the tent toward the back.

Protestant, Catholic, Jewish—men of all faiths gathered together for their ration of God's word. No rank here, with enlisted men, officers, and ground crew who still wore grease-covered overalls from working all night.

Men spoke quietly, all wet and cold, but patiently they waited. A deep hunger for spiritual nourishment drew them together, the uncertainty of the future looming before them.

Chaplain John Eastwood arrived forty-five minutes late. Word spread that his jeep had gotten stuck in the muck, and he had to wait for help to arrive. Several men rushed out to carry in his small altar and portable organ.

A deep silence enveloped the gathering as the chaplain finally stood before them, clutching his Bible to his chest. He silently scanned the tent, looking compassionately into each face. The only sound was the rain drumming on the tent roof.

"Let us pray." The chaplain's kind, baritone rang out.

Everyone swept off their caps and bowed their heads.

The poignant prayer seemed to pierce Eaves' heart as the chaplain thanked the One who had suffered and died for them all, making a way for sinful men to enter that heavenly homeland.

Tears brimmed in his eyes. And he was not alone, as tears unashamedly flowed down many a face, with some men furtively wiping their cheeks and clearing their throats. A holy aura seemed to surround the gathering.

The chaplain moved to his organ and played the introduction to a familiar hymn, "Christ Arose." Then he looked up. "Let us sing."

The men lifted their voices, deep and resonant, rivaling the greatest of choirs in a magnificent cathedral. On they sang, two more stirring Easter hymns.

Finally, the chaplain stood behind the small altar and, lifting his Bible, read from Luke 24:13-36, the story of the resurrected Lord meeting His two discouraged followers on their way to Emmaus. As He walked with them, He explained the Scriptures—why it was necessary for the Christ to suffer and die to enter His Glory.

Men soaked in the words, rapt attention on each face.

The simple sermon ended with a final hymn, with every man's voice ringing out strong and true. "Rock of Ages, cleft for me. Let me hide myself in Thee."

All heads bowed as they recited together the familiar words of the Lord's Prayer.

"Jesus said, 'Surely, I am with you always, even to the end of the age.'" As the words of the Benediction fell from the chaplain's lips, Eaves' heart surged with the hope and joy of Easter as he had never felt it before, surrounded by these fellow fighting men, bravely willing to sacrifice all if necessary for freedom and homeland.

As the men quietly left the tent, he heard no complaints, although all were wet and shivering in the cold. Eaves' heart swelled with pride to be among them, galvanized to face tomorrow.

✈✈✈

12 APRIL 1944—OUDNA AIRFIELD, TUNISIA

It was a week after Easter before the 464th was back up in the air for another training flight. Rumors flew that they'd soon be leaving for a base in Italy.

Eaves focused on staying wing tip to wing tip in the tight box formation of the 777th. Suddenly his wingman, *Wise Wabbitt*, spun out of control, plunging straight down toward the Mediterranean.

Alarmed, he pressed his throat mic. "Did they pull out? Any chutes?"

Only silence filled the airwaves.

Finally, a subdued voice sounded over the intercom. "Ball turret here, sir. No chutes."

Eaves tried to swallow the huge lump in his throat. Fellow officers he had known, gone. A small hope flickered. Maybe some would survive the water landing.

The intercom crackled. "Christel here. Order to return to base, sir."

As he banked and turned the plane back toward Oudna, the words of the chaplain floated through his mind: "Even if called to make the greatest sacrifice, we rest in the confidence of the cross and know our Savior will be waiting with arms open wide to welcome us home."

So many sacrifices already made. And not even one bomb dropped on the enemy yet by the 464th Bomb Group.

✈✈✈

20 April 1944—Gioia del Colle Airfield, Italy

The orders finally arrived. All morning planes took off individually from Oudna heading for southern Italy. The major base at Pantanella was still not ready, and the 464th Bomb Group had been assigned to a smaller base at Gioia del Colle, southwest of Bari.

The routine flight took three hours and fifteen minutes. Eaves brought *Target for Tonite* down for a smooth landing on the matted steel, then hit a rough crater of sod in the center of the runway, jarring them all. Relieved to roll back onto steel matting, he taxied to a hardstand as directed. Emerging from the plane he found Sgt. Ryskeciski, their crew chief from Lincoln Army Airfield, standing before him.

"Welcome to Gioia, sir."

"You are a sight for sore eyes, Sergeant." Eaves pumped his hand. "Glad to have you back working on this girl. How long you been here?"

"About a month now. Long cruise over the pond on an overloaded tanker." He wrinkled his nose. "Been trying to get this base ready ever since we trucked over here from Bari."

"What happened to the runway?"

"A P-38 in distress attempted an unsuccessful landing. Exploded on impact and took out part of the runway." Both men were silent for a moment. "Filled it in with oiled sod. That's the best we can do for now."

Eaves nodded.

Sgt. Ryskeciski looked at the plane fondly. "*Target for Tonite*—that's a good name. How's the old girl been doing for you?"

"Well, it's a long story, but she pulled through like a champ. Got us to the Canary Islands on fumes." He looked up to see the transport truck arriving, and the crew beginning to load their barracks bags and equipment. "Gotta go but will fill you in later. No problems right now but relieved to know you'll be checking her out for us."

Chapter 9

21 April 1944—Gioia del Colle Airfield, Italy

COLONEL BONNER HAD ARRIVED EARLY in one of the first planes out of Oudna. A stickler for details, his first order of business was to plan and assign areas for the officers and enlisted men to set up their tents.

Rain poured down and Italy proved to be as wet as Oudna. Eaves never thought he'd miss the arid hills of West Texas like he did.

Slogging through the muck in drenching rain, the officers worked together to set up their tent. They dug a slit trench along a little ridge in case of air raids, which quickly filled with mud and water up to their knees.

Elder, the flight engineer, proved to be an exceptional scavenger. He found a spare airplane fuel tank and rigged up a stove for the officers.

Their neighbors turned out to be Lieutenant Tudor and his crew.

"You can hire an Italian kid from Gioia to pour a concrete floor for next to nothing," Tudor advised. "They do a good job. And their mothers are willing to do laundry too."

"Sounds good," Eaves said. "Got one you recommend?"

"You bet." He smiled. "And we traded cigarettes and K-rations for a home-cooked spaghetti dinner. No meat, but a delicious tomato sauce. Sure beats Army grub."

Settling in took a few days as rain fell in torrents, but before long rumors were flying that their "freshman" mission would be soon.

Sherman ducked into the tent. "Hey Red, the big buzz at the officers' club today was all about our first combat mission. Scuttlebutt says the policy of the Fifteenth is to plan an easy mission, a 'milk run,' for all new groups."

"Sounds good to me," Eaves grunted as he sat on his cot scraping the mud off his boots. "But we aren't going anywhere in this weather."

The skies finally cleared on the 29th and all planes in the bomb group did a quick formation training run, in the air for less than two hours. Sure enough, orders for the first mission were posted after the evening meal, briefing scheduled at 0500.

Eaves stared at his name on the alert list for tomorrow's mission. Finally, into the fight for real. Actual combat tomorrow. Mixed feelings rose inside as questions whirled through his mind.

What will the target be? Would they be dealing with anti-aircraft fire, enemy fighters, or both?

Tentacles of fear tangled his thoughts. Not of dying, but of failing to perform as expected under fire or making a wrong decision at a critical time. He couldn't let his men down.

His thoughts raced to Jean and home. Tomorrow was Sunday. He pictured his wife sitting with her folks in a pew at the little church they attended, bright light filtering through the stained- glass windows. Then, in the kitchen, helping Ollie with Sunday dinner. Just the thought of home-cooked Southern comfort food made his mouth water. A wave of homesickness swept over him.

He jerked his focus back to the mission tomorrow.

Help me do my best, Lord.

His fellow officers were quiet that night. Eaves stretched out on his cot and tried to relax. Sleep proved elusive. Finally, he dozed off, tossed and turned in a restless sleep, but woke when the quiet of the night was broken by trucks starting their engines. Soon the hum of traffic buzzed outside their tent.

A rustle—the tent flap lifted, and a flashlight bobbed toward his cot. The bright light glared into his eyes. "Lt. Eaves, sir, it's time to get up." The enlisted man stood beside him until Eaves sat up and started pulling on his long johns. Then he turned to wake the other officers in the tent.

Eaves heated some water and used his helmet as a basin while he shaved. Definitely using the oxygen masks today—high altitude bombing the norm here.

First, breakfast. He and the other officers walked briskly toward the mess tent. The smell of bacon and coffee wafting on the damp air failed to stir much of an appetite, even when real eggs greeted their eyes instead of the powdered ones they'd come to dread.

Eaves picked at his food but forced himself to eat a few bites, savoring the strong coffee. Low murmurs of conversation contrasted markedly from the usually boisterous mess hall.

Back at their tent, the officers grabbed their duffel bags stuffed with their heavy flight suits and caught the next truck taking them to the briefing room. A curtain covered the screen behind the podium. Conversation was subdued, but laughter bubbled up here and there until a voice announced, "Ten-hut!"

All the airmen stood as Colonel Bonner and his entourage strode into the room. At the command "At ease," the men settled onto the rough benches.

The chaplain gave a brief prayer, and Colonel Bonner stepped forward to address the group. "Good morning, men. I want to share the four main objectives of the Fifteenth Air Force that will define the missions of the 464th Bomb Group."

"Our number one priority is to achieve air superiority through the destruction of the German *Luftwaffe*, in the air and on the ground. Second priority is destruction of vital Axis industry, including aircraft factories, ball-bearing plants, oil refineries, armament production, and submarine bases. Our third objective is support for the battle here on the Italian peninsula, attacking transportation and communication centers, including those based in Austria. And the fourth priority is to attack German forces and facilities in the Balkans."

He paused and scanned the faces of the young men before him. "Today is the first true test of all you have been trained to do. I know you will perform well and bring honor to yourselves and your country." He nodded to the briefing officer, who stepped to the front.

The officer drew back the curtain covering the map of the target.

Eaves' lips parted and he let out a deep breath as the officer pointed at the red yarn stretching from Gioia upward to a spot in the northern part of Italy.

Good. Not known to be a terribly dangerous target area.

"Today you will be hitting the marshalling yards of Castel Maggiore and derailing any trains passing through the area. You will follow the 460th Bomb Group to the target." The officer described the importance of disrupting German transport of troops and supplies through this area and the resistance they might encounter. "Very little anti-aircraft coverage reported here, but be on the lookout for bandits. Good luck and God speed."

The pilots, navigators and bombardiers departed for their separate briefings. Before boarding the plane to prepare their stations, the enlisted men proceeded to the equipment shack to get their parachutes and flak vests.

Armorers had swarmed over *Target for Tonite* all night. The bomb bay bristled with live five-hundred--pound bombs when Eaves arrived and climbed inside. The gunners were checking the ammo belts for their .50-caliber machine guns. Even one bullet slightly off center could jam their gun.

Sherman and Elder waited on the flight deck. Eaves laid his flak jacket on the seat before he sat down. Too bulky to wear—maybe it would do some good there. He already felt like a penguin stuffed in his flight jacket with the silk muffler around his neck and two pairs of heavy gloves pulled snuggly over the silk ones.

Quickly they went through their checklist in preparation for flight. When the flare to start their engines lit up the sky, they were ready. Soon all four engines roared to life.

Leaning out the top hatch, Elder guided the way from the hardstand down the taxiway. "Right, to the right, sir."

Target for Tonite waddled into the line of planes waiting to take off. Eaves tightened his grip on the yoke. With live bombs and ammo, flak jackets, oxygen tanks and extra gasoline, the B-24H weighed about 70,000 pounds—the heaviest plane he'd ever flown. He eyed the sod insert in the runway, noting the interruption in the speed of the planes ahead of him as they hit it. Sweat trickled down his back. Every take-off was a challenge, especially with a damaged runway that was almost too short.

With the brakes on, he pushed the throttle forward, all engines full force. The B-24 vibrated violently. Twenty seconds after the plane in front of him roared down the runway, he and Sherman released the brakes and *Target for Tonite* raced forward, reluctantly gaining speed as it hurtled down the runway. Hitting the sod, the plane bounced roughly before finally rolling onto the solid steel tarmac where better traction helped acceleration.

All too soon they approached the end of the runway and Eaves pulled up the nose.

"Gear up," he ordered. Sherman flipped the switch, hydraulically retracting the three wheels into the wheel wells. The heavily loaded Liberator skimmed the ground.

"Flaps up."

"Flaps up, sir," Sherman confirmed.

Gradually the B-24 began to climb, at first barely above the treetops.

Whew—that was close, but we made it.

Plane after plane climbed into the sky. A yellow flare guided Eaves to the 777th squadron's lead ship, and they pulled in close, wing tip to wing tip.

The bomb group continued to meld together into the box formation. The 777th Bomb Squadron was flying in Baker, the upper combat wing to the right and above Able, the Lead Group. Forty B-24s stacked tightly in the air. They had every right to feel formidable.

"Great formation flying," came the brief message from the Wing Commander.

As they gained altitude, Eaves completed the routine check-ins with each crew member. As they passed over the Adriatic Sea, he ordered the gunners to test their weapons. A short burst of fire erupted individually from each turret and the waist as the gunners fired their machine guns.

"Bombardier, arm bombs," Eaves commanded.

Live bombs today. May they find their target.

"Roger." Lambert climbed into the bomb bay to pull the pins on each of the twelve bombs while they were still over the sea.

At an altitude of 10,000 feet, Eaves pressed his throat mic. "Plug in your oxygen, men."

The 464th continued to climb, leveling off at 22,000 feet. Temperatures plunged to twenty below zero. The cold penetrated his wool gloves and coat, and Eaves shivered despite all the heavy layering. Never felt cold like this in Texas. White frosty contrails streamed behind the bombers.

Water could freeze in the oxygen lines. He completed another routine check-in on the intercom with each crew member.

Land appeared to the north.

"Haverkos here. Don't know what's happening. We just passed landfall, but no 460th in sight."

Eaves sucked in his breath. What had gone wrong? This was the designated meeting spot. The 460th Bomb Group was to be here to lead the attack.

"Roger, Haverkos. Thanks for the heads up."

The Lead Group banked and began circling. The whole formation followed, creating a giant spiral of planes and white plumes in the cold blue sky.

Suddenly Eaves saw planes on the inside begin to stall. Alarmed, he watched pilots pull up to avoid crashing. Scanning the gauges, he noted airspeed was too slow.

His grip tightened on the yoke. Any moment he expected to see the flash of a collision.

Just then the lead plane of Eaves' squadron pulled out of the group circle and headed south. Eaves swung in behind him.

"Navigator, what is the heading?"

After a moment, Haverkos replied, "Looks like—back to Gioia, sir."

After a few minutes, Eaves pushed his throat mic. "Masterson, what do you see from the tail?"

"The whole group formed up behind us and are following us back to base, sir."

Eaves blinked and his gut clenched. Back to base, like a pup with his tail between his legs.

While over the Adriatic, the lead plane dropped its live bombs. Eaves sucked in his breathe and then ordered the bombardier to follow suit. Not safe to land with all that live ammo.

Disappointment sat like a heavy stone in his gut. Total failure—not what he expected on their first mission.

✈✈✈

2 MAY 1944—GIOIA DEL COLLE AIRFIELD, ITALY

Two days later they were back in the briefing room.

Colonel Bonner made it clear he was not pleased with the first mission. Frowning, he cleared his throat and said, "The last mission was a total failure. The 464th will receive no credit for this waste of time and ammunition. We must do better. The 779th Bomb Squad will lead the attack today and I will personally be aboard Shoemaker's plane as mission commander." He stepped back and looked at the intelligence officer, who hastily stepped forward as the curtain was drawn back to reveal their target. A red line stretched up into northern Italy.

"Assignment today—the marshalling yards in Parma, Italy, another transportation hub for German supplies and troop movement. Our intelligence reports indicate few anti-aircraft guns in the area, but you can expect fighter plane attacks. Stay in tight formation for protection, gunners alert. Men, this should be a 'milk run.' Take out the marshalling yards and any trains in the area."

The weather officer took front stage. "Weather in the target area is expected to be good. A storm front may be moving in later this afternoon."

After the chaplain prayed for the men, the officers headed for their special briefing.

Eaves tightened his jaw.

We must get those bombs to the target today.

The enlisted men headed out to pick up their parachutes and flak vests before catching the truck to the hardstand to prepare their stations.

Eaves learned at the pilots' meeting that the 777th lead plane had pulled out of formation in the last mission due to failure of the oxygen system.

Although it triggered the group to abort the mission due to the radio blackout, it probably saved lives from planes potentially crashing in that huge spiral. No one knew why the 460th Bomb Group failed to arrive at the scheduled time for the mission.

Today Eaves' squadron would be slotted in Charlie, the lower box to the left of the Lead Command bomb squadron.

Soon the 464th was back in the air without incident. Wing tip to wing tip, the formation pulled together. Cruising in the icy cold at 22,000 feet, they reached the Initial Point (IP) and turned north on the bomb run heading.

So far so good. Eaves turned over control of the plane. "Bombardier, your plane."

Leaving the Adriatic Sea to head inland, Eaves saw a port city coming up below.

"Location, Haverkos," Eaves called into the intercom.

"Harbor of La Spezia ahead. Ten minutes to target."

"Roger."

Deep ahead in the distance Eaves could see dark clouds looming. Bad weather arriving early—so much for predictions.

Suddenly black puffs appeared below the formation as they droned on toward the target. Flak! The menacing clouds of anti-aircraft gun-fire drew closer and closer to the Lead Group, intensity and accuracy obviously increasing by the minute.

Eaves sucked in his breath. Now on the bomb run, there could be no evasive maneuvers.

Eaves startled at a flash of red just off to his left. The acrid smell of explosives stung his nose as they passed through a veil of black smoke. He gripped the yoke tighter as sounds reverberated around him like gravel hitting the plane.

No defense here but hope and a prayer.

Lord, please be with us!

Target for Tonite plunged on. No apparent damage.

He exhaled deeply. A firestorm of destruction, too close for comfort.

Suddenly the Combat Lead plane of the 779th Squadron with Bonner onboard, Shoemaker's *Shoo Shoo Baby,* pulled up and banked to the right. Eaves watched as the second-in-command ship, Lt. Wingfield in Big Fat Mama, slid into the Combat Lead position, continuing toward the target.

In horror Eaves saw the wingman on the left attempt to follow *Shoo Shoo Baby,* turning right into the path of Lt. Wingfield. Its right rudder knifed into the front turret of *Big Fat Mama* and snapped off. The wingman spiraled and fell from the sky. *Big Fat Mama* was thrown on her back and was last seen in a dive headed straight down.

Stay focused. Stay focused!

Eaves took a ragged breath and punched his throat mic. "Bombardier! My plane!"

Eaves pushed down on the yoke and followed his squadron lead plane as it dove down to the left, away from the crash and into the storm clouds below. He struggled to stay in control as *Target for Tonite* bucked and swayed in the gusty winds. Emerging from the clouds, Eaves saw the formation had broken apart, their 777th Squadron alone in the sky.

The 777th lead plane leveled off at 18,000 feet and opened its bomb doors as it circled back toward the port.

Their target? The harbor at La Spezia, of course. Knock out the flak guns. Following their lead, he turned *Target for Tonite* toward the port, determination etched into the lines of his face.

"Bombardier, prepare to drop bombs on the harbor. Your plane."

Eaves watched air speed and altitude as moments ticked by. Bombs rained down from the lead plane.

"Bombs away," Lambert called out.

Target for Tonite leaped upward as twelve five-hundred-pound bombs fell from her belly.

"Masterson here. Direct hit on a ship in the harbor and the dock, sir."

Satisfaction warmed Eaves' chest. At last, a blow struck against the enemy. This mission wasn't a total failure. He spotted another small group of B-24s also dropping their bombs on the harbor.

"Your plane, sir." Lambert's voice sounded over the intercom.

"Roger. Good job, men. Keep watch for enemy fighters." Eaves' heart raced as he banked to follow the lead plane, circling back toward Gioia.

The skies stayed quiet as they winged back to base. Visions of the lost planes replayed in his mind. How many good men died today? And what in the world made Shoemaker pull up like that?

Eaves scowled. This was more than bad luck.

Chapter 10

3 May 1944—Gioia del Colle Airfield, Italy

ALL CREWS STOOD DOWN the day after the disastrous mission. Eaves and Tudor each grabbed a drink and nabbed a couple of seats in a corner of a packed officers' club.

Tudor leaned in close and spoke quietly. "The guys on Shoemaker's plane said he panicked. As soon as Bonner saw the flak rising, he jerked the controls away from Shoemaker. Pulled the plane out of formation and skedaddled back to Gioia." He shook his head. "What kind of leadership is that? Hard to respect a man who causes two planes to go down because of cowardice."

Eaves narrowed his eyes, bile burning behind his breastbone. "Only two parachutes reported out of *Southern Gal* before she crashed. And Wingfield's whole crew is listed as missing in action." He struggled to keep his voice low and to control the rage threatening to erupt. "What did Shoemaker do?"

Tudor shrugged. "Don't know who, but someone reported it. Bonner was called up to headquarters to answer to the brass. Maybe they'll get rid of him."

"Overheard some guys talking about shooting him down if he goes up to lead again." Eaves frowned. "I had to speak up. What about the other nine men flying with him? He may have a yellow streak a mile wide down his backside, but that's not the answer."

Tudor nodded. "Understand their feelings though. Can't trust a leader who can't take the heat."

Just then a voice rang out. “Hey guys! Wingfield just landed *Big Fat Mama* here in Gioia! He managed to make it to Corsica with that rudder sticking out of the nose. Most of the crew is with him.”

Eaves and Tudor rushed to join the crowd of men pouring out the door of the officers’ club and headed over to the tarmac to check it out.

“Can’t believe it—that’s some flying!” Tudor’s voice radiated the admiration and amazement they were all feeling.

Eaves agreed. An incredible feat of airmanship . . . and the grace of God.

When they arrived at the hardstand, they learned that four men had bailed out before Wingfield got the plane leveled out, including Lt. Colonel Hand, the Deputy Group Commander of the 464th. All four were still listed as missing in action.

Eaves mulled over this incredible turn of events as he and Tudor ambled over to the mess tent. They learned that Bonner had arrived back at Gioia later that day, along with officers from Wing Headquarters in Bari. An investigation was underway.

Word soon spread that Lt. Wingfield was so enraged to learn what Bonner had done that he marched over to the colonel’s tent to speak with him. Reportedly he vowed to never fly with him again.

Orders were posted after the evening meal. Eaves saw his name listed for the sortie, briefing at 0600. He took a deep breath and sent up a prayer. Two missions ending in apparent failure—things had to change.

✈✈✈

5 May 1944—Gioia del Colle Airfield, Italy

After another restless night and an early awakening, Eaves joined the other airmen gathered in the briefing room. Bonner entered with the brass from headquarters but didn’t speak. Chaplin John Eastwood rose as usual, praying for the men about to fly into combat and those who were missing.

One of the officers from headquarters jumped to his feet and curtly informed the group that this time of prayer would be discontinued. Murmurs of discontent filled the hall.

Eaves rocked back in shock. Chaplain Eastwood had gone out of his way to be available to the airmen for prayer and words of comfort. Eaves had come to appreciate the man’s faith and wisdom.

What were those guys thinking?

He clenched his fists as he thought of the men who had recently sacrificed all for their country.

We'll see about that—no one should have to fly off to combat without prayer.

Eaves forced his attention back to the briefing officer, who drew back the curtain to expose the huge map with a red yarn line going from Gioia to Podgorcia, Yugoslavia. Another short flight. The mission focused on a reported buildup of German troops in the area. They were assured again that this should be a 'milk run.'

"No known flak or enemy fighters in the area. Group to leave at 1030 hours."

Eaves breathed a sigh of relief. No mention of Bonner leading.

Men muttered in small groups as they left the briefing room. By the time the pilots reached their designated briefing room, someone had drafted a handwritten petition demanding the order concerning the chaplain be rescinded and added a quote from President Roosevelt:

"As Commander-in-Chief I take pleasure in commending the reading of the Bible to all who serve in the armed forces of the United States. Throughout the centuries, men of many faiths and diverse origins have found in the Sacred Book words of wisdom, counsel, and inspiration. It is a fountain of strength and now, as always, an aid in attaining the highest aspirations of the human soul."

Every pilot signed. No one wanted to fly into battle without prayer support.

This time the reconnaissance reports proved accurate. As they cleared the Adriatic Sea, the group emerged from clouds to clear skies. Eaves spotted tiny villages below in the Montenegro area.

Only a short two-hour flight to Podgorcia. After a successful payload drop with no flak or enemy fighter planes, all the aircraft of the 464th returned safely to base.

Eaves breathed a sigh of relief. Finally, a true milk run.

At the base, good news awaited. Due to the strong protest, the decision regarding prayer had been reversed. Chaplain Eastwood would be allowed to pray for the troops again before each mission.

A warm feeling of satisfaction spread over Eaves. Someone higher up had heard their voices and responded.

"We're posted for a mission again tomorrow," Tudor said, looking up at Eaves as he joined him at the dinner table in the mess tent.

"What?" Eaves swallowed hard, still feeling the exhaustion all B-24 pilots felt after horsing around the huge machine for several hours.

"Oh, well, bring it on," he said, determination edging his voice. "Another mission toward going home. Hope it goes as well as the one today."

They ate in silence, Eaves' mind filled with thoughts of home and those waiting for him there.

✈✈✈

6 MAY 1944—GIOA DEL COLLE AIRFIELD, ITALY

Voices buzzed in the briefing room as they waited for Bonner and the revelation of today's target.

After the entourage entered and the "At Ease" command was given, Chaplain John Eastwood stood first to pray for the men. Every cap was swept off, and a reverent hush fell. Appreciation was palpable in the room that the decision to cease prayer had been reversed.

The chaplain's eyes scanned the room as he clutched his Bible to his chest. Bowing his head, he said, "Oh Lord, hear our prayer.

Lord guard and guide the men who fly
Through the great spaces of the sky;

Be with them as they take to the air,
In morning light and sunshine fair.

Eternal Father, strong to save.
Give them courage and make them brave;

Protect them wheresoe'er they go,
From shell and flak and fire and foe;

Most loved Member of their crew,
Ride with them up in the blue.

Direct their bombs upon the foe,
But shelter those whom Thou dost know.

Keep them together upon their way,
Grant their work success today.

Deliver them from hate and sin,
And bring them back safely again.

O God bless the men who fly,
Through lonely ways across the sky."

He paused before adding the heartfelt ending, "In Jesus' Name. Amen."

The chaplain stepped back and the briefing officer took his place at the podium, nodding for the curtain to be pulled back. A few groans were heard as the red line stretched across the Adriatic to Romania.

"Our target today is the marshalling yards in Craiova, Romania. Expect to be over six hours in the air. Anti-aircraft batteries and enemy fighters known to be in the area. Stay in tight formation, gunners alert."

The weatherman advised that pilots could expect clear skies after leaving the Alps.

Then Colonel Bonner stood, and looking straight at Wingfield, announced, "I will be flying with Lt. Wingfield as Group Lead today. Assembly dismissed." With that, he turned and left the stage.

Murmurs filled the room as officers dispatched to their own briefing and the enlisted men headed for their stations. Eaves looked at Tudor across the room and shrugged.

In the pilots' meeting, Wingfield stood to protest Colonel Bonner's decision but was immediately overruled.

"That's an order, Lieutenant," the briefing officer barked. He proceeded to tell the pilots the position of each squadron in the group formation, which position each airplane had within the squadron formation, and gave more specific details on the mission, listing possible alternative targets.

Soon the 464th Bomb Group took to the air again. As they neared Craiova, the Germans threw up some flak, but the Lead plane stayed steady. *Target for Tonite* experienced no direct hits. Several German fighters circled the formation but they did not engage.

Except for a few extra flak holes in some of the B-24s, all returned safely and the mission was considered a success.

Only later in the officers' club in a private conversation did they learn that Wingfield and Colonel Bonner had a disagreement regarding the cylinder head temperatures.

Winfield explained his side to the pilots. "Due to a leak in the induction system of engine two, I had to apply extra power to the other three engines to maintain as group lead. Because of the increased fuel required, on the return trip I had to lean the mixtures to conserve enough fuel to make it back to the base." Wingfield rolled his eyes.

"Bonner insisted I return the mixture control to 'auto rich,' but I refused. He kept protesting, but I knew we couldn't make it back on 'auto rich.' Finally, the colonel reached over and moved the control himself. At that point I physically knocked his hand off the control pedestal."

"What did Bonner say?" Tudor asked, his eyes wide.

"Nothing. He said nothing for the rest of the mission."

Silence.

Eaves looked at Tudor, who just shook his head.

They still had no information about the investigation by headquarters. Bonner can't afford another black mark. Maybe Wingfield would escape without a reprimand for insubordination. And . . . maybe, just maybe, Bonner learned that when you sit in the right seat, you keep your hands to yourself unless help is requested.

For the third day in a row, the alert list was up after the evening meal. Another mission scheduled for Sunday morning. Eaves scanned the roster.

Relief. His name was not on it.

But Tudor was. "Hey, Red, you get a break. Better enjoy it."

Eaves had no trouble sleeping that night. He sent up a prayer for his friend, but as soon as he stretched out on his cot, exhaustion closed his eyelids.

✈✈✈

A day in town was just what the doctor ordered. After the chapel service, Eaves and the other three officers caught a ride on the truck that made regular runs back and forth from the base.

The small village of Gioia del Colle had a town square with a fountain. Sort of reminded Eaves of his little hometown in Texas. He noticed very little bombing damage downtown, with several small shops and cafes open for business.

Eaves and Haverkos made a beeline for the barber shop. For about ten dollars plus a tip Eaves got the royal treatment: a shampoo, head and neck massage, haircut, manicure and a shave. The pampering felt great.

At a small café, they enjoyed a spaghetti dinner with fresh baked bread and a bottle of wine. No meat, but a delicious tomato sauce tantalized their taste buds after the bland GI fare they were accustomed to receiving.

As they wandered the narrow, cobbled streets, the people smiled and seemed friendly. Mostly women and the elderly, all dressed in dark clothing, looking a little shabby and worse-for-wear.

Eaves felt a tug on his sleeve. He looked down into the brown eyes of a little street urchin, basically dressed in rags, lifting his other hand palm up. He kept repeating something in Italian.

Eaves' heart went out to the forlorn-looking child, probably about five or six years old. His own little brother popped into his mind. He dug in his pocket and pulled out hard candy and a stick of gum.

Not much, but he was rewarded with a smile and a heart-felt "*grazie mille!*"

The narrow streets were lined with very old two-story stone buildings. Shuttered windows above street level sported little wrought-iron balconies.

Turning a corner, they came upon an ancient Norman castle. Fascinated by the huge, magnificent monolith, they strolled under the archway to discover a lovely courtyard and peeking inside, they gaped at an elegant throne room. Eaves gazed at the splendor, grateful this medieval treasure had survived the war so far.

All too soon it was time to return to the base. Eaves was determined to send a V-mail off to Jean before dinner. He picked up her picture, cradling it his hands as he gazed into her dark eyes. Didn't know he could miss someone so intensely.

Tudor popped his head under the tent flap just as Eaves finished addressing his letter.

"Hey, heading over to the mess tent?"

Eaves nodded and grabbed his cap. "Gotta send this letter off to Jean and thought I might make mail call. How'd the mission go today?"

Tudor grimaced. "Aborted, no credit. The target was the railroad repair yard in Bucharest, Romania. Another long mission, over six hours, and we were almost to the target when they called us back. Weather was terrible, everything covered by clouds." He stared off into space, paused for a moment. "And we lost another plane. Lt. Gibbs disappeared in a cloud bank right after we took off. Reportedly they crashed twenty-five miles south of here. No survivors."

Eaves swallowed hard. More men gone, more wasted effort.

Help us, Lord. And please comfort their families.

✈✈✈

On 8 May the skies opened up and rain flooded down for two days. Missions were scrapped as the terrible weather obscured the targets. Eaves grew restless in the tight confinement of the musty tent and ventured out through the sea of mud to the headquarters building.

In the photo section room he caught a glimpse of a small bundle of gray and orange, dark eyes peering at him from a white face, hanging from a light pole. Eaves blinked. The little Brazilian monkey resurrected!

"Hey, what ya got there?" he asked.

"Our mascot," the sergeant at the desk looked up at him and grinned. "Someone brought him over the pond when we left Natal."

Eaves grimaced, remembering a similar creature and the havoc it had created over the Atlantic. He still didn't know who smuggled the monkey onboard. No one would admit to the feat nor reveal the culprit, and he had given up delving into that mystery.

Scuttlebutt had it that theirs was not the only plane with a stowaway. Wingfield's crew on *Big Fat Mama* had put a monkey in the ball turret for the journey over the Atlantic. After climbing to higher altitudes to clear mountains in Africa, they sadly discovered the little guy had expired and buried him at sea before landing at the Oudna Airfield.

But somehow, the sight of this little critter cheered Eaves up, bringing back memories of the restful beauty of Natal.

Survival—that's what it was. Some die, but others survive. Hope gleamed in that bundle of fur.

Slipping and sliding through the rain and mud, he trudged to the officers' club where he spotted Haverkos in the corner writing a letter.

Eaves smiled. "Hey, there. That doesn't happen to be a letter to Ginny, that pretty little blonde back home, does it?"

Haverkos just grinned and finished signing the V-mail. "Heading for the chow line?" he asked as he tucked the letter in his pocket and pulled on his cap.

Eaves nodded. Soon they had scooted into the mess tent and shook off the rain from their jackets. Eaves grabbed a tray and stood in line. Liver and onions tonight. Never his favorite meal, but it ranked higher than fried Spam.

After dinner, the alert list was up again. Eaves wasn't surprised to find his name on it. Briefing at 0500.

O dark thirty. Better hit the sack early. Who knew what tomorrow would hold?

Chapter 11

9 May 1944—Gioia del Colle Airfield, Italy

DESPITE HIS BEST INTENTIONS, Eaves' thoughts raced as he tossed and turned on his cot. Thoughts of home, of Jean, floated through his mind.

Odds were against them returning to the United States. Completion of the thirty missions required seemed an impossible feat. The casualty reports told the story—only one out of four crews made it through their tour in the Army Air Corps. He wasn't afraid to die, but failing to do his job or making an error that endangered the plane and his crew haunted him. In the dark of the night, the voice of doubt screamed the loudest.

"*Pray.*" That's what Jean would say. "*Just know the Lord is with you.*"

He sighed and rolled onto his side, winging up a prayer.

Give me the courage to face the challenges . . . and earn the respect of my men. Grant us success in completing our mission tomorrow, Lord. May we strike a blow against this enemy that threatens all I hold dear—family, freedom and righteousness. In Jesus' name I pray. Amen.

One day at a time, one mission at a time—he could handle that. Peace slipped over him.

His eyelids closed as his breathing slowed.

The sounds of truck motors broke through the silence in the predawn darkness. Eaves groaned. The wake-up call would come any moment now.

And there it was, the bobbing light . . .

All too soon they were gathered again in the briefing room. At 0500 the call, "Ten-hut," rang out, and the airmen leaped to their feet as Bonner and his entourage entered.

"At ease." The men settled back down on the wooden benches as Colonel Bonner stepped up to the podium.

Eaves' chest tightened. Would Bonner be leading again?

The colonel scanned the room, his face a frozen mask. "Today the 464th Bomb Group is honored to lead the entire 55th Bomb Wing to the target. A very formidable effort, with over four hundred Liberators and Fortresses deployed." He paused. "Major Clarence Poff, commander of the 778th Squadron, will be in Able Box leading the mission. Captain Hornbaker will fly Deputy Lead."

Eaves' shoulders relaxed as he exhaled deeply.

"You have trained well and I trust you are ready for this critical assignment." He nodded to the briefing officer, who took his place.

Groans and gasps cut through the air as the curtain swept back to reveal the huge map with the red line stretching from Gioia far across Austria, deep into enemy territory. A chill streaked down Eaves' spine.

"Wiener Neustadt, a city of 50,000, is located thirty miles south of Vienna and is vital to the German war effort. The Aircraft Assembly Plant here supplies over a third of all the German Me-109 fighter planes. Destruction of this facility is a priority of the Fifteenth Air Command and the mission of the 464th Bomb Group is to take it out."

The briefing officer cleared his throat. "Also located in Wiener Neustadt is the former locomotive factory, *Rax-Werke*, which has been converted to assemble A-4 missiles, with nearby facilities that supply steel, rubber and other critical elements. The rest of the 55th Wing will focus on these targets."

The intelligence officer took over. "Men, you have been tasked with a difficult mission." Silence deepened as he slowly scanned the room. "Wiener Neustadt is well-defended by a wall of anti-aircraft guns surrounding the city. A *Luftwaffe* base just outside city limits will launch more than a hundred German fighter planes in defense. So, count on bandits. Your best defense is to fly tight formation, and gunners—be on the alert. And . . . over two hundred Little Friends will accompany you today."

Murmurs of approval rose through the room. An escort of fighter planes would help.

"It's a long run. Expect over eight hours of flight time." He reminded the men that they would be over German territory. If forced to bail out, they were to seek German troops in the area to surrender to, as several reports of angry civilian mobs killing Allied airmen had surfaced. "Remember, give only name, rank, and serial number if captured," he stressed once again.

The meteorologist shared the report of two P-38 scouts. "Once you leave Italian air space, you should have clear skies to IP and over the target."

Chaplain Eastwood stood to pray for the men, his rich baritone speaking a blanket of comfort over them.

The mood was sober as Eaves and Sherman left for the pilots' meeting. Eaves kept his thoughts to himself as he received his assignment for position as right wingman in Baker, the box just above and slightly behind the Lead Squadron in Able.

He eyed the skies as he stepped outside into a gust of wind. Low-hanging, dense clouds. Takeoff could be difficult.

After the walk-around, the crew gathered under the wing, the strong smell of aircraft fuel enveloping them. The men looked expectantly at Eaves.

He took a deep breath and squared his shoulders. "Men, this will no doubt be our most challenging mission to date. I have utter confidence in each of you. Do your job well, as I know you can, and we'll prevail, with the help of God." He checked his watch. "Let's get aboard and prepare to start these engines."

When the green flare soared above, one by one the four engines roared to life. *Target for Tonite* taxied to the runway. Brakes were set, throttles thrust forward. Twenty seconds after the lead 777th plane roared down the runway, Eaves released the brakes and the heavily loaded B-24 rumbled over the steel matting.

Sherman called out the airspeed moment by moment. Bouncing over the rough sod insert, the ungainly B-24 gradually accelerated and lifted off into the air at the very end of the runway.

Up into dark clouds they soared. Zero visibility. *Target for Tonite* swayed in the blustery weather. Tension ratcheted up his shoulders as Eaves fought the wind. Gradually the Liberator gained altitude.

Minutes ticked by. Suddenly sunlight streamed into the cockpit as they popped up above the clouds. Eaves squinted in the bright light.

There it was—the yellow flare his squad leader released to bring the 777th squadron into formation as other B-24s rose through the cloud cover.

"Aircraft immediately below!" Petrone's warning rang out over the intercom.

Eaves yanked back on the yoke and banked starboard. The other plane stabilized and moved downward.

Whew—that was close. Thank You, Lord.

Eaves maneuvered into position, wing tip to wing tip in the box above the Lead Command Squadron. The bomb group climbed to 8,000 feet and as they passed over the Adriatic Sea, scattered showers persisted. The gunners tested their guns. Eaves called for Lambert to arm the bombs as the 464th continued to climb.

"Pilot to crew—put on your oxygen masks," Eaves ordered as they reached 10,000 feet in altitude.

The cold began to penetrate through his heavy fleece-lined flight jacket. At 22,000 feet the thermometer read thirty-five below Fahrenheit. He shivered as he checked in with each crew member to be sure oxygen still flowed and that everyone was ready for the battle ahead.

"Amazing sight from the tail, sir," Masterson's voice came over the intercom. "Hundreds of Liberators and Flying Fortresses have joined up and are strung out behind us for miles. Can see Little Friends up above. Looking good!"

Eaves pictured the massive formation in his mind. "Thanks for the report. Glad to know we have company."

Entering enemy air space, the bombers and their silvery vapor trails were a visible target to the Germans below. Knowing that the P-38 and P-51 fighters hovered above the formation provided some comfort.

The skies stayed peaceful as they reached the IP. Turning, they locked on the heading to the target.

"Bombardier, your plane."

Suddenly the skies exploded. Black clouds of flak filled the path before them.

Cold sweat formed on Eaves' forehead. There could be no evasive actions on the bomb run. The ship had to fly straight and level for the next fifteen minutes. He stared hard at the dreaded curtain of black billowing in front of them.

His jaw tightened as his hands clenched on the yoke. Flak was deadly. An exploding shell hurled over 1,500 deadly sharp fragments into an area covering 600 feet radius, at heights up to 40,000 feet. The bombers, with no defense, were forced to fly through the deadly barrage.

Gotta trust the steel helmet and flak jacket. And pray your name isn't written on a hunk of metal.

"Bandits! Two o'clock!" The cry came from Elder in the top turret. "Thirty, maybe forty gathering . . . but, looks like they're not entering this mess for now."

They're too smart to enter the flak cloud. Just hover above and wait for easy targets.

The 778th Lead Command Squadron entered the air space over the city and slipped into the inky cloud.

"Deputy Lead just took a direct hit, number four engine smoking," Sherman called out. "Looks like the top turret was knocked out, but Hornbaker's continuing toward the target."

Target for Tonite shuddered as she hit the curtain of flak, an explosive burst close enough to rock the plane. Gravel-like chunks pelted her aluminum sides, the smell of explosives filling the cockpit. Eaves' gut clenched as he scanned the gauges. He expelled his pent-up breath when it appeared no serious damage had occurred.

Another shell exploded with a fiery red flash in front of the plane on the starboard side.

A concussion shook *Target for Tonite* again. More sounds of metal colliding on metal. Time stood still as they plunged through the gauntlet of hellfire.

"Almost to target," came Lambert's voice.

Then, seconds later, "Bombs away!"

The B-24 leaped upward as the twelve five-hundred-pound bombs fell. Fires and explosions could be seen below, with clouds of smoke rising from the destroyed factory, flames raging.

"Your plane, sir," Lambert called out.

"Roger." Eaves pushed forward on the yoke and banked right, following the evasive maneuvers of the 777th lead plane as the whole formation dove down to escape the flak. After dropping over two thousand feet, the Lead Squadron leveled off and the 464th turned homeward.

Eaves pressed his throat microphone. "Check-in men. Anyone hurt? Damage to report?"

"Linneman here, sir. We're both okay. Lots of small holes in the waist, but nothing big."

"Masterson here, tail A-OK."

"Ball turret okay, sir."

"Haverkos here. Some flak holes and an ugly chunk of shrapnel landed in the greenhouse, but everybody is okay."

Sherman's voice broke in. "Hornbaker's dropping out of formation. Another plane moving into Deputy Lead position."

Eaves glanced down. Below the command group he spotted Hornbaker's plane slowly descending into the clouds like a wounded goose, smoke streaming from one engine. The lonely sight etched into his mind. The German fighters were sure to target a straggler.

God, be with them.

"Bandits, twelve o'clock high!" Elder's voice rang out from the top turret.

"Gunners, alert!" Eaves commanded.

Eaves watched three Me-109s bank and turn to approach him head-on, their 20 mm cannons blinking at him. His blood ran cold.

Guns from the nose turret opened up and spit out a steady stream of fire.

Like a game of chicken, the wave of fighters stayed the course, firing away, until just seconds from impact when they pulled up and over the Liberator.

The top turret guns burst into action, furiously ripping off round after round. The sound was deafening in the cockpit.

Target for Tonite plunged on. Amazingly the fighters had failed to hit any vital spots.

Elder cried out, "Think I got one! And here comes the cavalry! Two P-51s on their tail."

Suddenly Eaves saw black puffs appearing around the formation again.

Another pocket of anti-aircraft guns.

They've tracked our course and altitude, got us in their sights.

Fangman yelled into the intercom. "A command group plane, flak got the right wing!" Pause. "See chutes—one, two." A gasp. "Oh no—the whole plane just exploded."

A moment later, a subdued voice. "Petrone here. Saw a third chute . . . but it was on fire."

Silence.

Eaves gripped the yoke tighter, swallowed hard.

No hope for that man. Help us get through this, Lord.

Another shell burst rocked the Liberator, metallic sounds reverberating through the plane.

"Elder here. Bandits pulled up to get out of the flak and the Little Friends are after them."

Another concussion shook the plane, the smell of cordite and sounds of fragments hitting the hull.

Looking to the left, Eaves saw his wingman, *Red Hot Riding Hood*, run into an orange burst of flak. In horror he watched the bomber disappear into a dive straight down.

Moments later, "Ball turret here. Saw four chutes from *Riding Hood*."

Eaves knew that pilot. Lt. Latimer's face flashed before his eyes. He blinked to clear his vision.

The 778th Lead Group started evasive action once again to dodge the flak. Eaves struggled to stay tight in formation as they banked starboard and dropped lower in the sky.

"Sherman, check for damage."

"Losing pressure, engine four. Large hole in right wing," came the report.

Eaves sucked in his breath. "Feather four."

At least we've only lost one engine. Hope we can keep up with the group.

The German fighters lurked above for a while but didn't attack the formation. Probably after the stragglers.

Target for Tonite plodded gamely on.

The skies stayed clear. Eaves breathed a sigh of relief as the formation crossed over the snow-capped Alps and the sparkling blue of the Adriatic Sea came into focus.

✈✈✈

Once safely over the water, they dropped below 10,000 feet. Eaves yanked off his oxygen mask. After being on oxygen for more than five hours, he rubbed the chaffed skin and indentations the mask left on his nose, cheeks and chin.

Pressing his throat mic, he gave the order. "Okay to remove oxygen masks."

Almost to home base and *Target for Tonite* was still holding her own.

As the 464th reached Gioia, Eaves could see several planes shooting off red flares indicating casualties and serious battle-damage. Crash trucks and ambulance lights flashed around the runway.

"Fire the red flare," he ordered. Landing with even one engine out was serious business.

Eaves circled, waiting his turn to land, fighting the exhaustion from over eight hours of flight time. Finally, it was their turn.

"Landing gear down," he ordered.

"Gear indicator light isn't working, sir." Sherman's voice registered concern.

Eaves called the tower, notified them of the problems. "Flying on three engines and we don't know if the landing gear is down or not. Request permission to do a flyby to confirm."

The tower responded, "Roger. Do flyby at two hundred feet."

Eaves dropped the plane down. *Target for Tonite* made a pass in front of the control tower.

The tower came back on the air. "Only one wheel down. Right gear still up. Leave landing pattern and climb to 5,000 feet. Notify us after you lower gear manually."

"Roger." Eaves gripped the yoke tighter and pulled up. He took a deep breath as the plane slowly climbed.

"Elder, Linneman, get that right wheel down. Fangman, check from the waist windows and let me know when you see the yellow latches on both sides."

Flak must have cut the hydraulic line to the right wheel. Eaves felt sweat running down his back.

If we can't get that wheel down . . . little chance of surviving a belly-landing.

Moments passed. Eaves continued circling, noting the fuel level dropping toward zero. He pictured the engineer and waist gunner balanced on the bomb bay catwalk, taking turns pumping the hand crank that slowly lowered the right landing gear.

He squeezed his eyes shut for a moment.

The Canary Islands, flying on fumes . . . not again. Lord, help us.

A voice came over the intercom, interrupting his anxious thoughts. "Fangman here. Right landing gear down, can see the yellow latch on each side now, sir."

"Roger." A lightness filled his chest as Eaves notified the tower of the successful maneuver. But eyeing the fuel gauge, his gut tightened.

The tower confirmed. "Cleared to land."

"Prepare for emergency landing, men. Everyone aft." Eaves began the descent.

He could see the ambulance and emergency crash trucks standing by as they dropped down onto the runway.

Touch down. Smooth as glass. The right wheel gear held up.

A wave of relief washed over him as he and Sherman leaned back and applied the brakes. At the end of the runway, they slowly turned and taxied *Target for Tonite* toward the hardstand.

They rumbled to a halt in front of the crew chief, who flashed a thumbs-up. Eaves gestured back and cut the engines. He slumped forward over the yoke. He and Sherman sat for a moment in silence before Eaves sat up and pulled out the flight log to finish documentation. Sherman staggered to his feet and exited the flight deck.

Fatigue overtook Eaves as he finished the required forms. He struggled to muster enough strength to stand, his legs wobbling like a newborn calf's.

Sgt. Ryskeciski, the crew chief, stood waiting for him below the right wing. He pointed up at the gaping hole. "Only an inch more to the right or to the left and that shell would've hit the fuel tank or the wing support." He paused, not stating the obvious. It was a miracle they had survived. "Feathered engine four?"

Eaves nodded.

The crew chief looked down the plane. "The waist looks like a sieve and I see flak holes in the nose. Any other damage I should know about?"

"Right landing gear had to be manually lowered." Eaves took a deep breath. "Think you can fix her?"

"Do our best. She's a tough bird. We'll install a new engine. She'll be back into flying form again soon."

Eaves nodded and slowly trudged over to the truck where the crew waited. Haverkos reached down to give him a hand. Gratefully Eaves took it, pulling up and stepping into the cargo hold. He settled down on the hard wooden bench under the tarp next to Haverkos as the truck lurched toward the briefing room.

No one spoke, each man locked into their own thoughts and memories of a flight through hell. Eaves squeezed his eyes shut—fiery flashes in black clouds, planes falling from the sky played on the screen in his mind. He sucked in his breath. The horrible barrage of flak had taken so many young men's lives.

At the briefing center, no one turned down the standard shot of whiskey offered as they sat down with the briefing officer to describe the results of the mission. Each crew member was asked to give a report of the mission, any inconsistencies reconciled. Accuracy of bombs? How many German fighters? Did they see any aircraft go down? Any chutes? What damage did their plane incur? Any injuries?

Finally, the briefing officer wrapped it up. "Congratulations on a difficult mission accomplished—an accurate bomb drop, the aircraft factory reported to be almost completely obliterated."

He shuffled his papers into a neat pile on the table and folded his hands over them. Looking up, he spoke softly. "But it cost us dearly. Three planes from the 464th went down today, and Deputy Lead Hornbaker is listed as missing in action."

Chapter 12

11 MAY 1944—GIOIA DEL COLLE AIRFIELD, ITALY

THE 464TH STOOD DOWN from all missions the next day to let the ground crews repair the damaged planes. Practically every plane had flak holes to repair, and several had lost engines.

No one talked about the trauma, each one living his own nightmare and putting on a brave face.

Exhausted, Eaves slept hard after the mission, but violent dreams startled him awake early. Fighters diving at him, fiery explosions, planes dropping from the sky, black clouds of flak coming closer. Eaves got up and slipped out of the tent alone.

He walked over to the hardstand to see how the repairs were going on *Target for Tonite*. The ground crew had been busy. Most of the flak holes were already patched up, the damage concealed. Two men leaned over a new engine on a lift being installed on the right wing.

Drawing closer, he wrinkled his nose at the strong whiff of fresh paint lingering in the air. Surprised, he stared at the nine-foot twin tails gleaming with a fancy new paint job—the top half yellow with a black square, the bottom half black with a narrow yellow rectangle in the center.

Eaves spotted Sgt. Ryskeciski and waved him over. "What's the deal with the new tail colors? You guys getting bored?"

Ryskeciski laughed. "Yeah, right. No—orders from headquarters." He wiped sweat out of his eyes. "Yesterday they ordered all the tails of the 464th to be painted, top half yellow and bottom black. And they think specific markings for every bomb squadron will make identification easier in formation. So, your 777th got a yellow rectangle in the black, the 776th is red, 778th white, and the 779th all black."

"Looks pretty sharp!" Eaves grinned. "But that's a heck of a lot of painting. Didn't know you signed up to be an artist, did you?"

The crew chief gave him a tired smile and a thumbs-up sign as he turned back toward the plane. "Yep, talents galore."

Everywhere Eaves looked, he saw ground crews struggling with ladders, hoses, and sprayers, trying to get most of the planes done that day. He liked what he saw. Visual recognition of the other planes in their squadron should definitely help facilitate group formation in the air.

"Hey Red, there you are." He turned to see Haverkos' tall muscular form striding toward him, a serious look on his face, and the lanky Lambert tagging along behind. Haverkos wore his mitt on his hand, plunking a baseball into the pocket as he walked. "Got a challenge going on. Tudor thinks his crew can beat us in a ball game. I say no way!"

Eaves had to smile. "Are the guys up for a game?"

Haverkos nodded. "Elder is rounding them up right now."

Soon both crews gathered at an open field and warmed up. Eaves helped Tudor mark out the baselines. Good-natured catcalls echoed back and forth between the two crews.

Haverkos started pitching, with Eaves on the bench designated as backup. His eyes widened. Yes, Haverkos did have a wicked fastball.

Eaves smiled as he watched the men throw themselves into the game. A good way to work off some steam. Just play—and forget the horrors of yesterday, the fears of tomorrow.

Thank You, God, for these guys. Couldn't have a better crew.

The score was tied five to five in the sixth inning when thunder clouds rolled in and broke open. A torrent of rain began to fall.

"Guess we'll call it a tie. Beat you next time!" Tudor called out with a grin, as all the guys scrambled to gather their equipment and jogged for the tents.

After storing their gear, they slogged back through the muck to reach the mess tent for lunch. Standard fare. The menu sported fried Spam sandwiches and hashbrowns with coffee or powdered milk.

"How about catching a ride into town?" Eaves asked after cleaning his plate. "I want to spend some more time in that barber shop."

"Sounds good to me." Haverkos took a long swig of coffee to wash down the Spam. "You coming, Tudor?"

"Only if we can get another spaghetti dinner at the little village restaurant. I can already taste the homemade Italian bread and red wine. Mmm."

Haverkos smirked. "You mean the one with a cute little dark-haired waitress? Caught your fancy, did she?"

Tudor just tilted his head and smiled.

Soon after lunch they snagged a ride on a truck heading into the village of Gioia del Colle. After they enjoyed the spa-like treatment in the barbershop, the rain let up. They nosed around the little shops for a while before heading into the restaurant for a spaghetti dinner.

Tudor's face fell when a sturdy gray-haired matron greeted them as waitress. But the food lived up to their expectations. All too soon it was time to head back to the base.

Hopping off the cargo truck, they headed over for mail call. They had planned to go into the officers' club for a few drinks when they saw the alert list was up again on the bulletin board. Eaves and Tudor were both listed for tomorrow's mission. No drinks before a mission, and no rest for the weary.

Inside the mail room, more disappointment awaited. No mail.

But there was also some good news.

The orderly told them Captain Hornbaker had evaded the German fighters and threaded his way through the mountains. He made it to the Army Air Corps base at Foggia, where several wounded crew members received medical treatment. They lived to fly again.

✈✈✈

12 MAY 1944—GIOIA DEL COLLE AIR BASE, ITALY

Colonel Bonner addressed the airmen. "I know you've just emerged from an emotionally draining mission, our most difficult to date. Your courage and bravery in the face of incredible odds was commendable. Weiner Neustadt has been identified as the third most heavily defended target in the Third Reich—only Berlin and Vienna are more fortified. You effectively led the entire 55th Bomb Wing on a successful campaign, destroying vital facilities of the German war machine, even at the staggering loss of twenty-seven bombers from the Fifteenth Air Force."

He cleared his throat. "May their sacrifice never be forgotten." He turned toward the chaplain. "Chaplain Eastwood, lead us in prayer, please."

The chaplain strode forward to the podium. "Let us remember our brave brothers who have paid the ultimate price for our nation." Every cap was swept off, all heads bowed. A deep hush filled the hall.

After several moments of silence, Eastwood's baritone rang out. "Lord, we commend these courageous souls to Your care, and we pray Your comfort over their friends and loved ones back home. May we have success in the mission today and protection over these men who are dedicated to fighting for liberty and country. Aid them in completing the tasks before them. In the name of Jesus. Amen."

The operations officer stood and pulled the cord. The curtains swept back to reveal the huge map with a red yarn line leading from Gioia north into the top part of Italy.

Eaves' shoulders lost some of the tension bunching his muscles as low murmurs of approval filled the hall. At least they weren't headed back to Austria.

"Today we'll be targeting the marshalling yards in Reggio Emilia in Northern Italy." The briefing officer paused, studying the grim faces of the young airmen gathered before him. "We must cut off the flow of supplies to the German troops in the area. It's critical to the success of our ground troops in pushing the enemy out of Italy."

The intelligence officer stepped forward. "I want to assure you that this mission should be a milk run. No known anti-aircraft guns in the vicinity or enemy fighters frequenting the area. Three hours of flight time to target."

The weatherman promised clear skies. Briefing ended with the "time-tick," as all the airmen synchronized their watches to the official time announced by the operations officer.

And no mention of Colonel Bonner leading.

Eaves breathed a sigh of relief.

At least we don't have to worry about him folding under pressure.

He and Sherman headed to the pilots' meeting.

He learned his squadron would again be in Baker, the upper box. The 778th would be Lead Squadron today. A good position. After final instructions, he hopped on a cargo truck and headed for the hardstand, packing his heavy fleece-lined flying gear and his parachute.

Climbing down from the truck, Eaves stopped for a moment to admire the new paint job on the huge dual tail. *Target for Tonite* looked like a hornet with her new yellow and black markings.

Hope she stings like one too.

Soon the green flare to start engines created a ground-shaking roar rolling across the base as all the heavies fanned their props into action.

Eaves and Sherman completed the long preflight checklist, and they taxied the big bird over to the runway to wait their turn. Soon they were bouncing over the rough sod insert again. The heavily loaded B-24 gradually built up just enough speed to lift wheels at the end of the short runway.

As *Target for Tonite* skimmed above the tree line and slowly climbed into the sky, Eaves' heart thudded in his chest, the rush of adrenalin coursing through his body. Every take-off was an exhilarating challenge. And after the recent combat-filled mission, the specter of danger loomed large in his mind like a menacing bird of prey seeking a victim.

He shook his head.

Stay focused, Eaves. Do your job.

Spotting the rest of the 777th was definitely easier with the new paint jobs. The squadron quickly formed into a box formation and bunched in tight above Able. Tudor was flying on his wing.

Clear skies continued over the Adriatic. The plane shuddered with bursts of machine gun fire as the gunners tested their weapons. Lambert climbed back into the bomb bay to pull the pins.

As they rose to 10,000 feet, Eaves gave the order for oxygen masks. The high altitude cold soon penetrated all the layers of heavy clothing, and Eaves ordered Sherman to check in with each crewman to be sure oxygen was flowing.

All was ready.

Another hour of freezing cold and a sharp turn at the IP set them on the bomb run. Iron rails were clearly visible below, leading to the large marshalling area straight ahead. A locomotive could be seen pulling out of the station with a long train of railcars. Too late to escape.

The Lead Group began to drop their bombs just as Lambert called out, "Bombs away!" The familiar upward lurch confirmed the twelve-hundred-pound load of bombs had dropped.

The reconnaissance reports were right. No flak, and no bandits, as yet.

"Your plane, sir."

"Roger." Following the lead plane down, Eaves banked with the group, turning back toward home base. He exhaled deeply. So far so good.

The skies stayed peaceful on the return trip. Soon the blue of the Adriatic gave way to land ahoy.

Looks like this mission was a success. One more down, twenty-five to go. Eaves hoped the rest could be as easy as this one—but little chance of that.

No red flares to be seen. All the planes landed safely. They breezed through final paperwork and the debriefing before heading to the mess tent.

Eaves frowned to see the alert list up again after dinner. After the six-hour flight, his whole body ached. Reluctantly he trudged up to the board. His lips curled up into a smile when he saw his name was not on it.

Stopping by the mail room for mail call brought an even bigger smile. Three letters and a package waited for Lt. William T. Eaves. Tucking the box under his arm, he strode back to the tent to savor the words from home.

Stepping inside, the familiar smell of damp canvas, cigarettes, and aviation fuel assaulted his nose. And there was silence.

Good, no one here. Nice to have some peace and quiet.

Settling down on his cot, he eyed his prizes.

First, he opened the V-mail from his older sister Ruth. Squinting at the tiny writing, he smiled as he read about the crazy Texas wind and a sudden sandstorm that almost blew her away walking home from the PX. Marc had been promoted to staff sergeant and recently attended a Texas A&M baseball game. He wished Eaves had been there with him.

Eaves sighed as he folded the letter back into the envelope and felt a twinge of longing for the familiar activities back home, fun times with Ruth and Marc. Seemed like another world now. Would he make it back to experience those simple joys again?

He picked up the letter from his family in Iraan. His younger brothers and sisters were anxious for school to be out. Levon and Lyall were practicing their golf. And it was already hot. They were praying for rain in the arid hills of West Texas and . . . praying for him.

Eaves smiled wryly, wishing he could send them some of this overabundant Italian rain.

He slowly opened Jean's letter. Just seeing her neat handwriting brought a tightness to his chest. Her description of walking along the seawall in Galveston and helping her mother cook Sunday dinner sent a little wave of nostalgia wafting through him. He read, then re-read her tender words of love. He pictured her lovely face as the longing to hold her close swept over him. Would he survive to see her again?

Can't go there.

He pulled out his pocketknife and cut the cords wrapped around the brown paper-covered box. Inside he discovered a couple dozen chocolate chip cookies. He licked his lips. One of his favorites. He pictured Jean in the kitchen baking them. Must've taken all their sugar rations. Not standard fare at the mess tent here. And he knew they were made with love. That would make them taste even better.

He bit into one, closing his eyes as sweetness burst on his taste buds.

His reverie was interrupted as Haverkos lifted the tent flap and strode into the tent, Sherman right behind him.

"What's in the package?" Haverkos lifted his eyebrows and gave Eaves an expectant look. "Share and share alike," he said with a chuckle as he eyed the cookies.

Eaves grinned. "I'll remember that when your package from Ginny arrives. Gotta save some for the rest of the crew. And Tudor too." He chuckled. "Amazing how sweets from home lift the spirits!"

He snatched one more and then raised the box toward them. They quickly scooped up two cookies each.

"Mmm . . . good!" Sherman said as he smacked his lips after his first bite. "Thanks, Red."

Eaves carefully wrapped two more cookies in a clean napkin and stuffed them in his pocket before storing the box in his locker. "Heading over to the club," he said, as he ducked under the tent flap.

He found Tudor back in a corner sprawled in an overstuffed chair. He smiled when he saw Eaves approaching.

"Hey buddy—want a beer?" Tudor got up and turned toward the counter.

"Sure," Eaves said as he sat down in the chair next to Tudor's. He reached into his pocket and pulled out the napkin-wrapped cookies.

When Tudor returned, he carried two glasses of beer.

"Thanks." Eaves took a big draught, then shook his head. "Don't think I'll ever be a fan of warm beer." He wiped his lips with the back of his hand. Refrigeration was something he took for granted back home—none here in the club.

He lifted the little bundle toward Tudor. "Here. A little gift from home for you."

Tudor grinned when he saw the contents. "Cookies! Thanks, Red. Sure glad you married a good cook, my friend."

Eaves nodded. They sat in silence for a few minutes while Tudor munched and Eaves sipped at his beer. "Glad today's mission went well. Heard everyone made it back in one piece."

"Yep." Tudor nodded. "For once they were right. It really was a milk run. And then, more good news . . . our names are not on the list for tomorrow's sortie. So, tonight we can down a few and hit the sack for a good night's rest."

"I'll drink to that," Eaves said with a smile as he lifted his glass. "Gotta celebrate the simple things."

✈✈✈

The afternoon of the next day, Eaves and Tudor joined the ground crews as they all waited, scanning the skies for the returning planes. A fireman dressed head to toe in a white asbestos suit looked like something from Halloween as he stood by the fire truck. Eaves spotted Colonel Bonner on the command tower scanning the horizon with his binoculars. The tension was palpable.

"Should've been here by now," Tudor said, checking his watch. "Heard it was another mission to more Northern Italy marshalling yards, about the same distance as the sortie yesterday."

"Listen!" Eaves cocked his head. "I think I hear them."

The faint drone of motors swelled minute by minute, as planes soon swept into sight. Ground crews cheered when they spotted their plane. No red flares, a welcome sight as the planes began to land.

Eaves watched the reactions, appreciating the hours of hard work and the dedication to excellence the maintenance guys and armorers brought to each plane. Their investment was so sincere, evident in their excitement now, and in the grief conveyed if their "girl" failed to make it back.

"Thirty-nine, forty," Tudor counted. "Looks like the whole group made it back safely, thank God." He turned to Eaves. "Heard they got a poker game going at the club this afternoon. Wanna play?"

"Sounds good to me," Eaves said with a smile. "How much are you ready to lose?"

"Ha-ha—I don't play to lose," Tudor cocked his head. "Maybe you do?"

Soon they arrived at the club and joined a small group of officers around a big table. Time flew by, their winnings going up and down. Eaves' tummy rumbled.

Eaves counted his money. "I'm a little ahead. How 'bout you?"

"More than I came with," Tudor said with a smile. "Let's head for the chow hall before we lose it."

"Gotta go, guys." Eaves and Tudor stood up, started pocketing their money. Moans and catcalls greeted their withdrawal. Then someone called out, "Never mind—we'll win it back plus more next time!"

A welcome gentle breeze and sunny skies greeted them as they hustled back toward the mess tent. "Look at that! The alert list is up again." Eaves eyed the bulletin board as they arrived. "That's three missions in a row."

And sure enough—both their names were on alert for tomorrow morning. Briefing at 0500.

Chapter 13

13 May 1944—Galveston, Texas

A FAN STIRRED THE HUMID AIR in the fellowship hall. Jean inhaled the sweet smell of gardenias wafting in through the open windows. She wiped the sweat from her brow with her handkerchief before tucking it back into her skirt pocket.

"Well, that's the last one," she said as she finished tucking two more books into the cardboard box and folded the flaps shut.

Her mother looked up and smiled. "I know the servicemen will appreciate having something to read while they're away from home. I'm really proud of our young people. They did a great job canvassing the neighborhood and they collected a lot more books than I expected."

Jean nodded and then sighed.

Another Saturday without Red. How long had it been since they'd said goodbye in Pocatello? Every Saturday reminded her of the special weekends they'd spent together during his final training sessions. The ache inside her chest almost brought tears to her eyes. Two do become one. She didn't know she could miss someone so much.

Jean took a deep breath and closed her eyes for a moment.

Stay focused. Red would be proud of us. At least we're doing something to help . . . collecting useful things that contribute to the war effort and support the troops.

She looked up and forced herself to smile at her mother.

Be thankful—I'm not alone.

A warm rush of gratitude for her parents and their loving ways stole over her heart.

Hearing the door open, she looked up to see her mother's friend Dorothy flounce into the room. Her wind-blown gray hair framed a troubled face. Something was wrong.

"Ollie, did you hear? Emma Smith lost another son!" Dorothy stopped to catch her breath. "Her oldest boy died at Pearl Harbor, and now Johnny . . . shot down over Germany."

She gave a little sob as she pulled out an embroidered hanky and dabbed at her eyes. "Oh my, it just breaks my heart. All these young men who grew up in our church gone, just gone."

Jean's eyes widened and her heart thudded in her chest.

Not John Smith.

He'd been in her Sunday school class. Blond hair, twinkling blue eyes, always smiling.

Jean's mother reached out and patted her friend's shoulder, a stricken look on her face. "Oh, no," she exclaimed. "Poor Emma."

Jean closed her eyes, remembering Johnny. He'd volunteered to join the Army Air Corps right after his brother's death and trained to become a fighter pilot. Tears sprang to her eyes, and she tried to swallow the lump in her throat. It could have been Red.

"I know, I know. So much loss. It's overwhelming." Ollie continued to pat Dorothy's shoulder.

"We were planning to stop by the grocery store on the way home." She looked over at Jean. "We'll get something to take over to Emma for supper. I don't think she will feel much like eating, but she'll need to keep her strength up."

Dorothy sniffled and blew her nose into her handkerchief. "I'll get the word out to the Ladies Guild. I'm sure there are others who'd be willing to bring food." She turned and headed out the door. Ollie stooped to gather her things before following her.

Jean flipped off the lights and closed the fellowship hall door. Emotions churned through her. Why did God let good young men like John and his brother die in this senseless war? None of this hate and violence made sense. Tears slipped down her cheeks.

Ollie looked back and then stopped as she reached out to put her arm around her daughter. "I know this is so hard for you, sweetheart."

"Why doesn't God do something?" she sobbed.

"There, there." She pulled Jean close to her. "He is doing something, through Johnny and Red and all the young men out there fighting for truth and freedom." She paused. "I think Paul said it best in Romans 8. 'For your sake we face death all day long; we are considered as sheep to be slaughtered.' But then he goes on to say, 'No, in all these things, we are more than conquerors through Him who loved us,' and that nothing—not death or evil or any powers that be—can separate us from the love of God in Christ Jesus our Lord."

Ollie looked up thoughtfully. "I know His ways are above our ways and His thoughts above our thoughts, but God is always loving and good. And in the end, I believe good will always triumph over the evil of this world."

She sighed as she gave Jean another gentle squeeze and released her. They walked on in silence. The humid blustery wind pushed them down the sidewalk, bringing with it the salty scent of the sea. Jean pondered her mother's words, her heart still heavy with loss and fear.

Ollie stopped in front of the grocery store steps. She reached into her purse.

"Where is that ration book?" She shuffled through the contents and finally pulled out the document from the Office of Price Administration.

"I still have some stamps for meat and butter because last time we were here they were totally out—again." She sighed. "Glad we have the Victory Garden your father planted. At least we can be thankful for fresh vegetables and the fruit trees. Poor Red probably doesn't get much of anything in the way of fresh fruits and vegetables overseas."

Jean wiped her face with her handkerchief and turned to her mother. "I sure appreciate you using the sugar rations for his care packages, Mom."

Ollie smiled. "Of course, dear. He needs it more than we do."

"In his last letter, he asked for some twenty-five-watt bulbs for their tent."

"Let's look. We can wrap them in the socks I just finished knitting for him, and put them inside an empty coffee can to mail."

The store was crowded with shoppers on their day off from work. The shelves were pretty bare, but they were in luck. They picked up the last two twenty-five-watt bulbs, a can of peaches, some potatoes, coffee, and a can of Ovaltine.

They waited in the long line at the meat counter in the back of the store. "Sorry, still no butter, but I do have some stew meat and margarine," the butcher said with a smile when it was finally their turn.

"We'll take two pounds of the stew meat, please," Ollie said. "And a pound sack of margarine."

They took their purchases to the cash register and surrendered the ration stamps needed for the meat and coffee. Jean carefully carried the light bulbs and the sack of margarine while her mother took the rest in a brown paper bag.

"What a blessing. Should be enough meat here to make a delicious stew that we can share with Emma," Ollie said. "You can pull some carrots and onions from the garden when we get home."

As they turned toward home, Jean noticed some young men piling scrap metal on the empty lot at the end of the block. A rusted fender, an old ice box, broken rakes, and a file cabinet caught her eye. A new sign stood next to the sidewalk. "Support the War. Metal Needed."

"Mom, maybe the toothpaste tubes and aluminum foil we've been saving can be donated here." She glanced at her mother. "Do we have any other metal we can spare?"

"We can ask. Your father has that old wheelbarrow with the flat tire and some extra tools he might part with. Every little bit can help."

After learning the saved tubes and foil were certainly welcome in the metal drive, they walked on in silence the few short blocks to home. Jean eyed the snug little white cottage with gratitude and a twinge of guilt. They had a roof over their heads, not a tent like Red was living in.

The backyard garden was just starting to produce, but Jean found tender carrots and green onions for the stew. After peeling the potatoes, she chopped all the vegetables into chunks.

"Jean, please look in the pantry," Ollie said as she browned the stew meat. "I think there are still a few jars of tomatoes that we canned last summer."

Jean found the tomatoes and handed the jar to her mother. "I'll fix the margarine."

Breaking open the yellow coloring packet, Jean whipped it into the pound of white margarine. Her arm ached as she scraped the final golden product into a small red bowl. She couldn't understand why the dairy industry was so opposed to adding the coloring at the factory. It would make it so much easier to use margarine, although it certainly wasn't as tasty as butter.

Jean mopped her brow with the kitchen towel. "Think I'm going to go lie down for a while, Mom, if you don't need me."

"Go ahead, sweetheart. Do you want to go over to Emma's with me in a bit?" Ollie asked. "And . . . were you planning to help serve at the USO Club dance tonight?"

"No. If it's all right with you, I think I'll just stay in my room. I want to write Red a letter to go in the package." She looked into her mom's brown eyes. "And thanks again—I know Red will be so pleased to get the light bulbs. And the peaches and Ovaltine you bought will be a sweet treat. You and Daddy are the best!"

"God provides all we need." Ollie smiled warmly at her daughter and turned back to stirring the stew simmering on the burner.

Jean walked down the hall to her little room. After she closed the door, she sat down on the edge of the bed and put her head into her hands, tears welling up.

Be brave . . . that's what Red said when I left Pocatello. Lord, I didn't know it was going to be so hard. So many dying in this awful war. And I just can't stand to go watch all those young soldiers putting their arms around their dance partners tonight—not when I ache to feel Red's arms around me.

She reached into her pocket for her handkerchief and blew her nose, folding it over and dabbing at her eyes. Taking a deep breath, she lifted her head and looked up.

Please help me to lean on You, Lord. I chose to trust You and Your promises. Send Your angels to watch over Red and his men, and please, please . . . bring him home to me.

Chapter 14

18 May 1944—Gioia del Colle Airfield, Italy

HAVERKOS GLANCED AROUND the briefing room. All the crews had gathered to wait for Bonner and the entourage. He turned to Eaves and grinned.

"Longnose," he quipped. "Pretty apropos for that last mission to Piombino since it took us over six hours to get there and back. Somebody's getting a little more creative with the callsigns." He chuckled. "Just hope we'll have another mission today like those last two runs to Northern Italy."

Eaves nodded. "Wish they could all be that easy. Rumors are flying that the mission today could be different, way different." He squinted at his watch. "They got us up an hour earlier, which says something."

"Ten-hut!" They all leaped to their feet as Bonner strode into the briefing room.

"At ease, men." Bonner grasped the edges of the podium as the airmen settled back down on the wooden benches, his eyes scanning the room. He took a deep breath and tightened his jaw before speaking. "Today you will have a challenging mission, but you are well-prepared. I trust you will accomplish our objectives."

He nodded to the operations officer, who pulled the cord, whipping the curtain back to reveal the red yarn once again stretching deep into enemy territory—across Yugoslavia and into Romania, all the way to Ploesti, one of the most talked about and feared targets in the war.

Haverkos' stomach lurched and he felt the hair on the nape of his neck lift. Groans and curses rang throughout the room. The refineries at Ploesti had been targeted several times by the Fifteenth Air Force, with disastrous losses.

The operations officer took the podium, his face grim. "Our target is the Concordia Vega Oil Refinery in Ploesti. The Germans depend on this rich oil field for a majority of their fuel. It is critical that we destroy this refinery and cut off the fuel supply to the Nazi war machine. This is a top priority from headquarters. Ploesti was severely damaged in the Fifteenth's last mission there, but the Germans have been busy rebuilding. It's our job to mop up anything left standing."

The meteorologist reported clear weather going, but the possibility of turbulence later in the day. Weather could make this mission more difficult than flak.

The intelligence officer took over. "As you know, Ploesti is well-defended with anti-aircraft guns and fighters. A new tactic they've employed is creating a dense smoke screen with generators set throughout the city. If the target is obscured, do a second flyover and hopefully prevailing winds will clear the smoke." He looked intently at the young men before him. "I stress again—destruction of these facilities is top priority for the Fifteenth."

Haverkos swallowed hard. No one wanted to do a second flyover with anti-aircraft guns zeroing in on them. He clenched his jaw. Have to try to get it done right the first time over the target.

Chaplin Eastwood stood to offer a heartfelt prayer to the Almighty. Men were subdued as they left the briefing. Haverkos nodded to Eaves and headed to the navigators' briefing to get final details of the flight.

When he arrived at the hardstand, Haverkos pulled on his heavy fleece-lined pants and jacket. The bulky flak jacket went on next and then the Mae West life-preserver that would inflate in the event of a water emergency.

Entering *Target for Tonite* through the bomb bay, he waddled his way carefully across the nine-inch catwalk in the heavy gear. He ducked down to crawl through the front wheel casing to reach his station just behind the nose. Lambert was already in the "greenhouse," the enclosed, multi-paned compartment in the nose section of the plane, checking his equipment and the nose gun.

Haverkos spread out his maps, then grabbed his protractors, ruler, and pencils as he settled down on his seat at the navigator's table situated right below the pilot's feet. No extra room here.

And—no room for errors.

The flight plan called for several legs at different angles to avoid heavy flak concentrations and to confuse the Germans. All known areas of intense anti-aircraft installations were highlighted in red on the map. All groups would fly the same course, which also enabled the fighter escort to provide better protection.

One by one the engines roared to life, and the plane lumbered to the line for take-off. *Target for Tonite* bounced over the infamous oiled sod insert and reluctantly accelerated. Finally reaching the end of the runway, the jarring vibrations and rattles ceased as the landing gear came up. Haverkos breathed easier as the big bird nosed smoothly upward. Every takeoff in a B-24 was a heart-stopping adventure for the whole crew, especially knowing the deadly cargo they carried.

After giving Eaves the heading, Haverkos rechecked the flight plan and secondary targets. This mission would be long, over nine hours of flight time even if everything went well. The weight of his responsibilities sat like a rock on his chest.

Target for Tonite slid tightly into formation, wing-tip to wing tip. At least the 777th Squadron was in Baker, the upper box. Definitely safer than the lower box.

Once they reached the Adriatic, Eaves ordered guns to be tested. Lambert fired off several test rounds from the nose guns, brass casing scattering on the floor.

"Bombardier, arm bombs."

"Roger." Lambert slipped back to the bomb bay to pull the pins.

The bomb group continued climbing. Haverkos checked his watch. They'd been airborne for about an hour.

Eaves again. "Men, we're at 10,000 feet. Oxygen masks on."

Haverkos pulled the mask up over his nose and flipped on the oxygen.

Suddenly Eaves' voice came back on the intercom. "Attention all hands, this is the pilot. We've got a major leak in the oxygen system. We're dropping out of formation and returning to base. Haverkos, plot our return heading."

Target for Tonite banked left and dove downward as they circled back.

Haverkos blinked. Good call. No way could they survive at twenty thousand feet without oxygen. He quickly pulled out his maps as a surge of adrenaline flooded through his system and started calculating the heading they'd need with the current wind flow.

Eaves' voice sounded over the intercom again. "Pilot to Bombardier, your plane. Drop those live bombs."

Conflicting emotions rushed through Haverkos. Relief that they wouldn't have to face this dangerous mission. Then a wave of suffocating guilt for leaving their duty undone, wasting their bombs, abandoning their friends. He shook his head.

It's not our fault we have to abort. Lord, go with our buddies and grant them success.

He took a deep breath.

Get focused, Haverkos. Get this baby back to base.

✈✈✈

Eaves shivered as he pulled the cord to wash off the soap. Having time to bathe was a luxury, but cold water pouring over his shivering body in the rough outdoor washroom was grueling. Not like the warm showers he remembered back home. Just get in—and get out.

Haverkos had finished his shower moments before and stood waiting when Eaves emerged. "About time for them to return," he said, wrapping his dirty uniform in his towel.

Eaves nodded, his gut tightening as he pictured the firestorm their squadron faced in Ploesti. He sent up a quick prayer for all the guys, especially Tudor and his crew. They were like family.

They headed back to their tent. Once inside, they stuffed their dirty uniforms and wet towels in the laundry bag. The young local who'd poured their concrete floor had convinced his mother to launder their uniforms each week for a few K-rations and a little currency. A little luxury they could afford. Laundry was not a chore Eaves missed.

He eyed the one bare bulb now lighting the tent.

Hope Jean can send more bulbs before that one burns out.

Eaves and Haverkos strode over to join the maintenance crews who had already gathered together in small groups. Emergency equipment lined the runway. Eaves scanned the sky for any sign of returning bombers. He jammed his hands into his pockets and glanced up to see Colonel Bonner pacing on the deck of the control tower, then stopping to peer at the eastern horizon through his binoculars.

"They should be back," Haverkos muttered, looking at his watch.

Eaves searched the sky, a tightness in his chest. Ploesti was a dreaded target. How many good men wouldn't make it back today?

The faint drone of a plane engine electrified the group. Someone yelled. "Here they come!"

The roar of engines swelled as more planes flew into view. Several red flares illuminated the sky, indicating casualties and serious mechanical issues. Men rushed to staff the ambulances and the firetrucks.

One by one the B-24s landed. Eaves finally spotted Tudor's plane. A red flare. One of the last to land, she turned and taxied toward the hardstand. He could see engine four was feathered, flak damage evident on the fuselage.

Eaves swallowed to ease his dry mouth and exhaled slowly.

Thank God, they made it.

He and Haverkos strode over to the hardstand. They waited till Tudor climbed out of the plane and finished talking with his crew chief.

"Hey, buddy, what happened? Saw you drop out of formation." A haggard-looking Tudor squinted up at Eaves.

"Major oxygen leak." Eaves shrugged. "No choice but to abort. How'd the mission go?"

"Rough. Weather turned bad, total cloud and smoke cover over the target when we got there. Flak everywhere. And bandits. Lots of bandits." Tudor coughed, rubbed his chin. "Dropped our bombs on secondary targets on the way home. Then flak took out an engine. No casualties, thank God. Just glad we made it back."

Eaves reached out and squeezed his friend's shoulder.

"It looked like the whole group made it back," Haverkos said. "But a lot of flak-damaged planes."

"Have to go report in. See you guys at the club after." Tudor turned and shuffled toward the cargo truck loading his crew for the trip to the debriefing.

Eaves stopped by *Target for Tonite*'s hardstand. Sgt. Ryskeciski, the crew chief, was there, still working on the oxygen system.

"How's it going?" Eaves called out.

"She'll be good as new soon," he said with a grin. "Go have a few for me."

Eaves flashed him a smile and a thumbs-up.

Haverkos was quiet as they hiked toward the mess tent, both men mulling over the recent events. Outside, the alert list was up. They were on it.

Mission tomorrow, briefing at 0500. Eaves sighed. No drinks at the officers' club for them.

✈✈✈

Three days in a row on the alert list. Exhaustion throbbed through his body, but anxiety pushed away sleep. Eaves squeezed his eyes closed, but tired as he was, his mind still raced. Even though they were in the air for only a couple of hours before discovering the oxygen leak, the early hours and adrenaline had taken a toll. Much as he craved sleep, his body wouldn't cooperate. He plumped his pillow with his fist.

Would *Target for Tonite* even be ready for the mission tomorrow? What would the target be? Another long trip into enemy territory?

Black flak clouds and enemy fighters crowded the screen in his mind. He opened his eyes in the damp night air, the smell of wet canvas, stale cigarettes and aviation fuel in his nostrils. He turned onto his side, taking a deep breath and sending up a prayer.

Help me get some rest, Lord. I need to be able to do my best tomorrow regardless of where they send us. Help us successfully complete the mission and get back safely. And . . . may the Allies continue to make progress against this evil regime.

His thoughts roamed to home and his sweetheart. His arms ached to hold her. Memories of happy times, magical moments, calmed his spirit. His breathing slowed.

The next thing he knew, a bright light shone in his eyes. The orderly holding the flashlight in his face shook his shoulder.

"Lt. Eaves, time to get up, sir. Briefing, 0500."

Eaves sat up and pulled on his long underwear, then his flight suit. Pouring water into his mess cup, he heated it on the stove. Dumping the hot water into his steel helmet, he washed his face and shaved. The other officers moved like shadows, preparing for the day.

After picking at their breakfast and downing lots of steaming hot coffee, the men found themselves back in the briefing room again.

Eaves took a deep breath and rolled his shoulders as they waited.

Colonel Bonner and his entourage arrived promptly at 0500. After the airmen seated themselves on the wooden planks, the colonel stood at the podium to address them.

"We are grateful to the Almighty that all planes returned after the long mission yesterday." He looked down at his hands gripping the edges of the podium, then raised his eyes to scan the room. "Weather prevented us from accomplishing our objectives at Ploesti, but we scored major hits on secondary targets. You are to be commended."

Stepping down, he relinquished the podium to the operations officer, who pulled the cord to reveal a red line going up into Northern Italy. Murmurs of approval mixed with a few inevitable groans.

"Our mission today is to take out the marshalling yards at Faenza, about thirty miles south of Bologna, a hub for transporting German troops and supplies. The Allied troops on the ground are depending on us to disrupt the flow of reinforcements and armaments." He paused. "Accuracy is critical today in dropping your payload directly on the marshalling yard. Be careful to avoid the cultural or religious buildings which are nearby. There are several medieval cathedrals in the area, and it is the policy of the Fifteenth Air Force to preserve them."

The intelligence officer reported little flak in the area but warned of the possibility of bandits. Next the weather officer addressed the men. "Expect some clouds before reaching the IP, clear skies reported over the marshalling yards."

The airmen "hacked" their watches and the briefing ended with a respectful silence as Chaplain Eastwood stood to pray for the men.

In the pilots' briefing, Eaves learned his squadron would fly in Charlie, the lower box, and he would be the last plane, lower left, the "Tail-end Charlie" spot.

He swallowed hard. The most dangerous position.

Flight time should be three hours to target. The good news was that *Target for Tonite* was back in service, thanks to Sgt. Ryskeciski and his crew.

After donning their heavy flight suits and grabbing their parachutes, the crew soon completed all the preflight checks. Engines roared to life, exhaust fumes filled the air and an incredible reverberation of sound covered the airfield as forty B-24s paraded to the runway and climbed into the clouds.

Popping up into bright sunlight, Eaves squinted as he searched the skies above the clouds for the yellow tail marks of the 777th Squadron and slipped into position in the lower box.

"Purple Heart Corner" some of the guys called it. Flying last over the target meant German gunners below could improve their aim as the formation passed above them. Flak deaths and injuries were higher for those slotted in this box, especially the plane in the last position. Eaves clutched the yoke tighter and prayed the reports of little antiaircraft artillery in the area were correct.

The formation slowly rose to a cruising altitude at 22,000 feet. Arriving at the IP, they did a sharp turn toward Faenza. The skies were clear and no flak rose to greet them over the city. So far so good.

"Bombardier, your plane," Eaves commanded.

"Roger."

Eaves could see the tall spire of a Gothic cathedral below. Masterpieces, amazing works of architecture that had survived for centuries could be rubble after an air strike. He was glad the Fifteenth Air Force sought to preserve them and proud that American forces also practiced strategic bombing, avoiding random bombing of German cities and the killing of innocent civilians. This was not true of their British allies, who believed that destroying German cities and homeland workers would bring a quicker end to the war. And after the repeated German bombings of London, he really couldn't blame them.

The marshalling yards came into view. A few trains stretched out below as the bomb bay doors of the Lead Group opened. Seconds later, five-hundred-pound bombs began to rain down.

"Bombs away," Lambert called out. *Target for Tonite* sprang upwards as the heavy missiles dropped one after another from the bomb bay. "Your plane, sir."

"Roger," Eaves replied. He pushed forward on the yoke and followed the lead plane to the right as the group dropped down two thousand feet before leveling off.

"Bandits at three o'clock!" The warning came from Linneman. "Wait. Those are P-47s. It's our Little Friends! Maybe they scared away the bad guys."

A warm feeling of relief flooded over Eaves. Nice to have backup from Allied fighters.

Turning for Gioia, the formation continued to drop lower in the sky as they reached the Adriatic Sea and oxygen masks came off.

All planes returned without damage. Another mission accomplished. Nine down, twenty-one to go—almost a third of the magic number of missions that spelled home.

After landing, they taxied to the hardstand. Eaves sagged into his seat. He closed his eyes, feeling lightheaded from exhaustion. Six hours of flying time. Three missions in three days had sapped all his strength. He leaned forward and closed his eyes for a few minutes before finishing the paperwork. Then he struggled to stand up and crawled out of the bomber.

After a quick debriefing, the officers went straight to the mess tent. Hours of flight after a breakfast they'd barely touched left them all famished. First food, then rest.

As soon as he finished eating, Eaves excused himself and headed back to the tent. He fell asleep the minute he stretched out on his cot.

A voice called out to him from far away. "Red. Hey Red." He blinked, struggling to open his eyes.

It was Haverkos, tapping his shoulder. "Hate to wake you, but you have a letter from Jean." He thrust a V-mail into Eaves' hands.

Sherman stepped out from behind Haverkos. "And . . . after mail call, we checked the alert list. Good news—we're not on it!"

Eaves struggled to focus his eyes, a slow smile creeping across his face. "Much as I want to get all our missions done, that's really good news." He pried open his letter. "Thanks, guys."

Pulling out a flashlight, he read and then re-read the letter from his sweetheart. Word from home, always a treasure. He slipped the letter under his pillow, and before his head hit the pillow, his eyes were closed.

He slept twelve solid hours.

Chapter 15

21 May 1944—Gioia del Colle Airfield, Italy

DARK CLOUDS OPENED AND DUMPED buckets of water for two days. When the downpour slacked and the clouds parted in the afternoon, Bonner called for a training run.

Reluctantly, the crews headed for their bombers, puddles of water still standing in low spots on the taxi lanes and runway, all slick with sludge oozing up through the steel matting.

"What's with the Old Man, calling for a training run in this weather?" Sherman glanced over at Eaves and rolled his eyes as they trudged through the sticky mess.

Eaves shrugged. "He's definitely a stickler about details. And he's still in command." He gave a thin-lipped smile. "Just be glad he hasn't requested a ride in *Target for Tonite*." He had no respect for the man, but orders were orders.

The group managed to get into the air without incident and practiced tight formation flying for about an hour.

"Oil pressure dropping in engine number two," Sherman noted.

Eaves looked out the window to his left and could see the engine closest to him was running rough. Even with adjustments, the oil pressure continued to drop and the prop began to slow.

"Feather engine two," Eaves said into the intercom. "Elder, cut the fuel. I'll call the lead plane to tell them we are dropping out of formation."

Eaves pushed forward on the yoke and banked left to turn back to Gioia del Colle.

Headquarters cleared them to land, and they found Sgt. Ryskeciski, the crew chief, waiting at the hardstand. Eaves explained the problem.

"Hmm, we'll check it out and slap a new engine in if we need to. We'll give all the engines a good look-see," the crew chief said. "May take a day or two."

After stowing their gear, the officers struggled through the muck to the mess tent. Tonight's menu featured beef stew, which at least was hot and warmed their bellies.

"Hey, Red!"

Eaves turned to see Tudor threading his way through the chow hall tables. "We're on the alert list again for tomorrow. Briefing at 0500."

✈✈✈

"At ease."

Eaves and his crew settled back down on the wooden benches as Bonner stepped up and gripped the podium. He glanced their way for a moment before turning to scan the briefing room.

"Today we will be assisting our ground troops as they push toward Rome." He cleared his throat. "The Fifteenth Air Force has been tasked with destroying an area where German troops are known to congregate. When the enemy uses medieval structures to protect their troops, we have no choice but to take them down. After your instructions for our last mission, you may wonder at this seeming change in policy, but this is war, men, and we must do whatever it takes to defeat this cunning enemy." He paused.

"And . . . if you don't take it out today, I can promise you'll be back there tomorrow." He grimly nodded to the operations officer.

The officer pulled the cord and the drapes opened to reveal the red yarn running toward a spot just south of Rome on the map.

"Our target today is Valmontone, a village on a hill about fifty kilometers south of Rome. The Germans are garrisoned in this ancient city, which has some massive walls surrounding a castle. Our priority is the large marshalling yard critical for transporting German supplies and reinforcements. The objective is to demolish this target so our boys can drive through to Rome. No known flak in the area but be alert for bandits. This will be a short run. Should be in the air a little over three hours. The 485th Bomb Group will join us on this mission, and the 777th Squadron will lead the attack today. Lt. Eaves will fly lead plane in Able Box."

Eaves blinked. He had no idea he would be called on to lead today. A heavy responsibility, but what an honor.

Haverkos leaned forward with a smile and flashed a thumbs-up. "Good choice. It's no secret that they only choose the best pilots to lead."

The weather man reported clear skies to and from the target. After the pilots hacked their watches, Chaplain Eastwood dismissed them with prayer.

At the pilots' briefing Eaves got the details for the mission. Bombing altitude to be 21,000 feet. Main target would be the marshalling yards, with secondary targets including the city walls, gates and the castle. Lt. Tudor would be Deputy Lead.

Target for Tonite was still out of commission. They'd be flying a loaner plane, a B-24J.

After connecting with Haverkos and Sherman, they loaded their winter flying gear, Mae Wests, and parachutes into the cargo truck that took them to the hardstand where the crew waited. This wasn't *Target for Tonite*, and Eaves wanted everything double-checked today for safety. He and Sherman walked around the plane, carefully checking out every area with Elder and the crew chief before meeting the rest of the guys under the wing. They all pulled on their heavy fleece gear and clipped on the inflatable vests.

Picking up his parachute, Eaves looked at his crew. "We have a big responsibility on our shoulders today men. I trust you all to do your jobs, and I pray we successfully complete our mission. Keep your eyes peeled for bandits, and notify me if you see any problems in the formation behind us."

As usual, Elder, the flight engineer, entered the plane first. Eaves ducked down and followed him, climbing up through the bomb bay. Balancing the parachute, he waddled across the nine-inch-wide catwalk above the live bombs. Passing Christel's spot in the radio compartment, he stepped onto the flight deck and settled into the seat on the left.

The crew completed their preflight checklists and, at the designated time, Eaves ordered Sherman to start the engines. The reverberation escalated as each engine rumbled to life, the smell of aviation fuel and exhaust filling the cockpit. Elder stood in the top hatch to guide them down the packed-clay taxiway.

Halting at the top of the runway, Eaves called out the final checklist, then pushed all four throttles forward. Rattling and vibrating, the plane strained like a dog pulling at its leash. The green flare flashed. He and Sherman released the brakes. The plane hurtled headlong down the runway, bounced over the sod insert, and then steadied itself on the remaining steel matting. Eaves pulled back gently on the control column and the B-24 nosed up. As the wheels lifted, the plane hummed, and the smooth feeling of flight replaced the vibrations. Eaves banked and spiraled up into the sky.

Now, to get the group into formation and head for Valmontone.

Eaves' Lead Group had just pulled into formation when his radio crackled.

"This is headquarters. There has been an accident. Hold at 8,000 feet while we clear the runway for the rest of the group to get into the air."

Eaves sucked in his breath. His grip tightened on the yoke.

Hope no one was killed. Wonder how long this will take? May have to abort.

He glanced at his watch, then touched his throat microphone to notify the crew of the delay and ask Christel to send out word to the rest of Able Box.

All they could do was circle and wait. And wait they did, wishing the cloud cover would lift as it prevented them from seeing what had occurred.

An hour later, headquarters came back on the air to say the planes were rolling down the runway and the mission could continue. Thankfully, this mission was a short hop and full fuel tanks would carry them through.

First Baker, the upper box popped up and came together, then Charlie, the lower box. The second unit formed, and the formation tightened, forty B-24s strong.

A flash of pride coursed through Eaves. The 464th Bomb Group was ready.

Now it was up to him to maintain a constant speed, altitude, and heading. That's what separated a good lead from a bad one. He didn't want his fellow pilots complaining that they'd had to constantly jockey throttles and elevators to stay in the proper position.

The loaner plane proved to be steady, although Eaves would have preferred to fly *Target For Tonite.*

Skies were clear and quiet as they headed out over the Adriatic. Gunners tested their guns and Lambert pulled the pins on the bombs. As they reached 10,000 feet, Eaves ordered the crew to put on their oxygen masks. Making a direct turn inland, Sherman checked in with each crew member as they reached bombing altitude of 21,000 feet. All was well.

The 485th Bomb Group appeared at the designated time and latched on behind. The massive fleet of eighty bombers continued toward the target.

An hour later the cold had penetrated through his fleece suit and three pairs of gloves. Twenty below zero. Eaves shivered as ice flakes fell on his shoulders from frost accumulating on the ceiling of the cockpit. Almost to the IP and the final leg to the target.

Making the last turn, he saw rolling hills below and a walled castle coming up ahead.

He pressed his throat mic. "Bombardier, your plane."

As lead plane, all other bombardiers would toggle when Lambert released his plane's bombs today.

"Roger," Lambert responded.

So far so good. No flak rising to greet them. Eaves could see railroad tracks and the marshalling yards with the castle close by.

"Bomb doors open." Minutes ticked by.

"Bombs away!"

The plane bucked upward as the weight of twelve five-hundred-pound bombs fell away. Relief rolled over Eaves.

We did our job.

"Pilot, your plane."

"Roger." Eaves pushed forward on the yoke. The B-24 dropped down, and he banked back toward home base.

"Petrone here. Good view from the bubble, sir. Saw several bombs dropped right into the marshalling yards and also a direct hit on the castle walls."

"Thanks, good to know. Masterson, how does the formation look from the tail?"

"Lined up behind us, tight formation, sir. Got some good photos of the target as we pulled away. The rest of the group hit the marshalling yards pretty hard, left a train burning."

"Good job men. Keep your eyes peeled for bandits."

A warm glow filled Eaves' chest.

Mission accomplished. And check eleven off the list of thirty. Now . . . just focus on returning safely.

No bandits appeared to harass them. As they reached Gioia del Colle, Eaves glanced at his watch. Only four and a half hours in the air.

Gratefully he noted no red flares today, as one by one the planes came in to land.

Eaves cringed as he looked at the broken hulk of a plane, debris scattered all around, in the field at the end of the runway.

What had happened here?

At the debriefing, they learned that *Off Limits* had lifted up and retracted its wheels too early. Caught in the prop wash from the plane ahead, the B-24 crashed back down onto the runway with a scream of crunching metal as props dug into the steel matting and parts scattered, sparks flying. Everyone had watched in horror, expecting the inevitable explosion and fireball.

Miraculously, the plane slid off the runway to rest in the field with a cloud of dust. Fire engines raced down to fight the fire sure to come as the crew crawled out, some with injuries, but none critical.

"No one could explain why the plane didn't explode on impact," the briefing officer said. He slowly shook his head. "It was a miracle. Only by the grace of God."

Eaves looked up, his chest filled with warmth.

So grateful, Lord. A successful mission and no loss of life on the day of my lead. Thank You, thank You!

Chapter 16

22 May 1944—Galveston, Texas

JEAN STOPPED TO READ the war poster in the store window.

"Use it up,
Wear it out
Make it do,
Or do without."

Hmm . . . that last line was getting to be more and more common. She sighed. Nylon was needed to make parachutes. She had no nylons left and she couldn't buy more. Some girls drew dark lines down the back of their legs with their eyebrow pencils, but with Red gone overseas, she didn't care enough to do that.

One of her shoes had a hole the size of a half-dollar worn in the sole, but she didn't have ration stamps for new ones. So, she cut a piece of cardboard to make a liner for it.

And even with ration stamps, meat hadn't been available the last two times she and her mother had gone to the market.

Of course, these were little sacrifices compared to what her beloved and all the other soldiers were giving up. Determined to win this war, President Roosevelt had asked the country to step up and support their troops. And the nation responded. She would do her part without complaining.

She had trouble listening to the radio reports about the battles and seeing the long list of casualties in the newspaper. The Allies were struggling to push the Germans out of Italy and the war just went on and on. Would it ever end?

Leaving the storefront, she headed toward the beach. A daily walk along the boardwalk helped clear her mind from worries. And she chose to be thankful, to focus on three gratitudes each day.

Warm humid air swept over her, carrying scents of gardenias and the salty, pungent smells of the Gulf. The weather in May was already balmy. Today she could thank the Lord for the lovely sunshine and the spring flowers.

The inspiring words from yesterday's sermon at church floated through her mind. The pastor had reminded them that God was still on the throne, regardless of a world in crisis. Another good thing to be thankful for.

And third, Red's letter arrived on Friday and was safely tucked in her purse.

She watched the brownish waves breaking on the shore, pushing piles of seaweed onto the beach, a common sight all along the seawall. The shipping lanes were close by and the huge tankers stirred up the sand, dirtying their coastal waters. No crystal-clear blue waters here.

Still, people enjoyed the beach. She stopped to smile at three small children splashing in the shallow waves while their parents watched. A little arrow poked at her heart. Would she and Red have children playing like that on the beach someday?

Jean ached to hold a child now, but her arms were empty.

Someday, Lord?

There was no answer. Resolutely, she turned away and resumed her walk.

Moisture beaded on her forehead, and she felt a trickle down her back. The sun beat down on her head. Temperatures had soared into the 80s the last two days and it was always humid in Galveston.

Striding up the boardwalk, Jean reached the long wooden gangway that stretched from the seawall to The Balinese Room. The elegant nightclub stood six hundred feet out in the Gulf, and she could see several fishermen casting their lines out into the water from spots along the walkway.

Sweet memories flooded her mind. Eaves holding her in his arms as they danced on the gleaming wooden floor in the ballroom, the twinkling stars shining down the night he proposed in the moonlight . . .

It all seemed like a dream now, so long ago.

She sighed and then determinedly strode away from the boardwalk, looking both ways before crossing Seawall Boulevard. She took the next street north, leading her back toward Avenue S½ and the little white cottage where her mother waited for her.

Thank you, Lord, for Your Presence—here with me and also with Red, so far away. Thank you for our love, and for providing what we need, even if it's not all we want. Forgive me for being selfish. Guide me, help me be sensitive to Your

Holy Spirit, and give me strength to do the tasks You have for me to do here. In Jesus' name. Amen.

The first thing she saw when she walked into the living room was something brown and wiggling in her dad's arms.

"What do you have there?" she exclaimed.

Her father grinned. "Well, now," he said in his slow Texas drawl, "this little fellow has been hanging around the shipyards for a couple of weeks. Been looking pretty hungry. I'd taken to sharing my lunch with him sometimes." He looked down affectionately at a small ragtag dog in his arms. "Nobody knew who he belonged to. We put up a lost dog sign, but no one stepped up to claim him." He looked up at Jean. "Seems like he needs someone to take care of him, and I thought of you."

The puppy's ribs showed and his fur was matted. But his brown eyes looked intelligent and bright.

Jean walked over and stretched out her hand. He sniffed, then licked her fingers. She grinned and gently stroked the top of his head until he squirmed and his tail began to wag.

Her father lifted the puppy toward her and she wrapped her arms around its little body. He stretched up to lick her cheek and she laughed out loud.

Her mother walked into the room wiping her hands on an embroidered dish towel. "Does me good to hear your sweet laugh, Jean," she said with a gentle smile. She cocked her head toward her husband. "Think you did good, dear, bringing home that bundle of joy."

Jean could feel the little dog's heart beat against her chest. Maybe she didn't have a baby in her arms, but she did have a sweet doggy to nurse back to health and an armload of love.

"Does he have a name, Dad?"

"Not that I know of," he answered.

"Hmm, I think I'll call him Ricky," Jean said, holding the little guy out and looking into his eyes. "I think we can get you looking better soon."

Cradling him tightly, she smiled.

Surely God had seen her pain and sent a gift of comfort.

Chapter 17

24 May 1944—Gioia del Colle Airfield, Italy

EAVES LOOKED AT HAVERKOS as they waited in the briefing room. "An hour earlier for wake-up means this will be a long trip. Not a good sign."

Haverkos rubbed his arm. "Heard the guys had to go back to Valmontone yesterday. The Germans were still holding the castle, blocking the ground troops, so the Fifteenth targeted the gates and the walls, the whole village. Reportedly, the town was pretty much leveled." Haverkos looked down and clasped his hands in front of him. "Glad we had the day off. All the guys were dog-tired after four missions almost back-to-back."

Eaves nodded. "Well, we did our part on the marshalling yards. And Bonner kept his promise. He said the group would be going back if the Germans maintained their position."

"Ten-hut," came the command, and all the men stood as Bonner and the entourage entered the room. "At ease" brought everyone back down on the wooden planks.

Bonner confirmed what they'd heard. The 464th Bomb Group had successfully completed the mission yesterday, and Allied ground troops were now marching toward Rome. Eaves felt a warm glow of satisfaction seep into his chest. Knowing that the bombers were helping defeat the enemy made what they were going through worthwhile.

Slow going, but progress was being made.

Bonner stepped away and the operations officer whipped back the curtain. Groans and curse words filled the air. The red line went across Austria, deep into enemy territory, back to Wiener-Neustadt.

Not again. The mission from hell. Eaves sucked in his breath as a cold chill tingled through him. The black curtain of flak, German fighters swarming like bees. The sight of Captain Hornbaker's plane descending into the clouds and *Red Hot Riding Hood* exploding in a ball of flame. Each vision indelibly etched in his memory banks, still haunting his dreams.

The operations officer stood silent, waiting until the room quieted and stilled into a deep, uneasy hush. "Yes, men, we're going back to Wiener-Neustadt." He paused, his jaw tight and his lips a grim line. "This time our target is the *Wollersdorf Airdrome* stores and machine shops, which provide vital support for the German *Luftwaffe*. Destruction of these resources is a high priority for the Fifteenth. Today the 464th will join forces with the 456th and 485th Bomb Groups to take them out. And we'll have some Little Friends out there to accompany us—the 332nd Fighter Group and some P-51 Mustangs. Good to have fighter planes with us that can go the distance."

After a murmur of approval subsided, he continued. "As you know, it's a long mission. Expect over seven hours in the air." He slowly scanned the room, gazing intently at each of the upturned young faces. "Remember, we do not want to go back there again. Consider yourselves dead already—and do your jobs."

Startled, Eaves pondered that last statement. Yes, the secret to beating fear—just accept the worst and do your job.

After all, that's what we're here for—to die, if necessary, for our families and our country. And . . . it's all in God's hands.

✈✈✈

Eaves patted the console. Facing this dangerous mission, it was comforting to be back in *Target for Tonite*. Sgt. Ryskeciski had gone over her with a fine-tooth comb after replacing engine number two and declared her fit as a fiddle. She'd proved herself reliable in the past.

He also put Jean's picture in his breast pocket, just for luck. A strong reminder of who he was fighting for, and the prayers he knew were flying for him and the whole crew. Today they needed all the prayer support they could get.

In the pilots' briefing Eaves learned the 464th would be following the other two bomber groups to the target. And the 777th Squadron was in Fox, the last box of the 464th formation. "Coffin corner," they called it, for good reason. Being in the lower element and flying last gave the Germans time to zero in with their 88 mm flak guns. And they were more susceptible to fighters. But someone had to do it. Today was their turn.

Remember—count yourself dead and do your job Eaves.

The 464th Bomb Group got up in the air without incident and pulled into tight formation, wing tip to wing tip. After testing their guns and arming the bombs over the Adriatic, they arrived at landfall at the designated time to connect with the other two bomber groups.

As they reached their 21,000-foot bombing altitude, Eaves and Sherman looked with awe at the massive armada of planes ahead of them. Over a hundred B-24s created an impressive sight, their icy contrails flowing behind them like veils of white lace.

Awed by the power emanating from a fleet of mighty warships, Eaves' confidence surged. Might and right rode on their side, and his chest swelled with the honor of being one of them.

An hour later, they made the final turn leading to the IP and the bomb run. So far, they'd managed to avoid any concentration of anti-aircraft batteries, but Eaves dreaded what he knew lay ahead at Weiner-Neustadt.

Eaves jockeyed the plane even closer to his wing mates, but the turbulence in the air stream from so many planes battered *Target for Tonite* like waves in an ocean, requiring constant adjustments. Still, the tighter they were, wing tip almost touching wing tip, the less likely a German fighter could infiltrate their ranks.

"Linneman here, sir. I can almost shake hands with Tudor's waist gunner!"

Eaves laughed and touched his throat mic. "This is the pilot to the crew. Safest place to be, Linneman." He then added more soberly, "Men, keep your eyes peeled for bandits. We're in their air space now."

"Christel here, sir. Just wanted you to know that from the top turret I can see some Little Friends right above us. Kind of comforting to know they're up there as promised."

"Roger. Thanks for the encouraging word." Fighter planes offered help against the bandits who were sure to be circling, waiting like vultures for the bombers to leave the deadly flak curtain. The *Luftwaffe* fighter base just outside the city limits could reportedly launch over a hundred German fighters.

"Navigator to pilot. IP in two minutes."

As the massive fleet began to turn, Eaves spoke into the throat mic one more time.

"Pilot to bombardier, your plane."

"Roger. Ten minutes to target," came the reply.

The ominous black puffs began to appear under the lead ships. Gradually a curtain of fog rose above the city. A sudden ball of flame ahead told Eaves the flak had found its first victim.

He ducked involuntarily at a brilliant orange flash just to the right of the cockpit. Cordite rattled against the hull and the smell of explosives filled the cockpit.

Whew, that was close. Eaves scanned the instruments. Nothing vital hit.

Streams of smoke shot above them, below them, bursting into velvety black clouds with red centers. Metal flew. A loud bang! and a horrific shudder rocked the plane. Eaves felt the plane list to the side and worked to stabilize her.

"Christel here. Big hole in the right rudder!"

Target for Tonite plunged ahead, running through the gauntlet of flak. There could be no evasive actions on the bomb run.

"Bomb bay open," Lambert called out.

Mesmerized, Eaves stared at the bombs raining down ahead of them, flowers of flame bursting below as explosions bloomed. The black cloud of flak mushroomed toward them. Eaves steeled himself, brushing his hand over Jean's picture in his pocket.

A fiery red explosion, this time to the left. A concussion shook *Target for Tonite* as a rain of shrapnel peppered the hull and the smell of explosives filled the cockpit.

"Waist to pilot. I can see a football-sized hole in the left wing and fluid running out of the wing tip. And we have a ragged hole in the top of the fuselage as big as a dinner table. No injuries, thank God."

Oh, no—shrapnel must had punctured the line to the wing tip fuel tank. "Roger. Elder, transfer all fuel out of the leftwing tip." Maybe they could save some.

"Bombs away," Lambert called.

Target for Tonite lurched upward as the load of deadly bombs fell from her belly.

"Bombardier to pilot. Your plane."

Eaves pushed forward on the yoke and banked to follow the lead plane in his squadron that had plunged downward to dodge the flak flying at them. Another turn to the right and they leveled off at 18,000 feet, moving beyond the air space above the city and leaving behind the wall of flak.

"Bandits, twelve o'clock high," Christel called from the top turret.

Eaves looked up to see a rounded grey shape flying head first toward them, a German *Focke-Wulf* 190, his cannon spitting and guns twinkling. The nose gunner began firing. Tracers filled the air.

Eaves gasped. He pushed down on the yoke in an attempt to dodge.

This is it. We're done for.

He flinched and his eyes automatically squeezed shut.

When his eyes snapped back open, he could see only wing tips . . . and a terrific red flash as the German plane exploded. A rain of debris showered them, but *Target for Tonite* powered on. Eaves leveled the ship.

Two Mustangs swooped down in front of them. The American fighter planes must have dropped down and shot the German fighter out of the air just in the nick of time.

Thank God. Little Friends had done their job.

The German fighters swarmed all around like angry bees. Some engaged in dogfights with the Little Friends.

The top turret gunner hammered away, hot brass casings falling down on the flight deck behind the pilots. Other gunners let lead fly whenever a bandit flew their way.

Eaves cringed when a Mustang took a hit and dove straight down trailing smoke. He saw a parachute mushroom.

Help him, Lord!

Suddenly another German FW-190 raked the right side of *Target for Tonite* with cannon blasts and machine guns stitching the fuselage. The plane shuddered. The yoke went limp under Eaves' hands.

"I got him," Linneman yelled. The German plane fell from the sky.

Eaves struggled for control. *Target for Tonite* listed to the side and wasn't responding.

"Fangman here, sir. Don't know what's happening, but we have some cables flying all around back here in the waist, and purple fluid running everywhere."

Oh, no—sounds like the rudder and hydraulic lines were cut.

Would explain the lack of response from the rudder on that side. He'd have to control the plane by adjusting the power on the engines. Without control, it wasn't safe to stay in formation, threatening his wing mates.

Eaves pushed forward on the yoke to lower the nose and banked left, maneuvering away from the other planes by pulling back the throttles on engines one and two, increasing power on three and four at the same time. He strained to push on the left rudder. No response. He reached up and pressed his throat mic. Have to get the flight engineer on it.

"Elder, damage report. See if you can splice those cables back together." The loss of hydraulics would mean no power to control the landing gear, flaps, bomb bay doors, or brakes.

Eaves clenched his jaw and gripped the yoke tighter. Loss of an engine now would render the aircraft uncontrollable. Cold sweat ran down his back. If the plane went into a flat spin, it was all but impossible to bail out.

Target for Tonite dropped lower in the sky, the main formation pulling away. Eaves looked around for cloud banks that might provide cover. A straggler, out of control, just what the German fighters looked for. Moments felt like hours.

"Elder here, sir. Hydraulic and rudder cables were severed. I shut off the hydraulics and spliced the cables as best I could. Fuselage has a multitude of punctures, huge one over the bomb bay and a couple of others bigger than a basketball. The left rudder has a hole the size of a door torn out of it. No one injured."

Eaves licked his lips and swallowed hard. "Roger."

Another voice broke in. "Christel here, sir. Four red-tailed P-47s directly above, have us under their wings. Looks like they're running cover for us."

A burst of gratitude warmed Eaves' chest.

God had sent some angels to help them.

✈✈✈

They'd cleared the Alps and Eaves could see the Adriatic coming up. *Target for Tonite* had been trying to flip over on her back and it took all the effort he and Sherman could muster to keep the 'dirty side' down. The bomber was sluggish, hard to trim, and they'd dropped lower and lower in the sky. Only good thing was the oxygen masks were off.

Eaves touched his throat mic. "Pilot to crew. Everyone check your parachutes and put them on. I'm going to try to take this plane into base, but if anyone wants to bail out over Italy, let me know."

As they reached the coastline, one of the red-tailed P-47s pulled up beside the bomber. Eaves blinked when he turned to see the pilot, a white scarf wrapped around his neck. A dark face smiled at him. Pointing toward Italy, the pilot saluted before he peeled off to join the other three fighter planes. The P-47s pulled into a tight formation and flew northwest.

Eaves spoke into the intercom. "Boys, those Thunderbolts were flown by the Tuskegee Airmen. I'd heard about them, but now we've seen 'em in action. They can't carry as much fuel as we can, but I sure appreciate them staying with us as long as they could."

He paused, scanning the instruments. "Don't know how much hydraulic fluid is left. Petrone, crank the ball turret up by hand. And we'll have to lower the landing gear by hand when we reach Gioia."

Eaves' shoulders ached. Hopefully they'd have enough hydraulics for the brakes. Without brakes, stopping a forty-thousand-pound bomber on the runway would be impossible.

Almost seven hours of airtime. At least they wouldn't have a load of extra fuel in the tanks when they landed.

The coastline of Italy was a welcome sight. No one called requesting permission to bail out.

No other planes in the air as they approached the airfield, coasting just above tree level.

"Masterson, fire the red flares," Eaves ordered. "Linneman and Christel, get the landing gear down. Fangman, watch out the waist window for the yellow latch. Lambert, crank that nose wheel down. Elder and Haverkos, lower the flaps manually."

Eaves wrestled *Target for Tonite* in line with the runway.

"Fangman here, sir. Yellow latch in sight, landing gear locked."

Eaves pursed his lips. The drag of the lowered gear helped slow the plane. Minutes ticked by. Lights flashed below as firetrucks and emergency vehicles waited by the runway.

"Everyone in the waist and brace for emergency landing" He looked at his copilot. "Get ready to hit those brakes, Dan."

Eaves sucked in his breath. "Here we go."

Target for Tonite touched down gently and then began to vibrate as Eaves and Sherman stomped on the brakes as hard as they could.

Just enough hydraulic fluid left—the plane continued to decelerate. Gradually slowing, *Target for Tonite* bounced over the infamous sod insert and came to a trembling stop at the end of the runway.

By the grace of God they'd made it.

Target for Tonite perched like a huge quivering bird of prey at the end of the runway. Eaves flipped off the fuel switches one by one. Silence filled the cockpit.

Thank You, Lord.

He slumped back in his seat, eyes closed. His hands slid off of the yoke and dangled limply at his sides. Sherman leaned forward and laid his head on the yoke.

Elder dropped down from the upper turret and poked his head into the cockpit. Eaves blinked, squinting at him through half-closed eyes.

After a long moment, Elder silently backed out, leaving the pilots alone.

Moments passed. Sherman roused himself and stood to leave.

"Hell of a ride," was all he said.

Eaves nodded. He pulled out the log book, glanced at his watch and recorded the flight time. Seven hours felt like five hundred.

He struggled to his feet and willed his rubbery legs to support him as he stepped out of the cockpit. He lurched down the catwalk toward the exit.

The skin of the bomber was pierced with a multitude of machine gun bullet holes, light streaming through like twinkling stars. The FW-190s' cannon blasts and flak had punched gashes in both sides of the fuselage. Eaves looked up at the sky through the massive flak hole above the bomb bay. He shook his head. With all that lead flying, it was a miracle the crew had escaped injury.

Reaching the exit, he dropped down to the tarmac. His legs trembled and he steadied himself before ducking under the bomb bay doors and stepping out into the fading light.

A crowd had gathered around the bomber. A firetruck, an ambulance, and several jeeps were randomly parked on the tarmac. He joined Sherman and they walked around the bomber, describing the known damage to the crew chief. Sgt. Ryskeciski just shook his head when he saw the massive hole in the rudder, the damaged wing, and the gashes in the fuselage.

That last task accomplished, Eaves stood rooted in place. Through a haze he saw Fangman and Masterson throwing their flight gear into the back of a cargo truck. He felt a hand on his arm.

"Lieutenant, you okay?"

He nodded, and turned to see a young staff sergeant, his blue eyes filled with concern.

"Give you a lift to the debriefing, sir?"

Again, he nodded, eyes glazed over and exhaustion rendering him totally detached from the scene, seeing it as through a gray fog. Doggedly he trudged to the truck with the young sergeant and accepted a hand-up from Haverkos. The crew remained silent, each processing the day's events.

A short bumpy ride and they arrived at the operations center. As they entered the debriefing room, he gulped down the standard shot of whiskey and gratefully accepted a cup of steaming hot coffee as the crew sat together to answer the routine questions of a not-so-routine mission. He struggled to focus and report the events of the mission accurately.

Totally drained and lightheaded, food was first on his agenda. After a stop at the mess tent, he trudged over to the officers' club. Tudor spotted him coming in and hurried over to greet him.

"Let me get you a beer," he said.

Eaves nodded and plopped down in a leather-covered easy chair by the stove.

"Heard about the damage. That was some flying, Red," he said as he handed him a beer.

Eaves took the beverage. Then he looked up questioningly. It was ice cold.

Tudor grinned. "The ground crew had stowed away a case of beer in the plane today. Great to have a cold one, isn't it?" He laughed out loud. "Been months with only warm beer. Pretty inventive."

Eaves gave him a brief smile, then looked down at his drink. Closing his eyes for a few moments, he was back in the battle. He looked at his friend.

"Your trip bad?"

Tudor pursed his lips as he slowly shook his head. "A few flak holes, no injuries."

Eaves tipped up his beer and took a gulp. "Was a miracle that we had no injuries with all that lead flying. And if those red-tailed Thunderbolts hadn't flown cover for us on the way back . . ." His voice just trailed off.

Tudor nodded solemnly. They stared into their drinks, lost in their thoughts. Some planes had not made it back that day. Numbness, guilt—it could have been them.

Finally, Tudor looked up. "Rumors are flying that we are moving to the new base at Pantanella in the next day or so. Don't know if it will be any better, but I sure hope we get out of this awful mud."

"Well, a solid tarmac will be better than the crater-pocked one we have here." Eaves took another sip of his drink.

After finishing their beers and listening to conversation around them, they slipped out and headed back toward their tents. The alert list was up on the bulletin board.

"What?" Tudor shook his head. "We're both on it again. Briefing at 0500."

"I don't believe it." Eaves squinted at the board. Sure enough, mission again tomorrow. After what they'd all been through, his whole crew was dog-tired. But so was everyone else.

Dazed by the thought of flying again tomorrow, Eaves walked silently toward the hard stand where *Target for Tonite* had been towed. The ground crew swarmed over her, circling the bullet and shrapnel holes with white chalk.

Eaves eyed the right rudder, a hole the size of the latrine door torn through it. Hard to believe they'd made it back to base with that much damage.

The crew chief spotted Eaves and turned toward him.

"Sir, she's got over 500 puncture wounds that we've counted so far, and so much damage that I don't know when . . . or if . . . we'll get her operational again," he said sadly.

Eaves gazed at his plane, a lump in his throat that he couldn't seem to swallow, a sudden mist in his eyes. She had been a magnificent war machine, home to him and his crew, faithful to get them back to the base time and time again.

A wounded warrior glinted in the light of the setting sun.

Chapter 18

25 May 1944—Gioia del Colle Airfield, Italy

AFTER A RESTLESS NIGHT fraught with anxiety, Eaves found himself back in the briefing room before dawn.

Colonel Bonner minced no words. "Men, I know you just returned from a very challenging mission and I commend you. But yesterday we received special orders from headquarters. The 464th has been assigned a new critical priority." He leaned forward above the podium and scanned the room with his gaze.

"As you know, the high command is preparing for the invasion of France sometime in the near future. The Fifteenth has been tasked with the immediate destruction of German transportation centers to disrupt Axis troop movement and supplies. I trust you to fulfill all that is being asked of us." He nodded to the operations officer.

Gasps cut through the room as the operations officer pulled the cord over the giant map. The red line led across the Mediterranean and deep into eastern France.

"Priority target today is the marshalling yards of the Saint-Etienne-Lyon railway that runs through the Gier Valley located near Givors. Expect a long mission, over nine hours in the air. Little anti-aircraft fire around the target, but reports of German fighters in the area. We will have some Little Friends escorting us there and back. Today the 779th Squadron will lead the attack."

No doubt another long and dangerous mission loomed ahead of them. Eaves got the mission details at the pilots' briefing. The callsign for the group was "Longstick."

He gave a tight-lipped smile. Pretty appropriate considering the distance to the target today.

His squadron would be in Baker, the upper box to the right of the 779th Lead Group, and he would fly a B-24J.

After picking up his parachute, Mae West, and heavy flying gear, Eaves got Sherman and Elder together with the crew chief to thoroughly check out the loaner plane.

The men moved slowly as they gathered under the wing to pull on their fleece-lined flying gear. Fatigue lined their faces and a palpable sense of sadness covered them. It was hard to think that *Target for Tonite* might be cannibalized to keep other planes flying.

"Shake it off, men. It was a long day yesterday, but we can do this. Focus on your job and doing it well." Eaves reached down to pick up his parachute and flak jacket. "Let's get going." He turned and ducked under the bomb bay doors to enter the plane behind the flight engineer.

Everyone completed their checklists and soon the heavily loaded B-24 launched into the air. The formation pulled together tightly and began the climb to bombing altitude. At the designated landfall, the 464th latched on behind the 465th Bomb Group. Over eighty mighty Liberators roared toward the coast of France.

Eaves ordered the gunners to test their .50-caliber machine guns once they were over the Mediterranean Sea. Lambert armed the bomb load.

The armada reached bombing altitude of 21,000 feet and turned on the Initial Point. They could see the Givors Canal and village ahead on the bomb run. At 1300 hours they dropped the bomb load on the marshalling yards. Only a few flak bursts mushroomed below them. So far so good.

The 464th banked left and continued down the Rhone Valley on the planned route toward the coast for the return leg.

"Christel here, sir. I see Me-109s circling along the edges of the formation. Probably looking for stragglers."

"Roger. Stay alert, gunners." The horrors of yesterday's air battle loomed fresh in his mind. A chill of apprehension ran up his spine. Ahead, he could see the French coastline.

Eaves touched his throat mic. "Navigator, where are we?"

"On course. North of Marseilles, near Cap Roux."

"Roger." Eaves shrugged his shoulders to relieve the tension.

An urgent voice crackled over the intercom. "Petrone here. Me-109s coming up, six o'clock!"

Christel called out, "Top turret, two FW-190s at twelve o'clock!"

Eaves gripped the yoke tighter as German fighters swarmed around the formation, attacking from above and below, tracers flying.

Stay focused, Eaves. Keep this plane flying straight and level.

Machine guns above and below threw out lead at the oncoming bandits. Hot brass casings from the top turret flew down behind the pilots, littering the flight deck.

The plane shuddered as .20 mm cannon bullets tore through the fuselage.

"Got one!" Christel cried out. "Here comes the cavalry. Mustangs dropping down into the fight."

Instinctively, Eaves jerked at a sudden bright flash to his right. Glancing at his wing mate, he saw a demolished nose and the number two engine in flames. The plane fell from formation.

Seconds later, a voice sounded on the intercom. "Masterson here. Lt. Trotter's plane just turned into a torch. Saw three chutes come out, but two were on fire."

Eaves swallowed hard. More good men gone. He gritted his teeth as pain of losing fellow airmen swept through him.

A few German fighters regrouped and focused their attack on the lead box. Captain Hornbaker's plane, *Strickly From Hunger*, already had two engines on fire on the left wing when Eaves saw another Me-109 swoop in to riddle the left side again with machine gun fire, shattering the cockpit. The plane bobbled in the air.

Flames extinguished in one engine. Probably activated the fire extinguisher bottle in the cowl. But with the other engine still burning, the plane fell from the sky.

Moments later. "Lambert here. Three chutes out of *Strickly From Hunger*."

Eaves felt cold sweat run down his back as he pulled the plane tighter into formation.

They had reached the coastline. Mustangs engaged some of the bandits and the other German fighters pulled back, probably going after stragglers.

Eaves glanced at his watch. Over eight hours of flight time.

"Check in, men. Damages, injuries?"

One by one the crew rang in. Minor damage, no personal injuries.

Once again, they had beaten the odds.

✈✈✈

Eaves logged in his time, the nine and a half hours in the air seemed like an eternity. "Longstick" indeed.

At the post-mission interrogation, the exhausted crew struggled to share what they had seen and experienced.

Eaves learned four planes had failed to return to base. Many returning planes suffered casualties and serious damage. The *Luftwaffe* had exacted a high price for the destruction of the marshalling yards but reportedly lost several fighters in the exchange.

At the mess hall the exhausted men were greeted with another alert list. Eaves scanned it quickly. His name was on it again for tomorrow's mission, briefing at 0430. An hour earlier.

He reeled back on his heels, a sinking feeling in his gut. Would he even be able to pilot a B-24 safely tomorrow? Three days in a row. The last two missions had left the whole crew exhausted and shell-shocked. Could they even do their jobs?

Maybe he should refuse the mission. No one would force them to fly. But this is why he volunteered. He chewed his lip, his stomach churning.

Failure galled him. His skin crawled to think he lacked the fortitude necessary to give all that was asked of him. He shook his head. He could decide to wait. He would see how he felt tomorrow morning before making the decision.

The officers silently entered the mess tent and filled their trays. No one seemed to have energy for conversation. After slurping down beef stew and eating two rolls, Eaves headed directly to his tent and crashed on his cot.

Chapter 19

26 May 1944—Gioia del Colle Airfield, Italy

THE BOBBING LIGHT AGAIN. "Lt. Eaves, it's 0300. Briefing is at 0430."

Eaves tried to focus. The young sergeant stood waiting until he sat up, groggily throwing his feet over the edge of the cot, and reached for his thermal underwear. Then the orderly moved on through the tent, waking the other officers.

Eaves stood up and stretched his arms overhead. His muscles ached from wrestling the huge machine the last two days. But he felt better than he thought he would.

He slipped into his flight suit and gathered his shaving mug. After heating the cup of water on the stove, he used his steel helmet to hold the warm water to wash his face and finished scraping off the day-old stubble.

He'd made his decision. One more mission, taking him one step closer to earning the right to go home. Tucking Jean's picture into his pocket, he gathered up the heavy flight gear and pulled on his fleece-lined flight boots.

Pulling out his flashlight, he called to the other officers. "Ready, guys?"

"Just a sec. Have to grab my cap," Haverkos said.

Trucks rumbled by as they hiked over to the mess tent. Other flashlights flickered like fireflies as small groups of officers headed for breakfast.

In the mess tent, men grabbed coffee. The cooks gave lean servings, having learned from experience that most of the food would be untouched the morning before combat. Too early for conversation.

Stars still glittered in the dark sky as Eaves waited with the other officers outside the mess tent. He shivered, hunching his shoulders in the damp morning air. When the cargo truck pulled up, they clambered into the back with their gear and headed to the briefing.

Leaving this early meant only one thing. Another long mission.

Colonel Bonner was brief. "Yesterday's mission was successful but cost us dearly. Four planes in the 464th failed to return, including Captain Hornbaker's. We lost many good men." He cleared his throat. "Despite the cost, we shall continue and we shall prevail over the enemy. Chaplain Eastwood, please lead us in prayer."

A rustle as caps were swept off heads. A reverent hush filled the room as heads bowed. After a long moment of silence, the chaplain lifted the fallen to the Almighty and prayed for success in today's mission.

When the operations officer stepped forward and pulled the cord, Eaves wasn't surprised to see the red yarn stretching deep into Eastern France. Curses and groans filled the air.

"Today the 464th will target the marshalling yards in Lyons, France, another urgent priority from headquarters. Reportedly Lyons has a high concentration of German troops, so anything we can do to disrupt transfer of ammunition and supplies to this area is critical. This will be another nine-hour flight. Expect some anti-aircraft units in the area. Two fighter groups will run cover for us."

The weather officer predicted clear skies on the approach and over the target.

In the pilots' briefing, Eaves was pleased to learn the 777th was back in Baker, the upper box above and to the right of the Lead Group in Able. Bombing altitude would be 21,000 feet. The route was planned to miss most areas of concentrated flak, which were identified. He was assigned the same B-24J they had flown yesterday. At least he had some familiarity with her.

After the routine check of the plane, the men stood under the wing to pull on their heavy flight gear. Christel walked up to Eaves and said quietly, "Captain, I thought you should know that Linneman has been under the weather with a bad cold for over a week. I told him to go to the doc and get it checked out, but he refused."

"Thanks for telling me, Bill. I'll check in with him." The waist gunners routinely faced open windows with frigid air roaring around them. At bombing altitudes over 20,000 feet, the wind chill hovered at forty to fifty below. Little wonder someone might succumb to illness.

Eaves sidled over to Linneman, noticing his pale countenance and the dark circles under his eyes. His ever-present smile was missing. "Hey Joe, how are you doing?"

Linneman raised his eyebrows and gave a weak grin. "I'm okay, sir."

"Well, you don't look okay. Are you sure you want to do this mission? We could call for a replacement."

"No, I'm okay. I can do this. We've got to stick together."

Eaves paused. "Well, alright, but only if you promise to see the doc when we get back."

Linneman nodded as he pulled his rounds over his shoulder, picked up his parachute and got ready to climb aboard.

The 464th got up in the air without a hitch. Eaves maneuvered into his position in the top box as the formation tightened up. As they climbed to bombing altitude, the gunners threw some lead out over the Mediterranean and Lambert pulled the pins on the bomb load.

Looking down, Eaves could see the island of Corsica below. Thankfully it was in Allied hands and had an emergency landing base there. Reassuring to know that option was there.

The formation droned on, time passing agonizingly slow. Four hours into the flight, the Lead Group turned on the last leg of the approach to the bomb run. No flak or bandits so far.

Eaves pressed his throat mic. "Pilot to Navigator, location."

"Ten minutes to IP," Haverkos replied.

Dark puffs could be seen rising below. Flak. Nothing hitting close enough yet to see the fiery red or orange centers. Eaves hoped it would stay that way.

The formation continued toward the target.

"Navigator to pilot, approaching IP in five minutes.

"Roger."

The lead plane banked north, and Eaves turned the plane down the last leg to the target. "Pilot to bombardier, your plane."

"Roger. Bomb bay opening."

Suddenly, a brilliant orange flash filled the cockpit. Flak had burst above their plane and shrapnel rained down on the nose and fuselage. The smell of cordite filled the air. The enemy had zeroed in on its targets.

Eaves checked the gauges as the plane powered on. Nothing vital had been hit.

"Two minutes to target." Lambert's voice came over the intercom.

Flak bursts below flashed red. Eaves sucked in his breath and gripped the yoke tighter. Running a gauntlet of hellfire with no defense brought that overpowering sense of vulnerability flooding over him.

God help us.

Sitting ducks, that's what they were. A carnival scene from long ago flashed across his mind, little ducks popping up on the revolving treadmill to be knocked down by his cork gun, a stuffed animal prize in the offing.

Now *they* were the ducks.

He jerked his mind back to the mission. Where's that marshalling yard?

Finally, rails below. Bombs fell from the Lead Group and Lambert's voice rang out, "Bombs away." The plane popped upward as over twelve hundred pounds dropped from her belly. Mission accomplished.

Seconds later. "Bombardier to pilot, your plane."

"Roger." Relief flooded his system as Eaves banked left and followed his lead plane as Able box dove down, down, down, dropping over 2,000 feet to get out of the flak range. The formation made another turn immediately as they headed toward the designated return leg along the coastline.

"Pilot to gunners, be alert." This is where the attack came yesterday, just before they reached the coast. Today the sky remained peaceful, but tension ratcheted up Eaves' spine and into his shoulders. Adrenaline rushed through him, overcoming the exhaustion.

Elder's voice crackled over the intercom. "Top turret here. Can see Little Friends covering above. No bandits in sight."

"Good to know." Time seemed to stand still as the planes roared on toward the coast. Finally, waves appeared below, open sea ahead. Eaves took a deep breath, shrugging his shoulders to relieve the tight knot in his upper back.

He started relaxing as the formation flew over Corsica. No German fighters had been sighted.

Maybe the *Luftwaffe* had bigger fish to fry today. Or maybe they hadn't bounced back from the serious beating they took yesterday. Could be that the constant Allied attacks on German oil refineries were finally making a difference.

In his gut, Eaves knew the U.S. Army Air Force would command the skies before this war ended.

Chapter 20

27 May 1944—Gioia del Colle Airfield, Italy

HAVERKOS STRETCHED HIS ARMS and rolled over on the cot. Sunlight streamed into the darkness of their canvas hovel through the crack in the tent door. He reveled in the luxury of sleeping as long as he wanted after those last three long missions. The alert list was up again last night, but thankfully they weren't on it. Didn't think he could've done another day.

He sat up and pulled on his uniform. Reaching into his locker for his razor, he picked up the ugly chunk of flak he'd saved. A chill tingled through him. Was a miracle it landed between him and Lambert when it crashed through the Plexiglas of the greenhouse. He blinked as visions of flak puffs and flaming planes brought back the horrors of the last three days.

Refocus, Haverkos—today is another day. And we don't have to fly today.

He put down the evil-looking lump of metal and picked up Ginny's picture. Would he make it back home to tell her how he felt? He mentally kicked himself for being so slow to recognize how sweet she was. Yes, she'd seemed like a younger kid sister, but he'd finally come to his senses. After setting her up to date his buddies a couple of times, he'd finally taken her out himself just before he left for the war.

He laughed to himself, thinking of them both crawling around on the floor under the table at a fancy restaurant looking for the silver wings he'd just received that day. Thank goodness she'd spotted them under the arched table leg. No way could he have gone back to base without them. He smiled. What a trooper she was.

His eyes fell on her letters he'd bundled together with string. He would have to scribble off a note to her today. She'd been so faithful in writing to him, and those words from home were a lifeline.

"Dreaming about your sweetheart?" Eaves words cut through his reverie.

Haverkos's face warmed. He grinned. "What was your first clue?"

Eaves laughed out loud. "That dreamy look on your face as you stared at her picture."

"Where do you think the mission went today?" Haverkos changed the subject as he carefully tucked her picture back into the locker and shut the lid.

"Well, seems to be a pattern lately. My guess is back to France." Eaves grabbed his cap. "Let's go get breakfast and check it out."

Soon they loaded their trays with powdered eggs and Spam, hash-browns, toast, and orange marmalade jelly. Always marmalade. Seems like someone could find grape or strawberry jam somewhere.

Grabbing steaming cups of coffee, they found an empty table.

Sherman entered the mess tent and joined them. "Hey, heard the mission today was the marshalling yards in Nimes, France." He took a sip of his coffee. "A long one again. All this focus on France makes me think the invasion is just around the corner."

"Hmm, just like you thought, Red." Haverkos cocked his head toward Eaves. "Can't be long now."

"Sure looks that way," Eaves said. "But enough about missions. We've got the day off and we'd better enjoy it. Let's head into Bari for a change of scenery. Maybe we can catch a ride with the supply truck if we hustle."

The three officers managed to talk the supply sergeant into letting them hitch a ride into town. They gratefully squeezed into the back of the cargo truck.

"We're off to see the wizard," Haverkos quipped. "Or at least . . . some of Italy."

They bounced along under the tarp-covered canopy. Over twenty miles of rutted roads felt more like forty.

"Not exactly the Italian sightseeing tour I'd choose." Sherman gripped the plank bench to steady himself as the truck lurched along. "But at least we're off the base."

"I heard Bari had a 'Pearl Harbor' of its own in December of '43 when the Fifteenth Air Force moved in to set up headquarters," Haverkos said. "A surprise bombing by the Germans sunk over seventeen ships and decimated a large portion of the city."

"You don't say!" Sherman cocked his head. "Well, here's hoping for a peaceful time today."

The truck rumbled to a halt and the sergeant pulled back the tarp cover. He nodded to Eaves. "Here you go, sir. Used to be a museum, but now it's the recreation center. You just might find some cute USO girlies and doughnuts waiting inside." He grinned and checked his watch.

"Interesting sights up in Old Bari, but be sure to be here ready to leave at 1600 hours . . . or you could find yourselves hoofing it back. Deadlines, sir." He saluted, then turned to climb back into the cab with his partner.

Haverkos craned his neck to look at the old city sprawled out around them. Many buildings still showed damage from the German bombing that had taken the Allies by surprise.

Ancient buildings loomed three stories high, fit together like a honeycomb with narrow cobbled streets between them.

The smell of the salt in the air and the low roar of crashing waves verified the sea was not far away. A medieval city with a natural harbor, Bari clung to rocky cliffs jutting out into the Adriatic.

"Let's go inside and see about those doughnuts," Eaves said.

Two attractive young American women stood behind the food bar, a neat row of ceramic mugs on the ledge by a pot of coffee. Haverkos heard male laughter coming from the room to the left. The smell of fresh-baked pastries wafted into his nostrils and his mouth filled with saliva.

"Welcome," the brunette called out with a smile. "Can we interest you in some coffee and doughnuts?"

Haverkos' smile stretched wider. "You sure can. And you don't know how long it's been since we saw such a pretty face, offering us doughnuts to boot."

The shy smile and pink flush in her cheeks made him chuckle. But it also brought Ginny's sweet face to mind, with a stab of pain.

He reached out to accept the glazed doughnut and steaming mug of hot coffee from the young woman's hand.

Don't get treats like this at the base.

"We also have a game room, a reading room, and can get mail out for you," she said, stretching her arm toward the open doorway.

Haverkos took a bite of the pastry.

"Mmm . . . good. Thank you very much." He licked sugar off his lip. "Any suggestions for seeing the sights here in Bari?"

"Well," the little redhead spoke up. "*Basilica San Nicola* is a beautiful cathedral and only a few blocks south out on the point by the harbor. Pilgrims come from all over the world to visit. Allegedly it contains the bones of Saint Nicholas."

"What! Santa Claus is dead?" Haverkos' quip brought more smiles and giggles from the girls.

Ignoring the bait, the pretty brunette chimed in. "Only a few blocks north of the cathedral is the *Castello Svevo*, a medieval fortress that dates back to Norman times. It's a fascinating place. The castle sustained damage in the bombing, but I think part of it is open to the public." Cocking her head, she added. "And you might enjoy the little cafés and barber shops that are open along the way."

"You suggesting I need a haircut?" Haverkos grinned. More giggles.

Eaves turned toward the door. "Thank you, ladies," he said. "We appreciate the treats and your suggestions."

The three officers strolled along mostly deserted streets, seeing only a few other American servicemen wandering the town. A little hole-in-the-wall shop sporting a red and white barber pole signaled an opportunity for a haircut and hopefully a massage.

Haverkos appreciated the chance to unwind and relax. As they left, the efficient and friendly Italian barber pointed the way to *Basilica San Nicola.*

Though damage marred buildings nearby, the spectacular cathedral showed none. It had escaped destruction. The heavy wooden doors opened to reveal a candle-lit sanctuary with a long aisle stretching toward an elaborate altar.

Haverkos tilted his head back in amazement as he studied the huge vaulted arches high overhead, suspended from ornate columns. Light filtered through two gleaming golden crosses of decorative stained glass in windows flanking the crucifix. Votive candles flickered before the rail surrounding the altar, the smell of scented wax filling the air.

The architecture was simple but astounding. Truly a work of art.

A door creaked open. A priest walked to the altar and, after making the sign of the cross, knelt and bowed his head in prayer.

Haverkos stood transfixed while Eaves and Sherman sank down on a wooden pew. A deep silence enveloped the cathedral. The stillness birthed a tranquility that was hard to describe.

He bowed his head.

Holy, holy, holy, Lord God Almighty. You are Creator and Savior, worthy of all praise. For You are Good and Compassionate. By Your mercy, we are here, and I thank You. Keep us in Your care.

He raised his eyes. Truly, this was a thin place, where heaven and earth touched.

Time seemed to stand still. Finally, Eaves stood up. Looking at Haverkos and Sherman, he whispered, "Shall we go?"

Haverkos nodded. Words didn't seem right in this holy place.

As they walked the cobbled streets that wound between ancient three-story buildings, an outdoor café with red-checkered tablecloths caught their eye. Knowing no Italian, they somehow ordered a delicious lasagna meal, with wine and French bread. The waiter brought *gelato* for dessert, which turned out to be a kind of ice cream.

Walking on, they turned the corner, and the twin towers of a massive castle filled the horizon. *Castello Svevo* stood before them, an impressive structure built of huge blocks of stone in three layers, with small arched openings in the top section. A formidable edifice. Charm and strength emanated from the mighty fortress that loomed over the city. Impregnable still—the doors were locked.

Eaves looked at his watch. "Hey, guys. We'd better hustle back to the rec center or we'll miss our ride."

Haverkos' long legs put him at the head of the group as Eaves and Sherman tried to keep up. All were breathing hard when they reached the rec center and sat down on the steps to wait.

"Well, it's been good to get away from the base," Sherman said, just as the cargo truck turned the corner and stopped in front of them.

"Yep, we sure needed a break," Eaves said with a tired smile.

For a few hours, they could almost forget about the horrors of war.

Chapter 21

EAVES LOOKED UP AS TUDOR approached their table, his face haggard with fatigue. "How'd the mission go?" he asked, shoving a chair out for him.

Tudor placed his tray on the table and crumpled into the seat. He slowly shook his head. "Flak everywhere around Nimes." His hand visibly trembled as he took a swig of coffee. He set the cup down and stared blankly at it.

Finally, he looked up. "*Old Granddad* exploded right in front of *Belzebub*." He swallowed hard. "No chutes. *Belzebub* just dropped from formation like a rock. Don't know what happened to them."

A shot of pain knifed through Eaves. Two planes from his squadron.

Lt. Parrish and his whole crew . . . gone? How many more friends will we lose?

He pushed down a wave of nausea and put his hand on his buddy's shoulder. "You did okay?"

Tudor nodded and reached for his fork. "We got a brand-new plane today. The boys named her *All Meat-No Potatoes*. Took a little flak damage, but no casualties."

The officers continued to eat. Tudor broke the heavy silence. "One piece of good news—the briefing officer told us no mission is scheduled for tomorrow as the base is preparing to move to Pantanella."

"Yeah, I noticed there was no alert posted. Guess we'd better get packed up." Eaves pushed back his chair and picked up his tray. "Can't say I'm sorry to leave this mud pit."

"Lt. Eaves?"

He turned around to see the operations officer standing behind him.

"Could I have a word?"

"Yes, of course, sir." Eaves set down the tray and walked over to him.

"You probably heard there are no missions scheduled for tomorrow, but the 464th has had a special request to send a few bombers to Yugoslavia to hit German troop concentrations there. So, we are looking for volunteers who didn't fly today. Would you be willing to take on this mission?"

Eaves thought for a moment. Yugoslavia would be a short hop, probably less than three hours. And it would be mission number fifteen for them—halfway to the magic number thirty.

"Yes, sir. You can count on us."

"Good. Briefing at 0700." The operations officer turned to scope out the room, and made his way to another table.

Eaves headed out to pass the word on to his crew, his mind zeroed in on Jean and home.

✈✈✈

28 MAY 1944—GIOIA DEL COLLE AIRFIELD, ITALY

A hacking cough. From inside the bomb bay, Eaves turned around and looked back.

Linneman's shoulders shook as another cough racked his body. He struggled to climb up into the bomber with his ammo belts and parachute. The pallor and listless look on the gunner's face triggered an urgent sense of concern.

"Did you go to the infirmary?"

"No, sir." Linneman hung his head. "Just rested. Thought I was feeling a little better."

"You check into the infirmary as soon as we get back. That's an order, sergeant." Eaves' voice was stern.

After a routine takeoff, Eaves pulled into formation with two other volunteer squadrons and headed east. In less than an hour the coast of Yugoslavia came into view. No flak arched toward them as the bombers dropped their payload on the designated target. Eaves followed the lead plane as it dropped lower and turned back toward Italy, relief washing over him.

A true milk run, mission accomplished.

When they got back to base, the official word was out. Everyone was to pack up for the move to the new base at Pantanella. The airfield was abuzz with activity.

In the tent, Haverkos was on his cot writing the almost daily letter to Ginny. Eaves finished packing his belongings into the foot locker and he realized he had enough time to get a V-mail off to Jean.

Babe,

I sure miss you sweetheart. Words can't say how much. Italy is pretty wet and miserable, mud everywhere. Never thought I'd miss the dryness of West Texas like I do.

Thanks for the care package – the cookies were delicious! Had to share them with the boys. Everyone knows when you get a letter or package at mail call, no hiding it. So, you just keep them coming—fifteen, at least, because Tudor and the officers next door include themselves in our crew when they see a package arrive.

I'm praying you have all the things you need and that we are together again soon. So glad you are there with your mom and dad. Give them both my love and thanks.

Hugs and kisses just for you.

All my love

Sug

He smiled as he folded the form and added the address. They had their code—she would know by the number mentioned that he had completed fifteen missions now, halfway through his tour. God willing, he would make it home in another month or so. He turned toward Haverkos. "Let's get these to the APO and head to the mess tent."

Haverkos scribbled the address on his V-mail and tucked it in his pocket. As they lifted the tent flap, they saw Tudor headed their way.

"Join you for supper?" Eaves asked.

"Only if Bob doesn't talk about Ginny the whole time," he replied, with a twinkle in his eye. Haverkos blushed and shook his head.

After another meal of liver and onions, Eaves stopped to check the bulletin board. An alert list up again. And they were on it.

He shook his head in disbelief.

What about the move?

Chapter 22

29 May 1944—Gioia del Colle Airfield, Italy

"LT. EAVES?" A VOICE SOUNDED from far away. A bright orb glared on his closed lids. "0300, sir. Briefing at 0500."

Eaves groaned. A restless night—seemed like he'd tossed and turned all night, but must have finally dozed off.

He sat up to clear his head as the light bobbed away toward Haverkos.

Another day, another mission. One day closer to the day he'd head home—to Jean.

Still dark in the musty tent, he reached under the cot for his flashlight, and the flight suit he'd laid out last night. After a close shave, he pulled on his flight jacket and made his way through the darkness toward the mess tent where he was greeted with odors of fried bacon and sausage.

Don't know why we get a good breakfast the day of a mission, even real eggs, when we can't eat much.

Grabbing a tray, he went through the line and joined the other officers.

Not much chitchat. They all picked at their food, but gulped down steaming cups of coffee.

They hiked back to their tent for the rest of their gear and waited at the rendezvous spot for the cargo truck ride to the briefing.

Soon the whole crew crowded together in a room that oozed a unique smell of leather, tobacco, sweat and anxiety. Warriors all, banter about the planned move and discussion of what today's target might be concealed any shakiness.

"Where's Linneman?" Eaves asked, noting the gunner was missing.

Christel spoke up. "They kept him in the infirmary last night."

"I'll request a substitute for him. He's got to rest if he wants to get well."

A captain called out, "Ten-hut." The men leaped to their feet and stood at attention as Colonel Bonner strode into the room.

Eaves looked past him, remembering the tragic results of Bonner's cowardice on that second mission. Hard to look at the man with any respect, but he was still in charge.

"At ease." The airmen settled back down on their seats.

"Good morning, men. This will be a three-pronged mission for the Fifteenth," Bonner announced. "We are throwing everything but the latrine at Hitler today."

At his signal, the operations officer pulled back the curtain, exposing the map.

Audible gasps and groans were heard throughout the room as the men recognized the targets. Red yarn led to the well-defended Wiener Neustadt, which they had hit twice in the last month. Two other red lines went to Vienna—highlighted was the Atzgersdorf aircraft factory and the *Wollersdorf Airdrome*. All the targets were critical to the German war effort and all heavily defended with flak and fighters.

No milk run today.

The operations officer stepped up. "Today we will be joining the Fifteenth Air Force in a massive three-pronged attack. Over a hundred Liberators will target Weiner Neustadt. Another three hundred bombers will hit the *Wollersdorf Airdrome*. Our assignment—join one hundred Liberators who are targeting the Atzgersdorf aircraft factory. This factory is located three miles south of Vienna's city center, and it produces most of the parts for the Me-109 fighter planes. Destruction of this plant will strike a significant blow to the *Luftwaffe*." He paused, gripping the podium tightly. "And . . . we will have backup today. Thunderbolts and P-51 Mustangs are pledged for escort."

Murmurs of approval rippled through the room at that announcement.

"Hope it's the Red Tails," Haverkos whispered. "They stick with the heavies."

A young intelligence officer strode forward to describe the nuts and bolts of the mission. "This is a long mission, at least eight hours of flight time to the target and back. Expect bandits. Reportedly over a hundred German fighters are protecting this vital aircraft factory, and Vienna is ringed with anti-aircraft flak units. Note a hospital and a school to avoid."

He reviewed the escape and evasion plans, pointing out the current Allied front lines in the area. "If shot down, seek out Tito's Partisans. The Partisans are actively engaging the Germans and aiding Allied airmen. They will help you get back to our lines. But beware of the Chetniks. They are known to be collaborating with the Germans."

The weather officer gave his report. "Clouds on takeoff, but clear over the Alps and, hopefully, clear over the targets."

Eaves sighed. The weather was always unpredictable. Usually worse than they anticipated, with the air currents in the Alps constantly shifting.

Bonner stepped forward again and he waited until the room grew still. "I will be leading the attack today." He looked around the room. "Chaplain Eastwood, a word of prayer, please."

After the prayer, the tension in the room was palpable. The unspoken question . . . would Bonner panic again?

Men muttered under their breath as they left the briefing room. Eaves looked straight ahead and kept his thoughts to himself.

In the pilots' briefing he got more bad news. With a sinking feeling, he found the 777th Squadron was in the lower element, positioned last over the target. Tail-End Charlie again—the most dangerous position.

Eaves' request for a substitute waist gunner was approved.

A twinge of sadness swept through him when he saw *Target for Tonite* listed out of service. Heading to the flight line, he looked for his plane assignment. It was *All Meat-No Potatoes*, Lt. Tudor's new plane.

As he arrived at the plane, he saw Tudor approaching, a serious look on his face.

"Say, just saw that you are scheduled for the mission in *All Meat-No Potatoes*," he said. "You know, she just came over and we've only had one mission in her. Hate to tell you, but she's a little sluggish. Doesn't handle as well as *Target for Tonite*." He looked at the line of planes, then down at his hands. "Sorry about her—heard they're scrapping her for parts. I'd hoped they might be able to put her back together again. She was a great plane."

Eaves nodded, his throat constricting. She had served them well. He cleared his throat. "What do you mean—sluggish?"

"Hard to nail down. She just doesn't respond well. Wish I could trade her in for another." He paused. "One good thing about the new B-24Hs though—reinforced steel plates under and behind the pilot and copilot's seats." His eyes crinkled at the corners. "Won't have to sit on the flak jackets anymore."

Eaves laughed with him. "Well, that's one good thing for sure. Thanks for the heads up. Gotta go. Enjoy your day off, buddy."

He caught up with the crew at the equipment shack. Took the heavy flak jacket he was issued. The sergeant handing out the parachutes had his usual banter going. "Here you go. Bring it back if it doesn't work."

Right.

Eaves gave him a wan smile.

Hope we never have to find out.

The Army Air Corps did not believe in practicing bailouts unless you were a paratrooper. Just strap 'em on and leap out.

Under the plane he pulled on the extra socks and heavy fleece flight trousers.

"Sergeant McMillan, sir. Understand you need a waist gunner today."

Eaves turned to see a young gunner saluting, his ammo belts crossed over his shoulders, parachute in hand.

"You're in the right spot, sergeant. Welcome aboard."

✈✈✈

Ominous black puffs filled the sky over Vienna. The inky cloud below looked solid enough to walk on. Eaves coolly stared at the barrage of German antiaircraft flak—far below for now. Fifteen missions had taught him something.

His fingertips briefly brushed his breast pocket containing Jean's picture.

Remember who you're fighting for, and the men who rely on you. Focus Eaves—let's get this job done.

So far so good. The flight from Italy had been routine. They'd reached the IP and Bonner hadn't panicked as the group made the final turn. The Atzgersdorf aircraft factory lay dead ahead. Those fighter plane parts were critical to the German war effort . . . Eaves knew the enemy would be throwing everything they had at the bombers.

"Pilot to bombardier, your ship," he said as he turned over control. For the next ten minutes their course could not be altered.

"Bombardier to pilot, roger."

Eaves' gut tightened. Flying last over the target, danger increased by the minute. He pictured the German gunners five miles below pulling the lanyards of the 88 mm cannons that propelled the twenty-pound shells skyward.

Black puffs rose higher. The enemy was calculating the bombers' air speed, course, and altitude, and improving their aim.

Without warning, a flash of orange filled the cockpit. Shrapnel rained down on the windshield and metal hull. The bomber shuddered as the acrid odor of explosives filled the air.

Eaves sucked in his breath, his grip tightening on the yoke. Strange how the roar of the motors silenced all other sounds except when shrapnel hit.

Sherman scanned the dials. "Direct hit on engine two."

Looking at the left wing, Eaves saw smoke pouring out of the closest engine, the propeller blades slowing to a stop.

The yoke went limp for a moment. Eaves pulled back ever so slightly to hold the nose up and in position. Too much drag.

"Feather the prop," he ordered.

Sherman hastily cut the fuel and pushed the button. The blades turned knife-edged to the wind, reducing the friction slowing them down. Unrelenting, the bomber pressed on, three motors continuing to carry the load.

"Elder here. Huge hole between engine number three and the fuselage, sir," he reported.

Petrone suddenly hollered. "Ball turret here. *Black-Z's* on fire!"

Eaves flinched. It was Lt. Jones, his wing mate.

Moments later, Petrone continued, more subdued. "I saw two chutes come out of her. Oh, wait. Two more."

Lord, help them all get out.

"Bombardier, how long to target?" Eaves asked.

"Three minutes," came the answer.

All Meat-No Potatoes lumbered on.

Moments later, "Bombardier to crew, bomb bay doors open."

As the lead plane spewed its bombs, Lambert called out, "Bombs away!" He made the drop and the arsenal of destruction rained down.

The twelve five-hundred-pound bombs hurtled accurately toward the aircraft factory already blooming with explosions from bombs bursting below. The eerie black fog of flak covered the rest of the landscape.

As she dropped her heavy load, *All Meat-No Potatoes* bucked upward like a colt let out to pasture.

"Bombardier to pilot, they're in the pickle barrel. Your ship."

Resuming control of the sluggish bomber and pressing his throat mic, Eaves said, "Roger. We did our job, men. Now—watch for bandits!"

Eaves banked left to follow the combat lead plane as it took evasive action to get out of the flak.

"Petrone here. I see three planes dropping behind. Must've taken hits, sir."

Eaves checked the instruments. Air speed dropping. Too much damage—*All Meat-No Potatoes* couldn't keep up with the formation. He made a quick decision.

"Christel, radio command that we are dropping out of formation to group up with the three stragglers. Tell 'em we'll see them in Gioia."

He peeled off to the right and regrouped with the other three bombers falling behind the main group.

Now we've all got more fire power. No Little Friends to help out on the way home. Those German fighters will be looking for lame-duck targets, easy pickings.

The skies stayed peaceful as they pulled away from Vienna. *All Meat-No Potatoes* was at 16,000 feet, airspeed 190 mph.

Hopefully it would stay this way.

✈✈✈

Eaves saw flak rising over Gaza, Austria. The four stragglers had dropped below 12,000 feet. Five miles ahead he could see the main group pulling away.

"You guys hungry?" Haverkos suddenly leaned into the flight deck. He had removed his oxygen mask and held an open K-ration in his hands.

Before Eaves could answer, Haverkos dropped the K-ration and pointed up. "Bandits! Two o'clock high!"

Two German Messerschmitts shot out of the clouds, wing guns twinkling.

The plane rocked. Direct hit under the pilots' seats.

Thank God we're in Tudor's plane with those reinforced steel plates around us. We'd be goners if we were in Target for Tonite.

The plane wasn't responding. He swallowed hard. The blast must have taken out part of the controls. Quickly he put the B-24 on autopilot to hold it steady.

Elder was manning the top turret and returned fire, brass casings raining down onto the flight deck.

Two more Me-109s came from the other side, guns blazing.

"I'm hit!" Christel called out from the nose turret.

"I've got him." Haverkos grabbed the first aid kit and rushed to his aid.

All Meat-No Potatoes struggled along and had dropped to 11,000 feet.

The fighters swarmed like bees, stitching both sides of the bomber. At least fifteen fighter planes circled the four stragglers for the kill.

Machine guns blazed. The gunners did a good job—first one fighter plane, then another fell from the sky, but more bandits took their place. Bullets ripped through the ship, piercing the bomber's skin.

"McMillan's hit!" cried Fangman, right waist gunner, just as engine three on the right wing coughed and sputtered out. Another man wounded. Eaves pulled up on the yoke and ordered Sherman to feather the prop.

With only two engines functioning, *All Meat-No Potatoes* sank lower in the sky.

Can't keep up.

The rest of the group powered on and they were alone against the enemy.

"Damage report," Eaves called, his eyes scanning the gauges.

Moments later Elder, the engineer, came on, "Direct hit on ball turret; Petrone unconscious. His intercom and line for the hydraulic lift is severed. Fangman's wounded. Left waist, McMillan, dead."

Dead—oh no. The substitute for Linneman.

The young man's face flashed before his eyes, a pang of grief seared through him. Eaves' jaw tightened.

Gotta think of the rest of the crew.

Just then the bomber was raked again by machine gun fire from another diving German fighter.

Someone in the rear of the plane yelled, "Fire!"

No time to lose—this bird could blow up. Touching his throat mic, Eaves gave the command as he flipped the alarm, "Pilot to crew. Bail out. I repeat, bail out now! All hands, abandon ship. God be with you." He turned to Sherman. "Go get'em out."

Eaves stayed at the controls.

Lord, help them all get out safely.

Chapter 23

HAVERKOS RUSHED TO THE NOSE TURRET with the first aid kit. Christel stood ankle-deep in spent cartridges holding his left arm, blood dripping from his fingertips, a bullet hole evident in the upper arm of the flight jacket.

Haverkos unzipped the heavy flight jacket and Christel grunted as Haverkos helped him slip his arm out, the sleeve wet with blood.

Grabbing gauze pads, he pressed against the wound to stem the blood flow. It appeared to be a flesh wound, no broken bones.

Haverkos applied the antiseptic powder and wrapped fresh pads firmly in place with strips of gauze and a couple wraps of tape.

Suddenly the bailout alarm sounded.

Oh no!

Haverkos helped Christel pull his flight jacket back on and grabbed both parachutes. He felt a tap on his shoulder and turned to find himself face to face with Sherman.

The copilot yelled, "Help me over here." He pointed toward the radio compartment. "We've got more wounded to get out. What's our location?"

"Yugoslavia—just north of Zagreb," Haverkos hollered back, realizing his interphone was out.

Fangman and Masterson lay on the floor of the radio compartment, blood everywhere. Light twinkled through hundreds of holes the machine gun fire had punctured throughout the skin of the fuselage. Smoke filled the air, stinging his nose and throat.

Haverkos knelt by Fangman and pulled off his bloody flight jacket. Over ten wounds riddled his arms and legs, but no lead appeared to have hit vital organs. Still conscious, Fangman moaned in pain. Haverkos grabbed a syringe from the first aid kit and administered a shot of morphine. Then he furiously applied the sulfanilamide powder, grabbing a dressing and gauze to wrap each wound as best he could.

He helped the man sit up and strapped him into his parachute harness. Checking his own parachute, he cinched it tightly in place.

He looked up to see Lambert with both arms wrapped around a vertical support column, his face chalky white. "I'm not jumping," he shouted at Christel.

Haverkos watched with amazement as the little man literally peeled the bombardier's fingers off the pole, despite his wounded arm.

"Oh yes, you are," Christel yelled as he pushed Lambert down the catwalk.

Sherman had finished administering first aid to Masterson and had him ready for bail out. When he hit the button for the bomb bay doors to open, nothing happened.

"The hydraulics are out!" he yelled.

Haverkos jumped into the bay and began to kick. Christel joined him. The doors burst open and wind roared in.

Haverkos glanced at his watch—1135.

Time to hit the silks.

He leaped, the first one out.

He seemed to be sitting in a comfortable chair. Surreal, no sensation of falling, just floating. He pulled up his arm and watched the sweep of the second hand on his watch until eighteen seconds had elapsed.

Time to pull the ripcord.

He pulled hard—nothing happened. The chute was hung up. Reaching up with his left hand, he frantically felt for the small jump chute cord.

Where was it?

Finally, his fingers locked around the elusive cord and he jerked downward.

A moment later he felt a tremendous jolt as the emergency chute mushroomed above him and stopped his free fall. He gasped for breath and swallowed to clear his plugged ears.

Looking north, he was elated to see two parachutes descending, one closer to his height, dropping toward dark woods below. Must be Christel. The other chute was still quite high.

He would head that way when he landed.

✈✈✈

Eaves contemplated that last painful message crackling over the intercom. "Sherman here. Confirming, McMillan KIA. Petrone unconscious, hydraulics out. Fangman, Elder, Christel, and Masterson all wounded. Haverkos and I are giving first aid as best we can." He added, "Haverkos reports our location just north of Zagreb, Yugoslavia. Will get them all out and be right behind them. See you below."

Eaves' thoughts swirled while he struggled to keep the bomber level. So many wounded. *God help them.*

And no way to raise the ball turret with hydraulics out—the only crank was inside the turret.

What could he do? If he got the bodies out, maybe they would be found and sent home to their families?

Suddenly Elder dropped down from the upper turret and climbed into the copilot's seat. "Captain, if you're trying to take her back to base, I'll help you."

The flight engineer was wounded, blood streaming down his face.

What's he still doing here? Got to stop the bleeding.

Eaves just shook his head. "No chance of that." Wiping the blood from Elder's eyes with his sleeve, Eaves stood up. "Let's go, Jim."

He pulled the wounded man to his feet and guided him back toward the bomb bay.

Strong odors of gasoline and acrid smoke filled the air. His eyes swept the area.

Good. They're all out.

Grabbing gauze and antiseptic from an open first aid kit, he quickly wrapped Elder's head and secured the bandage with tape. He checked Elder's parachute and steadied him as they crept down the catwalk to the open bomb bay doors.

"Get down," he yelled. He helped Elder kneel in the rushing wind, the position they'd been taught.

"Roll out." Elder hesitated. Eaves gave him a firm push and he was gone.

Kneeling down, he snapped his own parachute in place. Glancing below, all he could see was rugged mountains. Smoke billowed around him. He hesitated when he turned and saw McMillan's body through the smoke.

Could I get him out? No, no time. Gotta go. Help me, Lord.

Taking a deep breath, he rolled off the catwalk.

His first bailout—the wind sucked his breath away.

He drew in air as he fumbled for the ripcord and curled his fingers tightly around it. Hurtling downward, he counted—one thousand one, one thousand two, one thousand three.

He yanked on the ripcord. The chute streamed above him, opening with a violent jerk and a lurch that knocked the air out of his lungs.

He gasped as he floated in an eerily peaceful, quiet sky, so foreign to the echoing drone of the bomber's noise still ringing in his ears.

He scanned the sky for other chutes. None in sight.

Help them all to survive, Lord. Get them to friendly forces.

The sound of a plane's motor abruptly broke the silence. Turning his head, he saw an Me-109 headed straight at him.

Eaves stared at the fighter plane quickly closing the distance between them.

So, this is how it ends.

A puppet on a string, no way to evade the bullets that would rip through him.

Sorry for letting you down, Jean. Please take care of her, Lord.

The fighter zoomed closer. He could just make out the form of the pilot.

This is it.

Suddenly the plane waggled its wings. The pilot raised his arm and saluted. The fighter surged around him on the left, the parachute rocking in its wake.

A shocked rush of relief flooded over him.

A German man of honor. They were true, the stories of the *Luftwaffe's* code of chivalry—never shoot a helpless man dangling in a parachute.

An enemy had spared his life.

Hello—look out, Eaves. The ground is coming up fast.

Looking down, he saw a small grain field. Pulling firmly on the left side of his parachute did little to direct it, but thankfully the wind glided him toward the middle of the open field.

He took a deep breath.

Here we go.

Thump. Hitting the ground running at first, he collapsed in a heap as his right leg twisted under him.

Whoosh. The landing knocked the wind out of his lungs. The parachute billowed over him.

The pungent smell of fresh soil and faint odor of manure filled his nostrils, his face planted in the dirt. But never had solid ground felt so comforting. Dizzy, he wiped his face and struggled to catch his breath.

Taking assessment, he noted his right knee throbbing. The landing jarred the old football injury, but he could still bend it. He was scraped up a bit, but thankfully he had no broken bones.

Eaves pulled the parachute aside and peered through green stalks of wheat waving gently in the breeze. Dark forest surrounded the field on all sides, with massive mountains looming above the small valley. No houses in sight.

Better roll up this parachute and get out of here. The Germans will be looking for me.

He got to his knees and unclasped the harness, quickly drawing the chute toward him and folding it up as best he could. Sweat beads formed on his forehead and trickled down his back from the exertion.

Gotta get this flight suit off—way too hot.

Peeling off the heavy layers of sheepskin brought immediate relief.

Where to hide them?

Clutching the flight suit under his arm and dragging the parachute, he crawled toward the nearest edge of the field.

Cautiously, he raised up again. His heart lurched.

Two men were running toward him.

He automatically put his hand on his Colt 45.

Chapter 24

AS HE DRIFTED DOWN, Haverkos tried to get his bearings. Below, the Savo River made a long, lazy bend to the south, and two small villages flanked him on either side, tree-covered mountains looming around them.

The drone of an airplane motor startled him. He scanned the sky. To his horror, he recognized a Messerschmitt headed directly toward him, nose first.

Panic-struck, he grabbed the shrouds and tried to swing the chute but found he was too weak to make any difference.

To his amazement, the plane lazily circled him, then dipped its wings and flew off.

A man with a sense of sportsmanship, an enemy to boot.

Probably radioing my location to ground troops. They'll be looking for me.

Glancing below, he saw a uniformed man carrying a rifle running up a road to the far north, going away from him. Too far away to identify whether friend or foe.

He thought fast. As soon as he hit the ground, he should probably head north to try to connect with the crew members who had landed in the woods. The Yugoslav coast was about seventy-five miles southwest, and with the map in the escape kit to guide them, they could probably make that distance in about a week. Could try to work their way south at night, hide by day.

Ground, coming up fast. Better concentrate on landing.

The parachute floated toward the grassy slope of a small hill. Relief flooded over him—he wasn't landing in a tree.

Thump. He hit the ground hard, seeing stars for a moment.

Dazed, he struggled to wiggle out of the parachute harness. Rolling the parachute up as he pulled it toward him, he looked for a place to bury it. Finding a spot of loose earth, he dug a hole with a stick and stuffed the chute into it, scattering some leaves and rocks on top. Satisfied, he started up the small rise heading away from the river.

But after only a step or two, a wave of nausea struck him and stopped him in his tracks. Bending over, he gagged several times. Wiping his mouth, he stumbled on.

From the top of the rise, he saw a large wheat field stretched before him, an old run-down cemetery on the left side. The shelter of dark woods directly across the field beckoned.

To save time, he elected to brave the open field instead of skirting through the cemetery. Running low through the wavy green wheat, he had almost reached the woods when he heard a distant crack of rifles, the buzz of a bullet, and an immediate searing pain pierced his right leg.

He pitched forward to the ground, his heart beating like a trip-hammer.

He lay still, a minute, maybe five minutes. Nothing happened. He began to inch his way forward. Finally, he slowly raised his head to gain his bearings.

He found himself staring down the barrels of several rifles. A solid ring of blue uniformed soldiers surrounded him. Germans.

He was a prisoner of war.

✈✈✈

Eaves' gaze locked on the two men running toward him. When they saw him, they stopped and called out, "*Americanski? Englaise?*"

He hesitated, not knowing whether they were friends or foes. Both wore dark woolen clothing; one clean-shaven, the other, who looked older, had a small mustache. He did not see weapons on them.

He shouted back, "American, I'm American." He scrambled to his feet and faced them squarely, trying not to grimace as he put weight on his knee.

They smiled broadly and strode up to him. The man with the mustache appeared to be middle-aged and approached first. He enveloped Eaves in a huge bear hug, almost lifting him off his feet, and kissed him on each cheek. "*Americanski!*"

The younger man also hugged him in the same manner, slapping him on the back and exclaiming again and again, "Americanski!"

Taken aback by their boisterous welcome and a bit bewildered as to how best to respond, he nodded and smiled.

Friends—they seemed to be friends.

Thank You, God.

The man with the mustache scanned the landscape, then pointed at the parachute and gestured with his hands for Eaves to bring it to the younger man, who held out his arms. Eaves obliged and looked back toward the older man.

Beckoning with his arm that Eaves should follow, the man set off at a brisk pace toward the edge of the wheat field, not looking back. Eaves clutched his flight suit, limping along on his injured knee.

Leaving the wheat field behind, they launched down a path into the woods. After weaving through the dark forest for about a quarter of a mile, they came to a clearing. Eaves saw a gray stone hut with a thatched roof and an old-fashioned wooden cart leaning against a small barn. The men and the house reminded him of something from the Middle Ages.

The older man pushed open the rough wooden door and spoke rapidly in a strange-sounding dialect that Eaves did not understand. He turned and motioned again for Eaves to follow him.

Eaves stepped through the narrow doorway and as his eyes adjusted to the dim light of the interior, he saw an elderly man with a gray mustache and bushy eyebrows standing before him.

"Welcome Americanski," he said with a smile as he also reached out to hug Eaves tightly and kiss him on each cheek.

Startled, Eaves stuttered, "You . . . speak English?"

The patriarch of the family nodded, smiling, as he held his thumb and forefinger an inch or so apart. "Ja, little. Some time ago visit family in America. When I return, war comes." He shrugged and pointed to a crudely made chair by a table that appeared to be made of hand-hewn planks. "Sit," he said as he turned and spoke rapidly to a middle-aged woman with a scarf over her head. Also dressed in rough dark clothing, she stood quietly behind them in the dimly-lit corner of the room.

Patting his chest, he introduced himself to Eaves, but the unusual combination of consonants and vowels mashed together in a jumble. Eaves did not try to repeat the sounds, just nodded and smiled. "Eaves," he said. "Lt. W.T. Eaves."

The woman returned with two large water glasses and filled them with an amber liquid from a small wooden cask, smiling shyly as she handed one to him and to the elderly man. Eaves eyed the glass and realized how thirsty he was.

"Drink," the man said as he raised his glass toward Eaves and took a huge gulp.

Eaves followed suit, and then choked and coughed as the strong drink burned inside. The men and the woman laughed, then nodded at him.

"*Rakija*," the old man said smiling. "We make, plums. *Rakija*—goot."

He spoke rapidly again to the woman, and she turned to open rough cupboard doors along the wall, pulling out plates and cloth-wrapped bundles.

"We honored you here," the older man said. He pointed to the south. "Germans, over mountain. Look for you." He frowned, spat on the floor. "Eat, be strong. Then . . . we go."

"Where are we going?" Eaves asked.

The older man just nodded and smiled, motioning for the younger men to join them at the table.

The woman brought plates to each of them containing a chunk of strong-smelling cheese, a few onions and a small crust of dark bread.

The patriarch spoke to the younger men, and they bowed their heads. He looked at Eaves. "We pray." Eaves bowed his head also.

"Thank You for food. Protect *Americanski*." He spoke in broken English, then continued in his own language before pronouncing, "Amen."

The men looked expectantly toward him, indicating that he should eat. It dawned on Eaves that they were waiting for him as their guest to take the first bite.

Eaves' stomach rolled as he looked at the plate before him. He had no appetite at all, but he had to respect the hospitality being offered him by these gracious people. And he needed nourishment to survive. So, he crunched on the dry bread, almost choked, and washed it down with more *rakija*.

Soon the spreading warmth in his belly helped the cheese and onions go down too, and he noticed his knee wasn't hurting as much either.

"You go now." The older man nodded to the two younger men, speaking rapidly. They rose and gathered some belongings.

Eaves recognized the word "Partisans."

"You have contact with the Partisans?" he asked.

"Ja. They help you."

These were the underground fighters he had been told to connect with. Thank God for landing here, with men who could lead him to these allies. Maybe this meant he'd soon find a way back to Italy.

Chapter 25

A LITTLE DISMAYED AND SAD to leave the only English-speaking person he had met, Eaves trudged behind the man with the mustache who strode rapidly along a rocky goat trail winding up into the mountains. They walked without speaking for about two hours. The younger man brought up the rear.

Eaves had rolled up his flight jacket and pants. Tying them with cords from the parachute, he made a backpack where he also strapped the bottle of water he'd been given, a blanket-sized piece of parachute material, and his emergency escape kit.

Gravel crunched beneath his boots.

Wonder where I am? And where we are going? Sure wish Haverkos was here with his knowledge of the area.

Concern for his men filled his mind before his thoughts turned to Jean and family.

Lord, please help her to somehow know I'm okay when she gets the missing in action telegram. Keep her spirits up, and the rest of the family's, too.

Thirst became his focus and his knee throbbed as the numbing effect of the *rakija* wore off. They came to a spring and stopped. When the older man squatted down on his haunches, Eaves realized it was time for a break. Gratefully, he sank down on a log.

The leader lifted his water bottle and drank deeply, pointing to Eaves to indicate he should drink also. Then he filled his bottle from the spring, motioning for Eaves to do the same. Immediately they started off again at the same pace.

The drone of an airplane pierced the crisp mountain air. The leader stopped and looked up, scanning the sky. He hissed in his guttural language. "*Švabo, Švabo!*"

Eaves' heart pounded in his chest. He recognized two German fighters to the north, heading their way. Probably surveillance, searching for the resistance fighters. Or . . . looking for him and the rest of the crew?

Signaling with his arm that Eaves should follow, the leader ran toward a rocky outcropping off the trail and squatted behind some huge granite boulders.

Eaves scrambled over the rocky terrain, boots sliding on the broken fragments. Scrunched against the boulder, the older man indicated Eaves should lie down in the hollow behind the rock. The younger man squeezed in beside them.

His breathing ragged, Eaves crouched low against the massive rock and prayed the Germans would not see them.

The whine of the oncoming planes changed and began fading away. Eaves warily raised up and peered over the rock. The planes had veered to the east. Something else had their attention. With the drone of the engines fading, the distant sound of gunfire split the air as the fighters strafed a ridge to the east.

Eaves breathed a sigh of relief, and the men slowly got to their feet. The older man spat on the ground, shook his fist toward the now distant planes, speaking strongly to the younger man, "*Švabo!*" Then he abruptly turned and stomped toward the trail.

They trudged ever upward for an hour before they reached a summit where snow still clung to the shaded areas along the path. Eaves gasped for breath, relieved to see the trail curving downhill. After another hour of following twisting turns with forks that led in various directions, the leader stopped and pointed at the mountainside ahead.

Eaves studied the mountain, puzzled at first, until he spotted it. A well-camouflaged stone house, two stories high, built into the cliff with a stone-slab roof.

"Partisans," the leader said. Then he yelled out something in his language, ending with "*Americanski.*"

Several young men and women in an array of dark clothing poured out of the building holding rifles. Eaves noticed that they each wore caps with a red star sewn on them. Surprised to see young women with rifles, he concluded they were evidently part of the Partisan fighting force. Some appeared very young, barely in their early teen years.

"*Americanski*," the leader yelled out again. The group rushed toward them, jabbering excitedly in their own language. Once again Eaves endured backbreaking hugs and kisses from the men, back slaps, and cries of "*Americanski*!"

Looking up, he noticed someone else walking out of the house who was dressed differently. A man in a flight suit.

He couldn't believe his eyes. Could it be? Dan Sherman, his copilot?

"Dan," he called out, a grin splitting his face. "Is that you?"

Sherman ran to him. They hugged briefly, clapping each other on the back.

"Man, you're a sight for sore eyes," Eaves said. "How did you get here?"

Sherman told him that his parachute landed by a family tending their sheep. They'd greeted him with hugs, gave him water and had him wait with them until they herded the sheep back to a small village. Two young Partisans escorted him here. They'd arrived a few hours ago.

Sherman filled him in on how all the crew had been helped to bail out. Fangman had been the most seriously wounded, barely conscious, and they put the ripcord in his hand as they pushed him out. They were elated when they saw the chute open.

"I just hope he was found by someone who could get him to medical care," Sherman said, concern edging his voice.

"Have you heard anything about the rest of the crew?"

Sherman shook his head. "No one here speaks English. The only words I recognize are *Americanski* and Partisan."

Eaves told him about the family patriarch he had met. "Amazing to meet someone who understood English. Only by the grace of God. Sure wish he had been able to come with us. Did you see any German reconnaissance planes?"

"No. Did you?"

Eaves told the story of the two German fighters in the mountains.

The Partisans had been conversing among themselves and now indicated by pointing that they wanted Eaves and Sherman to follow them back to the stone house.

Several rough tables and chairs filled the open room on the lower floor. Two older women came in dressed in dark woolen clothing. Both wore long skirts, short jackets with wide sleeves, and black kerchiefs tied under their chins. They carried large platters piled with chunks of what appeared to be a flat cornbread, surrounded by cooked turnips, and set them down on two of the tables.

A young man with piercing dark eyes, bushy black eyebrows and a scar on his cheek appeared to be the leader of the small group of Partisans. He indicated Eaves and Sherman should sit beside him at one of the tables.

The women quickly returned with glasses filled with an amber liquid. Eaves soon recognized more *rakija*, obviously a favorite beverage here in Yugoslavia.

The others stood back and watched as the Americans were encouraged with gestures to eat.

Eaves gratefully accepted the food, hunger clenching his gut. He bit into the flat cornbread. It was dry and hard, not the sweet cornbread his family baked back home in Texas. Coarsely ground cornmeal appeared to be glued together with a little water and he could hardly swallow it.

Eaves looked at Dan, and then washed the corn bread down with the *rakija*. His throat burned, but soon the familiar warmth spread through his body. Sherman followed suit, and they both ate some vegetables.

"This might be all the food they have. We better leave some for the rest of the group," Eaves said quietly to Sherman, who nodded in understanding.

When offered more, Eaves shook his head and then rubbed his stomach, "Mmmm," he smiled.

His host smiled and nodded, speaking rapidly and gesturing to the others to sit and partake, now that their guests had eaten. Soon the table was empty, even the crumbs carefully picked up and consumed.

Sudden shouting erupted outside the building. The young Partisans leaped to their feet, grabbed their guns, and headed for the door, jabbering rapidly in their language.

Pulse pounding, Eaves looked at Dan. "Germans?"

They both quickly rose to their feet, uncertain as to what the commotion was about and what they should do.

They moved toward the door. Then, a familiar cry pierced the air. "*Americanski*!"

They pulled open the door and peered outside. The sun was dropping behind the mountains. In the dim light, two young Partisan women with guns strode toward the group gathered in front of the house. As Eaves' eyes gradually adjusted to the twilight, he spotted someone else coming down the trail. A man in a flight suit.

Joy mixed with relief as he recognized Jim Elder, the flight engineer, his bloody bandage drooping over his forehead.

After being honored by the Partisans' now familiar greeting of hugs, kisses, and back-slapping, Eaves and Sherman made their way up to him. Elder appeared pale, looked exhausted.

"Are you okay, Jim?" Eaves reached out his hand to pat him on the shoulder.

Jim slowly nodded. "Yes, sir. Sorta rough getting here." He gave a rueful smile. "Luckily, I landed by a small village and they rushed out to help me. Seemed to want to get me out of the village as fast as possible, probably afraid the Germans would be looking for me. Rode in an oxcart covered up under some hay for quite a while, till we arrived at the hut where these two young women were."

He nodded toward the young girls with red stars on their caps. "They guided me here. Had to stop a few times along the way." He grimaced but then looked up at Eaves and Sherman with another smile. "You don't know how glad I am to see you two."

"Let's get you inside and check that wound." Eaves said. "Do you need some help?"

"No, sir. If I made it this far, I can make into the house," he said.

Soon they had Elder seated at the table and a young woman brought him a tall glass of *rakija*. Jim took a big drink, then sputtered.

"Drink it down, Jim. You'll feel better." Eaves laughed. "It's a plum brandy." Then he pulled out his emergency kit and prepared to remove the old dressing from Jim's head.

An older woman brought a simple oil lamp, a flat dish with oil and a wick, and set it on the table. Eaves smiled and nodded to her, thankful for the light.

The wound had drained into the dressing, and Jim winced as Eaves pulled off the blood-crusted gauze. The wound had jagged edges, a little red and angry-looking. Eaves washed it, sprinkled it with antiseptic powder, and applied a fresh bandage.

"Thanks, that feels better." Jim gingerly touched his forehead.

"I don't know how long we'll be here or what to expect, but we'd better take inventory of what we have," Eaves said. He pointed to his makeshift backpack. "Kept my flight suit and some parachute material. Thought I might need them for warmth. And I still have my emergency escape kit with the silk map, first aid supplies, compass, and a K-ration."

Elder had given the candy to the kids in the village, but he and Sherman both still had their emergency escape kits too. Sherman also had a K-ration tucked in a pant pocket.

"I think we better save the K-rations as long as we can," Eaves said.

Just then several young Partisans entered and stacked the other table and chairs in a corner of the room. One young woman removed the oil lamp from the table where Eaves, Elder, and Sherman sat, moving it to the fireplace mantle. The men stood and each grabbed a chair to help clear the room.

Two of the older women returned with arms filled with roughly woven woolen blankets and knitted wraps. They handed one to each of the airmen and their guides, smiling and bowing as they backed away.

One of the young men stoked the fire in the fireplace and placed extra wood in a wooden bin by the rough hearth. The leader pointed toward the area in front of the fire, indicating that it was time for their guests to lie down and rest for the night in the spot of honor by the fire.

The young Partisans pulled out blankets and found places around the room to lie down. Both men and women, like brothers and sisters, scattered about the room.

Eaves sank down onto the hard floor, pulling his backpack under his head, grateful for the warmth of the fire and the woolen blanket as coolness stole into the dark room.

Thank You, Lord, for shelter. And for these Partisans connecting me with Dan and Jim. Pray the rest of the crew joins us soon.

Slumber slipped over his frame, his last thoughts circling around what the morrow might bring.

✈✈✈

Sounds of movement awakened Eaves as the young Partisans scurried about the dark room. He stretched briefly, then turned toward Sherman and Elder. "Morning, guys. Looks like they start their day early. Guess we better gather our things together. How are you doing, Jim?"

"Helped to rest. Think I'm doing a little better today," he said.

They tried to return the blankets, but the young men shook their heads and pointed at their backpacks.

"Thank you," Eaves said, realizing they were to take the blankets with them.

"*Americanski*!"

Eaves turned. The Partisan leader gestured toward them and pointed to two young teens with rifles. The taller one had unruly dark brown hair poking out from under his cap, and the other, a little younger and scrawnier, had black hair and hawk-like eyes. He spoke briefly and the young men headed toward the door.

Apparently, they were their new guides. Picking up his backpack, Eaves followed them outside and the other two airmen trailed behind.

The sun had not peeked over the mountains yet. As they headed out into the clearing, Eaves turned to wave at the young Partisan leader. Standing like a sentinel outside the rock house and flanked by Eaves' former guides, he returned the greeting with a closed fist salute.

"Where do you think we're going?" Sherman asked, as they turned to follow the young men.

Eaves shrugged. "I don't know, but away from the Germans who are looking for us."

In the predawn light, Eaves pushed to keep up with the young men's pace, striding along single file on the rocky trail. Eaves' knee had stiffened up overnight and throbbed at first but gradually loosened up with the rhythmic action.

The path led upward, higher into the mountains. A wolf howl bounced eerily off the rocky cliffs. Startled, Eaves felt the hair on the back of his neck stand up. The young Partisan didn't waver or look back, just continued to stride along as the cry continued, twice, then three times.

Eaves hoped the wolves had other food in mind. The men drew a little closer together.

The path grew steeper as they climbed up, up, up. The sun rose in the early morning sky. A few small white clouds floated in an otherwise clear blue firmament. After about an hour, the leader stopped and pointed at some boulders, pulling out his water bottle. Eaves took a seat on a large flat rock, glad for a break. No apparent water source here. He was careful to take only a couple of swallows to conserve his supply.

The young Partisans stood alert, scanning the sky and listening, muttering to each other in their guttural language. Eaves remembered the fighter planes from yesterday. Must still be in territory patrolled by Germans.

After a brief rest, the group was off again. Their boots crunched on the rocky trail, with little birds trilling in the distance.

Eaves thought of home and remembered hiking up the little mountain behind Camp One in the early mornings, enjoying the quiet and the smell of the cedars. Solitude was a precious commodity when living with a big family.

Fondly he pictured each one—his father and stepmother, Levon and Lyall, Laverne and little Lou Ann, Ruth and Marcus. He imagined the scene when the telegram arrived. Missing in action—no way to know whether he was dead or alive. They'd pray, he was sure of that. He sighed. If only he could somehow send a message to them.

Steep climb again, the footpath always leading upward. His breath came hard now, muscles tight in his hamstrings, his boots heavier with each step. Stubby shrubs and boulders lined the trail. He glanced back. Elder was moving slowly and he stumbled once, but kept climbing.

Finally, a summit. A magnificent vista stretched out before them, a ribbon of a river winding through a green valley far below, more jagged mountains looming in the distance. His breath caught as he contemplated the expanse of the territory before them.

Their guides scanned the skies, then quickly moved on. No rest stop here, the area far too open. The trail started to wend downward through the boulders, toward the valley. The young men kept a fast pace, confidently choosing a path at each of the many forks in the trail. They didn't slow until they reached the tree line.

In a little grove, the leader finally stopped and searched the ground off the trail a bit to the left. Moving a dead limb, he uncovered a small spring, gurgling into a wooden trough. Again, Eaves appreciated the young men and their knowledge of the terrain. Fresh water. They would never have found it alone.

The Partisans squatted on their haunches, reached for their water flasks and took a big draught. Rummaging in their knapsacks, they pulled out chunks of dark bread and offered some to the Americans.

Gratefully, Eaves accepted the bread and chewed slowly on the hard tack, hoping to satiate the hunger ache in his gut. He and Elder perched on a log, while Sherman sat cross-legged on the ground.

"You guys doing okay?" Eaves asked.

Sherman nodded. "Little stiff from the landing yesterday, but sure glad we found each other. What luck, falling into the hands of the very underground fighters we were told to look for."

Elder looked a little pasty, his bandage drooped just above his eyes, but it was not crusted with blood. "I know I'm slow, but I keep putting one foot in front of the other. Any idea how much farther we have to go?"

Eaves shook his head. He wondered that himself. Nothing in sight looked like a destination.

After they refilled their water bottles, they were back on the trail heading down toward the green valley they had viewed from above. Several hours passed before the sun dropped behind the mountains to the west. The young men slowed. Eaves noticed they seemed to be searching for something.

The older one pointed at a mark on a tree, and after rapid words with his companion, he motioned for the Americans to wait. He disappeared into the forest.

Within a few minutes he returned, and with a big smile, nodded to his compadre. Motioning the American to follow, they wound through the forest to a limestone cliff. Climbing up a short rocky trail in the fading light, they arrived at the dark mouth of a cave, partially hidden by a large boulder.

The young Partisans ducked down to enter the cave, stopping to wave for the Americans to follow them. As Eaves straightened up inside, musky, damp air greeted his nostrils and in the dim light he surveyed a large room nature had carved into the limestone. This must be their home for the night.

After sharing a few small pieces of dried meat, the young men pulled out their blankets and rolled over, keeping their rifles close at their side. They lit no fire.

Elder rubbed his eyes. "Reminds me of my first Boy Scout camping trip. We slept in a cave. Spiders were my biggest worry."

Eaves's body ached from exhaustion. "In Texas caves, it's rattlesnakes we worry about. Wonder if they have snakes here?" He nodded at the Partisans. "Our guides don't seem worried, so guess I won't worry either." He yawned as he shook out his blanket and pulled his pack under his head.

Light faded from the cave entrance and a pitch-black darkness surrounded them. Exhausted from a long day of walking, all five men were soon fast asleep on the rocky floor.

✈✈✈

Faint light filtered through the cave opening. Eaves slowly opened his eyes, his body stiff and cramped from sleeping on the hard, cold floor of the cave. Turning his head, he saw the older teen was gone, the younger one rolling up his blanket.

Sherman sat up and stretched his arms overhead. "Looks like the day starts early again," he said.

"Yep, let's move it." Eaves got up and repacked his bed roll.

The young teen set his red star cap on his head at a jaunty angle and gestured for the Americans to follow him outside. In the fresh morning air, the other Partisan stood waiting, with his gun slung over his shoulder. He led them back down the steep narrow path from the cave. As they reached the main trail sprawling downward through the forest, he put his finger to his lips, indicating a need to be quiet. Motioning them to follow, he strode away.

Hmm . . . could be other ears in this territory? Eaves adjusted his backpack and stepped out behind him.

The black-haired teen dropped back as a rear guard.

Moments later the shriek of a hawk cut through the clear air, as powerful wings lifted the raptor off a dead tree branch just above their heads. Other bird calls echoed through the woodland as they trudged along.

The forest sounds soothed Eaves' spirit as he savored the peaceful aura of the dark woods. Warm morning sunlight shone down in patches on the trail and his shoulders relaxed.

Time marched on, with a short break about midmorning, and a longer break with another chunk of dark bread around midday when the sun was high overhead.

After walking another hour, they came out of the woods into a clearing with a primitive road running through it.

A sign of civilization at last.

But the leader abruptly stopped and gestured for the airmen to sit down. He spoke quietly to the younger teen, who disappeared into the brush on their left. After about ten minutes he reappeared and conferred in a normal tone with his partner. Apparently satisfied that it was safe, their guides stepped forward onto the road and motioned the Americans to follow them.

Eaves pulled out his compass and noticed they continued to head northward. Within minutes, he heard the gurgle of rushing water. As they walked around a bend, a river on their right swirled over boulders and out of its banks, with small shrubs and trees bending in the powerful force of the muddy spring run-off.

The road followed the twists and turns of the river. An hour passed, then two. Still, they walked on. Sometimes the young Partisans would stop, listen, and examine the sky.

At a huge stump, the leader halted the group. He squeezed through some bushes on the right side of the road, tramping back and forth slowly, his eyes searching the ground. Then he turned and motioned for the men to follow.

A faint trail ran through the trees and brush, emerging along the riverbank. They arrived at a spot where the river slowed and broadened. Logs had jammed together to form a small dam, creating a wide pond. Tall bushes grew on each side of the river.

The teens seemed to be looking for something along the bank.

The sound of a motor echoed through the forest.

Eaves sucked in his breath, his heart thudding in his chest. Only the Germans would have vehicles out here.

Ducking down, the Partisans scurried behind some larger clumps of brush and flattened to the earth, pulling their rifles off their shoulders. Eaves and the other two airmen dropped to a prone position, wiggling into a dip out of sight of the road. Eaves drew his pistol.

The sounds grew louder. Eaves recognized the roar of a truck motor, laboring up the road they'd just left. Faint sounds of voices and the tromp of many feet. The truck moved toward them, a cloud of dust revealing its path through the forest.

A German patrol. Maybe looking for food. Or looking for us.

Lord, help us!

He realized he was holding his breath and forced himself to breathe through his nose. Time seemed suspended, each second like an hour.

A loud order rang out. The truck ground to a halt just past them. A jumble of German voices could be heard.

Would their fresh tracks give them away?

Chapter 26

30 May 1944—Zagreb, Yugoslavia

HAVERKOS HEARD THE CLANK of keys in the jail cell door. Two German soldiers roughly shoved another airman into the cell and slammed the door shut. The man lay crumpled on the cell floor.

"Christel, is that you?" He stared in amazement at his friend. "Are you okay?"

Christel grimaced as he opened his eyes. "Tore something in my foot when I landed. Was trying to get out of the parachute when these goons appeared."

Haverkos jumped up and reached out a hand to him, balancing on his good leg. "Here, let me help you. I took a slug in my right leg, but it's just a flesh wound. The Krauts wrapped it up."

He grasped Haverkos' hand, pulled hard to get on his feet and then hobbled over to the bunk. Haverkos saw the Germans had taken Christel's belt and boots, just like they'd taken his.

"Any word on the rest of the crew?" Christel asked, breathing hard as he sat down.

Haverkos shook his head. "You and I were the first ones out. Just hope the others landed farther up in the mountains and were able to get away." He patted Christel on the back. "Glad to see you again buddy, but just wish we weren't in this jail."

Christel nodded, a grim look on his face. "Wonder if we can get word to our families. My mother will worry herself sick when she gets that telegram saying I'm missing in action." He chewed on his lip and looked down at the concrete floor. "You know, before we flew yesterday, I swung by the dispensary to see Linneman. Told him I just didn't have a good feeling about this mission. If we didn't make it back, I asked him to write a letter to my mother and tell her I'd be okay. And that I'll make it home, somehow. Sure hope he keeps that promise."

Ginny's sweet face crossed Haverkos's mind.

How would she take the news? Would he ever see her again?

He focused back on the reality before them. "Remember—only name, rank, and serial number. And they get pretty ugly when you stick with it. They tried the friendly approach first, a Kraut who spoke English pretty well." His jaw tightened. "The bayonet in your back doesn't feel good, but it could get worse, I'm sure."

The eerie wail of an air-raid siren abruptly cut off the conversation. They heard the guards shouting.

"Listen." Haverkos cocked his head.

The drone of bomber engines grew closer.

"Those are ours. Bombers." His eyes widened. "I saw the railroad yards only a block away from the jail. Bet that's their target."

"Sweet Mother of Jesus." Christel pulled out his rosary, bowed his head and began to pray.

Haverkos peered through the cell window. B-17s covered the sky above.

Ack-ack guns began to fire. A crescendo of rhythmic thumps escalated into a frenzy, heaving flack heavenward toward the oncoming silver bombers.

The hum of many bombers swelled like the buzz of a thousand angry bees.

Screaming bombs rained down. The ground shook violently as an incredible blast showered rocks and debris on the cell window. Haverkos covered his head with his arms, heart pounding, and prayed.

Lord, please help them be accurate. If ever those bombs needed to be in the pickle barrel, it's today. Protect our bombers too.

The anti-aircraft batteries kept firing. Blast after blast numbed their ears. The earth quaked beneath them.

Haverkos counted at least three bomb groups passing overhead, any moment expecting to breathe his last. Thirty-six bombers per group, an arsenal of firepower falling on the marshalling yards a hairsbreadth away.

He remembered Chaplain Eastwood, always praying for those on the ground in harm's way who were God's own.

That's us, Lord. Please—keep us safe.

✈✈✈

Twigs snapped. Someone was walking toward them. Eaves peered through the brush. A young German soldier stopped behind a tree. Taking off his rifle, he leaned it against the trunk. He took a long swig of water from his canteen before undoing his belt and dropping his pants.

Maybe just a rest break. Relief flooded through Eaves, and his breathing slowed slightly as the soldier stood, tightened his belt and picked up his rifle. He turned to stride back toward the road.

Minutes passed. Another loud command. The truck roared to life and the patrol moved on down the road. Moments felt like hours before the sound of the truck motor faded in the distance.

But for the grace of God, it could have been so different.

Eaves sighed as he stood and brushed the debris off his clothing.

"Whew—that was close." Sherman picked up his backpack. "Lucky that we'd just moved off the road."

Elder looked up at them. "You can say that again."

Eaves noticed how the injured man grimaced as he struggled to his feet.

Hope it isn't too much farther before we can stop for food and rest.

The young guides walked back and forth along the river, searching the ground. Suddenly they jabbered with excitement as they scrambled down a steep bank and motioned the airmen to follow.

Standing on a shelf of limestone, Eaves saw the opening to a small cave, partially covered by piled brush. The Partisans pulled the brush back to reveal a wooden rowboat and oars. Their smiles showed relief.

So, they did have a plan for crossing the river. The boat looked small, holding three people at best.

The young men lifted it into the river, the leader stepping in at the back. He pointed at Eaves and Elder, indicating that they should get in and sit on the rough plank at the front of the boat.

Scanning the sky one last time, the young man rowed out into the river. He bent his back, dipping the blades deep into the water and pulling firmly on the oars. Stronger than he looked, he rapidly covered the distance to the other side. Depositing Eaves and Elder on the far shore, he returned to pick up Sherman and the younger teen.

After pulling the boat onto the shore and covering it with brush, the Partisans strode up the hill and into the forest. Another half hour passed before the trail ended at the edge of a small clearing. A thatched-roof cottage, small barn and a garden stood before them, a few goats in the barnyard.

The leader stopped and whistled three times. Hearing an echoing whistle, he stepped into the clearing as a family poured out the doorway. A middle-aged couple stood before them smiling. Two young girls peered out from behind their mother's dark skirt.

"*Americanski*," the young Partisan exclaimed, and then continued speaking in his guttural language. He appeared to know these people.

After welcoming hugs and kisses all around, the man Eaves guessed to be the father stepped aside and motioned the airmen into his home.

Soon the Americans were seated at the family table with the father and the young Partisans. A simple oil lamp with a wick flickered in the center of the table. Odors of cooked cabbage and onions wafted from the pot over the fire. Eaves' mouth filled with saliva as the tantalizing odors revealed how ravenous he was.

The matron of the family served them each a wooden bowl containing a maize porridge with vegetables. And more *rakija*. The girls perched on their stools, watching as the men ate. Then the mother brought the pot to the table and pointed at Eaves' bowl with her ladle.

They haven't eaten yet.

He covered his bowl with his hand before saying "Thank you," as he nodded and rubbed his stomach. "Mmmm."

Under her kerchief, the mother smiled and nodded. She seemed happy that he appreciated her efforts.

The men rose from the table, and the Partisans helped the father move the two long wooden benches to spots along the wall. The girls each pulled a small stool up to the table as the mother divided the remaining porridge into three smaller bowls. Each child also received a small cup of milk, probably from the goats.

When the family had finished eating, the mother cleared the table. The father bent over to speak softly to the oldest daughter, who appeared to be nine or ten. She disappeared into the bedroom and then returned, shyly edging forward as she pulled out a hand-carved flute from behind her skirt. Putting it to her lips, she played a haunting tune. Her father smiled broadly and tapped his toe.

Eaves pictured his little sister Lou Ann in his mind and the lilting melodies she played on the recorder she brought home from school. A sudden mist filled his eyes. He looked down and blinked. Turning his head, he noticed Sherman listening intently with his head cocked, Elder with a smile on his face. How long had it been since music touched their ears?

As the last note faded, the Americans clapped.

"Bravo," Sherman said.

The little girl flushed and smiled, lifting her skirt to curtsy before darting behind her mother again.

The father conversed with the young Partisans and they began to unroll their bedding on the family room floor. Then, he gestured toward the bedroom off to the right and pointed at the airmen.

Not wanting to insult their hosts, Eaves nodded and smiled, moving through the doorway.

"I'll bunk on the floor," said Sherman, eyeing the one double bed in the room.

"Me too. Elder, you take the bed. You need rest to be able to travel again tomorrow." Eaves shook out his blanket.

"Yes sir," Elder said without protest, exhaustion showing on his face as he sank down onto the bed. He looked up at them. "Not grandmother's feather bed," he said with a chuckle. "But better than the floor. Thanks."

Eaves looked out the window in the twilight to see the father and mother carrying blankets and entering the small barn, the little ones following them.

This family had given up their bed, shared their food and music with us. His eyes glistened as he contemplated their generosity and courage. They would pay with their lives if the Germans discovered them hiding and abetting the airmen.

Protect these kind people and bless them, Lord, as they have blessed us.

Chapter 27

4 June 1944—Zagreb, Yugoslavia

Bombed-out ruins lined the streets, torn buildings revealing sheared off rooms like cells of a honeycomb. The Germans marched Haverkos and a small group of American officers through the rubble toward the railroad yards. The screech of brakes and chug of locomotives told him the railways were back in operation. He was amazed at how quickly the Germans had managed to use conquered slave labor to reconnect the lines.

Wonder where they are sending us?

He wished he knew how Christel was doing. The morning after the Allied bomb raid, the Krauts had taken Christel out of their cell, and he had not returned. Haverkos realized the Germans separated enlisted men from officers, so he wasn't totally surprised.

Just hope the little guy is holding up okay.

A German soldier shoved Haverkos toward a ramp leading into an open boxcar door. Inside the dark car, the putrid stench of urine and other foul odors caused him to gag. The car was already full of captured airmen, packed so tightly he and the new men squeezed in shoulder to shoulder as the door slammed shut. Men muttered curses and groans as the train lurched into action, throwing them against each other. No room to even sit down.

"How long have you been in here?" Haverkos asked the man in front of him.

"Two days. Captured in Romania. And we spent the last twelve hours stalled on the tracks."

"Any idea where they're taking us?"

"One of the guys who speaks a little German overhead them say something about *Dulag Luft*. Heard it's the interrogation center close to Frankfurt where they grill us to get every scrap of information they can before shipping us to a POW camp. Think we might be there in a day or two." He paused, then cleared his throat. "That is, unless we get strafed by B-25s. They don't know what the Krauts might be hauling."

Haverkos digested his words, the cold reality of the situation sending a chill down his spine.

✈✈✈

Eaves awoke to scraping sounds and low voices drifting through the wall in the cool darkness. Morning had come early.

He lay for a moment with his eyes closed, listening to Elder's light snoring and deep breathing coming from Sherman. He'd slept hard, but startled awake with dreams of black flak clouds blossoming into orange/red bursts and a German fighter diving toward his plane, guns blazing.

Jean's sweet face flashed before his eyes.

Keep her safe and help us get home soon, please Lord.

Stiff from sleeping on the hard floor, he forced himself to sit up in the semi-darkness, stretching his arms above his head, and then twisting side to side.

"Hey, guys, time to rise and shine," he said quietly as he shook out his blanket and rolled it tightly. Opening his emergency escape kit, he took out the candy and stuffed it in his pocket.

Sherman rolled over. "It's still dark," he protested. Elder just groaned.

"Our hosts are already stirring." He strapped up his pack. "I'll go see what's up."

Shouldering the backpack, he pulled open the bedroom door. The young Partisans were seated at the table with the father speaking softly, the mother stirring something in a black pot over the fire. Warmth drew him into the room, and the aroma of food made his mouth water. They smiled and nodded to him, pointing to the empty chair at the table.

As he seated himself and placed the pack at his feet, the woman ladled a yellowish-colored mush into four bowls and began to serve them. Eaves smiled his thanks, and picked up the hand-carved wooden spoon.

Hmm . . . reminds me of grits back home. A quick prayer wafted upward.

Thank you for food, Lord.

Gratefully, he dug in, hunger making every bite of the maize mush taste good. He washed it down with a warm tea-like beverage that she set before him.

Eaves had just finished eating when Elder and Sherman entered the room. He and the Partisans stood. "Here, take our seats," he said.

As the airmen ate, the young Partisans picked up their belongings. They pulled out their water bottles and the mother filled them from a goatskin bag. She looked at Eaves, so he pulled out his water bottle too. After she filled it, she turned to wrap a chunk of goat cheese in a cloth and handed it to one of the young men.

Obviously, they were preparing to travel again.

"Let's head out men," Eaves said as soon as Elder and Sherman finished eating their mush. Each one grabbed their bedding and filled their water flasks, heaving the makeshift packs to their shoulders.

Just then the two little girls poked their heads in the door. They moved toward their mother with braids that needed combing, rubbing sleepy eyes.

Eaves smiled at them and dug into his pocket. He held out the candy. "For you," he said.

They smiled shyly and their eyes brightened, but they stood rooted in place as they first looked at their father. He nodded and waved them forward. The older girl grabbed her little sister's hand and stepped closer. She timidly reached up to accept the offering. They curtsied their thanks but quickly retreated behind their mother's skirts.

Eaves wondered how long it had been since they last enjoyed a sweet treat. War and poverty, such a sad combination.

The father smiled broadly, speaking softly to his daughters, and then repeating "*Americanski*" as he administered the now-expected bear hugs and kisses on each airman.

"Thank you," Eaves said, as he tried to communicate his heartfelt appreciation with his voice and his eyes. Stepping out the door, he turned to wave goodbye to the family before hustling across the clearing to catch up with the group just as the sun peeked over the mountains.

Another day on the move, going to who knows where.

✈✈✈

JUNE 1944 – GALVESTON, TEXAS

Just looking at the blue star in the window tangled Jean's emotions. Her heart burned with pride in her man and the important work he performed for his country. But then a finger of fear knifed into her heart. Her anxiety and apprehension increased as he flew mission after mission in the cold blue skies over Europe.

Jean couldn't read the news of the war anymore. The long lists of names of local young men not returning, the number of planes lost that month. She cringed at the sight of new gold stars appearing in windows for young men who would never come home.

As she reached for the door knob, she whispered the prayer repeated so many times daily.

Please watch over him Lord. Keep him safe and bring him home soon.

"Hi Mom. I'm home." Jean opened the front door and shut it firmly against the constant Galveston wind. "Any mail today for me?" She looked hopefully toward her mother who was settled into the blue rocker in the front room.

The little brown dog leaped off the couch and ran to Jean, his tail beating the air. Jean bent down to give him a pat. "Hi Ricky. Good dog."

Ollie's dark eyes reflected the sadness that now filled her voice. "No, honey. Nothing again today."

Jean's stomach lurched. No word. It wasn't like Red. No mail now for weeks when he'd been so faithful to write every day or every other day.

"Oh, Mom. I'm so worried. We should be hearing something by now." She slumped down on the couch and pulled the little dog into her arms.

"Now, now," her mother reached over to pat her knee. "You know how the mail is in wartime. Sometimes it comes in clumps." Ollie leaned back thoughtfully. "God is faithful and keeps His promises. We just have to keep praying." After a moment, she asked, "How did the drive for aluminum foil and cooking oil go at the church?"

"Good. We had fifteen volunteers helping make posters and a lot of people have already donated." She looked up, absentmindedly scratching behind the little dog's ears. "I'm glad we can do something to help." Tears filled her eyes. "I just wish the war was over. I miss him so much."

"I know, sweetheart. But the Lord is good to help us. He promises to not give us more than we can bear in His strength."

Jean nodded. "I know. I shouldn't complain. I'm so blessed to have Red in my life."

A knock interrupted their conversation. Jean watched her mother open the door. Two men in military uniforms stood on the porch. Her breath caught in her throat, the scene etched upon her heart. She pushed Ricky off her lap and rose to her feet.

Oh no! Please, it can't be! Not my Red!

"Yes, she's here. Please, come in." Her mother said quietly as she motioned them into the living room. She walked over to put her arm around Jean.

Tucking his cap under his arm, the young officer's blue eyes held pain. "I'm sorry to have to bring this news, Mrs. Eaves," he said as he held a telegram toward her. Moving as if in a dream, she stretched out a trembling hand to receive it.

Her quivering fingers had difficulty opening the envelope. Her eyes filled with tears as the words blurred in front of her.

MISSING IN ACTION.

She leaned against her mother for support, her knees wobbly. "He's missing in action," she whispered as she sank down on the couch. Ricky whined and laid his head on her knee.

She sobbed quietly as her mother thanked the young men for coming and walked with them to the door. Ollie leaned against the door as she shut it behind them, tears now sliding down her cheeks.

After a few moments, her mother raised her head. "Honey, we don't know for sure what has happened to Red." She pulled a handkerchief out of her pocket, wiped her eyes and blew her nose. "We will just keep praying, and trust God to care for him."

Jean looked at her mother through a fog of tears.

What if he is gone? I can't bear it. Oh Lord, help me!

✈✈✈

June 1944—Iraan, Texas

Lyall watched out the window as the black car pulled up in front of their home in Camp One and a man in uniform stepped out.

"Daddy, there's an Army guy walking up toward our house," Lyall called out to his father.

Tom Eaves finished drying his hands and hung up the towel before stepping into the front room, his dark face a frozen mask.

Tom opened the door after the knock. The young officer looked in his eyes and took a deep breath.

"Tom Eaves?" he asked.

Tom nodded.

"This telegram is for you." The young officer extended his arm, an envelope in his hand. "I'm really sorry, sir." He abruptly turned and walked back to the car.

Tom shut the door and tore open the envelope. He silently read the message. His hand holding the telegram dropped slowly to his side as he gazed blankly straight ahead. Tears began to roll down his leathery cheeks.

Shocked, Lyall stared at his father. He had never seen his daddy cry.

Chapter 28

6 JUNE 1944—DULAG LUFT, FRANKFORT, GERMANY

THE RAILROAD CAR SHUDDERED TO A HALT. German voices could be heard outside before the door slid open.

The sudden glare of sunlight was blinding after being in almost total darkness for two days. Haverkos closed his eyes briefly and then squinted at the blue uniformed soldier pointing a rifle at him and waving it toward the ground, shouting commands at him in German.

He moved toward the open doorway and jumped down into the gravel, stumbling and falling to his knees when he hit the ground. Immediately he felt a gun poking into his back and heard more yelling. He staggered to his feet and soon was lined up with several other prisoners in a group of ten officers, marched in pairs away from the train toward a truck idling by the tracks.

A group of townspeople stared at them with open hostility, some with shovels and pitchforks in their hands.

Haverkos could see the effects of Allied bombing all around him, the town in almost total ruins. He'd heard stories of airmen killed by civilians with pitchforks after bailing out over Germany.

Men at the front of the group yelled and brandished their weapons as they advanced toward them.

Haverkos' heart pounded in his chest. He averted his eyes and looked toward the ground, not wanting to appear arrogant and insensitive to their loss.

"Don't look at them, guys. Look down," he said quietly.

Suddenly a German *Luftwaffe* officer stepped in front of the prisoners and gave a loud command. Murmuring, the people halted briefly but then started toward the Americans again. The officer uttered another loud command. All the soldiers guarding the prisoners turned their guns toward the townspeople. He obviously had ordered them to halt, the threat of gunfire enforcing his orders.

The angry townspeople stopped in their tracks. After a moment's hesitation, still muttering, they slowly dispersed, some shaking their fists at the airmen and shouting angry words.

Haverkos took a deep breath and he slowly looked up. Again, his life had been spared by the enemy, an officer of honor not allowing helpless POWs to be slaughtered by an angry mob. A rush of gratitude, then a reluctant feeling of respect surprised him. Not what he expected to feel toward his captors—even if possible information was the only inducement for mercy, information he was determined not to give.

✈✈✈

June 1944—Galveston, Texas

Rap, rap, rap. "Jean, get up. It's time for breakfast."

Jean's swollen eyelids fluttered open, her mother's voice faintly calling from far away. Dimly, she realized her mother was knocking on the door to her room.

Must have finally dozed off, after sobbing until she had no more tears, tossing and turning through the long night. Another day of not knowing what had happened to Red.

She forced herself to answer. "Okay, Mother. I'm coming."

She swung her legs over the edge of the bed and reached for her housecoat. Pulling it on over her blue nightgown, she opened the door and padded down the hall to the bathroom. Sighing, she splashed water on her face and brushed at her hair before walking down the hall to the kitchen.

"Good morning, sweetheart. How did you sleep?" Her mom stood by the stove, bacon sizzling in the pan. A rare treat.

Jean just shook her head. "Not well, I'm afraid. Tossed and turned most of the night." She had no appetite but obediently sat down at the table, already set for two. Her father always left early for work.

Her mother took the skillet off the burner and ladled the bacon onto a platter heaped with scrambled eggs and toast. Carrying it to the table, she placed it between them and sat down across from her daughter. Looking deep into Jean's dark eyes, she reached out for her daughter's hand and cradled it in her own.

"Honey, I know Red is okay," she said with a huge smile.

Jean's eyes widened. "How could you know that? Did another telegram come?"

"No. But last night the Lord showed me in a dream." She leaned forward, looking intently at Jean. "I saw Red and another airman huddled in some bushes while the Germans marched by on the road. The Germans didn't see them." She paused, then spoke with confidence. "I know he is still alive and hiding from the Germans somewhere."

Jean stared deep into her mother's warm brown eyes. Her mother had dreams from the Lord that proved true before. Could it be?

Her mother continued. "We just have to trust and believe. Every day we'll pray for protection for Red and his men, and for provision of food and shelter until they can make it back home." Her mother bowed her head and squeezed Jean's hand as she prayed aloud.

"Thank You for letting us know Red is okay, Lord. Help him and his men to stay safe and to evade the enemy. Protect them and provide all they need. Please send people to aid them and heal any of the men that need Your healing touch. Thank You for this food and for Your presence with us and with them. You are so good! In Jesus' name. Amen."

A rush of peace flowed over Jean's heart as her mother lifted her voice in earnest prayer.

Yes, I think it is true. Thank You, Lord. I trust You.

She would choose to believe and pray.

Chapter 29

June 1944—somewhere in Yugoslavia

EAVES GRIMACED. HIS BOOTS were rubbing a huge blister on his heel. Not made for hiking these rugged mountain trails.

"Hawk" was leading the way again. Eaves had decided to give their Partisan guides each a nickname, and the older teen was observant, quick in his decisions, definitely the leader here. He sent "Scout" out on patrol, checking the terrain and searching out trails, a quiet shadow who appeared and disappeared.

Eaves looked up. Cirrus clouds streaked the blue sky, the sun hot overhead. He wiped the sweat from his brow and wrinkled his nose at the rank odor his filthy clothes emitted.

Been on this trek a week now. Sure wish we could shower.

The rocky trail bent downward again, weaving through another forested area. Hawk stopped, eyeing the fork in the trail briefly before choosing the fainter path to the right. For another half hour, they trudged along a shaded path through the trees. Then the forest opened to a valley, with a stream flowing along limestone cliffs.

Hawk strode to some boulders lining the creek. He looked around carefully, seemed relaxed here. After waving Scout off to the north, he threw down his pack and began removing his clothes. He smiled at the airmen and then jumped off a boulder into a deep blue pool.

"Hey, guys, it's bath time!" Eaves laughed out loud, as he quickly followed suit. Stripping to his skivvies, he leaped in. The plunge into the cool water was refreshing and stimulating, the pool deeper than he first thought. Popping up, he flipped over on his back and paddled gently, sucking in his breath as the water brought a sharp sting to his blistered heel.

"Bombs away!"

Splash! Eaves sputtered as he jerked upright to wipe the water from his eyes.

Sherman laughed. "Had to do that cannonball. Sorry, Red."

Soon all four guys were whooping and hollering as they splashed water on each other. Even Hawk seemed to be enjoying the fun.

After the horseplay subsided, Eaves waded to a shallower section of the river. He rubbed some sand over his body as a kind of scouring agent and reveled in the tingling feeling of clean it evoked.

Climbing onto the bank, he picked up his uniform. Carefully emptying his pockets, he stopped to gaze at Jean's lovely face for a moment before placing the treasured photo in his pack. He wished he had some soap as he pulled the uniform into the water to scrub it. After ringing it out as best he could, he hung it on bushes to dry.

Glancing up river, far in the distance he spotted someone in the water. Must be Scout, probably bathing too. He waved at him.

He dried off using the silk parachute material he'd saved and lay down on a boulder to soak in some rays from the sun.

"Didn't know water could feel so good," Elder commented. He had washed out his flight suit too and stretched out across from Eaves, enjoying the warm sun.

Soon they all dozed from the exertion and the relaxing warmth. Time seemed to stand still.

Suddenly Scout broke through bushes along the creek and ran toward them. He jabbered rapidly to Hawk in their guttural tongue, fear etched on his face. Hawk's face turned ashen as he leaped up and began throwing on his clothes.

"*Švabo! Švabo!*" he exclaimed.

Eaves recognized that word from the day the German fighter plane came at them. Germans! He jumped up, his heart pounding as he struggled to pull on his still-damp flight suit. "Move it, boys. I guess that guy I waved at wasn't Scout—must have been a Nazi."

He scooped up his backpack and boots, following Scout to the edge of the woods before stopping to pull them on.

Hawk raced back to the trail they'd been on before and the airmen struggled to keep up. This time at the fork he took the path to the left, back into the forest, and he pressed on quickly toward the mountains.

The trail wound continuously upward, and Eaves' breath grew more labored. His calves ached. After about an hour, Hawk finally slowed the pace. Stopping in a clearing, he searched intently and chose an almost obscure trail along the mountainside. Soon they scrambled over rocky crags and around massive boulders.

Moments later they arrived at another limestone cave, bushes nearly covering the dark entrance. Following Hawk, they crouched to crawl into the dank hole in the cliff.

Hawk pulled off his backpack and squatted on the cave floor.

Eaves slumped to the ground, exhausted. He slipped off his boots, relieving the pressure on his blister.

"Where would we be without Hawk and Scout?" he said to Sherman, who nodded.

"They sure know the trails around here. Thank God for that," he answered.

Scout pulled out the cloth-wrapped goat cheese. He divided it into five small chunks and fished out a few dark crusts of bread that he shared with the airmen. Not much, but it eased the hunger pangs.

Again, they lit no fire, and as daylight faded, each curled up in their blankets on the cave floor.

Eaves dozed fitfully through the night—one eye on the cave entrance, his gun close by his hand.

✈✈✈

Eaves' eyes popped open. What was that strange snuffling sound? Peering through the semi-darkness, he saw Scout gutting a small animal. Looking closer, he saw it was a rabbit. Saliva moistened his mouth. How long had it been since they'd eaten meat?

Scout pulled dry moss and twigs from his backpack and piled them in a firepit which had obviously seen use before. Using a primitive flint stone, he fanned a spark into a small flame. After adding larger branches, he patiently sat back and waited for the blaze to die down.

They must be feeling pretty safe if they felt free to light a fire.

Eaves got up and sat down beside him.

Scout nodded and smiled a welcome. He pulled out his knife and tapered the end of a green branch. Inserting the sharpened stick through the carcass, he waited till the coals glowed bright and then suspended the rabbit between two rocks.

One by one the other men came to crouch around the small firepit. The flames painted shadows on the cave walls. Eaves basked in the warmth and inhaled the tantalizing odors. All seemed transfixed by the sizzling morsel roasting on the skewer that Scout occasionally turned. Not much for five guys, but he could almost taste the warm flesh.

Thank You, Lord, for these young men and their survival skills.

Hawk presided over the carving of their breakfast, handing each man a small chunk of rabbit meat.

Eaves nodded his thanks and bit in, chewing slowly to savor each delicious bite. Sucking on the bone, he licked his fingers. "Delicious!"

"Didn't know food could taste so good," Elder agreed.

Soon they were back on the trail, climbing higher into the hills. Hawk sent Scout on ahead. He seemed more relaxed, stopping for a long break by another spring that gurgled out of the mountainside.

The wind came up, whipping the trees and pushing the airmen along the trail. Large cumulous clouds rushed across the sky. When the sun was high overhead, Hawk stopped in the shade by three large boulders at the edge of a clearing. He squatted on his haunches, and indicated the airmen should sit. He kept watching the trail leading across the meadow. Time passed, but he seemed in no hurry to move on. Suddenly he cocked his head as a bird call rang out through the wind.

Hawk stood and repeated the plaintive whistle.

Eaves squinted. A dark form moved in the trees on the other side. Scout stepped out into the clearing, and three other dark forms followed.

Partisans. Eaves could see the identifying red stars on their caps, each man with a rifle on his shoulder.

Hawk stood and raised his fist in salute, then motioned for Eaves and his men to follow him across the meadow. The new group of Partisans and Hawk jabbered rapidly, the only familiar word being "*Americanski*." The now expected hugs and kisses of greeting followed.

A slender young man who looked to be in his early twenties, dark-haired with a neatly trimmed mustache, seemed to be in charge of the small band. He turned and led the group a short way into the forest, halting in a shaded grove. He pointed, indicating that they should all be seated and spoke quickly to his comrade, a shorter man with a thick black beard and bushy mustache. The man pulled a loaf of dark bread and dried chunks of meat from his pack. He offered food to the airmen first, and then to all the others.

Silence reigned, as each man eagerly consumed the food.

"Goot," the leader said as he rubbed his stomach and looked at Eaves.

"Yes," Eaves said, surprised at this communication. "Thank you." He smiled and nodded his thanks.

The leader bobbed his head. "*Americanski, Americanski,*" he stated, and then pointed toward the north.

Eaves gasped. "Hey, I think he is trying to tell us there are more Americans up ahead!"

Sherman's eyes lit up. "Well, that's the best news we've had for a while!"

"Just wondering . . . how far up ahead?" Elder said a little dubiously.

Hawk and Scout gathered their things and stood. Eaves realized this was goodbye. They were going back now, their part of the journey completed.

Eaves stood up and stuck out his hand, "You may not understand a word I say, but we thank you from the bottom of our hearts." He grabbed each man's hand and shook it up and down, then gave them each a bear hug. Sherman and Elder followed suit.

The young men smiled and nodded, accepting the appreciation being expressed. Hawk faced the Partisan leader, raising his arm in a fist salute, then turned and crossed back over the meadow, with Scout scurrying behind.

"Going to miss those guys," Eaves said. Sherman nodded.

The new Partisan leader swung his rifle over his shoulder and looked expectantly at the three airmen, motioning for them to follow. The other two young Partisans brought up the rear as they hiked along another mountain trail going north.

Sunlight filtered through the trees and little birds flitted overhead, their sweet songs comforting Eaves as he trudged along. Other Americans ahead. The thought filled him with hope of finding more of his crew.

The trail led upward, with switchbacks weaving back and forth across the steep mountain. The small group passed the tree line and progressed into rough barren terrain, boulders and scrub brush surrounding them. In the open area of the heights, Eaves noticed the Partisans were back on alert, scanning the horizon frequently.

Probably watching for German planes.

Toward the crest of the mountain, they stumbled upon the ruins of a small rock home, obviously strafed and burned by the enemy. The scouts poked through the rubble, kicked over some pots inside the house, but did not find food or anything worth keeping.

"*Švabo!*" The leader spat out the word and pumped his fist in the air. He turned abruptly and strode up the rocky trail.

As they topped the summit, all Eaves could see was another range of dark mountains in the distance and the glint of another small ribbon of blue in a green valley below. He sighed deeply. Somehow, he'd hoped to see something more, something indicating a way out of here.

The leader didn't stop, hustling down the steep trail toward the forest below. Probably need to get us off this open area. Eaves' blister throbbed with each step. He placed his feet with care on firm parts of the trail so he didn't slip on the loose gravel and rocks that littered the path.

The group had just entered the forest again when he heard it. The drone of a plane. Scanning the sky, he spotted a small plane far to the east but headed their way.

"German fighter. Thank God we're back under cover. Would've been sitting ducks on that ridge," he muttered to Sherman, who nodded his agreement.

The Partisan leader stopped to watch the plane briefly before striding deeper into the canopy of the forest, hustling off the main trail to pause under the shelter of larger trees until the sound of the plane's engine grew fainter and fainter.

Cautiously stepping out to scan the sky, he signaled his two comrades to go on ahead. He waited until they moved out of sight around a bend, then he turned and motioned the airmen to follow him. The trail wound downward toward the valley.

Eaves rubbed the stubble on his chin.

Could use a shave.

He glanced at Sherman and Elder.

Pretty scruffy. We'd never pass Bonner's inspection.

He chuckled to himself, the thought momentarily cheering him up.

He studied Elder. The head wound seemed to be healing pretty well, and his stride was stronger. He didn't fall behind as often.

The young Partisan kept a steady pace more than two hours before signaling another break. The two scouts had not returned.

Eaves shook his water bottle. Almost empty and no apparent water source here. He took a small swallow.

Hope we find water soon. But we have to trust these young men and their knowledge of the terrain.

The young guide wasted no time in getting them back on the trail.

The sun was dropping behind the trees as the group entered a small valley. The trail merged onto a rutted primitive road. Small cultivated fields appeared. Eaves squinted into the evening haze.

Was that a tiny village ahead?

Three small cottages, with a large barn, nestled against the hillside.

Drawing closer, he recognized the other two Partisan scouts standing outside talking with a couple of other men dressed in dark clothing. One exclaimed, "*Americanski!*" as they turned to face the approaching group.

Suddenly the barn door slid open and several men wearing flight suits poured out.

Eaves couldn't believe his eyes. Other Americans! He scanned the faces. Maybe some of his crew? No familiar countenance smiled back at him.

Hope plummeted. A familiar sick feeling rose in his gut. If only he knew what had happened to the rest of his men.

But . . . maybe there's news of a way out of here.

Chapter 30

June 1944—Stalag Luft III, Sagan, Germany

THE CHARCOAL-BURNING GERMAN ARMY truck belched and chugged up to the main gate. Haverkos had noticed a few horse-drawn wagons driven by civilians but saw no other trucks or cars on the roads.

He couldn't help but relish some small satisfaction. He'd done his part, helping Allied bombers destroy German refineries and depriving the enemy of much-needed gasoline.

Surrounded by pine forests, the prison camp appeared dismal and formidable. Haverkos eyed the two nine-foot-high barbed wire fences, separated by a space filled with coils of barbed wire, surrounding the exterior of two compounds. On each side of the camp, he counted three or four sentinel towers looming above the fences, guards armed with machine guns and searchlights. The trees had been cut behind towers, leaving a wide swath of no-man's land, open and barren, abutted by the dark piney woods.

Nothing would escape the guards' scrutiny.

The gate swung open and the truck lumbered to a halt in front of a headquarters building. German guards shouted commands and waved their guns toward the ground. The tightly packed American airmen jumped down and were roughly shoved into a line.

Haverkos scanned the area. Two other buildings stood across from the headquarters. The closest compound yard was filled with Brits and Canadians, who hollered out greetings and waved from behind the fences. "Welcome Yanks!"

A gun prodding his back, Haverkos staggered toward a stone wall where each new prisoner was photographed, then stripped and led to a shower. After emerging from the shower, each was given clean clothing and a blanket.

After all were processed, the new prisoners were marched two by two past the first compound along a wire fence running parallel to the exterior boundaries. Haverkos saw Americans ahead in the southern compound yard, and as they entered, the imprisoned airmen called out greetings, a few hollering names of friends.

No one called his name.

The wooden huts were long and narrow, about two feet off the ground. Haverkos was shoved toward the first hut, and when he stepped inside, he found it divided into several rooms. He peered into the first small room, about fifteen-by-fifteen feet, containing five triple-decker bunk beds made from rough two-by-fours.

"Hey buddy, you can have this one." A thin-faced lieutenant with sunken brown eyes stood up from a bottom bed and pointed to the middle bunk in a tier.

Haverkos poked at the burlap-covered bag on the bed. "Thought our straw mattresses at Gioia were bad. What's in it?"

The young man smiled. "Wood chips. Like sleeping on gravel, but you sorta get used to it." He paused. "How was *Dulag Luft*?"

Haverkos grimaced. "A mental pressure cooker. Sure glad to get out of there. Think I was there only about three days, but hard to tell in those isolation cells."

The man nodded. "Yeah, I know what you mean. Lights on all night and overheated rooms so you can't sleep. Those frosted windows kept me confused as to whether it was day or night, and the guards woke me up whenever I finally did close my eyes."

"Never saw another prisoner the whole time I was there." Haverkos shook his head. "They want you to feel alone, try to break you. I think the sheer number of guys coming through to be processed helped cut my time short."

He stretched out his hand. "I'm Bob, Bob Haverkos, from Cincinnati by the way. How long you been here?"

"Been here too long, about eight months now." He reached over and shook Haverkos' hand. "Sam Smith. Grew up in Leavenworth, Kansas."

Suddenly Sam grinned. "Say, bet you haven't heard the news. The Allies landed at Normandy on June 6th and are pushing toward Paris!"

Haverkos' eyebrows shot up and his heart pounded. "What? The invasion has started! How'd you find out?"

"Those wily Brits. They have a hidden radio that the goons can't find. We get the latest news before the guards do. Signal crews pass the info along, and we'll have our own radio working soon."

He paused, and his face took on a serious look. "We were all housed together in the north compound until last summer. Then they built this compound and in August moved all the American airmen down here. Guess we got along too good," he said with a lopsided grin.

"What do you mean?" Haverkos asked.

"Did you notice the sandy soil? Easy to dig. We were digging three separate escape tunnels all last year. That's our duty, you know, to escape." He cocked his head. "Guys tried escaping other ways too, but usually they were quickly caught and got slammed in the cooler for two weeks isolation on bread and water."

Sam looked away for a moment. "Just before the plan was to go into action, they moved us to this new compound." He slapped the bunk support beam. "I felt cheated! I'd been part of the excavation crew and hoped to be on the list to go. The goons found one tunnel and thought they had us beat when they blew it up." He lowered his voice. "But the true escape tunnel was still ready, and seventy-six guys slipped out one dark night about six weeks ago."

Haverkos blinked. "Over seventy? How in the world did they plan to survive out here in the middle of Germany?"

Sam smiled grimly. "You wouldn't believe the forgers and costume designers and all the preparation that created identities for each of them. Went in pairs or groups of three. Of course, we knew the odds. A lot of guys probably wouldn't make it and would end up with two weeks in the cooler. But there was a good chance some could get away. And, it forced thousands of Germans soldiers to scour the countryside looking for them instead of fighting."

Haverkos nodded. "A good diversion. Any news on who made it?"

"Fifteen were caught right away and returned here. Sent to the cooler. Then, we heard nothing for several weeks." Sam's jaw tightened, his hand dropped to his side and clenched into a fist.

"Couldn't believe it was true when we first heard what had happened." He sucked in his breath. "Fifty of the boys were shot."

"What? Doesn't that violate the Geneva Convention that Germany signed in 1929?" Haverkos' gut roiled.

"The official report says they all tried to run, but we don't believe it." Sam's voice shook with anger. "The report even shocked the new Kommandant here, Oberst Braune, a *Luftwaffe* officer with an Iron Cross."

Sam's eyes glistened and he swallowed hard. "The names were just posted a couple of days ago. Some were good friends of mine."

Haverkos felt bile rising in his throat. Unarmed men, defenseless prisoners. He saw his friend, Christel, in his mind. What if he had been one of those executed? He struggled to find something to say.

Sam looked away. "We were told the Germans will return their ashes here. The Kommandant has given permission for a work party to start building a vault in a nearby cemetery where other allied airmen from this camp have been buried." He straightened his shoulders and looked at Haverkos. "Their sacrifice won't be forgotten."

Haverkos did quick calculating. "Fifteen and fifty. I figure that leaves eleven guys not accounted for."

"Yep. Have to believe that some of them made it." Sam paused. "And by the way—the Krauts announced new rules. Anyone attempting to escape from now on will be executed."

Chapter 31

JUNE 1944—SOMEWHERE IN YUGOSLAVIA

EAVES SCRATCHED HIS CHEST as he hiked along, his body covered with bites from elusive fleas and lice. The sheep and goats that inhabited the barn had left the disgusting vermin in the hay where the airmen slept. Now they were all infested.

None of the airmen knew where they were or what the plan for their return to Italy might be. The small group of Americans had grown to twelve, all from different bomber groups located in Italy.

Eaves decided to call the young Partisan leader "George." George moved them rapidly from village to village, sometimes only a small cluster of two to three simple houses, always heading in a north to northeast direction through the mountains. Days had morphed into weeks. None of the Partisans were fluent in English, although George seemed interested in learning a few words. Eaves could only pray that these guerilla fighters were marching them toward some type of contact with the Allies.

Food was constantly an issue. The airmen were parceled out to different homes at each location. The villagers shared their meager food stuffs, but often one meal a day was it.

At one of their overnight stops in a cave, Eaves had offered the two K-rations he'd saved to the group. Two other K-rations appeared from others. Malnourished as they were, even a Spam soup tasted good.

Except for small basins of water offered occasionally to wash their faces or hands, none of the airmen had been able to shower or bathe. The stubble on their faces quickly grew into scruffy beards. Combined with filth, hunger, lice, and fleas, misery stalked their steps. Eaves noticed several of the men showed the yellowish signs of jaundice and weakness from gastrointestinal ailments.

The airmen's boots were not made for hiking the rocky trails. As the soles of his boots wore through, Eaves cut pieces of parachute material to line them and provide some protection.

Arriving at dusk on a ridge above another isolated valley high in the mountains, Eaves spotted a farmhouse with a large barn in a clearing below. As the group of exhausted airmen struggled down the incline into the clearing, Eaves fought to keep putting one foot in front of the other. The downhill stretches aggravated his old knee injury. But the thought of possible food ahead kept him moving.

The barn door swung open. Startled, Eaves saw several Allied airmen swarm out of the building, maybe another ten men. But no familiar faces greeted his searching gaze.

He sighed. He kept praying the rest of the crew made it to safety. His thoughts revolved back so often to McMillian and Petrone. Somehow, he felt he'd let them down. If only he'd been able to push their bodies out of the burning plane.

"Welcome, y'all. Just in time for dinner." A lanky lieutenant with a Southern drawl strode up to shake Eaves' hand. "Eddie Jones, from Tennessee." He smiled. "What group were you with?"

"W.T. Eaves, from the great state of Texas," Eaves replied as he shook the outstretched hand. "464th Bomb Group, out of Gioia del Colle. And you?"

"Heck, we're neighbors—463rd Bomb Group, stationed at Foggia."

"How long you been here?"

"About three weeks now. Seems to be a holding place, pretty safe from the Germans, but we keep an eye out for fighter planes." Eddie pointed to a large black pot beside the barn being tended by two peasant women in their rough handwoven black garb. "Soup's almost ready. Hungry?"

Eaves' mouth watered as tantalizing scents of cabbage, onions, and turnips wafted on the breeze. His stomach growled with anticipation.

"You bet!" Tension eased in his shoulders as he peeled off the makeshift pack.

Eaves followed the young lieutenant to the end of the line already forming. He glanced around and could see the airmen here looked better than he and his buddies did. Their uniforms appeared to have been laundered and their faces were clean-shaven.

Maybe there was hope for a bath.

He could see why the Partisans might choose this site to hide airmen. He'd seen no improved roads in the area, which would definitely hinder German troops from moving rapidly into the valley. And he'd observed a small group of young Partisans stationed at the top of the pass where any suspicious activity on the trail below could easily be spotted.

Finally, one of the women handed him a roughly carved wooden bowl filled with soup and a piece of crusty corn bread. He smiled and nodded his thanks, then found a place to sit on a log by the lanky lieutenant and Sherman, who were already chowing down.

First things first. He dipped a corner of the corn bread into the thin liquid and savored the warm vegetable flavors in his mouth, chewing slowly to enjoy every bite. After the corn bread was gone, he tipped the bowl up to his lips and slurped down the rest of the soup, leaving a big chunk of potato and cabbage in the bottom of his bowl. Carefully he poured them into his mouth, savoring every morsel.

Wiping his mouth with the back of his hand, he turned to the lieutenant. "Thanks for the welcome." He cocked his head. "Do you know if there are other guys from the 464th here? My copilot Sherman," he nodded toward Dan, "and our flight engineer Elder are here with me, but I keep hoping to connect up with the rest of our crew."

Eddie just shook his head. "Nope, sorry. Understand your feelings though."

"Have another question for you," Eaves said. "Do you know of any plans to get us back to Italy?" Eaves steeled himself to hear another dismal reply.

Eddie's smile grew wider. "Well, nothing definite, but today we got some really good news." He paused. "Two of the guys hiked over three days with Bara, the Partisan leader here, to a rendezvous with someone connected to the Allies." He leaned forward and pointed. "That's Bara over yonder, leaning against the barn door."

Eaves looked up to see a stout, dark-haired man with a scar running down his left cheek who wore his red-starred cap jauntily tilted to the side, talking with George.

"They connected with someone named Roger, a British underground officer who has a two-way radio. He made contact with the Allies in Italy. Guess what they found out?" Eddie's smile grew bigger, his blue eyes lit up. "They've landed! June 6th was D-Day! Allied ground troops are pushing through France."

"What?" Eaves' heart thudded in his chest, energy suddenly coursing through his body. "That's great news!" Those long flights into France—he was right, they were getting ready to invade.

"Yes, and that's not all. The Brit said he would notify the Allies about the number of downed airmen here with the Partisans and give them our location. He promised to get us an air drop of supplies soon, and to work on a plan to get us out of here."

"That's the best news I've had in a long time! I know I'll sleep better tonight knowing that we are pushing toward Berlin . . . and that someone knows we're here." Eaves looked at Sherman, who grinned ear to ear. "That calls for a celebration."

"Well, I reckon I'll see if our hosts might have a little plum brandy around for the occasion," Eddie said. He jumped up and trotted over to Bara. Eddie gestured with his hands, tipping an imaginary glass up to his lips.

Bara slowly nodded, and then smiled, calling out something toward the house in his strange dialect.

Eaves smiled as he recognized the now-familiar word "*Rakija*."

Bara turned and disappeared into the farmhouse. He emerged a few minutes later with a small wooden barrel on his shoulder, and one of the women carried a tray of glasses. He pulled out a hand-carved plug and began filling glasses, eager hands quickly reaching out and passing drinks around the circle. Not enough glasses for everyone, but the men didn't mind sharing at all.

A young man brought out a violin and began to play a haunting tune. Eaves let the music wash over him. As the violinist switched to an upbeat song, some of the men clapped along.

Eaves finally got a glass of the amber liquid and it burned as he gulped it down. A warmth welled up to fill his belly as he tapped his toe and smiled.

With God's help, we're on our way to winning this war. Maybe back to Italy soon. And then . . . home.

Hope burned brightly in his chest.

✈✈✈

The next morning, Eaves crawled out of the nest he'd made in the hay. Bright shafts of light illuminated the golden straw littering the floor of the stall he'd chosen for his quarters. He stood and stretched, still scratching itchy spots. Darned bugs.

Somehow all the airmen had managed to find a resting spot in the large barn. He'd slept soundly and felt refreshed, still energized by the hopeful news of last night.

Eddie poked his head around the stall wall where Eaves stood. "Morning, Eaves. Hey, after breakfast I can show y'all where to get a bath."

"Man am I ready for that!" Eaves threw back his head and laughed, tingling with anticipation. "Breakfast too? You don't know how good that sounds."

Eddie smiled. "I know. They prepare a big pot of hot gruel every morning. Not as good as the grits I'm used to back home, but it fills those empty spots in the belly. Sure do appreciate their generosity."

Eaves followed Eddie out to the side of the barn where a woman ladled out a warm mash from the big black pot. He took the wooden bowl and spoon offered to him, and once again tried to communicate his thanks with a nod and a smile.

He settled down onto the big log by Eddie to enjoy the meal. Soon Sherman and Elder joined them. "Eddie is going to show us where we can get a bath." He looked sideways at Eddie. "Don't suppose there's any chance of soap?"

Eddie grinned. "Yep. Y'all are in luck. The ladies made some just last week. And they have towels that they let us use. Amazing how grateful I am for the simple things of life now."

Taking a trail through the forest that bordered the clearing, Eddie led them to a small river that twisted and gurgled around gray boulders. He stopped by a sandy beach that led into a large deep pool.

"I'll leave you here." He handed Eaves a rough bar of yellowish soap and three towels. "Gotta go help the family with some weeding. They've got a big vegetable garden and some fields of wheat and corn south of the farmhouse. Least we can do to show our appreciation."

He started to leave, then turned back. "Almost forgot . . . I'll take y'all into the village later. There's a barber there who'll cut your hair and give you a shave for a little of that currency you've got in them escape kits. Does a darn good job too."

"What? A real barber! I can't wait." Eaves felt like dancing a jig.

He hummed as he started stripping off his flight suit, carefully taking out Jean's tattered picture and feasting his eyes on her sweet face. He laid it on top of a boulder with a small chunk of rock on it to hold it safe.

Thank You for Your blessings, Lord! And keep Jean safe for me until I make it home.

Chapter 32

THE NEXT MORNING, George and his two comrades left right after breakfast, heading up the trail to the north.

Eaves waved and yelled, "Goodbye!"

George looked back. He smiled and gave a closed fist salute. "Goot-by," he called back. Then, the young men turned to climb the ridge.

Wonder where they're going. Seem to be on a mission.

He rubbed his cheek, reveling in the smooth feel of his skin. Eddie was right—the barber was good at his job. The hot towels on his face had felt like a luxury long forgotten. Laundering his uniform yesterday after his bath left him feeling the cleanest he'd been in weeks. Now, if they only had an antidote for these pesky bugs.

Eaves joined the work crew heading out into the fields. These poor people farmed with handmade tools, nothing mechanical here. He attacked weeds growing between the beets and turnips in the garden with a primitive hoe, a slab of metal lashed onto a firm rod.

By midday the sun's rays beat down on him, and he wished he had a hat. Sweat trickled down the back of his neck. As he stopped to wipe his brow with the back of his hand, he winced. The salty sweat made his hand sting. Looking down, he saw both hands were cracked and red, couple of blisters starting.

Gritting his teeth, he determined to finish the last row before he retreated to the shade where the water jug sat.

Just as he finished taking a drink, Elder walked up from the other side of the garden where he'd been hoeing the cabbage patch.

"How you doing, Jim?" Eaves asked. "Water?"

Elder nodded, and Eaves handed him the small jug. He noticed the wound on Elder's head had finally healed, leaving a jagged scar.

Elder took a long drink and put the cork back in the jug. "Better, now that we got food and cleaned up some," he said with a wry grin. "And . . . got the good news that the Allies know we are here."

"It's a relief to know that someone is working on a plan to get us out of here." Eaves scratched at the back of his neck. "Wonder if they'll be able to do that food drop soon."

"Hope so," Elder said. He looked out across the garden. "Sure am hungry for some meat. Vegetables are better than nothing, but a man craves meat and potatoes sometimes."

Eaves salivated at just the mention of meat, alluring visions of home-cooked roasts and fried chicken taunting him. Suddenly a thought popped into his mind. "I wonder . . . if there might be some fish in that river."

Elder's eyes brightened at the thought. "Let's go see."

Soon he and Elder were quietly stalking along the river banks, looking for any signs of fish life. Circles appeared on the surface of the water indicating something was feeding in the calmer water of a narrow pool where a little stream fed into the river.

Eaves caught a grasshopper and tossed it into the stream just above the pool. He watched it drift down. Splash! A fairly large fish jumped out of the water to snatch it. Eaves could see several other fish swirling in the water.

Hmm . . . a school of fish. But how to catch them without a hook or line?

Backing away, he whispered, "Let's catch more grasshoppers. I'll get in the water and you drop them in one at a time. I'll try to flip the fish out on the bank."

"Worth a try." Elder cupped his hand over another hopper.

After catching a few more, Eaves stripped down and slowly waded into the water by the pool. They waited. The fish continued circling, occasionally feeding on the surface. Eaves moved closer.

Giving a thumbs-up, Eaves slowly slipped his hands under the water. Jim carefully tossed a still-kicking hopper into the water above the pool. As it floated in front of Eaves, he saw a fish rise up toward it. He scooped with both hands and tossed the fish out onto the bank.

"Wahoo! You got one!" Elder pounced on the squirming fish, pushing it away from the river. Finally wrapping his fingers around the slippery creature, he stuck a finger into its gills. Looking around, he broke off a green willow branch and stripped off the leaves before threading it through the gills and out the mouth. He grinned as he held up the eight-inch catch for Eaves to see. "Let's get some more."

Eaves grinned back. He could already taste them.

Elusive and wary, the fish were not as easy to catch as they first thought. Two hours later they had managed to only catch five fish. Eaves pulled out the knife from his escape kit to gut each one and scrape off the scales.

"Let's see if one of the ladies will cook 'em for us," Eaves said.

When they got back to the farmhouse, they found most of the guys were still out in the fields or in the village. Pointing at the fish and the fire pit, Eaves communicated what they wanted to an older woman who sat in her dark garb on the porch knitting.

Nodding and smiling, she took the fish, dusted them with some cornmeal, and began to cook them in a heavy iron skillet over the firepit.

Eaves sat down on the porch step to wait.

Can't feel guilty about eating the fish by ourselves—not enough to share with everyone.

Just then Sherman and their new friend Eddie strode around the barn.

"What ya got there, Eaves?" Eddie sniffed at the air. "Smells like a mess of fish, if I ever smelled one."

"Well, you got here just in time," Eaves said with a grin. "One fish for each of us and one for the little lady doing the cooking."

Soon they each had a plate with fish on it.

"Man, this is good, even without salt and pepper." Eaves licked his fingers after sucking every morsel of flesh off the backbone. "Gotta thank the good Lord for these fish. A feast, just like those stories we read in the Bible."

Chapter 33

JULY 1944—STALAG LUFT III, SAGAN, GERMANY

HAVERKOS FINALLY GOT TO THE FRONT of the line and reached out his hands to receive the Red Cross package. A lifeline, that's what it was. He tucked it under his arm and strode rapidly back to his barracks

He prayed the two postcards he had written, one to Ginny and one to his folks, made it through the German censor and would be released to the International Red Cross workers to be mailed to the USA. He wanted them to know that he was still alive and doing okay.

Opening the door, he walked down the hall to the kitchen area. Each hut had a double burner where meals were prepared, a dining room furnished with a few simple tables, and a small living room. In the corner of the living room sat a little coal-burning stove on a tiled hearth with a few shelves of books on the wall.

Haverkos' first impression of appreciation for the warmth the stove must provide was squashed when he learned that the coal ration they received daily in the winter heated the room for only a few hours each day.

But he had to be thankful that the *Luftwaffe* ran this camp for officers. German respect for fellow officers bought a few "luxuries" he'd come to appreciate. He shuddered to think of the SS being the ones in control. Just seeing the Gestapo officers who came for inspections gave him the creeps. Cold, steely blue eyes—evil seemed to radiate from them.

His little buddy, Christel, popped into his mind.

Lord, I just pray he's not in their clutches and is doing okay, wherever they sent him.

Haverkos' eyes lit up as he opened the parcel and examined the contents: K-rations, a can of powdered milk, margarine, raisins, sugar, coffee, cigarettes, toilet paper, soap, and the chocolate D-bar. Never thought he'd be excited to see Spam, but it was a delicacy when compared to the thin slice of black, sour-tasting bread the Krauts served as their main food ration twice daily. Occasionally the Germans brought in a truck-load of half-rotten potatoes or ladled out sauerkraut, but it was the Red Cross packages that arrived once a week or every other week that staved off starvation.

He quickly sorted the contents. The K-rations, powdered milk, raisins, margarine, sugar, and coffee all stayed in the kitchen. Some of the kriegies, the name he'd learned that the POWs chose to give themselves because it sounded somewhat like the German word for prisoners, "*kriegsgafanganen*," had volunteered to cook. They commandeered the basic food elements in all the Red Cross parcels and eked out two meals a day for the one hundred men living in the hut.

Everything in the parcels was used. The cans were shaped into bowls and cooking utensils, the cardboard became chessboards or liners for the soles of their shoes, the tasteless margarine served as oil for simple lamps or sealant for cans.

Each man kept the bar of soap, cigarettes, D-bar, and the toilet paper. Haverkos carried his treasures back down the hall to his room.

Once inside, he opened the D-bar, gnawing off a small chunk. He chewed slowly, savoring the bitterness of the chocolate food bar. Not the sweet Hershey bar he remembered from home. The D-bar was almost indestructible, a calorie-dense food product designed to sustain life on the front lines and in POW packages. Re-wrapping the rest for later, he stored it in his pocket.

"Hey, Haverkos." Sam poked his head through the doorway. "Stash your stuff for now. We're scheduled to play Barracks Four in the softball tournament."

"Give me a moment." Haverkos tucked the cigarettes, soap, and toilet paper—all luxury items here—under his lumpy mattress for safekeeping. "Better get the guys fired up. We may have a little competition here. Heard they've got some heavy hitters."

When the South Compound had been built, the Germans had Russian POWs cut down all the pine trees in the yard surrounding the barracks, leaving the stumps in the ground. The Kommandant had allowed the American airmen to use the "Klim" cans to dig the stumps out of the sandy soil to make a softball field. Haverkos smiled. "Klim" was milk spelled backward. The multipurpose containers of powdered milk that came in the Red Cross parcels made great little shovels.

The work kept them busy and helped fill the empty time they had on their hands. When the field was finally cleared, they'd set up leagues for competition. The rivalry was intense, guys betting food and cigarettes on the outcomes. Even the guards joined the action, wagering on which teams would win.

Haverkos was chosen as the pitcher for his hut's team. So far, they were undefeated, eighteen straight wins. But the weaker teams were falling, and now they faced serious contenders for the camp title.

Haverkos pulled out a Red Cross parcel box he'd labeled with his name in big letters from under the bunk bed where he stored a few personal items. When his own laundered uniform had been returned to him, he had to surrender the issued pants and shirt. But he still had some underwear, socks, his ceramic bowl, mug, spoon, fork, and knife.

He dug deep into the box to retrieve a ball and mitt. The International YMCA sent recreational equipment to the camp, and as pitcher for their team, he was responsible for his equipment.

When he reached the field, the guys were stretching and warming up. After a few warm-up pitches to the catcher, the umpire called for the game to begin.

Haverkos had been right. Barracks Four had impressive hitters and good defense. Equally matched, the score was five to five in the fifth inning. But at the bottom of the sixth, Haverkos sent a sizzling fastball over the plate only to have it hammered into a home run bringing in two base runners.

Even the guards heckled him, "Vat es wrong, Haverkos?!"

He just shook his head. Even though he struck out the next six batters, his team could not muster enough runs to win and the game ended in a tie, 8 to 8. Victory would have to come on another day.

As he and Sam trudged back toward their hut, Colonel Goodrich, the senior American officer of the camp stopped them.

"Sorry to see your winning streak broken today," he offered, with a smile. "Bob, I was wondering if I might have a word with you?"

"Sure," Haverkos said and looked at Sam.

"See you at supper. Heard we have Spam soup tonight—yum." Sam gave a half-grin, then walked on toward their barracks.

The officer looked around and said quietly, "Let's go to the library in my barracks, over there." He tilted his head toward the hut on the right.

No one was in the library when they arrived, and the senior officer closed the door. They sat down on the two wooden chairs facing each other.

Haverkos studied the colonel's lined, gaunt face, wondering why he had asked him here. He knew the man was well respected, a seasoned officer who had been in this camp for over two years.

"Bob, as you have probably figured out, we kriegies have organized ourselves to meet the needs of the whole group as best we can. And to continue to plan possible escapes, which is our duty." He paused and thoughtfully studied his hands, which he rubbed and then clasped together. Looking up, he continued. "I've noticed your ability to lead men and your athletic abilities. We need someone like you on our leadership team. Would you consider being part of the Commandos, the ten men I rely on for advice and leadership?"

Haverkos swallowed hard, honored to be approached with such an offer. "If you believe I can be of assistance, I am at your command, sir."

"The less you know, the safer you are. And the safer everyone else is." He looked deep into Haverkos' eyes. "Do not share any information with anyone."

Haverkos nodded soberly. "I understand, sir."

"We've heard rumors that Hitler may order the execution of all prisoners before the Allies can free us, so at our next meeting we'll devise a plan to overthrow the guards if it comes to that. We must be prepared. So, think about possibilities, and come here tomorrow at 1700 ready to discuss. That's all for now."

"Yes, sir. I'll be here."

Both men stood and shook hands.

Haverkos left and headed for his own barracks. He reflected on the trust expressed by his senior officer.

Don't know what all this means, but I can't let him down.

Glancing up at the goon box he could see the guards scanning the area and a machine gun pointing down at him. His scalp tingled with danger.

Lord, give us wisdom, and help me do my best to help in whatever ways I can.

Chapter 34

July 1944—somewhere in Yugoslavia

An orange flash, the sound of flak hitting the plane. Out of the black cloud emerged an FW-190 fighter plane headed straight toward him, guns blazing.

Eaves ducked to the side and awoke to the smell of manure and dust, struggling in the hay where he'd carved out a spot to sleep.

Nightmares again. He stared into the dark musky air of the barn, still trembling inside, and forced himself to take in a long, slow breath.

Out. In. Out. In. Focus Eaves. How long have we been here? Weeks now.

His mind flew back over the slow-moving moments, a kaleidoscope of events that seemed random, going nowhere. Every few days the Partisans had brought in one or two more downed airmen. More than thirty guys now, all wanting to get back to Italy.

He kept hoping for a familiar face, but the rest of his crew had not shown up. McMillian and Petrone's young faces floated into his mind, haunting him.

Why them? Why not him? How many more of his crew had died? If only he could have changed something . . .

He squeezed his eyes shut, a deep pain in his gut.

Other faces flashed before him. Friends and comrades gone, paying the ultimate price for freedom. Lt. Cummings, whose plane crashed before even reaching Brazil. Captain James Latimer in *Red Hot Riding Hood*, Lt. Parrish, Captain Hornbaker over France after evading the Germans once before . . . so many others.

Young men in their prime, lives snuffed out before they could live their hopes and dreams. Pain of loss seared through his soul like a flaming sword. He recoiled from the horrors of war, the cost.

So many questions . . . no answers.

He took another deep breath, stretched his legs, and turned over.

His mind flew back to the farm when he and Ruth had lived with Aunt Minnie and Uncle Otto. They didn't have much, but every day they bowed their heads and gave thanks to the Lord for His bounty in providing food, shelter, whatever they needed.

Be grateful, Eaves. Think about the positives. At least we're in a safe spot for the moment, even if it feels like we've gone back a century in time.

The food drop helped morale—cigs, K-rations, even some hard candy. And last week, Bara slaughtering that hog gave them some meat they'd all craved. The compassion and kindness of these people was amazing, sharing what little they had, treating the airmen like honored guests.

There was also the message that had come with the food drop.

"Be ready to move out when you get the notice. We are coming to get you out of there."

Yes, finally, a rescue plan. Hope had burned brighter.

But when? Anytime soon would be great.

His thoughts swirled upward.

Lord, I am grateful. Thank You for watching over us, and for sending help.

He took a deep breath, thinking again of those brave men who were gone.

I pray for those families back home who have lost their loved ones, and for those who don't know. Comfort them, Lord. And my family, not knowing if I'm dead or alive.

He squeezed his eyes shut and saw Jean's sweet face. Their time together had been so brief. The familiar ache, the need to hold her, almost brought tears to his eyes

Keep Jean safe for me, and please, provide for her needs.

Questions swirled and taunted him.

Why? Why? Finding love at last—but will it be taken from me again? First my mother. I can hardly remember her. Then, having to leave Aunt Minnie.

An overwhelming sadness covered his heart. His breath caught in his throat.

Does love ever last?

Silence. Only a creak of the old barn filled the emptiness.

Will she be true, still waiting for me when I get home? Or will I even make it home, to be the husband and father I want to be?

He pulled the blanket tighter. He listened but only heard the chirp of a cricket. The silence deepened as sadness enveloped him.

Then, inside, a shift.

He sucked in his breath as he remembered with Whom he spoke—the Holy One who had paid all for him, who knew pain and loss.

He exhaled and bowed his heart in quiet surrender.

You are Good, and Faithful, and True. All Your ways are above mine. Only You know, Lord . . . and I put it all into Your hands.

A deep peace stole over his frame. His muscles relaxed, his breathing slowed.

No longer elusive, sleep swept over him.

✈✈✈

The wheat heads, golden and full, lay in clumps on the ground. Harvest time had come. Eaves stopped to wipe his brow with the back of his hand. His shoulders ached from swinging the scythe into the yellow stalks. The sun beat down on him, the smell of dust, sweat, and fresh-cut straw filling his nostrils. He bent down to gather the wheat into a bundle and tied it with the last piece of cord in his pocket.

Trudging over to the water jug lying in the shade of the trees lining the field, he took a swig and looked up to see two men coming down the mountain pass trail. He squinted in the bright light. The first guy looked familiar.

"Hey Jim," he called out. "Look who's coming!"

Elder threw his bundle of wheat into the cart standing at the edge of the field and shaded his eyes to look in the direction Eaves was pointing.

"My gosh—it looks like George."

Sure enough, their former guide soon joined them in the shade. A dark-haired teenage boy, wearing the Partisans' red-starred cap, walked behind him with a rifle slung over his shoulder.

"*Americanski!*" George exclaimed, as he gave them each a bear hug and the traditional kiss on each cheek. Smiling broadly, he reached into his pocket and pulled out a folded piece of paper, presenting it to Eaves.

"Or-ders," he said carefully.

"You're learning English," Eaves said with a smile, as he reached for the document, his heart beating rapidly with anticipation. Unfolding the paper, he read aloud.

To: Allied Airmen

The plan is a go. Follow this man immediately to the destination he will show you. You will be passing through enemy territory, so proceed with utmost caution. God speed.

In His Majesty's Service,

Roger

Elder whooped and clapped Eaves on the back. "Can't believe it! They're coming to get us!"

Eaves grabbed George's hand and pumped it up and down. George grinned from ear to ear, his red-starred cap bobbing. "Is goot," he said.

"Gotta go tell the others." Eaves looked at George. "You tell Bara?"

George nodded several times before he turned on his heel and headed for the farmhouse.

Grabbing the tools and last bundles of wheat, Eaves and Elder pulled the cart toward the barn. He spotted Eddie in the garden behind the house.

"Hey Eddie, George is back. He brought a message from the Allies. Gather the guys!"

Eddie flashed a huge smile and dropped his hoe. He started jogging toward the outlying fields.

Eaves and Elder pulled the field wagon up beside the barn door and let the cart handles fall to the ground.

"Jim, go round up any guys you see and tell them to gather by the black pot." Eaves poked his head inside the barn. "Dan, you in here?"

Sherman had been fighting a cold for weeks, couldn't seem to shake the cough. This morning he'd said he thought he'd better just lay low, try to kick it.

Stepping into the barn, he saw Sherman wrapped in his blanket on the haystack. "Hey, buddy, how you doing?"

Sherman moaned. Slowly opening his eyes, he gave a crooked smile. "Hanging in there." Then his racking cough spoke louder than the brave words.

Eaves swallowed hard, wishing he had some medicine to give him. "George just brought us the orders to move out. They're coming to get us!"

Sherman smiled and struggled to sit up. "Good news," he said weakly, "really good news."

The effort brought more coughing, and Eaves could hear wheezing. Not a good sign. Sounded like pneumonia. Kneeling down, Eaves touched his forehead. Hot to the touch.

"You just rest here. Eddie went to call the guys in from the fields so we can come up with a plan." He reached out for Sherman's water bottle. Empty.

"I'll get you more water. And don't worry, we'll get you out of here." Eaves stood up and quickly slipped back out the barn door.

✈✈✈

The airmen clustered in front of the farmhouse before the sun had peeked over the mountains. Eaves helped Sherman and another ill airman to settle into a bed of golden straw crammed in a primitive ox cart with wooden-spoked wheels. A couple of long-horned oxen stood yoked together and ready to pull, switching their tails at the flies swarming around them,

Two ladies in their dark woolen garb stashed several cloth-wrapped bundles in the wagon and then stepped back up onto the porch to stand in the doorway. Gratitude for Bara's provision washed over Eaves.

George and his companion stood beside Bara on the porch, speaking rapidly in low guttural tones. They gave the one-arm fist salute and turned to step down in front of the airmen.

"We go," George said.

Eaves and Eddie stepped up to Bara. "Thank you, thank you." Eaves shook Bara's hand up and down. "The words don't seem like enough," he said to Eddie, as he, too, expressed his thanks.

Bara nodded and smiled, wrapping each of them in a huge bear hug and kissing them soundly on each check. Even the women stepped forward to clasp the airmen's hands and kiss them, nodding and smiling.

Bless them, Lord. We can never repay them for their kindness.

In the predawn light, Eaves and Eddie turned to follow their guides as the long train of airmen snaked up the mountain ahead of them.

"Can't believe we're finally going," Eddie said. "The guys were chomping at the bit last night, ready to leave then!"

"I know. Hard to wait till morning." Eaves nodded, just as he heard Sherman struggle with another fit of coughing. He lowered his voice. "I'm so grateful to Bara for sending that cart. Just pray we can find medical help soon—Sherman is burning up with fever and that wheezing is getting worse."

"Yep. Maybe the Brit has connections. Or medical supplies with him."

They fell silent as they strode up the steep incline behind the cart. As his breathing became labored, Eaves spotted two young Partisan guards above them at the top of the pass. Not far now.

The oxen kept their heads down and bellowed occasionally. The cart creaked along as they pulled it over the rocky ruts.

Sunlight streamed over the crest of the mountain, the clouds tinged in pink, as the sun rose in all its glory.

Finally, a light at the end of this tunnel, a walk toward freedom.

The shadow of a hawk fell across the rocky path.

Eaves shivered, a sense of foreboding stealing over him.

What lay ahead? Roger said they would be in enemy territory. How would a group this large hide from German scrutiny?

Only with your hand covering us, Lord, will we make it. And please, guide our steps to the medical help the men need.

Chapter 35

July 1944—somewhere in Yugoslavia

EAVES PEERED THROUGH THE TREES at the settlement below. Definitely the biggest town they'd seen. George waited in the forest till dusk, indicating with motions to be seated, stay quiet and out of sight.

Eaves watched George divide the airmen into small groups of three or four. He escorted one group at a time into the village. He assigned Eaves, Elder, and Eddie to the cart. Leaving them till last, he finally led the oxen down winding cobblestone streets and stopped in front of a two-story stone house with shuttered windows.

After looking up and down the street, George climbed the stone steps leading to the carved front door and knocked twice. After several moments, he repeated the two knocks. The door creaked open. He spoke quietly to whoever stood inside. Eaves heard "*Americanski*" repeated twice. Stepping back, he motioned to the airmen.

"You, here," George said, pointing at Sherman, Elder, and Eaves.

Eddie waited by the cart as Eaves and Elder helped Sherman to his feet.

"Hey Dan, lean on us," Eaves said.

Slipping his arms over their shoulders, Sherman's legs wobbled as he tackled the four steps. They lifted him onto the porch and through the doorway.

Inside, an older couple dressed in dark, formal attire greeted them and seemed to quickly assess the situation. The diminutive grey-haired matron motioned the men toward a small door under the staircase on the main floor.

Squeezing into a narrow room, they helped Sherman onto the single cot, and Eaves pulled the covers over him. Then he and Elder backed out of the room.

Their hostess walked down the hall and returned with a cloth over her arm and a bowl of water. After bathing the sick man's face and hands, she came back to bring a glass of water.

Sherman was receiving tender care here. Maybe it would help.

The elderly gentleman was slightly hunched, with a bushy grey mustache and sharp dark eyes. He led Eaves and Elder up a narrow staircase to a large open attic room with two beds. He gestured toward a table with a wash basin, a pitcher of water and a small towel. Eaves appreciated the thoughtfulness of his host in providing water to wash their hands and face.

Eaves nodded and smiled. "Thank you."

The old man nodded, then pointed downstairs as he backed out of the room.

"I think he wants us to wash up and go downstairs," Eaves said.

"Maybe some dinner?" Elder said hopefully.

Their deduction soon proved correct. And for the first time, Eaves and Elder were seated at a dining table covered with a white tablecloth and set with linen napkins, silver flatware, and crystal glasses. Their host nodded and smiled at them under the warm light of a small candle chandelier flicking above their heads.

Eaves' eyes widened and saliva wet his dry mouth as the petite hostess served each of them a small portion of mutton, with cabbage and carrots, on porcelain plates. She returned to pour a familiar amber liquid into their glasses.

"Rakija?" Eaves asked.

"Ja," his host replied, nodding, his eyes twinkling with surprise.

Obviously, this couple had been affluent before the war. Eaves wondered what his occupation had been. Somehow they'd managed to keep some of their finer things, even under the German occupation.

Their host bowed his head and spoke rapidly in his harsh dialect, making the sign of the cross as he finished. He look up to smile at the airmen. He nodded and pointed with his fork, waiting for his guests to take the first bite.

Eaves didn't need more encouragement. He carefully cut a small piece of meat and took a bite. Mutton was not his favorite, but he relished every delicious morsel.

His hostess stood watching the men from the doorway, a pleased smile on her face. She disappeared down the hall, and Eaves watched as she returned with a steaming bowl of soup in her hands. She ducked under the doorway to Sherman's little room. Eaves sensed she recognized the weakened condition of the copilot and appreciated her thoughtful concern in bringing food that perhaps he could tolerate.

After the meal, their host rose and motioned for the men to follow him into the parlor. He picked up a portrait of a young man and gazed at it with a sad look in his eyes. He turned and held it before Eaves and Elder. Eaves saw the same dark eyes and strong jaw of the father in the young man.

"Your son?" he asked, pointing at his host and back to the picture.

"Ja," the father replied. "Partisan," he added with a proud smile, then lifted his hand in a wave toward the door.

Eaves realized the young man had left to fight for his country. Eyeing the rich draperies and luxuriant furnishing of the room, he understood the young man had courageously left loving parents and an affluent lifestyle to defend his homeland. Eaves had nothing but respect for the valiant young men and women he'd met who were helping him and other Allied airmen.

Eaves nodded and solemnly laid his hand over his heart. The old man smiled.

"We'd better check on Dan," Eaves said to Elder, as he pointed toward the stairs.

Holding a spoon up to the copilot's lips, the hostess looked up as Eaves peered into the room. She still held an almost full bowl of soup and just shook her head gently, her brown eyes speaking concern.

Putting his fingertips on Sherman's brow, Eaves grew alarmed. His forehead was moist with sweat, his eyes glazed.

"Dan, can you eat a little more of this soup?"

Sherman licked his lips but didn't respond.

Their hostess got up from the chair and slipped out of the small room.

Elder's eyes widened. "What can we do?"

Eaves took the cloth and dipped it in the bowl of water before wiping Sherman's forehead with it. "We can try to reduce the fever by keeping him cool." He unzipped the top of the flight suit and wiped his face and neck. "And pray."

✈✈✈

Eaves heard the knock in the predawn twilight. Looking out the window he saw the cart on the cobbled street. Must be George.

He heard quiet voices as the door creaked open.

"Come on, Jim. George is here. I'm heading down." He grabbed his backpack.

When he reached the entryway, George was already in Sherman's room. where the ill man moaned, his feverish words incoherent.

Looking at Eaves, George pointed to Sherman and to the cart. "Hos-pi-tal."

What—medical help here? Eaves nodded. Elder filed down the stairs just in time to help carry Sherman to the cart, covering him with a blanket.

The cobblestone streets wound around ancient two-story stone houses. All remained quiet as they pushed on toward the west side of the town. No streetlights and no one stirring. George stopped in front of another large rock house on the outskirts of town. Again, he knocked his two knocks, waited, then knocked again.

A shaft of light pierced the dark, illuminating the rough boards on the porch as the door open. Murmured words. George came down the steps to help them carry Sherman into the building. A stout middle-aged woman in traditional garb held the heavy door open as they scrambled onto the porch and through the doorway. She pointed them to a large, open room on the left with four beds and gestured toward the only unoccupied one.

Carefully, they laid Sherman on the bed. Speaking quickly to George, she turned to Sherman and began to remove his uniform, pulling a sheet and blanket over him.

Eaves recognized the other sick Allied airman who had been in the cart on the cot nearby, but the other two men were unknown to him.

"Hmmumf, vat do we have here?"

Eaves twirled around, surprised to hear the broken English. The grey-haired man was of thin build and wore a tweed suit coat over his black woolen pants. He held out his hand. "I'm Dr. Schwatzki."

"Where . . . did you learn English?" Eaves asked.

"Before the war, I spend time in England. My medical training there."

George frowned, waved his arm impatiently. "Must go."

Eaves' jaw tightened.

What? I can't just leave my friend here.

He turned to face the doctor. "I think it's pneumonia. Had a bad cough that went down in his lungs and then the fever came."

The doctor pursed his lips and nodded. "He must rest. Do not worry. We care for him." He put his hand on Eaves' shoulder and looked deep into his eyes. "But you, must go—now. Make plane. He, go later." The doctor looked toward George. "You endanger more by staying."

George had moved toward the door and now he turned, motioning for Eaves and Elder to follow.

Eaves eyes misted.

Could he trust this man? Leave his buddy?

He blinked. There's no way Sherman could hike those steep mountain trails they'd traversed, but was it safe to leave him here? "The Germans—they don't come here?"

"No, Partisans control here. The British send some medical supplies. We are careful, watch for German sympathizers. Safe for now." The doctor gave a tight-lipped smile. "Have plan to move, if necessary. But your time is short—must cover over one hundred kilometers distance."

Eaves hesitated. Maybe this was God's plan. These men had risked all to help them get this far. He would have to trust them.

Slowly he nodded. Walking over to Sherman, he took his hand and squeezed it. "You'll be okay here. Get well."

Sherman didn't respond.

Eaves looked at the doctor. "Tell him for me—that we'll be waiting for him in Italy."

✈✈✈

The forest trail led higher, giving way to boulders and low-lying brush. Eaves' legs ached from the upward climb and his feet hurt from the rocks that poked through the holes in his boots. He grimaced as another pebble wormed its way under the ball of his foot.

He prayed Sherman was doing better. He saw now why George had sent the cart back to Bara. No way a cart could've maneuvered these narrow, rocky goat trails.

George had kept them in the thick of the forest most of the day, but now as dusk fell, he led them upward toward the summit. He motioned for them to stop by some boulders, as he climbed up on one. Cocking his head, he listened and scanned the skies. Always the danger of German planes.

Eaves dumped out the pebble and pulled his boot back on, carefully wrapping his foot in the silk parachute material he'd used as a liner. He scratched his chest. Disgusting vermin.

As they'd hiked along, some of the men had talked about sports, then starlets and favorite singers. But somehow the conversation always led back to favorite foods, and those loved ones they missed at home. Eventually, they fell silent as hunger gnawed at them and the reality of the situation stimulated only apprehension. Hope of rescue seemed to flit away like a butterfly, just out of reach.

George had pushed them relentlessly. Now he hopped down from the boulder perch and motioned them on, striding quickly through the broken rock chips to the barren top of the mountain. The young leader's endurance and courage inspired Eaves to continue putting one foot in front of the other, despite his own weakened condition.

Eaves breathed a sigh of relief as they crested the pass and headed downward toward the safety of the woods. Dusk turned to dark, but George continued to trudge down the mountain. Eaves' foot slipped on a loose rock, but he caught his balance without falling.

The sound of running water told Eaves they were approaching another river. Suddenly George held up his hand to stop the group. Motioning them to wait, he signaled one of the young men with him to scout ahead.

Eaves slumped down onto the ground, grateful for a rest. Elder sank down beside him.

"Where do you think we are?" he whispered.

Eaves shrugged. "Don't know. But we covered a heck of a lot of territory today."

He raised his eyes to see the young Partisan return and speak quietly to George. After a brief consultation, George held his finger to his lips and motioned the airmen to follow.

Emerging from the forest, Eaves saw a rutted single-lane road before them. The group made better time as they strode down the road, moonlight helping to illuminate potholes and rocks.

His stomach growled. It had been hours since they stopped to eat anything. The small chunk of sour goat cheese and a crust of dark bread hadn't eased the ache of hunger. His flight suit hung loosely on him now. Not a diet he'd recommend to anyone. He swallowed hard, envisioning Aunt Minnie's sweet corn bread and a big bowl of beans before him. Saliva filled his mouth.

His daydream stopped abruptly as George stepped off the road and headed down another narrow trail toward the river. Eaves peered at the dark trail warily as he followed, trying not to trip on a root or rock. The rush of water sounded closer. Upon reaching the bank of the river, George moved even more cautiously, suddenly motioning for the group to stop and drop down.

As he dropped to his knees, Eaves looked up to see a railroad bridge looming across the river ahead. And he could just make out the shadowed form of a man walking across the trestle. A match flared as he stopped and lit a cigarette. Eaves saw the rifle on his shoulder. A German guard.

He sucked in his breath and his gut tightened.

George whispered to the two young Partisans and they slunk away into the darkness, moving like shadows. Again, George touched his lips with his finger as he crept back along the group of airmen, making sure they all saw, motioning them into the bushes.

Eaves sprawled behind a large bush, his heart pounding in his chest.

Dear Lord, please keep us all safe from our enemies.

He strained to listen for any sounds that would reveal other German soldiers. The gurgle of rushing water, a croak of a frog and the heavy breathing of the men around him was all he could hear.

Chapter 36

JULY 1944—STALAG LUFT III, SAGAN, GERMANY

HAVERKOS GLANCED OVER THE TITLES of the books on the two shelves lining the library wall. All books he'd already read, some of them twice.

The small room served as both a living room and library. Thankfully the International YMCA through Sweden was allowed to provide new reading material occasionally for the kriegies. He'd seen their representative, a sandy-haired Swedish lawyer, Henry Söderberg, once at the theater when he'd made one of his regular visits to the camp, personally checking to be sure the prisoners actually received the supplies.

Haverkos had learned that besides the books, the YMCA also supplied musical instruments, scripts for the theater productions, and religious supplies for the chaplains.

Stepping back, Haverkos leaned against the wall and studied the men who slipped into the room one by one. He nodded to a couple of guys he knew, but the rest were strangers.

"Close the door," Colonel Goodrich said after the tenth man had entered the small room.

The senior American officer introduced Haverkos to the group. "Remember—what is said in this room and who is here must stay locked in the confines of your mind. The fewer people involved, the safer we all are." The colonel paused and looked solemnly at each man in the room.

"Now, let's get down to the business at hand. The North Compound sent some interesting information today." He nodded to a lean lieutenant with intense blue eyes and blonde hair who was seated on one of the wooden chairs.

"You all know we were told that anyone trying to escape from now on would be executed." The lieutenant looked around the circle. "Well, a lad from Scotland in the North Compound was adamant in requesting the chance to try to escape and test that threat. The X Committee finally agreed. The day before yesterday he hid under an empty tin in the garbage truck and got out the gate. He managed to slip out of the truck and had walked an hour or so when some Wehrmacht soldiers happened by. They snagged him and hauled him back to the camp. Oberst Braune was furious. He had him thrown into the cooler for two weeks. So . . . it looks like the new Kommandant isn't going to follow through with the order to execute." He paused, then cocked his head. "Now, if it had been the Gestapo who found him, it might have been a different story."

The colonel leaned forward and spoke firmly. "The Brits have continued with their escape plans. There's another tunnel in the works, hopefully to the wire before the snow flies. As many of you know, the major concern before us all is that when Germany falls, as we know it will, Hitler may order all Allied airmen executed. Colonel Wilson, the senior British officer, is creating a plan for a compound-wide effort to create self-defense diversions if worse comes to worst. He asked if we will join in with them." He looked intently into each face. "What say you?"

The reality of the threat could not be denied. Haverkos' chest tightened thinking of the fifty unarmed POWs ruthlessly executed just a month ago.

A gaunt, dark-haired lieutenant spoke up. "Better to do something than just sit on our hands and wait."

A chorus of voices rang out in agreement, heads nodding.

"All right then, we'll send word back to him and find out what they want from us." Colonel Goodrich gave a tight-lipped smile.

"Meanwhile, we will continue with our own plans. The other alternative we may face is being marched to the west as the Russians advance on the Eastern Front. Start having the men in your barracks think about preparing to carry what they may need on a forced march. Questions?" He glanced around the group, but no one spoke up.

"We'll meet in the Barracks Four library in two days, around 1300. Be careful not to draw the attention of the guards. Glimnetz has been especially nosy lately, and his ferrets are everywhere."

Haverkos had seen the stern-faced chief German security supervisor just that morning at *appell*, the required roll-call where they stood outside in blocks to be counted twice a day. Glimnetz stood rigid with his arms crossed, coldly observing the prisoners. He wore his stiff peaked cap and was in complete uniform, as usual. His stooges dressed more casually, usually in overalls as they were often ordered to crawl under barracks to eavesdrop. Haverkos had learned the ferrets were susceptible to bribes, with some even sympathetic to the POWs.

To the contrary, Glimnetz was always formal and serious about his job. Haverkos had never seen him let down his guard. If a block count didn't add up, the kriegies would be called up one by one for a photo comparison, which could mean several hours of standing regardless of the weather, sometimes even into the night.

"Glimnetz has been walking up to airmen and demanding to know, 'How many tunnels now?' Just shrug and ignore him when he does that," Goodrich said. "Oh, yes—one piece of good news. Last week we got a coded letter from one of the men who escaped in March—Bob Van Der Stok. His plan was to go the Southern Route. The underground must have helped him reach Madrid, and the British Counsel flew him back to England."

The guys smiled and gave soft cheers, patting each other on the back.

Colonel Goodrich offered a slight smile. "Yes, that's the third one we know for sure made it back to Allied lines. Eight men are still unaccounted for."

The colonel stood and the men began to depart.

Haverkos waited at the barracks door for a few minutes until the man ahead of him ducked into the compound cookhouse. All the "goon food" was prepared there by conscripted Allied prisoners.

For the past two weeks no Red Cross parcels had been distributed. The Germans claimed the Allies had bombed the supply trains, saying with a laugh, "They destroyed your food."

Haverkos didn't believe that, but who knew? So, rations had consisted of a thin slice of dark, sour-tasting goon bread twice a day. He found if he toasted it on the little two-burner stove in the dining room, it went down easier.

He checked again to see if the coast was clear before stepping out and then nonchalantly headed toward the walking path winding along the inside row of barbed wire. With fifteen guys in his room, a walk around the perimeter provided an opportunity for a little solitude and to stretch his legs. Thoughtfully he mulled over the information that had been shared in the meeting. Then Ginny and home came to mind.

Would he ever see her again?

His stomach growled. Almost dinnertime.

Visions of the day-old bread and rolls from Haggenhoffer's bakery made his mouth water. Back home in Cincinnati, the kind-hearted baker next door had sold a whole sack of bread to his family for ten cents during the hard times of the Depression.

He shook his head.

Can't go there.

He gritted his teeth. Just have to wait and see if anything better than goon bread is offered tonight.

The theater sat on his right. Besides the softball games, he enjoyed the theater productions that the guys put on every month or so. Some were so professionally done he'd heard that Kommandant Oberst Von Lindeiner had even brought his wife to a show once before the big escape. He slowed down by the bulletin board to see the next offering before continuing on toward his barracks.

The dismal empty time after dinner loomed large in his mind. Every night after the evening meal, the kriegies were confined to their barracks. Bored and crammed together, they'd play cards or read till ten, the appointed time for lights out.

Then the guards marched about the compound, barring the doors of each barracks with wooden beams. A lighted window could draw a bullet. Guard dogs were turned loose to roam free all night, good deterrents to any thoughts of a nighttime escape attempt.

At *appell*, the vicious, snarling creatures strained at their leashes to nip any kriegies not shuffling into line fast enough. Once, one tore a pocket off his pants. Thank goodness, it didn't bite his leg.

Pockets. That's a good idea.

Sewing pockets into their blankets might be a good way to carry extra food and personal items on a forced march. He'd talk to Sam about that.

Chapter 37

JULY 1944—SOMEWHERE IN YUGOSLAVIA

EAVES' HAMSTRING CRAMPED as he lay flattened to the earth, and he stretched out his leg to relieve it.

A distinct bird call trilled through the night air and George cocked his head. Moments later, the call repeated. George scrambled to his feet and motioned for the airmen to follow him down the narrow path that wound along the riverbank.

Eaves looked up but saw no one on the railroad bridge. Silently, the column of airmen moved toward the bridge looming in the twilight. As they reached the embankment leading up to the tracks, George stopped. The shadowy forms of the two young Partisans rose above them.

Eaves whispered to George, "What about the German?"

George looked at him, his lips tightening into a thin line under his dark mustache. He slowly raised his arm and drew his finger across his throat, then turned to start up the embankment.

Eaves' eyes widened, and his heart thudded against his rib cage. Just young teens, these Partisans were hardened soldiers, patriots willing to risk all to take him and the other airmen to safety. An enemy had been killed for their lives.

Eaves started climbing, but after only two steps his foot slipped on a loose rock. It careened down the incline as he stumbled, then fell to his knees before regaining his footing.

Glancing up, he saw George looked back at him but then resumed his climb.

Guess he's not worried that other enemy ears might hear.

Puffing from exertion as he reached the railroad tracks, Eaves stood behind George and waited for the rest of the group to join them.

George scanned the area before motioning the group to follow him across the bridge.

Eaves looked to the right and the left by the guardhouse. No sign of the German guard.

In the darkness, a tight, eerie feeling coursed through him. A man had just died here. The Partisans probably disposed of the body so the Germans would not find it right away and seek retaliation.

George and the villagers who helped them were risking their very lives. His jaw clenched and his gut tightened remembering the ruthlessness of the Germans. Airmen who had recently joined them told of a whole village of more than a hundred people, mostly old men, women and children, who had been executed by the Germans because they had helped Americans and would not tell where they had gone. His heart broke to hear of their sacrifice.

The sound of boots thumping on the wooden trestle echoed through the night, sending a cold wave of fear cascading through him.

Did other enemy soldiers lurk within hearing distance?

But George strode confidently ahead.

Eaves exhaled deeply as they reached the safety of the far side. George continued following the rails, stepping from beam to beam. In the moonlight the tracks provided a stable walkway and the group marched steadily into the night.

Suddenly, a train whistle cut through the silence.

George bolted off the tracks to the left, rushing up the mountainside into thick forest. The airmen ran after him, scrambling through the bushes and into the trees. Eaves felt the sting of thin branches slapping him in the face. He threw up his arms to ward them off as they fled deeper into the woods.

Another blare from the train pierced the night, probably to alert the crossing guard. The train was getting closer.

Eaves stopped to catch his breath just as the light of the engine cut through the dark, illuminating the rails immediately in front of it, chugging upward toward the bridge. A cloud of steam rose from the locomotive's engine as it hissed up the incline. No other lights gleamed from the train.

A blacked-out train, probably an attempt to evade any Allied B-25s seeking to strafe German supply trains.

In the safety of the trees, Eaves hunkered down, listening to the clanking wheels and feeling the vibration as the dark train cars rocked by.

Thank You, God, that You got us off the tracks. Timing couldn't have been much closer.

The train whistle faded into the distance. Stillness once more filled the night. Eaves heard the ragged breathing of the men close to him and an owl's plaintive call.

Finally, George stood and brushed off his dark clothing. He whispered with the two young Partisans, who immediately disappeared into the forest. Turning to the airmen, George said, "We wait."

Eaves fumbled in his pack for his water bottle. Only a few sips left. He took a small drink and sloshed it around in his dry mouth before swallowing.

Leaning back against a tree trunk, he checked his watch. Ten minutes. Twenty minutes. His eyelids drooped.

A shuffling noise in the bushes behind him startled him awake. The two scouts reappeared and slipped over to George.

After conferring, George motioned to the airmen. Some men groaned, but Eaves staggered to his feet and followed George deeper into the forest. Higher on the mountainside, George turned down a narrow trail apparently familiar to him.

Eaves struggled to keep putting one foot in front of the other as he scratched at the elusive lice and fleas that tormented him. How much farther did they have to go tonight?

After another half hour of walking, they entered a small clearing. The faint gurgle of water revealed the presence of a small spring emerging from behind a large boulder. Eaves waited his turn to gratefully plunge his bottle into the cool, clear water and took a deep draught to quench his thirst.

He turned to see George rolling out his blanket in a grassy area. Eaves slipped off his backpack and glanced at his watch. After midnight. How many more days like this could he handle?

✈✈✈

George roused the airmen before the sun had crested the mountains. Eaves gratefully received a small chunk of smelly goat cheese and a crust of dark bread from the young Partisans, chewing slowly and washing it down with a swig of water. Carefully he tied his blanket to the makeshift pack and filled his water bottle. Determined to be ready, he pushed to his feet when George announced, "We go."

Cumulus clouds floated by in an azure sky. Staying on narrow trails leading through the forest, the men silently trudged like ants, one after another. A refreshing gentle breeze brought bird sounds, and random wildflowers brightened the path. In the peaceful forest Eaves could almost forget there was a war going on.

The plaintive whistle of a distant train broke the silence. Eaves' skin crawled. They were still in enemy territory. The Germans were actively moving men and supplies through this area.

It was late afternoon before George signaled another rest stop by a small stream. Only a small piece of jerky for each man. Again, they filled water bottles before pressing on.

As the sun dropped lower in the western sky, Eaves noticed that they were moving downward on switchback trails into a valley. Soon sounds of rushing water told him a river was up ahead. George slowed his pace, pausing to listen carefully before crossing a wide clearing. He stopped in a grove of trees on the other side and motioned the airmen down.

Elder squatted down by Eaves. "We must have come over twenty miles today."

Eaves nodded. "Covered a lot of ground. How are you doing?"

"Okay, just hoping we get there, wherever there is, soon."

George left with the two scouts but returned in about ten minutes. Motioning to Eaves, Elder, and the two men closest to them, he turned and led the four of them down to the river. A rope stretched across wide, rushing water and a small handmade rowboat lay pulled up against the bank, a stranger in a dark cap and rough garb at the helm.

George motioned for them to climb into the boat. If they squeezed together, four men could fit on the two empty plank seats. Eaves took off his backpack and stepped in, sticking it between his knees as he settled into the boat that sank lower into the river as the men loaded. The boat was coupled to the rope, and the oarsman pushed away from the bank. He leaned back and took one or two powerful strokes with the oars when the growl of a motor startled them all.

"*Švabo! Švabo!*" George spewed out more sharp words in his dialect. The young man rapidly returned the boat to the shore.

Eaves' heart pounded. Germans. Must be a road on the far bank.

"Out, out," George motioned toward the bushes on the bank. Eaves and the other men leaped out and ran, throwing themselves down in a small ditch behind the biggest shrubs they could see. He pressed himself against the rough ground, breathing in dust and the smell of fresh grass.

He lifted his head to peer through the bushes. The boat had disappeared behind some reeds and willows. The rope was gone. Maybe submerged in the water.

The growl of a truck motor grew louder.

Eaves ducked down and reached for his pistol. He hoped he wouldn't need to use it.

A German voice barked out orders. Time seemed frozen in place as Eaves stayed rooted in position. He listened as the whine of the truck motor and the tromp of many feet faded into the distance.

Maybe the Germans had been on patrol or seeking local produce. Whatever their mission, they hadn't noticed the Allied airmen on the far bank.

Eaves relaxed as he held his position. No movement from George.

Thirty minutes after the sounds of the Germans melted away, George stood and stretched. He slid the rowboat out of its hiding place and connected it to the dripping rope tautly stretched across the surging water.

Eaves and Elder climbed back into the boat, but this time with the two young Partisan scouts. The oarsman dipped the rough-hewn paddles deep into the water and his muscular arms pulled rhythmically, delivering them swiftly to the other bank. Clambering onto the shore, one young Partisan led them across the road and deeper into the forest on another narrow trail that ended in a small clearing, where he motioned for them to wait. He turned and rapidly strode back toward the river.

Eaves sank down and leaned against a log, grateful for time to rest while the others were being ferried across the river. His last reserves were fading. He couldn't believe how weak he felt. Hunger, bugs, and three days of hard hiking had taken a toll.

Elder closed his eyes. Moments later gentle snoring told Eaves the flight engineer was spent, too.

Eaves let his heavy eyelids droop shut as he contemplated the last three days. How far could they be from the destination? Everyone was worn out, gastrointestinal issues affected all of them. Would they arrive in time? Where would planes be able to land, if they did come?

So many questions. He had no answers, only hope in the promise that they were coming to rescue them.

A rustling in the bushes. Eaves opened his eyes to see four more airmen trudge into the clearing led by the young scout, who quickly retreated back to the river. He nodded to Eddie, who sank down beside him.

Eddie tugged at his sock. "Well, I reckon that was a little excitement I could do without. Hope those boys don't come back this way."

"Sure wish we had a map, or knew how far we still have to go," Eaves said. "You doin' okay?"

"Been better, that's for sure. Hoping we reach another village soon. Appreciate those folks sharing their grub with us." Eddie pulled out a canteen and took a deep draught before rolling over and closing his eyes.

Eaves leaned back.

Gotta grab a wink of sleep while we can. Lord, help us make it to that rendezvous spot on time.

Chapter 38

August 1944—somewhere in Yugoslavia

THE VILLAGE SAT TUCKED into the hillside, stone huts with thatched straw roofs. Eaves squinted through the dusk. Maybe ten cottages.

George strode forward to talk with the elders who greeted them and quickly assigned three men to each house.

Eaves, Elder, and Eddie were welcomed into a small cottage by a tiny gray-haired matron, slightly bent over, with her black kerchief tied under her wrinkled chin and rough woolen clothing covering her from head to toe. She clucked over them, nodding and smiling, pointing to a rough plank table and crude chairs close to the fireplace where a black pot bubbled, emitting tantalizing odors. Eaves' mouth filled with saliva.

She stirred the pot and dipped up three bowls of stew. Eaves smiled his thanks and looked into a wooden bowl filled with vegetables and even small chunks of meat. He briefly wondered what kind of meat it was but his stomach didn't care.

As he and the two men slurped down the soup, she returned with a small loaf of dark bread, which she then chopped into four chunks. The familiar smell of goat cheese wafted through the air as she unwrapped a cloth-covered bundle and cut a slice for each of them. A feast.

When they'd finished, she hobbled to the door with a gnarled cane and led them to a small barn behind the cottage. A pen held a spotted goat, and two scrawny chickens scurried about. She tugged open a creaky barn door and motioned toward the haystack.

Elder grinned. "This must be the guest bedroom. Better than the open field we slept in last night."

Eaves agreed. "Beggars can't be choosers." Again, he nodded and smiled his thanks.

She pulled the door closed. Eaves drew the blanket from his pack and folded his fleece flight pants into a pillow. Settling down into the fragrant hay in the darkness, he hardly closed his eyes before sleep overtook him.

George roused them from the barn before daylight. Their hostess stood outside the cottage door and beckoned them inside. Three bowls of gruel and another small chunk of dark bread waited for them on the table lit by a small oil lamp.

The three airmen hastily gulped down the hot porridge and grabbed the bread to eat on the way. They each bowed and smiled their thanks to the tiny woman, who stood in the doorway with a gentle smile, nodding to them as they hurried out.

George rounded up all the men and headed into the mountains before the sun peeked over the horizon. On the rocky goat trails, Eaves felt safer, away from the roads and railways frequented by the Germans.

The men were silent as they trudged up the mountain. Eaves thought of the blessings they had just experienced. Such generosity and kindness.

Thank You, Lord. This is the day You have made, and I will rejoice in it. Please bless the little woman who shared her food and gave us shelter. We have been blessed by so many ordinary folks on this journey—Your angels of mercy. George and the other Partisans who have guided us. I'm so grateful for Your provision for us. Help us get back to Italy soon. In Jesus' name. Amen

The sun rose above them and the trail led up, up, up—another mountain range to scale.

Eaves stumbled along, his muscles aching and his lungs sucking in air as his body strained to climb the steep incline. When they reached a summit in the trees George gave them a rest before heading down switchback trails into another wide valley.

George seemed more relaxed, whistling a haunting tune as he strode along and confidently choosing a trail each time the path split into divergent ways. As the sun passed its zenith, George motioned them to sit as the two young Partisans distributed some jerky to each man.

Eaves chewed slowly, savoring the small offering before finally washing it down with a swallow of water, grateful for the sustenance and the rest.

George seemed in no hurry this time, leaning back against a tree trunk. He looked at Eaves and held up two fingers about an inch apart. "No far," he said with a wink.

Eaves grinned. "Not far. Good," he said with a laugh. He was proud of George working to improve his English. Hearing they were close to their destination was music to his ears.

Finally, George rose and motioned for the men to follow. The trail wound down into the valley. They had walked another hour when Eaves caught a glimpse of tents amid the trees. George stopped and called out, "*Americanski! Americanski!*"

People emerged from among the tents and rushed toward them. Young men and women, Partisans with their trademark red stars sewn on their caps and in dark garb. And others in flight suits—more Americans.

Eaves' heart pounded in his chest. This has got to be it.

The rendezvous spot!

✈✈✈

"Well, the word is out that the planes are expected today. Just hope they're right." Eddie rubbed his jaw as he surveyed the valley in front of them. "This is the place they're supposed to land."

Eaves peered out from the protection of the forest. A wide pasture with a few cows munching grass did not look much like a landing field. But that was exactly what the Partisans wanted the Germans to think if they flew over. A good disguise.

Some Partisans moved into the pasture, shooing the cattle toward a barn at the far end of the field.

"The planes were supposed to arrive last night, but the fog was too thick." Eddie chewed his lip. "Hoping for a rerun today."

The encampment contained a large contingency of rebel fighters, tents carefully hidden among the trees. Eaves had noticed some wounded, obviously needing medical care, apparently from a recent battle with the Germans. An additional twenty-some Allied airmen were also gathered here waiting for rescue. No one he recognized.

Eaves turned to head back to the tents. "They say the Allies have been routinely sending supplies and food to the Partisans here. They pick up downed airmen and take the injured to the hospital in Bari."

He squinted as a bright shaft of sunlight filtered through the trees and glared into his eyes. "Wish I knew how Sherman was doing. I hated leaving him in that hospital, but we have to trust these Partisans. They've sacrificed a lot to bring us here, and I've got to believe they'll get him out when he can travel."

Eddie plucked a grass stem and chewed on the end. "Well, we got no choice but to trust 'em. Been straight arrows so far."

After walking about fifteen minutes, they reached the tent where they'd spent the last night. It was U.S. government issue, like most of the tents here. Eaves lifted the canvas flap and they ducked down to enter.

"Well, lieutenant," Elder said, looking up at them from his spot on the ground. "What do you think?"

"Little rough for a runway but looks possible for planes to land." Eaves said. "Wait a minute." He cocked his head. "Listen."

A dull roar greeted their ears.

Eddie whooped. "Planes—I hear planes! Let's go!"

All three men grabbed their packs and ran back toward the field. Other airmen flowed out of the adjoining tents and joined them, all shouting with excitement.

As they surged into the clearing, four C-47s were already on the ground, with bands of Partisans scurrying about, carrying boxes of food, medical supplies and ammunition back toward the encampment. Four Spitfires circled overhead.

Adrenaline pulsed through him. Eaves could scarcely believe his eyes. He didn't dare blink. Was it a dream? Tears stung his eyes.

They really are here, behind German lines. Thank You, Jesus!

By the time he reached the planes, the supplies were almost all unloaded. George waved them toward the first plane. Eaves stopped and pumped his hand.

"*Americanski!*" George gave him a huge bear hug and kissed each cheek.

Eaves looked deep in his eyes. "Thank you so, so much." It just didn't seem enough.

Suddenly he looked at George's threadbare coat and thought about the cold winter coming. He dropped his pack and jerked out his leather fleece-lined jacket. He held it out, putting it in George's hands. "For you. Stay warm. I won't ever forget what you did for us."

George's eyes widened, then he grinned. Clutching the jacket to his chest, he dipped his head and then looked up. "Dank you . . . Eaves."

"Hurry, men. Load up!" A sergeant reached down to pull one airman after another into the plane through the cargo door. Eaves reached up and grasped the outstretched hand.

Once inside, Eaves pulled on his fleece-lined flight pants and wrapped his blanket around his shoulders as he settled down with his back against the ribs of the fuselage. Elder and Eddie plopped down on each side. Soon twenty men had crammed together into the cargo hold. A crew member handed out more blankets.

Propellers rotated. The two Pratt &Whitney Twin Wasp engines roared as the cargo plane taxied toward the middle of the field and braked. The plane vibrated wildly as the pilot accelerated for takeoff.

Finally, the pilot released the quivering plane, and it raced forward down the field, bouncing over the rough turf. Eaves felt a thrill explode into his chest as the plane lifted off and the smooth feeling of flight replaced the jarring ride. Gradually, the plane gained altitude and wheels tucked up into their casings.

Eaves pinched his arm. Yep, he really was awake. He still couldn't believe it.

The whine of the twin engines resonated through the fuselage with a noise both physically irritating and strange to Eaves' ears. Usually, he was in the cockpit with the roar of engines thrumming around him, busy with piloting the plane and staying in touch with the crew.

He leaned backed and closed his eyes. None of those responsibilities today.

After two months behind German lines, he was finally headed back to Italy.

✈✈✈

The plane shuddered.

Eaves jerked awake. The all-too-familiar smell of cordite filled the fuselage, the pepper of shrapnel pelting the skin of the plane, pinpoints of light appearing above them. Flak!

His gut constricted as the plane suddenly dropped downward.

Eaves clenched his jaw. The pilot was probably trying defensive maneuvers to dive out of range. He pulled his ragged blanket tighter around his shoulder and took a deep breath, sending up a quick prayer.

Lord, keep us safe. Almost there.

The engines whined as the plane accelerated. Eaves found himself holding his breath. He released the air in his lungs and inhaled a ragged breath. In. Out.

He checked his watch. Five minutes. Ten minutes. No more hits.

Eaves began to relax.

Thirty minutes. Forty minutes. Time crept by.

The plane began to descend. Eaves heard the grind of the landing gear setting in place.

Finally, the plane touched down and vibrated roughly as the pilots applied the brakes. The C-47 slowly turned, taxied to its revetment, and parked.

A sergeant poked his head into the fuselage. "Welcome to Bari!"

The men shouted and cheered. Eaves grinned and clapped Elder on the back.

"Bari—We made it! Praise the Lord!"

Chapter 39

27 July 1944—American 36th General Hospital, Bari, Italy

"HOW CAN WE LET our families know we're okay?" The desire to ease their worry was the first thing on Eaves' mind when he arrived at the hospital.

"Sorry, Lieutenant. First things first. We have to get you all deloused and have the doc check you over."

The corpsman-in-charge waved Eaves and the other airmen toward a large shower room. Eaves pulled Jean's picture from his breast pocket and stripped off his ragged flight suit and boots. Besides the picture, nothing of value remained but his dog-tags and his silver wings.

Eaves stuffed everything else into the bag the corpsman held with gloved hands. Finding a safe ledge for Jean's picture and the silver wings, he stepped under the shower head. Hot water poured over his body.

How long had it been since he'd had a shower? Months. He reveled in the incredible feeling of warm streams of water cascading over his frame, massaging his aching muscles. Eaves closed his eyes. He could stay here forever.

"Lieutenant, use the soap, please," a voice interrupted his revelry. "And hurry, sir. Other men are waiting to shower."

Eaves reached for the bar of yellow soap and scrubbed his head and his body. Soap. Another luxury he'd taken for granted.

He rinsed the soap suds off and reluctantly turned off the hot water, accepting the white towel held out to him by the corpsman.

He dried off quickly and wrapped the towel firmly around his waist. After he gathered his silver wings and Jean's picture from the ledge, he headed through the doorway. The corpsman in charge called out, "Next!" and waved another airman from the line into the shower room.

Another corpsman greeted him with a packet in hand. "This is DDT," the corpsman said. "Delousing procedure, sir. Cover every inch of your body with this powder and then put these on." He handed Eaves hospital pajamas and pointed him toward curtained booths along the wall.

He ripped open the packet, and the smell of strong chemicals almost choked him as he sprinkled the DDT over his head. He massaged it into his scalp, then dropped his towel and rubbed the powder over his entire body, holding his breath. His only consolation was hope for relief from the demon bugs that had tormented him for so long.

Reaching for the pajamas, he held them to his nose and inhaled the sweet odor of freshly laundered clothing. His eyes closed as thoughts of home flooded over him and the hope of being with Jean again stirred an ache deep inside.

Emerging from the small, curtained cubicle, he felt almost human again. The corpsman smiled as he handed Eaves a razor and toothbrush, pointing him toward one of the sinks against the wall.

Eaves squinted at the sunburned, scruffy face in the mirror, an image he hardly recognized. Picking up a tube of toothpaste, he squeezed a dab on the bristles and reveled in the simple pleasure of brushing his teeth. After rinsing his mouth, he lathered his face and struggled to scrape off the straggly red beard. Splashing warm water on his face, he glanced up after patting it dry. A new man appeared in the mirror, gaunt but vaguely familiar.

Eaves watched the miraculous change in several other airmen as they completed these simple tasks, hardly recognizable as the disheveled men who had arrived an hour earlier.

A corpsman escorted Eaves and five other men down the hall to exam rooms. A doctor popped in to give him a cursory physical exam before assigning him to a room. Diagnosed as dehydrated and malnourished, Eaves also had general gastrointestinal issues but no serious ailments, thank God.

He was led to a room with four beds. He reveled at the sight of white sheets and a real pillow. He climbed in and pulled up the covers, snuggling into the comfort of a soft mattress for the first time in months.

"Put this under your tongue." He turned his head to see a genuine American female nurse, an angel in white, who had appeared holding a thermometer and a blood pressure cuff.

Eaves had to ask. "Is it possible to get a message to my wife that I'm okay?"

"First, your temperature," she said firmly. "Rest is what you need right now, Lieutenant. Tomorrow is soon enough to meet with the intelligence officers and personnel department. As you know, they're the ones who must do the official contact with families."

Disappointed, he popped the thermometer under his tongue with a sigh. Wait, wait, wait—that's the Army Air Corps way. He's waited this long. He could wait a little bit longer.

And choose to be grateful for being safely out of Yugoslavia.

After recording the data on his chart, she handed him a menu. "What can I bring you to eat?" She hung the chart on the end of his bed. "Anytime you are hungry, you just call. And if you wake up in the middle of the night and are hungry, you're welcome to get up and get yourself some Post Toasties, milk, and sugar from the ward kitchen."

"Post Toasties and milk sound real good right now, ma'am," Eaves said.

She turned to leave. He leaned his head back on the pillow and closed his eyes. Too good to be true. Like coming back from the dead.

Thank You, Lord! Back in Italy with real angels serving us. Only by Your Grace. I pray for the rest of the crew, and especially for Sherman. May he heal and be here soon.

He'd barely finished the Post Toasties before his eyelids drooped and he drifted into a deep sleep.

Chapter 40

1 August 1944—Pantanella Air Field, Italy

ONLY FIVE DAYS LATER, Eaves climbed out of the cargo truck in front of a stone building that housed the 464th Bomb Group's new headquarters and briefing room.

From the hillside where the base was located, he saw twin airstrips of pierced steel planking in the valley below running side-by-side. Hardstands for the bombers branched off the outer edges, surrounded by a small city of tents and buildings providing housing for the crew chiefs and armorers who liked to stay close to their ships.

He squinted at the large cluster of tents and buildings on the adjacent hill to the north. Must be the 465th Bomb Group, a sister B-24 group he'd heard had joined them at the Pantanella Air Field.

Hmm . . . definitely a step up from Gioia del Colle.

His mind flew back to the promise the intelligence officer at Bari had made after his interrogation session—said he'd send a telegram to Jean and his family as soon as possible.

I sure hope they know by now I'm alive and doing okay.

He took a deep breath and squared his shoulders.

Can't control that. Now . . . let's see what my next assignment will be.

Stepping inside, he addressed the orderly seated at the desk in front of a closed office door. "Lieutenant W.T. Eaves, reporting for duty."

"The colonel is expecting you, sir. Go right in."

The man with curly brown hair and a neatly trimmed mustache who sat behind the desk was not Colonel Bonner. The small desk sign read "Colonel A.L. Schroeder."

Eaves stood at attention and saluted. "Lieutenant W.T. Eaves reporting for duty, sir."

"At ease, Captain," the colonel replied.

Eaves blinked.

Captain? Was the colonel confused?

The colonel smiled. "Welcome to Pantanella, Captain Eaves. Congratulations on surviving a difficult journey and on your well-deserved promotion, which came through on 7 July while you were still MIA. Have a seat, Captain." He nodded to the chair in front of the desk.

Eaves removed his cap and sat down on the wooden chair, questions swirling in his mind.

"You probably wonder why I'm seated here instead of Colonel Bonner?"

"Yes, sir."

"Regretfully, the colonel was killed on a mission to the *Florisdorf* Oil Refinery in Vienna on 26 June. I was appointed to replace him."

Eaves felt no grief at the unexpected news.

The colonel paused, looking deeply into Eaves' eyes. "And . . . I understand that you would also like to know if we have any information about your crew." He shuffled through the papers on his desk. "I can tell you that all the men who bailed out with you on 29 May survived."

A surge of joy tingled through Eaves as relief flooded over him.

Tears pricked at his eyes and he struggled to maintain his composure. He could scarcely believe it. "All of them, sir?"

"Three were seriously wounded and in need of medical care when found by the Partisans. Headquarters expedited an airlift to the 36th General Hospital in Bari, which I understand you are now familiar with." He lifted a paper, scanning it quickly. "Lt. Lambert had a broken leg. Sgt. Masterson, wounds to the arms and legs. And your waist gunner, Sgt. Fangman, had twelve wounds in his arms and legs. They all recovered and have been reassigned."

Only by Your grace, Lord! Thank you so much.

"What about Lt. Haverkos and Sgt. Christel, sir?"

"I'm sorry to inform you that both men were captured and are being held in German POW camps. The International Red Cross informs us that Lt. Haverkos is in Stalag Luft III in Sagan, and Sgt. Christel in Stalag Luft IV."

Eaves blinked, as a cold sensation flooded through him and his muscles tensed. POWs. In the hands of the Germans. He swallowed hard.

God help them.

Colonel Schroeder gazed at Eaves, compassion in his eyes. "I understand Sgt. Elder returned from enemy territory with you, but what is the status of your copilot, Lt. Dan Sherman?"

Eaves cleared his throat. "Lt. Sherman fell ill with pneumonia and required hospitalization. The Partisans assured me he would be dispatched to the airfield we were rescued from as soon as he was able to travel."

The colonel made a note and laid the paperwork down before he looked up. "I must commend you, Captain Eaves, for your bravery and endurance. Reportedly, you provided assistance to three stragglers 29 May by pulling your aircraft back to add your fire power to theirs. Staying at the helm of a burning plane, you maintained control of the ship to enable your men to bail out. And you aided and supported your copilot and flight engineer in your two-month saga evading the enemy. I've written you up for a Silver Star, Captain."

Eaves flushed. Shaking his head, the faces of Petrone and McMillan flashed through his mind. If only . . .

"Sir, I only did my duty. I'm no hero. The real heroes are the men who died."

"I understand, Captain. Their sacrifices will never be forgotten." He sighed, his eyes darkened with pain. "I've had to write far too many letters to families at home."

Both men sat in the sadness for a moment.

The colonel cleared his throat. "I understand that your gunners performed incredibly well under extreme pressure. Reportedly, they knocked down two, maybe three German fighter planes. So, I'm also recommending that all five receive a Silver Star."

Eaves throat tightened, his eyes filled with tears. "That means so much. Thank you, sir, thank you."

The colonel lifted his eyebrows. "By the way, Captain, do you think you might remember how to fly an older B-24?"

"Yes, sir. The very planes I learned on."

"Good. Here are your orders." He picked up some documents and handed them to Eaves with a slight smile tugging at his lips. "On 3 August you are to pilot your Operations Officer, Captain Fred Hunt, and others to Naples. You will accompany him on a boat ride . . . out to the Isle of Capri for a few days of rest." His eyes twinkled and then crinkled in the corners as his smile widened. "Hope it's all that it's cracked up to be. You deserve it."

Eaves sucked in breath. Back as a pilot but headed for R & R—too good to be true.

Captain Hunt was a good egg. Hanging with him would hardly be a problem.

Colonel Schroeder glanced down at the stack of documents crowding his desktop before he slowly looked up again. "Please check with the orderly out front regarding your immediate needs, Captain. That's all."

"Thank you, sir." Eaves stood and saluted.

This was one order he could hardly wait to obey.

✈✈✈

Tudor was waiting outside headquarters, a smile stretching from ear to ear. "Aren't you a sight for sore eyes!" He pounded Eaves on the back. "Rumors spread faster than wildfire here. They said you were back. How the heck are you?"

Eaves grinned at his friend. "Still in one piece. Maybe a little lighter and pretty dehydrated when I got to Bari. Hated the DDT dusting, but it relieved me of some pesky vermin I was plenty ready to be rid of. And . . . I'll never take warm water or a toothbrush for granted again."

"Where's Sherman? Heard the rest of your crew survived but hated to hear that Haverkos and Christel are guests of the Germans."

"Had to leave him in a hospital with the Partisans. They promised to help him leave as soon as he can travel."

Tudor nodded. "By the way, we've got room in our little casa for an extra cot. Had some downtime right after our arrival and we managed to get native Tufa rock to make the floor and walls. The tent just covers the top." He paused, then frowned.

"Gotta tell you . . . the whole group was locked down for over a week in early June and rumors flew. Some thought Bonner was finally gone for sure, but others thought we were headed for the Pacific." He shook his head. "The brass visited Bonner and then he started flying more missions. We never did find out why the whole 464th was grounded, but . . . you've probably heard about Bonner?"

Eaves nodded, feeling a small stab of guilt that he felt no grief at his passing.

"Colonel Schroeder is a regular guy. He actually buzzed the landing strip the day he arrived. Been leading most of the missions himself since he got here and holds people accountable. He definitely is earning the respect of the men."

"We've needed a commanding officer we can look up to. He gave me a good welcome to Pantanella today." Eaves paused, then smiled. "And . . . a surprise gift—R&R for a week on the Isle of Capri!"

Tudor's eyebrows popped up, and he gave a low whistle. "What I wouldn't give for a few more days of that. Colonel Schroeder realized right away that the crews needed a little R&R or we'd all be flak-happy. Had a week in Naples myself." He cocked his head. "Any room in your suitcase for a buddy?"

Eaves laughed. "Wish I could sneak you onboard. My orders are to fly Captain Hunt there on the 3rd and accompany him." He looked sideways at Tudor. "I thought you might've reached the magic thirty missions and earned the right to head home by now."

Tudor just shook his head. His eyes looked sad as he gazed away. "Bad weather still shuts down a lot of missions, like the one today. And they upped the ante. Now it takes fifty missions to earn the right to go home." He sighed "I hate to tell you, but there are only three crews left in the 777th Squadron that started with us in Gioia."

Fifty missions? I'll never make it home. Only three crews left in the 777th?

Eaves felt his eyes widen in disbelief, a sick feeling in his gut.

Dear God. Three-fourths of his original squadron . . . gone.

Friends flashed through his mind, the faces of Petrone and McMillian lingering. He sucked in his breath and struggled to keep his composure. So much loss. And only God knew why he was still here and they weren't.

As they turned and silently walked down the hill, the strident voice of Winston Churchill played in his mind. He had never forgotten the stirring eloquence of his 1940 radio broadcast. "We shall not flag or fail. We shall go on to the end. We shall fight in France, we shall fight on the seas and the oceans, we shall fight in the air. Whatever the cost . . . we shall never give up." Churchill had refused to consider surrender or compromise with the Germans.

Roosevelt echoed the same message after Pearl Harbor. Peace demanded total commitment to fight to the end. And . . . the Army Air Corps was making a difference. He was doing his part in this war, and the Allies were pushing toward Germany itself.

Eaves' eyes stung. The price of freedom and ultimate victory was high . . . very high.

✈✈✈

7 AUGUST 1944—PANTANELLA AIR BASE, ITALY

Touted as one of the favorite spots for rest and relaxation, the Isle of Capri had lived up to its reputation. Eaves had no trouble piloting the "hackship" he'd been assigned, an older B-24A retired from combat duty. As he headed back to Pantanella with a plane-load of men returning from R&R, he reflected on the past few days that seemed like a fairy tale.

He and Captain Hunt had taken a two-hour boat ride from Naples to the island, then rode on the *Funicolare,* a small cable car that ran up the steep cliffs to hotels where the men stayed. The officers bunked at the *Qusianna,* while Elder and the other enlisted men reported to the *Bella Sojorno.* Both hotels had beds with real mattresses and sheets, with tile floors, hot and cold running water, and toilets that flushed. The food was excellent, much better than the fare at the base, and they even served ice cream twice.

Eaves found all kinds of things to do on the island. Every day he enjoyed a dip in crystal blue waters and time on sandy beaches relaxing in the sun. Lots of little shops to explore, with vendors eager to accept military script for souvenirs, haircuts, and drinks of all kinds.

He and Captain Hunt toured the ruins of the Villa of Tiberius high on a bluff and took the boat ride around the island to the Blue Grotto, an incredibly beautiful cave at sea level. When the boat floated inside, Eaves gaped at the incandescent blue light reflecting up through the water and cascading onto the walls. Reportedly fifteen to twenty feet deep, the blue pool appeared so shallow he thought he could wade in it.

As the older B-24 lumbered back to Pantanella, Eaves mused over how the time had flown by so fast. The only thing that would have made it better was if Jean were there to share it with him. He had written letters to her and all the family from Pantanella and again while on leave.

After shutting off the engines and completing his flight record, Eaves climbed out of the bomber and headed toward the hardstand for *All Meat-No Potatoes.* Tudor had named the new replacement B-24 with the same handle. He could hardly wait to tell Tudor about the adventures on the Isle of Capri.

Empty. Must not be back yet from today's mission.

He caught the eye of the crew chief, who was heading toward the staging area. His grimy fatigue cap was pushed up, his hands stained with oil and hydraulic fluids. Eaves reflected on the many sleepless nights the ground crews put in to keep their "baby" in the air.

"Hey, Sergeant, where was the mission today?"

A concerned look passed over the crew chief's face. "Blechhammer," he said. "They should be returning soon, Captain. Last three missions, all the planes made it back. Just hoping the lucky streak continues. Colonel Schroeder was flying the lead."

Eaves felt a shiver pass through him, and his gut tightened.

Blechhammer. . . heard of it. Another notoriously difficult target with synthetic oil refineries the Germans fought desperately to protect.

Eaves and the crew chief strode briskly toward the tower where the emergency crews had already gathered. The low rumble of a plane motor cut through the air. Eaves squinted in the bright sunlight and raised his hand to shield his eyes from the glare of the sun as he spotted the first planes headed toward the runway.

His heart pounded and he licked his dry lips. A nauseous feeling swept over him as visions of his last mission swam through his mind. He shook his head—*that's over, stay in today.*

Red flares flew as planes approached the base. Crews rushed to man the ambulances and fire trucks. One after another the aircraft landed, but Eaves had still not spotted Tudor's plane. Then the sky was quiet, no more planes in sight.

"How many planes went out today?" he asked the crew chief, a sick feeling deepening inside.

"Twenty-eight, but two returned with mechanical problems. I counted twenty-three planes in so far. We're missing three."

A lone P-38 appeared on the horizon. Eaves watched as the twin-tailed fighter plane made a pass at the runway and then pulled up, turned around and made another low pass over the runway. Some buzz job. Must know someone here. Eaves wondered briefly what that was about, but had more urgent questions on his mind.

"Let's go to the briefing room and see what we can learn about Tudor from the crews coming out." Eaves jogged toward a cargo truck where airmen were loading for the post-flight interrogation.

The crew chief nodded and ran with him toward the truck.

Eaves recognized the pilot waiting to climb into the back of the rig as one of the last remaining crews from the 777th. He called out, "Hey, do you know anything about Captain Tudor?"

The pilot turned with a stricken look on his face, the fog of combat and battle fatigue reflected on his countenance. A glimmer of recognition flickered in his eyes. "Lt. Eaves."

He paused, then spoke slowly. "Tudor was my wingman today. We were over Poland when we hit flak. Engine number one was blown completely off his left wing. Then he lost both engines on the other side. Went down in a spiral dive." He cleared his throat. "My crew counted five chutes out of her." He held Eaves' gaze for a moment. "Sorry." He reached up to grab his copilot's hand and disappeared under the canvas covering.

All the air left Eaves' lungs. He felt like he'd been kicked in the gut.

Not Tudor.

The crew chief had tears in his eyes. Eaves searched for a feeling, but only shock and numbness filled him. A hollow deadness stole over him.

Missing in Action . . .

Though the air was warm, he shivered. Vacant cots awaited him in the little rock casa. As he stumbled away, a prayer flew upward.

Lord, I pray he made it out of the plane. Please, Lord, help him and his men.

✈✈✈

8 AUGUST 1944—PANTANELLA AIR BASE, ITALY

"Captain Eaves, Colonel Schroeder would like to see you." The orderly poked his head into the empty casa. "I'll wait outside in the jeep and give you a ride to headquarters."

Eaves swung his legs over the edge of his cot and grabbed his cap. "Roger. Be right there."

He hated being alone in the casa, not knowing if Tudor and his men were dead or alive. He grabbed the V-mail he'd written to Jean. So difficult to encourage her when he had no idea when or if he'd be coming home.

The colonel was bent over his desk again when Eaves arrived.

"Captain Eaves, reporting for duty, sir." Eaves stiffened to attention and saluted.

"At ease, Captain. Have a seat." He finished writing and moved the paper to the top of the bin on his desk, his face serious when he looked up.

"Last month the 464th flew a total of nineteen missions and lost eighteen planes to enemy fighters and flak. Another rough month for the group. The new crews are green, lacking discipline and combat skills. We must step up to the challenge. Plans are in the works to open a gunnery school and also to employ the use of chaff to confuse the German radar."

Eaves listened intently, but baffled.

Why was the colonel sharing that with him?

"You spent two months behind enemy lines. Policy prohibits you from continuing to fly combat missions in the same arena. You have too much knowledge of the underground Partisan network, creating a dangerous situation if you fell into German hands."

Startled, Eaves sucked in his breath.

Was he being reassigned to the war in the Pacific?

The colonel continued. "As an experienced combat pilot, I believe you can best serve your country by providing training for the new crews arriving.

Your orders are to be available as needed to pilot short flights here in Italy, and to fly as a copilot in training new crews."

Eaves released his breath as a huge weight of dread slipped off his shoulders. No more combat missions. It was too good to be true. The fifty missions now required to earn the right to return home had seemed an impossible hurdle.

But, why him? He didn't deserve the right to step down from his duty. So many men had sacrificed all. Confusing feelings swept through him. He took a deep breath before responding.

"Yes, sir. If that's what you want me to do, I'll do my best."

"By the way, are you familiar with Lt. Ernie Latham?"

"Yes, sir," A bit puzzled, Eaves replied. "I remember him well."

"I thought you might. He transferred into a fighter unit recently, and that buzz job yesterday was a little hello to his buddies. Now he runs escort for us."

Eaves knew Latham had chomped at the bit in piloting the lumbering bombers, always wanted to be a fighter pilot. Now he had his wish. "I'm sure he'll do a fine job, sir."

The colonel nodded and gave a tight-lipped smile. "That's all, captain."

Eaves arrived back at the little casa to find a new crew of officers unpacking their barracks bags. Eaves cringed as a man settled into Tudor's spot.

Young, fresh-looking faces, joking and kidding each other.

Did we look that green when we first got here?

A thick wall seemed to encircle him, as if he watched the scene from another dimension. He swallowed hard.

The young lieutenant closest to him turned and saluted. "Captain Eaves?" he asked.

Eaves nodded. "At ease, men."

The young man's blue eyes shone with admiration. "We are so proud to be here with you, sir. Can't wait to give those Germans what's coming to them. What's combat like, sir?"

Eaves looked into the young lieutenant's eyes but saw instead young men he had trained with, men who were no longer here.

What it's like to run the gauntlet of flak or face a German ME-109 with guns blazing?

He slowly shook his head. "Something you just have to experience."

Eaves excused himself and walked toward the officers' club.

Can't afford to get close to any of them. Yet, I'm required to train them.

Eaves swallowed the lump in his throat, knowing he would do his level best to prepare them for what lay ahead, but right now it hurt too much to care about men who might not be back tomorrow.

✈✈✈

18 AUGUST 1944—PANTANELLA AIR BASE, ITALY

Eaves wiped the sweat off his brow and put down the trowel. Stepping back to admire the white Tufa rock wall of the chapel, he appreciated the progress they'd made today. The chapel was almost done.

He watched Chaplain Eastwood directing the placement of the last stones. The chaplain had labored side by side with the men who volunteered their free time to build a real place of worship, complete with a bell tower. Nothing like the sagging wet tent in Oudna.

Behind the chapel, a new dispensary had sprung up. Eaves had learned of a new miracle drug called penicillin. Reportedly, penicillin had helped Sgt. Fangman survive life-threatening infections in the twelve wounds from the firefight the day the plane had gone down. Truly amazing, a gift from the Almighty at a critical time in this long war.

In the last two weeks, the base had expanded and grown as new crews arrived. Entertainment improved too, with even a USO show and an outdoor theater built to the east of the chapel that now showed the latest flicks.

"Captain Eaves?" He turned to see a young orderly saluting. "Report to headquarters, sir."

Eaves hustled to Administration, where he was directed to Schroeder's office. As soon as he rapped on the door, Eaves heard Colonel Schroeder's voice. "Come in."

After formalities, Colonel Schroeder smiled encouragingly. "Captain Eaves, I have some news for you. First of all, I understand you were close friends with Captain James Tudor?"

Eaves nodded. "Yes, sir. He had been my copilot before his promotion."

"Well, we just received notice from the International Red Cross that Captain Tudor and four of his crew survived." The colonel's jaw tightened. "The bad news is they are in German hands. I just finished writing their families to notify them."

Eaves nodded, a mash of feelings pushing through him. First, a stab of joy, knowing his friend had survived, but then his gut had tightened with angst because Tudor was now in enemy hands.

"Thank you for letting me know, sir."

"And secondly, I have new orders for you, just arrived today." The colonel picked up a memo from his desk and began reading. "Return to the United States of America, all personnel who have evaded capture by the enemy for over six weeks in enemy-held territory. They are to report for trans-shipment to the United States by first available surface transportation."

Eaves' heart pounded. His eyes widened.

Home. He was going home.

Captain Schroeder looked up as he handed Eaves the written orders. "Plan to fly to Naples on 21 August and stand by to leave on the next ship home, Captain. You have done an exceptional job working with the new crews and we will miss your expertise. I'm sending a recommendation that your next assignment be in training the four-engine crews coming over to end this war. They need someone like you with combat experience to prepare them for the missions ahead."

"Thank you, sir. I appreciate your confidence in me." A rush of adrenaline and pride flowed through Eaves till his chest felt like it might burst.

Jean. His heart melted. Couldn't believe he'd be seeing his sweetheart soon.

The colonel offered a tired smile. "Wish I was going with you." He sighed as he eyed the pile of paper on his desk. "That's all, Captain."

Eaves saluted and backed out of the office, clutching the orders to his chest.

Finally, homeward bound!

✈✈✈

4 OCTOBER 1944—FORT SAM HOUSTON, SAN ANTONIO, TEXAS

The train, loaded with soldiers heading home for leave, chugged slowly away from the station.

Eaves stared out the window. Galveston was only a few hours away now, and it seemed unreal.

The few days spent in Naples had been a pleasure. The beautiful city offered good food, a theater, and the real beds. Finally, his name worked its way up to the top of the list for the next ship home.

The cruise had been long, seven days across the Atlantic, but uneventful. His heart almost burst when he saw the Statue of Liberty greeting them in the New York harbor.

From the huge staging area at Camp Shanks, he boarded a train to Washington, D.C., where he endured another evasion debriefing before squeezing onto a fully loaded troop train headed south to his next destination, the Miami Beach AAC Distribution Center.

From there, the train ride continued for three more days as he headed west to Fort Sam Houston in San Antonio. Finally leaving the tree-covered hills of Arkansas, he thrilled to the sight of the plains of Texas, the cattle dotting the countryside. But as they say, "everything is bigger in Texas," and train ride across the Lone Star state to San Antonio was no exception.

Everything moved in slow motion in the Army Air Corps, like a sloth slogging through molasses. After already taking a month to travel from Pantanella to Texas, another three days passed in San Antonio waiting for his leave to be approved.

Had they changed their minds? B-24 pilots were desperately needed in the Pacific. Would he be ordered to report for combat duty again? Even if he got leave, what would his next orders be?

Visiting the Alamo in his free time and meandering along the River Walk, with its many cafes and little shops, helped divert his anxiety as pride in his Texas heritage swept through him. Men had fought and died here for freedom, to create the new state of Texas.

Then, finally, his orders for twenty-one days of leave came through.

Eaves glanced around the packed train car filled with military men and a few civilians. Some were very young and chatty, probably headed to training or home for a last leave. The kind of raw cadets he would be training, if Colonel Schroeder's recommendation held sway.

Others appeared older, their eyes staring and blank. Distant and more reserved. Were they combat veterans too?

He had changed, he knew. He'd left something of himself on those missions and in the mountains of Yugoslavia. Combat had hardened him, but his faith had grown.

Last night, haunting visions filled his dreams again, faces of men lost, flashes of exploding flak, and diving fighter planes. Sudden sounds triggered flashes of panic.

Would Jean still be able to love the man who was coming home to her?

Anticipation gripped him as the Texas countryside flashed by with cotton fields and maize and windmills turning.

Would she be waiting?

He couldn't get a call through but had sent a telegram from Fort Sam Houston when he finally received his orders for leave.

As the train crossed the bay and reached the outskirts of Galveston, his heart thudded in his chest. Palm trees and crepe myrtle were familiar, but he'd never entered Galveston on a train. Everything looked strangely different, not the city he remembered.

The train slowed and finally ground to a halt. His heart felt like it might burst. He leaped up to grab his kit bag and joined the mass of men crowding into the aisle to exit the train.

Stepping onto the platform, the humid sea air carried scents of magnolia. He scanned the throngs of people shouting and waving by the train station.

Then he saw her, the familiar lovely face. Jean. Her gaze locked on his as they both struggled through the crowd toward each other.

"Red, oh, Red!" she cried out, as tears streaked down her pink cheeks.

"Jean!" He hurried his steps, pushing through the crush of people, and dropped his kit bag as he pulled her into his arms. Her tears spilled onto his chest and he inhaled the scent of her, bringing back memories of the moments they'd shared before he'd left for war.

"I've missed you so much," she said over and over. He clung to her, like he would never let go. Finally, he pushed her to arm's length and reached up a finger to touch her tear-streaked but beautiful face, then stroked her glistening dark hair.

"I almost died when the telegram came, saying you were missing in action." Jean gulped back her tears.

Eaves drew her into his arms again and patted her back. "There, there," he said soothingly. "I'm here now."

She wiped at her tears and looked up at him. "But we knew you were alive, and I prayed every day that you'd come back to me," she said. "I could hardly believe your telegram that arrived yesterday saying you would be here today!"

Eaves cocked his head. "How could you be so sure I was still alive?"

"Mom knew." Jean glanced to her right, and Eaves turned to see her parents, Bill and Ollie, standing together, waiting patiently.

"Praise God! You are home safe!" Ollie said with a smile, tears glistening in her eyes. Eaves let go of Jean long enough to give each of them a huge hug.

"How did we know? God showed me." Ollie slipped her arm back through her husband's elbow and smiled into Bill's eyes before gazing at Eaves. "It was right after we got the telegram saying you were missing in action. We were devastated. But then, the Lord sent a vivid dream."

She paused and closed her eyes, then continued. "I saw you and another man by a rushing river. You were both lying face down behind some bushes. Not far away was a road where German soldiers marched by, following a large truck. They didn't see you. When I awoke, I knew God was confirming that you and your men were alive and hiding from the Germans." She smiled. "So, every day we prayed for you and your men—that God would guide you, provide what you needed, and bring you home."

Eaves' eyes widened and goosebumps sent chills through him, even on a blazing hot Galveston day.

"Only God could have shown you that," he murmured. "What He showed you was an actual moment in time in the mountains of Yugoslavia when we were hiding from the Germans."

He blinked back tears, gratitude filling his soul.

God had provided comfort for Jean, like he'd asked. And she and her parents provided daily prayer coverage for him and his men. Incredibly, God's plan had connected them across the globe.

Eaves straightened his shoulders. He didn't need to worry.

God held him and his future in His good hands.

"You'll have to excuse us." Eaves cleared his throat, and looked at Bill and Ollie as he picked up his kit bag. Wrapping his arm around Jean, he pulled her close to his side. She slid her arm around his waist, and he smiled down into her eyes.

"I reserved a honeymoon suite at the Buccaneer Hotel. We have a lot of catching up to do."

Thank You, Lord, for home and family, and yes, for a sweet love that lasts.

Epilogue

THE REST OF THE STORY ...

CAPTAIN W.T. EAVES and his crew exemplified the courage, camaraderie, and endurance of the gallant young men called to aerial combat in the Fifteenth Air Force during WWII. Day after day they faced fear and performed their duties, flying through flak and enemy fighters to decimate the *Luftwaffe* and destroy the German war machine, preparing the way for D-Day and turning the tide of the war.

By the grace of God, all eight men who bailed out of *All Meat-No Potatoes* that fateful day survived and eventually returned home, as did their former copilot, Captain James Tudor. Forever changed by their combat experiences and fight for survival, these warriors remained brothers for life. All are now deceased, and most did not share freely about their war experiences, even with family, until more than fifty years had passed. Unrecognized then, Post-Traumatic Stress Disorder was as real in the past as it is now. Burying their memories, these brave men committed themselves to facing the future with integrity and plunged into work, devoting themselves to caring for their families.

The navigator, 1st Lt. Robert E. "Bob" Haverkos, remained confined in Stalag Luft III until January 27, 1945. As the Russians advanced on the Eastern Front, prisoners could hear shells exploding and gunfire drawing closer. Early that morning, guards entered each barracks and forced the men into groups of two hundred.

Marching through the snow of the German winter for three days with little food or water, Haverkos and his group reached an overflowing prison camp,

Lt. W.T. Eaves in his pilot gear, above, and with his newlywed bride, Jean, while below are Bill Christel, left, and Daniel Sherman

Jean Eaves with her puppy, above, and with her husband, Lt. W.T Eaves

Stalag Luft XIII-D at Nuremburg, where they were detained in squalid conditions. In early April, the POWs were evacuated again, forced to march to Stalag Luft VII-A in Moosburg, where over 10,000 prisoners were crammed. They were finally freed by General George Patton's forces on April 19, 1945.

Haverkos was awarded the Silver Star and a Purple Heart, among other awards. He returned to Cincinnati, Ohio, in May and married his sweetheart, Ginny, a month later. Bob fathered three sons, was an avid golfer and fisherman, and went on to serve as an executive with Proctor & Gamble, part of the team that developed the Pringle brand.

The radio operator and nose gunner, S/Sgt. William C. "Bill" Christel, was imprisoned in Stalag Luft IV, a camp located by the Baltic Sea and Poland. In February of 1945, as the Russians pushed over the Polish border, the Kommandant ordered the whole camp to march west. The ensuing six hundred mile "Death March" through the icy winter weather claimed the lives of almost half of the more than 7,000 Allied prisoners who were forced to keep moving through the frozen German countryside for months. Finally freed by British troops in May, Christel suffered malnutrition, severe frostbite, and untreated damage to his legs from his parachute landing.

Discharged due to disability, he received a Silver Star and a Purple Heart, among twelve other awards. Bill returned home to his mother in Wisconsin as he had promised, married and fathered a son of his own. He worked for Nestle and held several other jobs before establishing his own business.

My uncle, Captain William T. Eaves, received the Silver Star, a Distinguished Unit Award on December 14, 1945 and other awards. A humble man, he firmly believed the true heroes were the men who never came home, and he put away all his medals. Even his younger brother, Lyall, was unaware of his Silver Star and other awards until the day of his funeral, July 17, 2009.

Assigned and trained as an instructor for all four-engine bombers, Eaves was stationed in Florida after his return to the States. He also test-flew and trained crews to fly the giant B-29s that carried the nuclear bombs that ended World War II. Jean accompanied him to Florida and in January of 1947, their daughter was born, followed through the years by three sons. He was honorably discharged from the Army Air Corps as a major, US Air Force Reserve operations officer, in December of 1947, and returned to Iraan, Texas, to work for the Ohio Oil Company, which later became Marathon Oil. A true love that endured, his marriage to Jean lasted sixty-one years.

The copilot, 2nd Lt. Daniel W. Sherman, recovered from pneumonia and evaded the enemy in Yugoslavia for a total of fifteen weeks before arriving at

Split on the Adriatic Sea. He returned to Italy by boat. He received the Distinguished Flying Cross and a Purple Heart, among other awards. After the war he served in the Coast Guard and Merchant Marines until being discharged on July 2, 1946, as a lieutenant colonel, but he remained in the Army Air Corps until he retired from the US Air Force Reserves on March 1, 1967. After the war, he returned to New York State where he married and fathered eight children, five of whom followed him into military service. Later in life, he stayed busy managing farms, building homes, selling real estate, and serving as a U.S. civil servant.

All five gunners on the crew were cited for gallantry in action as they engaged in the heroic battle against twenty enemy planes on May 29, 1944. They were credited with destroying two, maybe three, German fighters despite the overwhelming odds. S/Sgt. George R. Masterson, Sgt. Sylester A. Fangman, and S/Sgt. James H. Elder each received the Silver Star and a Purple Heart, Sgt. Robert L. McMillian and Stg. James J. Petrone received the same medals posthumously.

Waist gunner Sylvester Fangman recovered from his twelve wounds to return to his home in Texas, where he married and fathered eight children. When Sy succumbed to an early death in 1973, Sgt. Joseph F. Linneman and his wife adopted Fangman's two youngest children, then middle school-aged, and took them home to St. Louis, Missouri, where Joe owned and managed several nursing homes.

Many of these men were lifelong friends, meeting at reunions and traveling thousands of miles to gather together at special events. Christel and Linneman remained best friends throughout their lives.

In 1966 my uncle moved to southern Illinois with Marathon Oil to become foreman of the pipeline terminal there. He and Jean often visited the Linnemans' home in St. Louis. Eaves' son-in-law, Dan Jouett, heard Joe Linneman say many times, "A great pilot. I'm alive today because of this man."

Eaves, Haverkos, and Sherman stayed in contact throughout their lives. At the request of Dan Sherman in 2005, my uncle and Bob Haverkos recorded written memories of the day they were shot down.

May we never forget the sacrifices made by this generation at home and in combat for our freedoms, and the restoration of freedom for countries enslaved by the Axis powers. Praise God for heroic warriors who did their best and gave their all. And for the victory over evil that came by the grace of the Almighty God.

Author's Notes and Acknowledgments

As a reader of historical fiction, I love to know what is true and what came from the imagination of the author. *Silver Wings Falling Down* is my attempt to relate as closely as possible the true WWII story of my uncle, 1st Lt. William T. Eaves, and his crew. Sadly, by the time I decided to write their stories, all of them were gone.

I'm relating the true names, dates, missions and known facts. But because much of the dialogue and setting details had to be created, the book is categorized as historical fiction. Silver Wings Falling Down is based on the written memories of my uncle and some of the crew, as well as oral stories passed down to their families, my uncle's stack of WWII papers and his flight log, the history of *The 464th Bomb Group in World War II* by Michael Hill and Betty Harle, online memories of men from the 464th Bomb Group, and the *Forgotten Fifteenth* by Barrett Tillman. Any mistakes or omissions are mine.

Not being a pilot nor ever having served in the military, my research consisted of digesting more than seventy WWII books, visiting WWII museums, touring both *Diamond Lil* and *Witchcraft*, the only two still flying B-24s in the United States, and interviewing veterans.

When my uncle W.T. Eaves retired from Marathon Oil, he and my Aunt Jean moved back to Texas. In the final years of their lives, they lived with their daughter JaNeen and her husband, Dan Jouett. Although my uncle chose not to talk about the war for almost fifty years, Dan began to ask him questions that revealed new facts.

My uncle told Dan of the stowaway monkey and the violent storm crossing the Atlantic, and he stated they did not have enough fuel to taxi off the runway after the emergency landing on the Canary Islands. *The 464th Bomb Group in World War II* included stories of other monkeys being smuggled aboard B-24s leaving Brazil for Africa and noted that one who did survive became the mascot of the photography unit at the Gioia del Colle Airfield in Italy.

My uncle spoke briefly of the lack of respect for their commanding officer, Colonel Bonner, which is well-documented in *The 464th Bomb Group in World War II.*

Haverkos commented on the temporary base at Gioia del Colle in his written memories and the worn-out tent that housed the four officers. He mentioned the early failed missions, also documented in *The 464th Bomb Group in World War II,* and the one-thousand-foot oiled-sod insert in the center of the runway where an unsuccessful forced landing of a P-38 had destroyed the steel matting.

The flight log confirmed that Eaves was Lead Pilot of the 464th on the mission to Valmontone on May 22, 1944, and that he was not in *Target for Tonite,* but flying B-24J. *The 464th Bomb Group in World War II* related the delay of the mission that day caused by the accident after the Lead Group was in the air, and the miracle of the heavily loaded plane not exploding on impact.

My uncle also told Dan Jouett that the Red Tails were their escorts on two of his last missions, and he expressed admiration for the skill of the Tuskegee Airmen and their devotion in "sticking with the heavies." After the mission to Weiner-Neustadt on May 24, 1944, *Target for Tonite* returned so damaged that it never flew again, and my uncle mentioned over five hundred puncture wounds in the plane. My imagination created the return coverage being provided by the Red Tails.

In the stack of fragile and yellowed WWII papers, I found a Galveston training record of gunnery range results showing my uncle with twelve hits among the three officers listed. Below on the same page were enlisted men, and William Christel had the highest score of all with sixteen hits. Certainly, it was a blessing to later have Christel assigned to his crew as the radio operator/gunner.

Bill Christel's daughter-in-law, Cherie Christel, and grandson, Matt Christel, shared a recorded interview and written memories not revealed by Bill until late in his life. They described Bill's description of his first encounter with Joe Linneman and their ensuing lifelong friendship.

Most of the details from the day they were shot down came from my uncle and Bob Haverkos in their written memories sent to Dan Sherman in 2005, copies of which they also shared with each other. Dan had wanted to chronicle their incredible journey, but health issues prevented him from finishing the book he intended to write.

Both my uncle and Bob Haverkos told of being spared by a German fighter plane when dangling in their parachutes and each described their landing on the ground. My uncle wrote of the two men running toward him in the wheat field and his surprise in meeting an older gentleman at the farmhouse who spoke broken English.

Bill Christel wrote of being thrown into the Zagreb jail with Haverkos and the terrifying moments as the Allied bombers dropped their lethal loads on the railroad yards only one block from the jail. The *Forgotten Fifteenth* also records a bombing mission involving three B-17 bomb groups targeting the marshalling yards in Zagreb that day. Christel spoke of being separated from Haverkos and shipped out in a railroad car where Allied airmen stood packed so tightly there was no room to sit or to lie down.

Haverkos arrived at Stalag Luft III approximately nine to ten weeks after the Great Escape, well-known from the movie based on *The Great Escape* by Paul Brickhill. Additional information was found online, and also provided by Haverkos' sons: Bob, Bruce and Mark Haverkos. Bruce shared a YouTube video of his father in his nineties talking of his early days, stories about Ginny, and for the first time his sons heard memories from the POW camp. He spoke about creating the softball field with Klim cans and being teased by the guards when their barracks' winning streak was broken with a tie. He said he was asked to serve as one of the ten Commandos in the American compound and told of the forced march into the German winter as the Russians approached. (See Bibliography, online resources)

The Partisans did unite Eaves, Elder, and Sherman on the ground in Yugoslavia, and they traveled together, walking for three to four weeks before arriving at the safe house high in the mountains. My uncle did not record any names or places, but he did write about sleeping in the barn, visiting the village barber, and the big black cook pot. Also true was the story of catching fish with his hands and how "they tasted really good, even without salt or pepper."

While at the safe house in the mountains, my uncle wrote about contact with a British underground officer who radioed the Allies for a food drop and a rescue plan. The four days of hard hiking to reach the rendezvous spot included the death of a German guard on a railroad bridge and the group of Allied airmen being ferried across a river in a small rowboat, interrupted by enemy troops on the other side.

Eaves documented that Dan Sherman had to be left in a hospital and wrote of flak hitting the C-47 as he left Yugoslavia in the daring rescue. He also mentioned being deloused during a short stay in the hospital in Bari, Italy.

Two of Dan Sherman's children, Peggy Sherman Ball and Joseph P. Sherman contributed valuable information, including documentation of the Silver Star Award to all five gunners for the mission on May 29, 1944. They confirmed that after their father recovered in Yugoslavia, he had returned to Italy by boat and, like Eaves, soon deployed back to the States due to the length of time behind enemy lines. Another confirmation of the close relationships and respect within the crew, Dan Sherman's son Joseph was told that he was named after Joseph Linneman.

After arriving in Italy following the rescue, Eaves described learning of the safe return of his wounded crew members and listed their reported conditions. Also, in a newspaper clipping from a 1970 reunion of the 464th Bomb Group, Sylvester Fangman reiterated being hit twelve times on the day they were shot down and returning to Texas to father eight children. Both Peggy Sherman Ball and my cousin JaNeen Eaves Jouett confirmed that Joseph and Babe Linneman adopted Fangman's two youngest daughters, middle school-aged.

In researching Pantanella, the new base that housed the 464th and the 465th Bomb Groups after my uncle's return from Yugoslavia, I was shocked to discover that his best friend, Captain James Tudor, had been shot down over Poland the same day my uncle's flight log indicated his return from R&R on the Isle of Capri. *The 464th Bomb Group in World War II* noted the capture of Tudor and four of his crew members by the Germans. Tudor was wounded in the thigh by shrapnel and taken to a hospital. My cousin, JaNeen Eaves Jouett, confirmed that Tudor survived and had contact with Eaves in the years following the war.

Eaves wrote that after his return to Pantanella, he "flew the brass around" and helped train some of the new crews. A document found in his WWII papers confirmed that anyone behind enemy lines more than six weeks was not allowed to continue to fly combat flights over the same territory.

Orders of August 18, 1944, were for Eaves to report to Naples for the next available ship home, and he wrote of enjoying the beautiful city of Naples while waiting to be shipped out. Another yellowed WWII paper indicated his arrival on September 26th, 1944, at Camp Shanks Staging Area, New York, from "an overseas destination."

Traveling from New York to Florida by train, Eaves wrote of stopping in Washington, D.C. for another evasion debriefing. Orders show him arriving in Fort Sam Houston in San Antonio, Texas, on September 29th and his twenty-one days of leave officially being granted on October 4, 1944.

My Aunt Jean shared about her mother's miracle vision when I spoke with her by phone the day after my Uncle W.T. passed away at age eighty-eight in July of 2009. I had never heard that story before. She also shared that her only sibling, her brother Johnny, had died from appendicitis at age twelve, and that she regarded my mother, Ruth, as her sister. Her mother, Ollie, did have a special relationship with the Lord, serving as a pastor after the war. Ollie lived with my Uncle W.T. and Jean in Illinois after the death her husband Bill. My uncle found in her the mother he always craved.

Eaves did take Jean back to Iraan to meet his family before the wedding, and the stories about Eaves' family were all true. My parents, Ruth and Marcus, did have to request a change in rules by the school board to marry and were shivareed by their students in Iraan. My uncle shared with me about the West Coast road trip and being upset when my mother refused to let him drive the car up Pikes Peak.

My cousin, JaNeen Eaves Jouett, shared details about her dad and mom dating in Galveston and Jean's fond memories of seeing the Harrisons at the Balinese Room. Her mother also told her about traveling to Pocatello with other military wives to be with my uncle during the final months of training before he left for the war. JaNeen shared family wartime photos with me and an old photograph of Jean with Ricky, the little dog that brought comfort.

This story could not have been told without the encouragement and support from my critique group and writing friends: Lindy Jacobs, Julie Johnson, Rosanne Croft, Anna Snyder, Lisa Ham, and Jan Sherrin. Also, the expertise and thoughtful comments from those who were either veterans, pilots, and/or family members with fathers who served in the Army Air Corp during WWII who encouraged me and loved the story: Peggy Sherman Ball, Scott Borden, Michael Puppos, Bill Ham, Al Lindberg, and Charlie Rowles. Thank you all!

I must thank my husband Keith Kays for always supporting my writing journey, and I acknowledge all my family and friends who prayed for me, especially my two brothers, Dan and Eddie Hale and their wives.

So grateful to my Uncle Lyall Eaves and his wife Jo Ann, who contributed their family memories and encouragement. Lyall described the scene when the telegram arrived at his father's home in Camp One and said he'd "never seen Daddy cry before."

To those who faithfully read chapters, giving me valuable insight and edits, I'm most grateful: Linda Jones, Nancy Simonson, Darlene Warrick, Diana Hoven, Jacinta Bushong, and Chris Kirkwood.

This work would not have been completed without the inspiration and encouragement from my many mentors and coaches connected with Oregon Christian Writers who shared their experience and expertise. My most grateful thanks to Melanie Dobson, Jane Kirkpatrick, Lynn Austin, Julie McDonald Zander, Paul Smith. Sherri Langton, David Sanford, Dan Walsh, Nick Harrison and Greg Johnson.

Bibliography

Ackerman, Diane. *The Zookeeper's Wife: A War Story.* New York: W.W. Norton & Company, Inc., 2007.

Alling, Charles. *A Mighty Fortress: Lead Bomber Over Europe.* Pennsylvania: Casemate, 2002.

Ambrose, Stephen E. *Band of Brothers: E Company, 506th Regiment, 101st Airborne From Normandy to Hitler's Eagle's Nest.* New York: Simon and Schuster, 1992.

Ambrose, Stephen E. *The Wild Blue: The Men and Boys Who Flew the B-24s Over Germany.* New York: Simon and Schuster, 2001.

Austin, Lynn. *A Woman's Place.* Minnesota: Bethany House Publishers, 2006.

Avriett, Carole Engle with Starks, Capt. George W. *Coffin Corner Boys.* Washington, DC: Regnery History, 2018.

Bowman, Martin. *B-17 Combat Missions: Fighters, Flak and Forts: First-hand Accounts of the Mighty 8th Operations Over Germany.* New York: Metro Books, 2007.

Boyne, Walter J. *The Smithsonian Book of Flight.* New York: Orion Books, 1987.

Bradley, James. *Flyboys: A True Story of Courage.* New York: Little, Brown and Company, 2003.

Brickhill, Paul. *The Great Escape.* New York: W. W. Norton & Company, 2004.

Brokaw, Tom. *The Greatest Generation.* New York: Random House, 1998.

Burch, Robert R. *World War II: A Pilot's Experience.* Victoria, BC: Trafford Publishing, 2005.

Caine, Phillip D. *Aircraft Down! Evading Capture in WWII Europe.* Washington, DC: Brassey's, 1997.

Davis, James M. and Snead, David L. eds. *An American B-24 Pilot in World War II.* Texas: University of North Texas Press, 2006.

Dobson, Melanie. *Chateau of Secrets.* New York: Howard Books, 2014.

Doerr, Anthony. *All the Light We Cannot See.* New York: Scribner, 2014.

Freeman, Gregory A. *The Forgotten 500: The Untold Story of the Men Who Risked All for the Greatest Rescue Mission of World War II.* New York: Penguin Books, 2007.

Grimes, Lee T. as told to Zander, Julie McDonald. *The Miracle Museum.* Washington: Chapters of Life, 2014.

Hannah, Kristin. *The Nightingale.* New York: St. Martin's Press, 2015.

Hill, Michael and Harle, Betty. *The 464th Bomb Group in World War II: On Action Over the Third Reich with the B-24 Liberator.* Pennsylvania:

Schiffer Military History, 2001.
Hillenbrand, Laura. *Unbroken: A World War II Story of Survival, Resilience, and Redemption.* New York: Random House, 2010.
Hodges, Andrew Gerow Jr. and George, Denise. *Behind Nazi Lines: My Father's Heroic Quest to Save 149 World War II POWs.* New York: Penguin Random House, 2015.
Hughes, Kay. *Searching for Stanley: Unforgotten Hero of World War II.* Nebraska: Dime Publishing, 2013.
Lihou, Maurice G. *Out of the Italian Night: Wellington Bomber Operations 1944-45.* England: Airlife Publishing, 2000.
Lineberry, Cate. *The Secret Rescue: An Untold Story of American Nurses and Medics Behind Nazi Lines.* New York: Little, Brown and Company, 2013.
Makos, Adam with Alexander, Larry. *A Higher Call.* New York: Berkley Caliber, 2012.
Malarkey, Sgt. Don with Welch, Bob. *Easy Company Soldier.* New York: St. Martin's Griffin, 2008.
Murphy, Audie. *To Hell and Back: The Classic Memoir of World War II by America's Most Decorated Soldier.* New York: Picador, 1949.
Novey, Jack. *The Cold Blue Sky: A B-17 Gunner in World War Two.* Virginia: Howell Press, 1997.
Parker, Ray. Down in Flames. Minnesota: Mill City Press, Inc. 2009.
Rust, Kenn C. *Fifteenth Air Force Story: In World War II.* California: Historical Aviation Album, 1976.
Sundin, Sarah. *With Every Letter.* Michigan: Revel, 2012.
Sundin, Sarah. *On Distant Shores.* Michigan: Revel, 2013.
Steinbeck, John. *Bombs Away: The Story of a Bomber Group.* New York: Penguin Books, 1942.
Stewart, John L. *The Forbidden Diary: A B-24 Navigator Remembers.* New York: McGraw Hill, 1998.
Tillman, Barrett. *Forgotten Fifteenth: The Daring Airmen Who Crippled Hitler's War Machine.* Washington, DC: Regnery History, 2014.
Tomasevic, Bato. *Life and Death in the Balkans: A Family Saga in a Century of Conflict.* New York: Columbia University Press, 2008.
Underhill, Robert. *Blechhammer on the Oder.* Iowa: DeVenture Publishing, 2000.
Waller, Douglas. Wild Bill Donovan: *The Spymaster Who Created the OSS and Modern American Espionage.* New York: Free Press, 2011.
Zander, Julie McDonald. *Life on the Home Front: Stories of those who worked, waited and worried during WWII.* Washington: Chapters of Life,

2005.

Zellmer, David. *The Spectator: A World War II Bomber Pilot's Journal of the Artist as Warrior.* Connecticut: Praeger Publishers, 1999.

Online resources:

The 464th Bombardment Group:
https://www.armyaircorpsmuseum.org/464th_Bombardment_Group.cfm

The 464th Bombardment Group in WWII: Our War Stories:
http://464thbombgroup.com/story.htm

B-24 Liberator Willow Run Assembly Plant:
https://www.youtube.com/embed/iKlt6rNciTo?rel=0.

Consolidated B-24J Liberator, The Collings Foundation:
https://www.collingsfoundation.org/aircrafts/consolidated-b-24-liberator/

American Airmen Rescued in Croatia, Bosnia, and Hercegovina by Croatian and Bosnian Partisans in World War II by Eterovich, Adam S:
http://www.croatia.org/crown/croatians/www.croatians.com/MILITARY-AIRMEN-PILOTS.htm

YouTube video, Bob Haverkos sharing:
https://www.youtube.com/watch?v=dMRk8CQRjDM

YVONNE KAYS, an award-winning author of short stories and poetry, was inspired by the true WWII stories of two bomber boys in her own family—her uncles, Lt. W.T. Eaves, a Silver Star recipient, and Tech/Sgt. Walker "Spike" Hale Jr., with a Purple Heart. Research uncovered unsung heroes with incredible stories of courage and danger, romance and faith, tales that needed to be told. Yvonne has a master's in teaching from Lewis and Clark College. She and her husband live in beautiful Central Oregon.

To learn more about Yvonne, visit her website at https://yvonnekays.com. Sign up for Yvonne's newsletter at https://dashboard.mailerlite.com/forms/65768/57358761159820960/share.

Printed in Dunstable, United Kingdom

80908743R00153